By A Woman's Hand

SECOND EDITION

By A Woman's Hand

A GUIDE TO MYSTERY FICTION BY WOMEN

SECOND EDITION

Jean Swanson and Dean James

BERKLEY PRIME CRIME, NEW YORK

BY A WOMAN'S HAND

A Berkley Prime Crime Book / published by arrangement with
the authors

PRINTING HISTORY
Berkley Prime Crime edition / September 1996

The Putnam Berkley World Wide Web site address is
http://www.berkley.com

ISBN: 0-425-15472-6

Berkley Prime Crime Books are published
by The Berkley Publishing Group,
200 Madison Avenue, New York, NY 10016.
The name BERKLEY PRIME CRIME and the BERKLEY PRIME CRIME
design are trademarks belonging to Berkley Publishing Corporation.

PRINTED IN THE UNITED STATES OF AMERICA

10 9 8 7 6 5 4 3 2 1

For James,
and in memory of Ellen Strid Swanson.

JS

For my mother,
and in memory of my father.

DJ

Contents

Acknowledgments

From both of us, special thanks to Martha Farrington, owner of Murder by the Book Bookstore in Houston, for her friendship to us both, for introducing us in the first place, and for providing such a wonderful environment for mystery-lovers; to the interlibrary loan staff of the University of Redlands Library and the Houston Academy of Medicine–Texas Medical Center Library, for helping to find much-needed books quickly and efficiently; to our editor, Natalee Rosenstein, for answering questions patiently and cheerfully and for making this experience considerably less nerve-racking than it might have been; to Carolyn G. Hart, for encouragement; and to Jim Thompson and Edith Brown, for assistance with information on certain authors. We owe a special thanks to our agent, Nancy Yost, for her energy, enthusiasm, and expertise; thanks for being an important part of the team.

We owe a big—and belated—thanks to Dave Thomas, Berkley sales representative extraordinaire, for taking the original proposal to New York in the first place. Thanks to Dave, we became part of the Berkley family.

We owe another big thanks to Victoria Nichols and Susan Thompson, who paved the way for us and others with their pioneering reference book, *Silk Stalkings: When Women Write of Murder*, now sadly out of print.

From Dean: Thanks to my friends and coworkers at Murder by the Book, Megan Bladen-Blinkoff, Edith Brown, Barbara Douglas, and David Thompson, who have graciously endured the painful birthing process and have offered friendship and encouragement when they were sorely needed.

From Jean: Thanks to Art Plotnik, for help in developing the original idea; thanks to the Orkney Public Library for granting me the privilege of using their excellent collection; to Trisha Aurelio and Jean Higginson for their support; and, most of all, to my father, Arthur Swanson, for teaching me how to write in the first place and for editing my work; and to my husband, Jim Thompson, for reading the manuscript and making valuable suggestions, and for his unfailing encouragement and moral support.

Preface

I recall that when I'd read every book by Agatha Christie that I could find, I despaired of ever discovering any other writer like her. I didn't want to try other mystery writers. What if they weren't as good? What if I wasted my money or time on their books? And how could I even begin to guess which ones among all of those other mystery novels at the libraries and bookstores might offer me a reading experience that was even close to the joy I obtained from a good Christie? If only I'd had this book!

There is, of course, no writer just like any other, but with a volume like this one in hand, I could have turned to an entry for Christie, Agatha—who was still alive at that time and so would have been included as a contemporary author—and I might have read: "Readers who enjoy English settings might also try the work of Dorothy L. Sayers, Josephine Tey, and Ngaio Marsh."

I'd have been a happy reader! I think you will be, too, with this masterful compendium to assist you. Jean Swanson and Dean James have created a tour de force of a reference source on contemporary women mystery writers, an armchair detective's dream, a veritable Fodor's—that is, a guidebook—of mystery, which may gently and tactfully but firmly and knowledgeably point you down the roads you most want to travel in your mystery reading.

I envy you this book! As you travel happily from Christie to Hart to Churchill, or from Muller to MacGregor to Dunlap, or from

Melville to O'Donnell to Maron and beyond, think of those earlier adventurers, like me, who traversed this terrain without a map.

This is your map to the grand world of mysteries written by contemporary women, and you may safely follow its expert recommendations to five-star reading pleasure.

NANCY PICKARD

Introduction

Women writers have always held an important place in the development of mystery fiction in the English-speaking world. Agatha Christie is probably the best-known mystery writer in much of the world; even those who are not devoted and regular mystery readers know the name of Christie and the type of literature with which it is associated. Christie, moreover, has exerted a powerful influence on the development of the mystery novel, either because writers have attempted to follow her patterns of plot and timing or because writers consciously have worked to escape many of the conventions that seemed to control Christie's writing.

As eminent as Christie's place has been in mystery fiction, she is certainly not the only woman writer of historical importance to the genre. Mary Roberts Rinehart, Mignon G. Eberhart, and Phoebe Atwood Taylor in America and Margery Allingham, Ngaio Marsh, Dorothy L. Sayers, and Josephine Tey in England all lent their distinctive voices to give an impressive imprimatur to the mystery novel as written by women. The mysteries written by these women are, in many ways, reflective of the societies in which the authors themselves were raised. These societies were convention-bound, and the roles of women in them were restricted. Perhaps in consequence, these women from earlier in the century wrote novels of mystery that steered clear of the mean streets so beloved of the hard-boiled, wise-cracking private eye school and centered rather upon the drawing room, the family in both its nuclear and extended definitions, or some other form of the small, enclosed community in which murder is bred from the relationships of the persons involved.

As the decades have passed and the social rules have changed, the number of women mystery writers has increased greatly. These authors come from widely varying backgrounds, and their personal attitudes and styles lend many different perspectives to the fiction they write and the characters they create. In consequence, mystery fiction is richer in diversity than ever before, for the range of women authors and women characters is wider and is expanding all the time. Writers like Pat Burden, Betty Rowlands, and Carolyn G. Hart may write mysteries in the vein of Agatha Christie but with a decidedly modern twist. Sue Grafton, Marcia Muller, Sara Paretsky, and many other authors write about strong women characters who have little relation to an earlier version of the female detective, Miss Jane Marple. Ruth Rendell, Margaret Millar, and Frances Hegarty (Fyfield) write novels of psychological complexity and realism very unlike mainstream mystery fiction from the Golden Age.

There is much to celebrate in the current boom in mystery fiction, which is in many ways dominated by women writers. Unfortunately, the supportive and reference literature has not caught up with this trend yet; women writers often have been ignored or undervalued by critics in the field. This led to the formation by Sara Paretsky of the group, Sisters in Crime, which has, with some success, lobbied for more book reviews of women authors and greater critical consideration. We hope that our book will help to fill this gap in the critical literature.

The overwhelming bounty of mystery fiction can cause problems for readers with definite likes and dislikes among mystery styles and types of characters. Readers who love psychological suspense novels might not care for the cozy, traditional mysteries in the Christie vein, for example. Once readers identify a particular type of mystery, a typical kind of series character, or mysteries with a regional setting, they often try to find similar writers. Thus, one common question in libraries and bookstores alike is; "I've just read my last novel by P. D. James [or Sue Grafton or Elizabeth Peters or whomever]. If I like her, whom should I read next?"

By a Woman's Hand is an attempt to help readers answer this question. This guide is arranged alphabetically by author, and each author entry offers a description of the salient features of the author's style, series characters, and other important characteristics. We include the title and the original American publication information of initial books in series, along with other books of importance among the more prolific writers' work. (This is not intended to be a bibliography; there are a number of reference works that fill that need.) These entries are intended as an analysis of the particular author, not to render our own opinions of the writer's standing in the genre as a whole, but rather to assess what there is about this writer's work that appeals to readers. We are well aware, however, of the critical reputation of the writers included in this guide, and we have attempted to indicate those writers who consistently are judged among the best in the field by critics. (P. D. James and Ruth Rendell are obvious examples.) We have also mentioned award-winning works whenever possible. The Edgars are given by the Mystery Writers of America organization in various categories, and the Gold and Silver Daggers are awarded by the British Crime Writers' Association. Other than these peer awards, we have also mentioned awards given by fans: the Agatha, bestowed by the Malice Domestic mystery convention (which is devoted to the traditional mystery), the Anthony, awarded by the Bouchercon (the World Mystery Convention), and the Macavity, given by the readership of the *Mystery Readers Journal* of Mystery Readers International. Finally, each entry ends with recommendations of other writers who might share some characteristic with the writer under discussion. These recommendations are based on our own extensive reading in the field. Most often, the recommendations given are to other women writers covered in this guide, if those are the most appropriate references.

One important question in the reader's mind is, no doubt, how we chose the writers included in this guide. We concentrate upon contemporary women mystery writers. We took as our rough starting date the year 1977, when Marcia Muller's first Sharon McCone novel, *Edwin of the Iron Shoes* (McKay Washburn), was published. Muller's book is often considered to have ushered in the era of the modern female private eye. From the late 1970s to the present day, we see the result of this trend in many types of women characters no longer bound by the conventions of the Golden Age mystery novel. In drawing up our list of writers for this guide, we chose authors whose first work has been published since 1977, such as

Elizabeth George or Frances Fyfield, or writers published before that time who are still consistently producing, such as P. D. James and Ellis Peters. We have tended to concentrate mostly on writers of mystery and detective fiction, though we have also included writers of suspense novels, such as Mary Higgins Clark, Mary Stewart, and Margaret Millar, because of their importance to the field. We have not included writers like Evelyn Anthony or Helen MacInnes, whose chief output is in the field of espionage thrillers. We cover primarily English-language writers, with an emphasis on American, Canadian, and British authors. We have not analyzed short stories, but we provide a bibliography of important short story anthologies that contain stories by women authors. Finally, we have also included women who have written a minimum of three books. As space and time have permitted, we have included authors who have written two books and whose third book seems imminent. No doubt readers will come up with writers who we failed to include for some reason, but we have included as many writers as we could without going blind and broke in the process.

In the appendices of the book, readers will find various index lists categorized by type of detective (such as private eye, amateur, police), regional setting, and series character and author. Finally, a word on definitions. The terms *cozy* and *traditional mystery* are used interchangeably throughout the book to refer to mysteries written largely in the tradition of Agatha Christie and other Golden Age authors. In other words, traditional mysteries are those with an enclosed setting, a series detective, little explicit violence, and a good puzzle to be solved. Cozies have come a long way since *The Body in the Library*, with gifted writers like Nancy Pickard, Carolyn G. Hart, and Frances Fyfield, among many others, stretching the boundaries. *Hard-boiled* refers to mysteries in which there might be violence and lots of action, but chiefly the term indicates a mood, a connection to what Raymond Chandler called the "mean streets." A great deal of upheaval has occurred in the hard-boiled mystery tradition in recent years, with the addition of female private eyes created by fine authors like Sara Paretsky, Liza Cody, and Sue Grafton. *Psychological* suspense refers to those books in which the emphasis is more on whydunit than whodunit, though writers like Ruth Rendell and Margaret Millar can fascinate the reader easily with both questions. A *thriller* or *suspense* novel might be defined as a story that keeps the reader turning the pages to find out what's going to happen next, with the emphasis on how it's going to turn out, rather than simply 'whodunit'. Readers may look for classic practitioners of this art like Mary Higgins Clark and Dorothy Dunnett. The *police procedural* can be a detective story or a thriller, but generally this type of novel relies on the routines of police activity in order to answer the vital questions, whodunit, whydunit, or howdunit. The emergence of policewomen as protagonists in novels by Susan Dunlap, Lillian O'Donnell, Katherine V. Forrest, and other women writers has created welcome change in this area.

The mystery reader's motto might easily be, "So many books, so little time." We certainly discovered that, as we immersed ourselves in the wealth of diversity of mystery fiction written by women. We hope that *By a Woman's Hand* can serve to help readers find those books and authors who most fit their tastes. This book was a voyage of discovery for its authors; may it be no less for its readers.

©JEAN SWANSON AND DEAN JAMES

A Note on the Second Edition

In this second edition, we have followed the principles for selection laid down in the introduction. Fortunately for mystery readers, new and interesting women mystery writers continue to appear on the publishers' lists every year. For this second edition, we have added over seventy new writers—once again, as many as time, money, and tired eyes would permit. In two or three more years, there may well be seventy more writers to add; time, and the publishing world, will tell.

A number of the writers included in the first edition of the book have since that time apparently ceased writing mysteries or gone completely out of print. With an eye to this, we have taken the entries for some of these writers from the body of the book for this new edition, but we have included a list of them among the index lists at the back of the book. We did not delete the cross references to authors whose entries we removed. These authors are still worth reading; we simply were trying to keep the crowding to a minimum. We trust that readers will understand.

Finally, we would both like to say a heartfelt thank you to the many readers who helped make the first edition a success: Thank you for your continued support and enthusiasm.

Authors Included in the Book

Deborah Adams
Catherine Aird
Susan Wittig Albert
Margot Arnold
Nancy Atherton
Marian Babson
✓Nikki Baker
Mignon F. Ballard
Jo Bannister
Linda Barnes
Nevada Barr
M. C. Beaton
K. K. Beck
Sophie Belfort
Carole Berry
Claudia Bishop
Malacai Black
Veronica Black
Anne Blaisdell
Eleanor Taylor Bland
J. S. Borthwick
D. B. Borton
Gail Bowen

Eleanor Boylan
Lilian Jackson Braun
Carol Brennan
Emily Brightwell
D. C. Brod
Rita Mae Brown
Edna Buchanan
Pat Burden
Jan Burke
Gwendoline Butler
Dorothy Cannell
P. M. Carlson
Sarah Caudwell
Elizabeth Chaplin
Kate Charles
Joyce Christmas
Jill Churchill
Carol Higgins Clark
Mary Higgins Clark
Anna Clarke
Melissa Cleary
Ann Cleeves
Liza Cody

Janet Cohen
Carolyn Coker
B. Comfort
Susan Conant
Natasha Cooper
Susan Rogers Cooper
Patricia D. Cornwell
Alisa Craig
Caroline Crane
Hamilton Crane
Trella Crespi
Deborah Crombie
Amanda Cross
Clare Curzon
Mary Daheim
Catherine Dain
Barbara D'Amato
Diane Mott Davidson
Dorothy Salisbury Davis
Lindsey Davis
Janet Dawson
Marele Day
Jane Dentinger
Eileen Dewhurst
R. B. Dominic
Anabel Donald
Carole Nelson Douglas
Lauren Wright Douglas
Alison Drake
Sarah Dreher
Peter Dunant
Sarah Dunant
Susan Dunlap
Dorothy Dunnett
Jack Early
Marjorie Eccles
Ruth Dudley Edwards
Lesley Egan
P. N. Elrod
Elizabeth Eyre

Ann C. Fallon
Quinn Fawcett
Tony Fennelly
E. X. Ferrars
Katherine V. Forrest
Earlene Fowler
Valerie Frankel
Anthea Fraser
Antonia Fraser
Margaret Frazer
Celia Fremlin
Mickey Friedman
Frances Fyfield
Kate Gallison
Judith Garwood
Susan Geason
Elizabeth George
B. M. Gill
Dorothy Gilman
Jaqueline Girdner
E. X. Giroux
Ellen Godfrey
Alison Gordon
Paula Gosling
Sue Grafton
Caroline Graham
Ann Granger
Linda Grant
Lesley Grant-Adamson
Gallagher Gray
Christine Green
Kate Green
D. M. Greenwood
Kerry Greenwood
Martha Grimes
Sally Gunning
Batya Gur
Jane Haddam
Joan Hadley
Jean Hager

Patricia Hall
Mollie Hardwick
Charlaine Harris
Lee Harris
Cynthia Harrod-Eagles
Carolyn G. Hart
✓Ellen Hart
S. T. Haymon
Frances Hegarty
Sue Henry
Joan Hess
Patricia Highsmith
Lynn S. Hightower
Isabelle Holland
Hazel Holt
Wendy Hornsby
Tanya Huff
Susan Isaacs
Marian J. A. Jackson
Nancy Baker Jacobs
P. D. James
J. A. Jance
Trish Janeshutz
Velda Johnston
Lucille Kallen
Faye Kellerman
Mary Anne Kelly
Nora Kelly
Susan Kelly
Susan B. Kelly
Judith Kelman
Toni L. P. Kelner
Susan Kenney
Karen Kijewski
✓Laurie R. King
Kate Kingsbury
Mary Kittredge
Alanna Knight
Kathryn Lasky Knight
Gabrielle Kraft

Rochelle Majer Krich
Sarah Lacey
Mercedes Lackey
Marsha Landreth
Jane Langton
Janet LaPierre
Emma Lathen
Janet Laurence
Janice Law
Elizabeth Lemarchand
Donna Leon
Elizabeth Linington
Gillian Linscott
Nancy Livingston
Caroline Llewellyn
Margaret Logan
M. K. Lorens
T. J. MacGregor
Charlotte MacLeod
✓Jaye Maiman
Jessica Mann
Margaret Maron
Lee Martin
Sarah J. Mason
Lia Matera
Stefanie Matteson
A. E. Maxwell
Taylor McCafferty
Tierney McClellan
Sharyn McCrumb
✓Val McDermid
Janet McGiffin
Jill McGown
Bridget McKenna
✓Claire McNab
Karin McQuillan
M. R. D. Meek
Jennie Melville
D. R. Meredith
Barbara Mertz

Annette Meyers
Maan Meyers
Barbara Michaels
Margaret Millar
Marlys Millhiser
D. F. Mills
Kay Mitchell
Gwen Moffat
Miriam Grace Monfredo
Susan Moody
Kate Morgan
Anne Morice
B. J. Morison
Patricia Moyes
Marcia Muller
Amy Myers
Magdalen Nabb
Janet Neel
Barbara Neely
Sharan Newman
Meg O'Brien
Maxine O'Callaghan
Carol O'Connell
Lillian O'Donnell
Susan Oleksiw
B. J. Oliphant
Sister Carol Anne O'Marie
A. J. Orde
Abigail Padgett
Katherine Hall Page
Robin Paige
Orania Papazoglou
Sara Paretsky
Barbara Paul
Joanne Pence
Anne Perry
Elizabeth Peters
Ellis Peters
Audrey Peterson
Nancy Pickard

Marissa Piesman
Elizabeth Pincus
Sandra West Prowell
Dianne G. Pugh
Mary Monica Pulver
Sheila Radley
J. M. Redmann
Ruth Rendell
Virginia Rich
Candace M. Robb
Gillian Roberts
Lora Roberts
Lynda S. Robinson
Nancy Taylor Rosenberg
Kate Ross
Rebecca Rothenberg
Jennifer Rowe
Betty Rowlands
Medora Sale
Eve K. Sandstrom
Corinne Holt Sawyer
Sandra Scoppettone
Lisa Scottoline
Kate Sedley
Sarah Shankman
Dell Shannon
Stella Shepherd
Celestine Sibley
Sheila Simonson
Dorothy Simpson
Shelley Singer
Gillian Slovo
Evelyn E. Smith
Janet L. Smith
Joan Smith
Julie Smith
Lora R. Smith
Rosamond Smith
Patricia H. Sprinkle

AUTHORS

Elizabeth Daniels Squire
Dana Stabenow
Susannah Stacey
Veronica Stallwood
Jill Staynes
Mary Stewart
Alice Storey
Margaret Storey
Elizabeth Atwood Taylor
June Thomson
Kathy Hogan Trocheck
Margaret Truman
Kerry Tucker
Dorothy Uhnak
Judith Van Gieson
Barbara Vine
Mary Willis Walker
Marilyn Wallace
Minette Walters
Martha G. Webb
Charlene Weir

Valerie Wilson Wesley
Carolyn Wheat
Gloria White
Teri White
Barbara Whitehead
Phyllis A. Whitney
Kate Wilhelm
✓Barbara Wilson
Chris Wiltz
Anne Wingate
✓Mary Wings
Valerie Wolzien
Sara Woods
Sherryl Woods
M. K. Wren
L. R. Wright
Chelsea Quinn Yarbro
Dorian Yeager
Margaret Yorke
✓Eve Zaremba
Sharon Zukowski

Adams, Deborah. This Tennessee author has taken the unusual tack of having a town serve as her series "character," rather than using a single person as the focal point of her books. The town is named Jesus Creek, and that should be a signal to the reader to expect Southern eccentricity to be a chief ingredient of the mix. In the first of the series, *All the Great Pretenders* (Ballantine, 1992), a rich young woman disappears, and a psychic tries to find her, while Jesus Creek is in the midst of its sesquicentennial celebrations. The third, *All the Dark Disguises* (Ballantine, 1993), offers a serial killer working in the area, dispatching pretty blondes to eternal rest, while the town concentrates on its St. Patrick's Day festivities. As the series progresses, some characters become regulars, like the police chief, the town's librarian, the town's beauty queen hopeful, and, of all things, an eccentric Yankee. Adams pitches her mélange of eccentricity and gently satiric humor in a low key, so there is never an extravagance of humor or character to veer off into caricature. Adams also demonstrates the ability to write affectingly about social issues in the framework of the mystery novel. In *All the Hungry Mothers* (Ballantine, 1994), she uses her experience in counseling battered women to chilling effect. Jesus Creek might be an unusual place, but it's a charmingly offbeat one to visit on a tour of the fictional South. *All the Great Pretenders* was nominated for an Agatha for Best First Novel. Adams won a Macavity Award for Best Short Story for "Cast Your Fate to the Wind" in *Malice Domestic 3* (Pocket, 1994).

Readers looking for other Southern mysteries with humor might try the Elizabeth MacPherson novels of Sharyn McCrumb, the work of Charlaine Harris, or the Samantha Adams novels of Sarah Shankman. Other Southern writers to note are Taylor Mc-Cafferty, Rita Mae Brown, Celestine Sibley, and Patricia H. Sprinkle.

Aird, Catherine.   Aird created the English county of Calleshire for her series of mysteries featuring Detective Inspector C. D. Sloan ("Seedy" to his friends) and amusingly annoying Sergeant Crosby. Calleshire owes much to the England of the Golden Age; village life in this county is much like what readers encounter in the works of Christie or Marsh, with a more modern face, though Aird's territory is not quite the modern English village of Dorothy Simpson or Peter Robinson. In his debut, *The Religious Body* (Doubleday, 1966), Sloan solves a murder at a nunnery, and Aird describes the life of the community of nuns well. A later book, *The Stately Home Murder* (Doubleday, 1970; English title, *The Complete Steel*), allows Aird to display at full steam a deliciously wry sense of humor, as tourists invade a stately home full of armor and the remnants of feudalism. This novel's solution contains one of the great literary jokes of mystery fiction, and Aird pulls it off with great panache. Indeed, through much of her work, Aird's sense of humor is a strong undercurrent, lending a light touch that distinguishes Aird from some contemporaries for whom humor is sometimes a mystery in itself. Though she writes a little too infrequently for her fans, Aird provides solid entertainment in the field of the traditional English mystery.

Those who have enjoyed Aird might try in addition the work of Elizabeth Lemarchand, June Thomson, Patricia Moyes, Caroline Graham, or E. X. Ferrars. Other writers who use humor to good effect in their traditional English mysteries are Sarah J. Mason, who also writes as Hamilton Crane, M. C. Beaton, and Nancy Livingston.

Albert, Susan Wittig/Robin Paige.   A former university administrator and professor of medieval literature, Albert gave up the academic life to write mysteries, often in collaboration with her husband, William Albert. Albert's first novel, *Thyme of Death* (Scribner, 1992), introduced China Bayles, formerly a corporate lawyer in Houston. China left the stresses of life in the big city and moved to the small town of Pecan Springs, Texas, where she runs her own shop, specializing in herbs. Besides running her own business, China has found time to have a relationship with an attractive man, in this case Mike McQuaid, a former cop, now a professor of criminal justice at a nearby university. Though she left the rat race behind in Houston, China soon discovers that the tensions of small-town life can frequently lead to murder, as she tries to balance work and relationship and her new sideline, detection. Albert weaves the lore of the herb garden into each book of the series. *Thyme of Death* was nominated for the Agatha and the Anthony Awards for Best First Novel.

With her husband William, Albert is writing another series under the pseudonym Robin Paige. The first book in the series is *Death at Bishop's Keep* (Avon, 1994). The setting is the Victorian era, and the main character is a young American woman, half-English and half-Irish in heritage, named Kathryn Ardleigh. Making her own way in the world in 1894, Kathryn secretly writes thrillers, or "penny dreadfuls." Summoned to England to meet an aunt she never knew existed, Kathryn finds herself embroiled in a plot just as lurid as one of her own concoctions. Kathryn, like China Bayles, is intelligent, forceful, and very appealing.

Fans of the China Bayles books might also try the work of Janet L. Smith, Judith Van Gieson, and Jean Hager. Readers looking for other mysteries with Victorian settings should try the work of Anne Perry, Miriam Grace Monfredo, and Amy Myers.

Arnold, Margot. An anthropologist and educator in real life, the pseudonymous Arnold makes excellent use of her own background to endow her sprightly series of mysteries with authentic settings and archaeological detail. Her series characters, American anthropologist Penny Spring and Welsh archaeologist Toby (Sir Tobias) Glendower, are long-standing friends and fellows in different Oxford colleges. These two eminent professionals somehow manage to combine crime-solving with anthropology and archaeology, much to the delight of the reader. They also demonstrate that sixty-something sleuths can be just as capable at crime-solving as their younger counterparts. Both Penny and Toby bring a wealth of experience, both academic and otherwise, to their investigations. Beginning with *Exit Actors, Dying* (Playboy, 1979), which is set in

Greece, Penny and Toby have traveled widely: Hawaii (*The Menehune Murders*; Foul Play, 1989); Israel (*Zadok's Treasure*; Playboy, 1979); Scotland (*Lament for a Lady Laird*; Playboy, 1982); and New Orleans (*Death of a Voodoo Doll*; Playboy, 1982), among other places. Whatever the venue, the result, in Arnold's hands, is sheer fun. Arnold has also written three novels in the thriller vein, deft mixtures of suspense, intrigue, and romance, including the recent *Sinister Purposes* (Fawcett, 1988).

Other writers who effectively use archaeology, anthropology, or art history as background for their work are Elizabeth Peters, Caroline Llewellyn, and Mary Stewart. Readers interested in other series about older sleuths should try the work of Eleanor Boylan, B. Comfort, Gallagher Gray, and Dorothy Gilman.

Atherton, Nancy. This is probably the only series in contemporary mystery fiction in which the series character is a ghost, Miss Dimity Westwood. In the first novel in the series, *Aunt Dimity's Death* (Viking, 1992), young Lori Shepherd is trying to recover from a series of painful events in her life when she learns of yet another death, that of her mother's beloved English friend, Dimity Westwood. Lori grew up on wonderful stories of ''Aunt'' Dimity's adventures, and she half-assumed that Aunt Dimity was simply a figment of her mother's imagination. But Aunt Dimity *was* real, she was rich, and she left Lori a fortune. Once Lori goes to England to claim her legacy, the real adventure begins, and she discovers that, though Aunt Dimity may be dead, her comforting presence is never far away. In the second book, *Aunt Dimity and the Duke* (Viking, 1994), another young American, Emma Porter, with a passion for English gardens, finds her own romantic adventure in England when she ends up helping the fourteenth duke of Penford restore his grandmother's garden. The mysteries in Atherton's novels are usually puzzles of the heart rather than puzzles of murder, and Aunt Dimity is the guiding spirit who gently oversees the proceedings, helping the characters resolve their dilemmas. Atherton offers a mixture of gentle warmth and fairy-tale charm, where readers will gladly escape the world around them.

Readers fond of the gentle whimsy of Nancy Atherton might also enjoy the mirth and mayhem of Charlotte MacLeod and Dorothy Cannell.

Babson, Marian.   Babson is an American author, long resident in England, who has written more than thirty mysteries in the traditional English style. Babson's skill with words, adroit depictions of quirky characters, and careful plot structures turn her novels into enjoyable reading experiences. *Pretty Lady* (Walker, 1990), for example, is a brief, suspenseful story of one violent incident and what happened in each character's life to lead up to it. Babson has used Douglas Perkins, a partner in the London public relations firm of Perkins & Tate, as a series character in some of her novels. The Perkins series begins with *Cover-up Story*. Babson also has written a series of humorous mysteries featuring Trixie Dolan and Evangeline Sinclair, who were movie stars in the Golden Age of Hollywood. The two elderly actors are attempting to revive their careers in London theater, but inevitably they become involved in murder. The series begins with *Reel Murder* (St. Martin's Press, 1986). American readers be warned: some of Babson's books change titles when they are published in the U.S., and certain novels have appeared in America years after their initial British publication.

Babson's first mystery was *Cover-up Story* (St. Martin's Press, 1988; London: Collins, 1971).

Readers who enjoy traditional cozy mysteries with idiosyncratic characters and humorous situations should look for the works of M. C. Beaton, K. K. Beck, Carolyn G. Hart, and Jill Churchill.

Baker, Nikki. With her African-American lesbian sleuth, Virginia Kelly, Baker brings the viewpoint of a double minority to the mystery world. In the series opener, *In the Game* (Naiad, 1991), investment counselor Ginny tries to help out an old and dear friend, Beverly, when Bev's lover is found dead behind a Chicago lesbian bar. The police think it may be a hate crime, but Ginny knows enough about the dead woman to believe that the motivation was a lot more personal. In the second book, *The Lavender House Murder* (Naiad, 1992), Ginny takes a vacation in Provincetown with her acerbic, chain-smoking friend, Naomi Wolf. There is a strange mix of characters staying at Lavender House, and even Naomi seems to be hiding something when an aggressive lesbian journalist is murdered. Ginny is an attractive and appealing character who shows good instincts for sleuthing, though she can't seem to solve the problems in her personal life. Her relationship with her lover, Emily, has hit a rough patch, and Ginny tries to sort out her own life as she solves other people's problems. Baker's style fits comfortably into the mold of the traditional mystery, but through Virginia Kelly she offers her own individual slant on life, racism, and lesbianism in the 1990s in America.

Readers acquainted with Nikki Baker might also want to try Barbara Neely, Eleanor Taylor Bland, and Valerie Wilson Wesley for other strong and appealing African-American heroines.

Ballard, Mignon F. Ballard writes romantic suspense novels with a strong atmosphere of lurking menace. Touches of the supernatural and convoluted twists in the plot are characteristic Ballard plot devices. Her first novel was *Raven Rock* (Dodd, Mead, 1986). *Deadly Promise* (Carroll & Graf, 1989) is set in the small town of Harmony, Georgia. Molly Stonehouse, a young widow, has come back to her husband's ancestral home to investigate his death. Ballard effectively creates a rural Southern atmosphere for her story. In *The Widow's Woods* (Carroll & Graf, 1991), Jane Cannon returns to her hometown in South Carolina after being jilted. One day she finds that her neighbor has disappeared, leaving a pan of beans burning on the stove. This small domestic crisis leads Jane into a maelstrom of evil, Satanism, and murder. *Final Curtain* (Carroll & Graf, 1992) is the most ghostly and atmospheric of Ballard's novels. A young woman, Ginger Cameron, comes to Plumb-Nelly Tavern in Fiddler's Glen, North Carolina, to look into the long-ago death of her great-aunt. The ghost of her aunt helps her in her search for the truth. Ballard's novels are as much Southern Gothics as they are mysteries.

Readers of Ballard may want to look for romantic mysteries by Barbara Michaels, Sherryl Woods, Velda Johnston, and Carolyn G. Hart. Charlaine Harris and Virginia Lanier write atmospheric Southern crime novels.

Bannister, Jo. Born in Lancashire, England, Bannister now lives in Northern Ireland. Trained as a journalist, she left a position as editor to write full-time, and she has published numerous novels of mystery and science fiction. Her first mystery, *Striving with Gods* (Doubleday, 1984), introduced physician-turned-mystery-writer Clio Rees. Asked to identify a body by Chief Inspector Harry Marsh, Clio quickly realizes that her friend was murdered, and soon she's tangling with the police as well as the murderer. In her second appearance, *Gilgamesh* (Doubleday, 1989), Clio is Mrs. Harry Marsh, and her sleuthing instincts help complicate her relationship with her husband. With *A Bleeding of Innocents* (St. Martin's Press, 1993), Bannister began a second series that features a trio of interesting detectives. The central character is Inspector Liz Graham, who is brought in to the understaffed force at Castlemere to help an old friend in a tight spot. The old friend is Detective Chief Inspector Frank Shapiro, who has just lost his right-hand man. Complicating the situation is Sergeant Cal Donovan, a rogue Irishman intent on finding out who murdered his partner, no matter what trouble he causes. With this trio of complex and well-drawn characters at the center of her work, Bannister offers tightly crafted and thought-provoking police procedurals. Bannister has also written suspenseful thrillers, such as *The Mason Codex* (Doubleday, 1988), in which Welsh schoolteacher Annie Meredith travels to Texas and Mexico to discover the fate of her illegitimate half-brother, an illegal immigrant.

Readers acquainted with Bannister's work might also read Jill McGown, Cynthia Harrod-Eagles, Sheila Radley, and Susan B. Kelly.

Barnes, Linda. The first series Linda Barnes wrote featured Michael Spraggue, an independently wealthy actor and detective. These stories are located in Boston, the Napa Valley, and New Orleans, and the first, *Blood Will Have Blood* (Avon, 1982), has a theatrical setting. Barnes's more recent series stars Carlotta Carlyle, Boston private eye and cab driver. Carlotta is six feet tall, half-Irish and half-Jewish, a former policewoman, and she is truly a memorable character. Barnes has endowed Carlotta with an active sense of humor and a wry outlook on life. Readers may enjoy Carlotta's personality as much as the lively and thought-provoking plots. The secondary characters are striking creations as well. Carlotta's tenant, Roz, is an eccentric artist. Sam Gianelli is a son (supposedly honest) of the local Mafia don; he and Carlotta have an occasional fling. Through the Little Sisters organization, Carlotta has found a young sister, Paolina, with whom she has a strong and fond connection. And of course a private eye may sometimes need a friend in the police department; Carlotta has Mooney, an old buddy from her days as a cop.

The first Carlotta Carlyle novel is *A Trouble of Fools* (St. Martin's Press, 1987), and it was nominated for an Edgar Award for Best Novel.

Strongly characterized private eyes include Sue Grafton's Kinsey Millhone, Sarah Dunant's Hannah Wolfe, and Karen Kijewski's Kat Colorado. Other mysteries set in the Boston-Cambridge area are written by Susan Conant, Susan Kelly, Kathryn Lasky Knight, and Jane Langton. P. M. Carlson and Jane Dentinger also have mysteries with theatrical connections.

Barr, Nevada. Barr is a national park ranger who brings her love for nature and wildlife to her novels. Her first book, *Bittersweet* (St. Martin's Press, 1984), is about two nineteenth-century women who try to live independent lives in the frontier West. The women live for many years in the Nevada desert, and Barr's skill in describing the elusive beauty of wild places is readily apparent in this novel. Barr brought this ability to her first mystery, *Track of the Cat* (Putnam, 1993), which won both the Agatha and the Anthony Awards for Best First Mystery Novel. The heroine is Anna Pigeon, a National Park Service ranger. Anna is a smart, thoughtful, gutsy outdoorswoman, and a widow who is still mourning her dead husband. Anna left New York City after his death, and now she finds her solace in the wild, lonely country of the Guadalupe Mountains in west Texas, where people can't get too close to her. Anna cares deeply about the animals, especially the endangered mountain lions. Barr also provides an inside look at the politics of the park service, the loss of wildlife because of local ranchers, and the career scramblings of petty bureaucrats. In *A Superior Death* (Putnam, 1994), Anna is reassigned to Isle Royal National Park in northern Michigan, on Lake Superior. She has trouble adjusting to a colder climate and to the necessity for deep dives into the frigid lake in order to investigate crimes. As with all of Barr's novels, the secondary characters are well-drawn, but Anna and the lake and the islands are the stars here. The descriptions of the park make the reader feel the cold, the beauty, and the wild fecundity of the summer flowers. With this novel, Barr again displays her considerable talent for writing about nature. *Ill Wind* (Putnam, 1995) takes Anna to Mesa Verde National Park in Colorado. Anna thinks of this park as being more human-oriented than a wilderness park, and she is somewhat disconcerted by the crowds of tourists. The descriptions of Anna's daily work life enable the reader to know what it would feel like to work at a national park, and Barr creates a distinctive, spooky setting for her story.

Judith Van Gieson, Janet LaPierre, and Jane Langton write mysteries that feature environmental concerns. Sandy Dengler has a character who is a park ranger, and Lee Wallingford portrays a forest ranger in her mysteries.

Beaton, M. C. Marion Chesney, a prolific writer of historical romances under her own name and the pseudonyms of Ann Fairfax, Jennie Tremaine, Helen Crampton, and Charlotte Ward, began writing mysteries in the 1980s under the name of M. C. Beaton. Her first mysteries have been a series of unusual police procedurals: witty, light, and full of eccentric characters. The novels are British cozies with an endearing Gaelic twist. The first mystery in the series is *Death of a Gossip* (St. Martin's Press, 1985). The hero is Hamish Macbeth, constable of the small village of Lochdubh in northwestern Scotland. In his role as village bobby, Hamish sometimes acts deliberately stupid, and he uses the stereotype of the lazy gormless Highlander to his advantage in dealing with suspects (especially snobbish English visitors). Hamish is also a crofter in the community, and so he knows the characters and the idiosyncracies of the villagers only too well. This understanding allows him to solve murders in spite of the interference of his crass and bigoted superior in the police bureaucracy. Unfortunately, Hamish has to keep downplaying his successes; the last thing he wants is to be promoted out of his comfortable rural sinecure. Some of the Hamish Macbeth novels have been filmed for television.

Beaton has begun a new series with *Agatha Raisin and the Quiche of Death* (St. Martin's Press, 1992). Agatha is a hard-hearted businesswoman who retires to a cottage in the Cotswolds and finds more than she had bargained for when she discovers that she must learn new social skills in order to get along with the locals, as well as dealing with mysterious deaths. Beaton's novels combine gentle comedy and memorable rural settings with the traditional British mystery format.

Readers of Beaton's mysteries may also enjoy Marian Babson's novels, with their unusual character studies, Gloria Dank's humorous mysteries, and Susannah Stacey's stories about Robert Bone, an English police superintendent. Alanna Knight sets her historical mysteries in Victorian Scotland.

Beck, K. K. A journalist and magazine editor in Seattle, Beck has shown herself to be a versatile mystery writer. Beck has a marvelous light touch, bringing sprightly humor and an engaging sense of fun to many of her books. Beck's first novel, *Death in a Deck Chair* (Walker, 1984), introduced one series character, 1920s college student Iris Cooper. Returning from a visit to England on an ocean liner, Iris and her aunt encounter murder on board ship. With the aid of charmingly roguish reporter Jack Clancy, Iris solves the crime. In a similar light vein, Beck penned a novel of romantic intrigue, set in pre–World War I America and Europe, *Mrs. Cavendish and the Kaiser's Men* (Walker, 1987). Lately, she has begun a new series with *A Hopeless Case* (Mysterious, 1992), featuring Jane da Silva as an investigator into seemingly hopeless cases. Jane inherited the business from a wealthy but eccentric uncle. All these works are entertaining evidence of Beck's skill with the light and breezy, but she has demonstrated that she can write a gripping suspense novel as well. In *Unwanted Attentions* (Walker, 1988), Beck offers a tense variation on the stalker novel, proving that she can handle the darker side just as well as she handles the light.

Readers looking for other Seattle-based mysteries might try the work of Mary Daheim and Janet L. Smith. Marian Babson also has an enjoyable light touch in many of her novels.

Belfort, Sophie. The academic mystery is a staple of contemporary mystery fiction, for the enclosed community of the academic world offers the mystery writer a ready-made setting for murder and mayhem. Belfort, a pseudonymous historian who lives in Massachusetts, writes novels that, to date, have combined the worlds of academia and politics in a readable and informative mixture. The main characters of the series are history professor Molly Rafferty, a specialist in the Renaissance and Reformation era, and Jesuit-educated policeman Nick Hannibal. The first novel in the series, *The Lace Curtain Murders* (Atheneum, 1986), is subtitled *A Romance* and is as much the story of Molly and Nick falling in love as it is the investigation of a politically motivated murder in Boston. In this first novel, Belfort tackles the thorny issues, both political and moral, surrounding American support of the IRA. In a later work, *Eyewitness to Murder* (Donald I. Fine, 1992), Molly and Nick are involved in a case revolving around the prosecution of a Catholic priest accused of being a Nazi war criminal. Much of the novel takes place in Eastern Europe after the Soviet breakdown. Molly and Nick make appealing characters, and they make no bones about their opinions on issues both political and ethical. Subtle and complex, the plots of the novels offer much to the reader looking for an unusual twist on the academic mystery.

Fans of Amanda Cross and Nora Kelly will find much to enjoy in Belfort's work. Also, those who admire writers who weave in the world of politics and contemporary ethics, like Sara Paretsky and Cross, should also enjoy Belfort. Other recommendations are the archaeological-anthropological mysteries of Margot Arnold, and the series by Gillian Roberts that features a thirty-something high school teacher involved with a homicide detective.

Berry, Carole. Berry's heroine in a continuing series is Bonnie Indermill, who has made a career of working as an office temporary. Berry uses the format of presenting a limited number of murder suspects in a colorful, insular setting. Bonnie has worked in a law office, a large corporation, a ballet company, and a resort hotel. Bonnie is personable, observant, casual, and funny. The first book in the series is *The Letter of the Law* (St. Martin's Press, 1987). In *Goodnight, Sweet Prince* (St. Martin's Press, 1990), Bonnie goes to work at a major ballet company, doing fund-raising. She inadvertently helps a famous Soviet dancer to defect; he is then murdered. In *Island Girl* (St. Martin's Press, 1991), Bonnie is working at a rather seedy, down-at-the-heels resort in the Bahamas where she teaches fitness classes and finds herself in the midst of murder. The Bonnie Indermill books are light and entertaining reading. Berry also has written a novel of suspense, *Nightmare Point* (St. Martin's Press, 1993), about a thirteen-year-old girl who is kidnapped while on vacation with her family on Cape Cod.

Other writers in a similar vein that readers might like include Annette Meyers, who writes about New York office workers from a more affluent viewpoint, and Trella Crespi, whose advertising agency employee and sleuth Simona Griffo is as perpetually broke as Bonnie Indermill.

Bishop, Claudia. Bishop is a pseudonym for science fiction novelist Mary Stanton. The setting for this charming series is Upstate New York, a mythical town called Hemlock Falls, somewhere near Ithaca. Sarah Quilliam, a burned-out artist from the Big Apple, is the owner of the Hemlock Falls Inn, and her sister Meg is the chef. Quill—as everyone calls Sarah—is warm and impulsive, and Meg is a temperamental culinary genius. Among the inn's staff are several regular characters: John Raintree, the manager, and Doreen Muxworthy, the eccentric head housekeeper, whose enthusiasms change as often as the weather. Another regular is the sheriff, Myles McHale, and he and Quill are romantically involved. Other residents of Hemlock Falls figure in each book as well, serving as something of a Greek chorus. In the first novel in the series, *A Taste for Murder* (Berkley, 1994), Hemlock Falls is gearing up for its annual History Days celebration, but when one of Quill's guests turns up dead, Quill turns sleuth to keep the inn from being hurt by the adverse publicity. Spiced with Bishop's lively wit and endearing characters, this series is a feast for fans of the traditional mystery. Each book includes one recipe from the Hemlock Falls Inn.

Readers who have sampled Bishop's work might also enjoy the books of Katherine Hall Page, Janet Laurence, Diane Mott Davidson, and the late Virginia Rich.

Black, Malacai. See **D'Amato, Barbara.**

Black, Veronica. Black is a pseudonym for English author Maureen Peters, who also writes romance novels. *Last Seen Wearing* (St. Martin's Press, 1990) is a suspense novel about the kidnapping of a three-year-old girl. It explores the tension and anguish of waiting by the child's mother, and adds a touch of romance. With *A Vow of Silence* (St. Martin's Press, 1990), Black began a series of clerical mysteries featuring Sister Joan. Sister Joan is a nun of the Order of the Daughters of Compassion; she lives in a convent in Cornwall and teaches at a small school on the moors. The strength of Black's clerical novels is in her detailed descriptions of the closely regulated lives of cloistered nuns. The outside world, with its evil and uncertainties, intrudes upon the nuns' peaceful routines, but never shakes Sister Joan's faith. The world inside the convent has its terrors as well; in *A Vow of Silence*, mysterious disappearances and deaths occur within the sisterhood. *A Vow of Chastity* (St. Martin's Press, 1991) continues the series with a story about the disappearance of a Gypsy child from Sister Joan's school. Black also has written a ghostly suspense novel, *My Name is Polly Winter* (St. Martin's Press, 1993). Jessica Cameron, a historical researcher, encounters murder and the specter of a long-dead child when she rents a room in a gloomy Victorian house in Liverpool.

Readers may also wish to look for clerical mysteries by Sister Carol Anne O'Marie, Kate Charles, Barbara Whitehead, Isabelle Holland, and D. M. Greenwood.

Blaisdell, Anne. See **Linington, Elizabeth.**

Bland, Eleanor Taylor. African-American women are beginning to make their mark in crime fiction, and Bland is among the first. Her series character is Marti MacAlister, who left her job in the Chicago Police Department to get her family away from the tragedy of her husband's death. They now live in the small town of Lincoln Prairie, Illinois, and Marti thinks she's traded her big-city worries for small-town problems. She has managed to establish a somewhat comfortable relationship with her partner, Vik Jessenovik, even though he still has problems with her gender. Physically imposing, bright, and tough, Marti is a good cop, and her strengths shine in her first appearance, *Dead Time* (St. Martin's Press, 1992), when she and Vik investigate the death of a former mental patient at a run-down hotel. Bland writes very effectively about ordinary people caught up in tragic events beyond their control.

Readers looking for other African-American women mystery writers should read Barbara Neely and Valerie Wilson Wesley. Those interested in women police officers as series characters might try P. M. Carlson, Margaret Maron, and Lee Martin.

Borthwick, J. S. Sarah Deane, graduate student in English literature and later a teaching fellow at a small college in Maine, is the central character in this series of traditional mysteries. In the first of the series, *The Case of the Hook-Billed Kites* (St. Martin's Press, 1982), Sarah has joined her boyfriend in southern Texas for a birdwatching expedition. Sarah's hapless boyfriend is soon murdered, and Sarah turns to Dr. Alex McKenzie, another bird-watcher, for help in solving the murder. Subsequent novels in the series find Sarah and Alex back on home ground in New England. In *The Student Body* (St. Martin's Press, 1988), Sarah is a teaching fellow when she finds herself involved in a perplexing academic mystery. In the latest, *Dude on Arrival* (St. Martin's Press, 1992), Sarah and Alex spend Christmas vacation on an Arizona dude ranch as a gift from one of Sarah's eccentric relatives, and they become embroiled in another murder. Borthwick has a leisurely writing style; she unfolds her stories deliberately and carefully. Sarah and Alex are an appealing couple, and their combined expertise in literature and medicine makes them a formidable sleuthing duo.

Readers who have enjoyed Borthwick might try the work of Sally Gunning, Susan Kenney, Jane Langton, B. J. Morison, and Katherine Hall Page, all of whom have made effective use of New England settings. Readers looking for more about bird-watching should try the work of English writer Ann Cleeves.

Borton, D. B. Borton is a pseudonym used by Lynette Carpenter, an English professor at a small Midwestern college, for her series of mysteries set in Cincinnati. Borton's protagonist is Cat Caliban, a widow who has decided to change her life radically after thirty-eight years of marriage and motherhood. Cat always has been good at investigating unusual events (who put that frog in the washing machine?), so she decides to adopt the life of a private investigator. She moves out of suburbia, buys a small apartment house in the city, and reads up on detection at the library. Cat is an active, bright, and friendly sleuth with an eccentric band of assistants who are her friends, tenants, local homeless people, and the neighborhood kids. In *One for the Money* (Berkley, 1993), she finds the body of a bag lady in the next apartment, and she decides that this is an excellent opportunity to learn her newfound trade. In *Two Points for Murder* (Berkley, 1993), the author and her heroine both display increased confidence in their skills, and the plot is an absorbing one about the death of a teenage basketball star. *Three Is a Crowd* (Berkley, 1994) concerns the murder of a former sixties activist. Cat's client is a homeless man who is accused of the crime.

The Cat Caliban books are light, amusing novels with appealing and unusual characters, but Borton also brings social issues, particularly the plight of the homeless, into her stories.

Other writers who portray lively older sleuths include Mary Bowen Hall, Corinne Holt Sawyer, B. J. Oliphant, Kate Morgan, Stefanie Matteson, and Elizabeth Daniels Squire.

Bowen, Gail. Canadian writer Bowen is an English professor in Regina, Saskatchewan. Her continuing protagonist is Joanne Kilbourn, a political writer, commentator, and professor. Joanne's husband, a rising young political figure, has been murdered before the series begins with *Deadly Appearances* (Vancouver: Douglas & McIntyre, 1990). Joanne is writing speeches for a Saskatchewan politician, and he is murdered while delivering a speech at a rally. Bowen conveys a particularly effective setting for murder on the prairies of Saskatchewan and in the cities of Regina and Saskatoon. The books in the series also have a recurring cast of characters who are mainly politicians, artists, and journalists, as well as Joanne's children and friends. Joanne has a big, comfortable house, and she is a busy, smart, and nurturing woman who cares deeply about her family. She is an amateur sleuth, who stumbles on murder in the time-honored tradition of classic mysteries. *Murder at the Mendel* (Toronto: Douglas & McIntyre, 1991), published in the U.S. as *Love and Murder* (St. Martin's Press, 1993), concerns murder in the depth of winter at a Saskatoon art museum. The woman who is killed is Joanne's old friend, Sally Love, a free-spirited and very talented artist who has hung a controversial exhibit at the museum. The social issues of censorship, eroticism in art, and community standards all come into play in this thought-provoking, atmospheric novel. Winner of the Alfred Ellis Award for Best Novel from the Canadian Crime Writers Association, *A Colder Kind of Death* (St. Martin's Press, 1995) begins, appropriately enough, at Halloween. The man who killed Joanne's husband is killed in prison, and his wife returns to taunt Joanne. The stage for murder is set, and for

Joanne's inevitable status as a prime suspect. Joanne slowly unwinds the true story about the day her husband died, and she finds that she must investigate people who have been her friends and her husband's political colleagues for years. Bowen provides a vivid and intelligent backdrop of Canadian politics and culture in all of her novels, and they are well worth searching out.

Ellen Godfrey, L. R. Wright, Medora Sale, and Alison Gordon also write mysteries set in Canada. Janet LaPierre and Kathryn Lasky Knight provide another sense of the comfort of domesticity and the warmth of family life.

Boylan, Eleanor.   Few contemporary American mystery writers (other than Sue Grafton, perhaps) have the pedigree belonging to both Boylan and her series character, Clara Gamadge. Boylan is the niece of the late Elizabeth Daly, whom Dame Agatha Christie once proclaimed her favorite American mystery writer. Daly's detective was the bibliophile Henry Gamadge, and Boylan has adopted Gamadge's wife, Clara, now widowed, as her detective. In her late sixties, Clara Gamadge is an active, intelligent, and attractive character. Surrounded by her children and grandchildren and a beloved cousin her own age, Clara first appeared in *Working Murder* (Henry Holt, 1990). Delving into a mystery that involves friends from the past, Clara proves herself as capable as her dear, departed Henry in getting to the bottom of things. This first novel was a nominee for an Agatha Award for Best First Novel. In a recent outing, *Murder Machree* (Henry Holt, 1992), Clara and her cousin Charles "Sadd" Saddlier travel to Ireland to aid an old friend who may fall victim to a murderous deception. Harking back to the classic mystery tradition so beautifully practiced by her aunt, Boylan holds up the family tradition quite well.

Other writers who feature older women detectives are Mary Bowen Hall, Corinne Holt Sawyer, Gallagher Gray, and E. X. Ferrars. Readers unacquainted with the work of Elizabeth Daly might also enjoy seeking out these tales of Clara and her beloved Henry, in many ways an American cousin of Lord Peter Wimsey.

Braun, Lilian Jackson.   Braun began writing about newspaperman Jim Qwilleran and his two talented Siamese cats in 1966. She wrote *The Cat Who Could Read Backwards* (Dutton, 1966) and two more Cat Who . . . novels, then took a break from writing books for eighteen years. Her first mystery in the revived series was *The Cat Who Saw Red* (Berkley, 1986), which was nominated for an Edgar Award. In the earlier books in the series, Braun's main character, Qwill, lives in a Midwestern city and works as a journalist at the *Daily Fluxion*. The extravagantly mustachioed Qwill is grumpy, crotchety, and a confirmed bachelor. In *The Cat Who Played Brahms* (Berkley, 1987), he inherits the Klingenschoen fortune, which is contingent upon his living in rural Pickax City in Moose County. Qwill retires and moves north, but he continues to produce columns for a local newspaper and to become involved (along with his cats) in local crime-solving. Pickax City is described as 400 miles north of anywhere, and the later books in the series have a distinctly Upper Midwest ambience. The other main characters in the series are Qwill's cats, Koko and Yum Yum, who have extraordinary powers of perception and a close bond with Qwilleran, while he spoils them shamelessly. Each cat, too, has a firmly established personality: Koko is notedly psychic, intelligent, and curious, while Yum Yum is coy, playful, and affectionate. Koko especially noses out evidence and clues, and thus sends Qwill hints on crimes that have been committed. In each book, Qwill eventually understands what the cats are trying to communicate to him and thus is able to solve a mystery.

Braun also has written a collection of feline-centered short stories, *The Cat Who Had 14 Tales* (Berkley, 1988).

Other writers who have created lively animal characters include Carole Nelson Douglas, Rita Mae Brown, and Susan Conant.

Brennan, Carol. Brennan has written mysteries in two series, both with New York City settings. The first series features Liz Wareham, a public relations specialist. Liz is twice-divorced, with two kids in college, and now she is worried about the possibility of being alone in life. Her job, however, is always a challenge. In *Headhunt* (Carroll & Graf, 1991), Liz discovers an executive headhunter dead at his desk. She is a tough, able publicist, but dealing with murder is another matter. *Full Commission* (Carroll & Graf, 1993) finds Liz dealing with real estate and murder at the same time she is trying to cope with a new romantic relationship with the investigating detective, Ike O'Hanlon.

The second series stars Emily Silver, an actress in Los Angeles, who is just about to get a big break when the suspenseful *In the*

Dark (Putnam, 1994) opens. Her lover Mike is killed and his murder may be linked to her tragic background. Her parents were killed when she was nine, and she survived by hiding. But she remembers hearing a mysterious, distinctive voice, which she assumes is the voice of the killer. She hears that voice again twenty years later in a movie theater, and she must return to New York City to find the killer. She enlists the help of Dev, an old friend of Mike's, and they begin to fall in love. Emily returns in *Chill of Summer* (Putnam, 1995). She has inherited her family's home in Upstate New York and is living there. She meets an old school friend again and befriends a teenage girl with emotional problems rather like the ones Emily had as a child. The stage is set, inevitably, for murder. Emily is a realistic and memorable character; she makes her share of personal mistakes and is an attractive amateur sleuth.

Readers also may enjoy the suspense novels of Carol and Mary Higgins Clark, Nancy Baker Jacobs, and Barbara Nickolae. Marissa Piesman's *Unorthodox Practices* gives another amusing view of murder over New York real estate.

Brightwell, Emily. Mrs. Hepzibah Jeffries, the widow of a Yorkshire policeman and now the housekeeper of a Scotland Yard detective, is the central character in this series of mysteries set in Victorian England. Mrs. Jeffries's employer, Inspector Witherspoon, is a nice man, but not terribly skilled at doing his job, which involves tracking down murderers. Luckily for Witherspoon, he inherited a fortune and a houseful of intelligent servants from an elderly aunt. Mrs. Jeffries, along with Mrs. Goodge, the cook, Betsy, the housemaid, Wiggins, the footman, and Smythe, the coachman, work diligently behind the scenes to gather information on Witherspoon's cases. They bring their information to Mrs. Jeffries, who in turn feeds it to the inspector, who seems rather bemused by his continued success in solving all these murder mysteries. The ensemble cast is engaging, and the stories have their own light charm. First in the series is *The Inspector and Mrs. Jeffries* (Berkley, 1993).

Readers who have enjoyed the exploits of Mrs. Jeffries and her crew might try as well the works of Kate Kingsbury. Amy Myers also writes an engaging series set in late Victorian England, but readers looking for a more in-depth portrayal of Victorian England should try the works of Anne Perry.

Brod, D. C.   Quint McCauley is the private eye created by Brod for her series of novels. Quint is a PI very much in the style of Philip Marlowe: laconic, principled, and sardonic. In Brod's first novel, *Murder in Store* (Walker, 1989), Quint, a former policeman, is in charge of security for a Chicago department store that seems rather akin to Marshall Field. Quint's life is complicated because he has been dumped by his girlfriend for a younger man and then has been reprimanded for catching his boss's wife shoplifting. When his boss is murdered, Quint, in the tradition of Marlowe, pursues truth doggedly while trying to keep his principles intact. In later novels, Quint moves to Foxport, a mythical suburb of Chicago on the Fox River. Even when everyone in Foxport (including the chief of police) is against him, Quint is persistent in solving mysteries. Inevitably, Quint gets beaten up, threatened, and car-bombed in the pursuit of truth. Brod's prose is unadorned and hard-boiled; her stories are tightly plotted.

Brod's readers might also be interested in the writings of Nancy Baker Jacobs, M. K. Wren, and Sara Paretsky.

Brown, Rita Mae.   Already a well-established novelist with a string of successful books to her credit, Brown recently, with the aid of her tiger cat, Sneaky Pie Brown, turned to writing mysteries. The setting for this series is the small town of Crozet, Virginia, near Charlottesville, and Brown has filled the town with engaging and believable characters, both animal and human. Mary Minor "Harry" Haristeen, the town's young postmistress, is the central human character. Watched over lovingly by Mrs. Murphy and Tee Tucker, her cat and dog, the central animal characters, Harry learns to live with the aftermath of divorce in a small and close-knit community. Her ex-husband, "Fair" (for Pharamond), is the town's veterinarian. In the first of the series, *Wish You Were Here* (Bantam, 1990), Harry starts noting strange postcards, which are heralds to murder. Prodded when necessary by Mrs. Murphy and Tee Tucker and other animal characters, Harry solves the mystery. Brown intersperses the narrative from the human point of view with engaging and amusing conversations among the animals (presumably these are the contributions of Sneaky Pie), which enhance the plot and offer another dimension of observation, with some quite satirical comments on the foibles of human behavior. Rich in character and small-town Southern ambience, the Mrs. Murphy mysteries are great fun. Each book includes illustrations by artist Wendy Wray.

For readers eager to enjoy the exploits of animal crime-solvers, The Cat Who . . . series of Lilian Jackson Braun remains the most popular, though the works of canine experts Susan Conant, Melissa Cleary, and cat fancier Carole Nelson Douglas are fast gaining an audience. Readers who like the Southern settings of Brown's work might also try the work of Charlaine Harris, Deborah Adams, Sarah Shankman, or Sharyn McCrumb.

Buchanan, Edna. Buchanan's first two books, *Never Let Them See You Cry* (Random House, 1992) and *The Corpse Had a Familiar Face* (Random House, 1987), are autobiographical. She tells, tersely and vividly, of the memorable crimes that she covered as a reporter for the Miami *Herald.* Buchanan, a Pulitzer Prize winner for her journalism, then turned to fiction with *Nobody Lives Forever* (Random House, 1990). She paints portraits of three police officers, all affected by a serial killer. As with all of her books, Buchanan provides a gritty, tough Miami background for her riveting story.

With *Contents Under Pressure* (Hyperion, 1992), Buchanan begins a series of mysteries featuring crime reporter Britt Montero. Britt is relentlessly curious and ready to drop anything (including her personal life) to go after a story. She loves the crime beat although many others, especially her mother, think it's no place for a woman. Britt always wants to prove them wrong. The Edgar-nominated *Miami, It's Murder* (Hyperion, 1994) tells the story of the Downtown Rapist, who is terrorizing Miamians, along with a mysterious series of events that appear to be revenge crimes. In *Suitable for Framing* (Hyperion, 1995), Buchanan tells two interwoven stories: one about a group of teenagers who steal cars and shoot the drivers, the other about a woman reporter who becomes a protégée to Britt.

Buchanan's stories of criminal events often focus on the people involved, and her characters come sharply alive for the reader. She is particularly notable for her skill in depicting how devastating violent crime is for the families of victims. Buchanan's concise prose is well-suited to her staccato, story telling style.

Readers who enjoy Buchanan's hard-edged urban tales may also like books by Dorothy Uhnak, Lillian O'Donnell, and Faye Kellerman. Meg O'Brien, Barbara D'Amato, Mickey Friedman, and Lesley

Grant-Adamson write mysteries that feature reporters, and Sherryl Woods and T. J. MacGregor write mysteries set in Miami.

Burden, Pat.   In this cozy series of English mysteries, retired policeman Henry Bassett has settled into a comfortable life in a Herefordshire cottage, tending his pigs and chickens and his garden. But a bizarre crime intrudes upon this rustic calm in *Screaming Bones* (Doubleday, 1990), the first novel in the series, and Bassett finds himself itching to become involved. Burden depicts the rural and village settings in Herefordshire with a loving eye and peoples her works with engaging descendants of the classic English mystery novel. There is a comforting sense of familiarity in Burden's novels, but rather than breeding contempt, familiarity in this case brings the cheering sense of recognition of yet another skilled practitioner of an established form. Burden's little corner of England is definitely part of the England of the 1990s but with recognizable ties to the past. *Screaming Bones* was an Agatha Award nominee for Best First Malice Domestic Mystery Novel.

Like Burden, June Thomson, Dorothy Simpson, and Susan B. Kelly infuse their works with a strong sense of rural and smaller-town England. Readers might also enjoy the work of Anne Granger and Ann Cleeves.

Burke, Jan.   Burke writes hard-boiled novels set in a Southern California beach city with protagonist Irene Kelly. In the first book in the series, *Goodnight, Irene* (Simon & Schuster, 1993), Irene has quit her job as a reporter and is working as a publicist and hates it. All that changes when her best friend and mentor, the veteran reporter O'Connor, is blown to bits one morning by a bomb. She returns to the newspaper to finish up some stories that O'Connor was working on and begins compulsively to look into his death, especially after she is attacked. Irene also begins a relationship again with an old boyfriend, Frank Harriman, who is a local homicide detective. *Goodnight, Irene* was nominated for the Anthony and Agatha Awards for best first mystery. Irene is back at the newspaper full-time in *Sweet Dreams, Irene* (Simon & Schuster, 1994), working on stories about local political campaigns. On Halloween, the teenage son of a local candidate tells her that a story alleging that he is a Satanist will initiate a smear campaign against his father. Irene begins to investigate, and the story quickly escalates into brutal murder and intimidation. Unfortunately, she is not allowed to work on crime stories anymore in case she leaks information to Frank, and he is under constant suspicion of leaking items to her as well. Burke provides a masterly depiction of the professional and personal difficulties of such a relationship in a realistic, not overly sentimental, way. Irene also must deal with a great deal of violence in this novel, much of it directed at her. In *Dear Irene,* (Simon & Schuster, 1995), Irene is still recovering from the physical and emotional injuries suffered in her previous case. She begins to get letters from a serial killer who is apparently obsessed with Greek mythology and signs himself Thanatos. The killer may also be obsessed with her, and the suspense is riveting. Burke's Southern California setting and her use of the history of women defense workers in World War II in her plot give a particularly strong backdrop to this novel.

Hannah Wolfe, in Sarah Dunant's *Fatlands,* must also address questions of the emotional repercussions of violence, as does V. I. Warshawski in Sara Paretsky's novels. Other Southern California sleuths are depicted in the mysteries of Maxine O'Callaghan, Wendy Hornsby, Abigail Padgett, Dianne G. Pugh, Rochelle Majer Krich, Faye Kellerman, and A. E. Maxwell.

Butler, Gwendoline.   This veteran author has penned over fifty novels under her own name and as Jennie Melville since the late 1950s. As Butler, she began writing mysteries, most of which featured Inspector Winter and his sergeant, John Coffin; the first is *Dead in a Row* (Geoffrey Bles, 1957). Then 0Coffin became the main character in a long series of novels, through the mid-1970s. Butler abandoned him for a while, writing instead historical novels with elements of mystery and suspense, like *Sarsen Place* (Coward McCann, 1974). Then, in 1986, she resurrected Coffin in *Coffin on the Water,* (St. Martin's Press, 1989), recreated some of the details of his personal life, and the series was reborn.

As Jennie Melville, she created policewoman Charmian Daniels, born and reared in Scotland, but working in Deerham Hills, near London. Daniels first appeared in *Come Home and Be Killed* (London House and Maxwell, 1964). Besides the Daniels books, Melville has written novels in the romantic suspense vein, like *Dragon's Eye* (Simon & Schuster, 1976).

Both Charmian Daniels and John Coffin are intelligent, intense, and curious about their fellow human beings. Whether writing as

Butler or Melville, the author has a style quite different from any of her peers. She creates a chilling sense of unease unlike anyone else, except perhaps Ruth Rendell. The murderer's presence is eerily tangible throughout each novel, like a goblin hovering on the periphery of vision. Readers looking for an unusual variation on the traditional English mystery will find Butler worth a visit.

Those who are familiar with Butler/Melville might try the Wexford novels of Ruth Rendell and the works of Minette Walters and S. T. Haymon. Readers looking for other writings of historical or contemporary romantic suspense might enjoy the work of Victoria Holt and her pseudonym Philippa Carr, Jean Stubbs, or Jessica Stirling.

C

Cannell, Dorothy. Cannell's first novel, *The Thin Woman* (St. Martin's Press, 1984) has been a perennial favorite with mystery readers. In this charming, eccentric comedy-mystery, the heroine, Ellie Simons, is an overweight interior decorator who becomes embroiled in a romantic fantasy straight out of her dreams. The problem is that she has to lose weight (sixty-three pounds!) and find a hidden treasure in six months in order to inherit a castle and win her true love. The leading man, Ben Haskell, is an aspiring chef and writer of great literature who makes ends meet by writing trashy stories and working (innocently enough) for an escort service. Cannell's second novel, *Down the Garden Path* (St. Martin's Press, 1985) introduces Hyacinth and Primrose Tramwell, elderly (and odd) sisters with a bent for duplicity and investigation. Later novels continue Ellie's adventures in life and crime, sometimes with the assistance (or perhaps it's the hindrance) of the Tramwells. All are set in England, except *Mum's the Word* (Bantam, 1990), which takes place in the hilariously described small Midwestern town of Mud Creek, Illinois. Cannell's characters are endearingly dotty in the best tradition of English literary eccentrics.

Comedy-mysteries by Elizabeth Peters, Charlotte MacLeod, and Joan Hess also may be fun for readers of Cannell. *Aunt Dimity's Death* (Viking, 1992) by Nancy Atherton is a charming, gentle tale that may appeal to admirers of *The Thin Woman*.

Carlson, P. M.   The *P* stands for Patricia. Carlson holds a Ph.D. in the psychology of language and has coauthored a textbook called *Behavioral Statistics*. Some of this background is evident in her mysteries, for Carlson has endowed her series character, Maggie Ryan, with her own interest and abilities in statistics. In the first of the series, *Audition for Murder* (Avon, 1985), set in 1967, Maggie is an undergraduate in a small college in Upstate New York. Several professional actors are teaching at the college and starring in a production of *Hamlet.* Among the actors are Nick O'Connor and his wife Lisette, who has a troubled history of drug abuse. Maggie, lighting expert for the play, soon turns sleuth when someone seems bent on driving Lisette back to drugs with malicious pranks. In subsequent books, the relationship between Maggie and Nick grows, and by *Murder Unrenovated* (Bantam, 1988), they're married and expecting their first child. While Carlson constructs neat puzzles along with the best of them, the chief appeal in her series is the strong characterizations. Maggie Ryan, the centerpiece, is intelligent, intense, and fiercely loyal to her friends. Sometimes she seems like a superwoman, because she can handle just about anything thrown in her path, never ducking an emotion simply because it is painful. Strength of character is her long suit. With *Gravestone* (Pocket, 1993), Carlson introduces Marty Hopkins, a sheriff's deputy in southern Indiana. A working mother with an unreliable husband, Marty is bright and tough, like Maggie Ryan.

The characters of M. K. Lorens are also intense, though perhaps more eccentric than those of Carlson. Nevertheless, readers who enjoy one might well try the other. Another New York series with intriguing characters are the Sigrid Harald books of Margaret Maron. In addition, Carlson fans might also enjoy the works of Nancy Pickard, B. J. Oliphant, and Kate Wilhelm. Jane Dentinger and Anne Morice both have main characters who are actresses.

Caudwell, Sarah.   Though she has only three books thus far to her credit, Caudwell has achieved a wide following for her mirthful tales of murder and mayhem. With an erudition and precision of language worthy of the late Dorothy L. Sayers, Caudwell does what she does quite unlike anyone else writing contemporary mystery novels. The narrator of Caudwell's work is the androgynous Oxford professor of law, Hilary Tamar. Though readers may claim to know whether Hilary is male or female, Caudwell smilingly refuses ever to settle the debate. The affairs that Hilary so amusingly relates concern five young London barristers, each of whom has her or his own particular talent for running into trouble. In the brilliantly funny *Thus Was Adonis Murdered* (Scribner, 1981), Julia Larwood, who knows the Finance Act inside out but who can't quite remember where she left her passport, becomes embroiled in murder while she's on holiday in Venice. Hilary, of course, must come to the rescue. The combination of wit, humor, and intelligence makes Caudwell's work a rare vintage. Caudwell's third novel, *The Sirens Sang of Murder* (Delacorte, 1989), won the Anthony Award for Best Novel from the Bouchercon.

Though few mystery writers currently writing quite approach the combination of Caudwell's elegant wit and humor, readers hungering for other highly individual or humorous writing styles might browse the work of Margery Allingham, Mollie Hardwick, Elizabeth Peters, Charlotte MacLeod, Patricia Moyes, and Dorothy L. Sayers.

Chaplin, Elizabeth.   See **McGown, Jill.**

Charles, Kate.   An American currently living in Bedford, England, Charles uses her experience as a former Anglican church administrator and her love of English ecclesiastical history and architecture to provide a fascinating background for a series of mysteries starring solicitor David Middleton-Brown. Middleton-Brown is himself an expert of a sort on church architecture, and in this role he sometimes finds himself involved in mysterious goings-on. In the first book of the series, *A Drink of Deadly Wine* (Mysterious Press, 1992), David must confront difficult secrets out of his own past when he is called upon for help by a charismatic priest, Gabriel Neville. Neville is being blackmailed, and, because of the peculiar circumstances, he knows David Middleton-Brown is the one person who can solve the puzzle. In the course of his investigation, David meets the artist Lucy Kingsley, with whom he develops an unusual relationship that continues in later books. In *The Snares of Death* (Mysterious Press, 1993), David and Lucy agree to investigate the death of a prominent Evangelical minister who had a talent for rubbing people the wrong way. Full of church politics and intriguing characters, this series has much to offer the fan of the traditional English mystery.

Readers who enjoy mysteries with clerical settings or characters should try the work of D. M. Greenwood, Mollie Hardwick, and Barbara Whitehead. Those interested in American mysteries with clerical backgrounds could try the work of Isabelle Holland and Sister Carol Anne O'Marie.

Christmas, Joyce. After writing several novels, some nonfiction books, and children's plays, Christmas turned to the mystery novel. Her series detective is Lady Margaret Priam, a genteel English-woman living in New York City. In her first appearance, *Suddenly in Her Sorbet* (Fawcett, 1988), Lady Margaret is attending a charity fund-raiser when someone poisons the organizer, a grande dame of New York society. Aided by her young friend and fellow socialite, Prince Paul Castrocani, Lady Margaret dives into the case. Along the way she becomes interested in the investigating police officer, detective Sam de Vere, and in subsequent novels, the two pursue a romantic relationship. Christmas handles the intriguing social world of New York City with deft skill, her slightly ironic eye yielding the reader quiet amusement at the foibles of the rich and often tasteless. Though much of the action in the series takes place in New York and its environs, Lady Margaret occasionally investigates farther afield. In one novel, *Friend or Faux* (Fawcett, 1991), she returns to England to help her brother, the Earl of Brayfield, solve the murder of one of his guests.

Recently, Christmas has begun a second series, starring retired businesswoman Betty Trenka. In her debut, *This Business Is Murder* (Fawcett, 1993), Betty moves to Connecticut to start her retirement, but quickly bored, she takes a temporary job at a local business and turns sleuth when someone starts murdering the employees. Nosy, competent, and worldly, Betty demonstrates that older women make excellent detectives.

Female English aristocrats are scarce among today's crime-solvers, although former Member of Parliament Michael Spicer has written several novels about Lady Jane Hildreth. Evelyn E. Smith is writing a series about Miss Susan Melville, a well-bred American woman who just happens to be a hired assassin, based in New York City. Other entertaining series set in New York City are the works of Gallagher Gray and Annette Meyers. Fans of Betty Trenka might try the works of Eleanor Boylan and Corinne Holt Sawyer, as well as Gallagher Gray.

Churchill, Jill. Churchill's books are charming and unpretentious. Jane Jeffry, a widowed homemaker and mother, lives in the suburbs of Chicago. Jane has three kids, nosy neighbors, and a network of friends who do volunteer work for charities and help each other out of jams. And of course they get involved in local murders. Jane and her friends solve murders by deduction and the application of common sense. They confound the police, especially Detective Mel VanDyne, with conclusions drawn from their everyday knowledge of housework and neighborhood customs. In *Grime and Punishment*, for example, Jane makes a crucial deduction by knowing how women typically vacuum a room. Churchill uses the traditional format: the murders occur in a small town among a closed circle of suspects, and the puzzle is solved by the use of well-hidden clues and logical deductions made by the amateur sleuth. Jane is a younger Miss Marple figure. She observes human nature, suburban life, and people, and then combines her observations with her inborn intelligence to solve crimes. Aside from the mystery plot, the books are brimful of Churchill's wry comments on motherhood, carpooling, living in suburbia, raising teenagers, and other conditions of modern life.

The first Jane Jeffry book is *Grime and Punishment* (Bantam, 1989). It won an Agatha Award for Best First Mystery Novel.

Jill Churchill is a pseudonym of Janice Young Brooks, who also writes historical novels. Other crime novelists the reader might like include Charlotte MacLeod, Valerie Wolzien, Katherine Hall Page, and of course Agatha Christie, especially her Miss Marple books.

Clark, Carol Higgins. Clark is an actress and a writer as well as the daughter of best-selling novelist Mary Higgins Clark. Before she began writing, she learned her trade by doing research for her mother's novels. Her first mystery is *Decked* (Warner, 1992), which was nominated for an Agatha Award for Best First Novel. It is set on an ocean liner crossing the Atlantic. Clark's series heroine is Regan Reilly, a private eye who is headquartered in Los Angeles, but who finds murder even on her vacations away from the office. On the way back from a college reunion in Oxford, Regan is hired as a last-minute replacement for a companion to a rich, elderly woman. Unbeknownst to her, the echoes of a murder committed ten years ago have followed her and her charge onto the boat. Regan's father, a funeral director, and her mother, a famous suspense writer, play secondary roles in this shipboard adventure. Clark moves her action to Miami in *Snagged* (Warner, 1993). Her parents are present for a funeral home convention, and Regan has come for a friend's wedding. Much of the action is set at a panty-hose convention, and it proves to be a clever idea and setting for murder. Like her mother, Clark depicts decent, middle-class people who are caught up in violence, and she is particularly adept at portraying her characters, especially the elderly, with sympathy and affection. She also has a brisk sense of humor between the moments of suspense. Readers may also enjoy the suspense novels of Mary Higgins Clark, Carol Brennan, Judith Kelman, Meg O'Brien, and Barbara Nickolae.

Clark, Mary Higgins. Clark's well-crafted novels of suspense have been making the best-seller lists since the 1970s. The books generally have attractive heroines or children in danger from a killer who is stalking them. Positively portrayed authority figures—police officers, doctors, lawyers, detectives—help find the criminal and protect the vulnerable. Clark's protagonists are mostly upscale, sophisticated, and articulate people. She provides vividly realized settings, and wintry scenes of Northeastern cities and their suburbs abound. Her first novel, *Where Are the Children?* (Simon & Schuster, 1975), is set on Cape Cod, with a villain who kidnaps two small children in order to frame their mother, who had been accused earlier in her life of killing two other children. In this and subsequent novels, Clark slowly builds suspense with her clear prose and measured evocation of daily life, as the killer hovers and events move out of the control of the innocent. Incidents move inevitably toward a terrifying crisis that must occur before order can be restored at the end of the story. Meanwhile, Clark has given the reader a strong sense of the danger that can lurk even in the most protected and affluent lives.

Clark also has written two volumes of short stories, and she moved away a bit from the suspense novel to write a mystery in the classic format, *Weep No More, My Lady* (Simon & Schuster, 1987). She received the French Grand Prix de Litterature Policiere in 1980.

Other novelists of suspense include Judith Kelman, T. J. MacGregor, Nancy Baker Jacobs, Rochelle Majer Krich, Patricia Cornwell, D. F. Mills, and Kate Green.

Clarke, Anna.   The literary world and its denizens hold strong interest for Clarke, for in many of her novels central characters are writers, sometimes of mystery fiction of some sort. An early example is *Plot Counter-Plot* (Walker, 1975), in which a successful, older woman novelist takes under her wing a brash, unsuccessful young man, also a novelist. Their relationship, both literary and amorous, leads them down the path to destruction, and Clarke cleverly keeps the reader guessing all the way. Another novel, *The Lady in Black* (McKay, 1978), has a Victorian setting and revolves around a mysterious woman who had penned a suspenseful tale of murder and remorse that may be fact rather than fiction. Only recently has Clarke developed a series character. When she first appears in *Last Judgement* (Doubleday, 1985), University of London English professor Paula Glenning is actually a minor character, but she soon moves to the forefront, as in *Murder in Writing* (Doubleday, 1988).

Clarke's interest in psychology and the myriad quirks of human behavior makes the best of her work suspenseful; she can take clichés of the genre and make them seem refreshingly new. *Letter from the Dead* (Doubleday, 1981), along with *Plot Counter-Plot*, demonstrate this very well.

Those who have enjoyed the work of Clarke might try the novels of E. X. Ferrars, Margaret Yorke, and Celia Fremlin.

Cleary, Melissa.   The central character in Cleary's series of 'dog lovers' mysteries is Jackie Walsh, who has recently divorced her husband and forsaken her life as a suburban housewife to move back into the city and take up her career once again. Living with Jackie is her ten-year-old son, Peter. In the first book of the series, *A Tail of Two Murders* (Berkley, 1992), Jackie and Peter find an Alsatian shepherd with a bullet wound in his leg, and they adopt the dog and name him Jake. Jake turns out to be a retired police dog whose owner has been mysteriously murdered. An instructor in the Rodgers University film department, Jackie finds her department chairman dead in the film library one day. Lieutenant Michael McGowan is officially in charge of the case, and he elicits Jackie's help. Their relationship continues in further books in the series, edging a little closer to romance all the time. The presence of Jake the retired police dog involves Jackie and Peter in danger, for the murder of Jake's former master is still unsolved, and someone considers Jake a threat. This is an enjoyable cozy series, with an attractive single mother, her son, and their adopted dog as the centerpieces.

Readers acquainted with Cleary might try as well the series by Susan Conant and Dana Stabenow, in which dogs play important roles in the crime-solving.

Cleeves, Ann. The distinctive feature of one of the two series that Cleeves writes is the prominence of bird-watching and related environmental issues. The main character, former Home Office official George Palmer-Jones, is an avid bird-watcher, and the murders with which he becomes involved generally occur around some activity connected with bird-watching. For the uninitiated, Cleeves explains the enthusiasms of the activity well, though readers with no interest in the subject might prefer Cleeves's other series.

The second series features Inspector Stephen Ramsay as the detective, and the setting is Northumberland. This series follows conventional lines for the modern British police detective mystery.

Both series fit comfortably into the traditional or cozy mold. First in the Palmer-Jones series is *A Bird in the Hand* (Fawcett, 1988); first in the Inspector Ramsay series is *A Lesson in Dying* (Fawcett, 1990).

No other writers have made bird-watching such a prominent feature of their series, except perhaps J. S. Borthwick, though bird-watching characters do appear rather often in many English series. Other writers who touch upon environmental and animal rights issues with frequency are Gwen Moffat and Susan Conant.

Cody, Liza. Until recently, it has been unusual for British women to write hard-boiled crime fiction, but Liza Cody has done so successfully and has added a distinctly English and feminist twist to a largely American art form. Cody's heroine is Anna Lee, an operative with Brierly Security in London. Anna's boss doesn't think much of women investigators, so he tends to assign her "female" cases, like hunting for a missing daughter or providing security for a department store (in spite of Anna's five years' experience in the police). Anna is certainly the low person on the totem pole and her position is not improved by the perception in the agency that she handles her assignments in ways different from the male agents. Somehow she gets involved with the people in her cases, even when doing security for a difficult rock star in *Under*

Contract (Scribner, 1987). In the tradition of fictional private eyes, Anna tends to be a self-reliant lone wolf. When she has a day off, she's likely to spend it cleaning the spark plugs and tuning up the engine on her old Triumph. Anna does have friendly and eccentric neighbors, Bea and Selwyn Price, who leave her little privacy or quiet. Like Sue Grafton, Cody is interested in the routine minutiae of the investigator's day. Her books are set in a grimy London; details of the traffic, the Underground system, and the daily challenges of urban life are abundant.

Cody began a second series with *Bucket Nut* (Doubleday, 1993), a virtuoso character study of Eva Wylie, a female wrestler, petty criminal, and security guard. Anna Lee appears briefly in this novel, but the focus is on Eva, the "London Lassassin", and her daily struggle for survival and independence. Eva returns in *Monkey Wrench* (Mysterious, 1995).

Cody has also written *Rift* (Scribner, 1988), a novel about a naive young woman's harrowing trip through a drought-stricken Ethiopia in 1974, and she has edited several short story anthologies.

Cody's first Anna Lee novel, *Dupe* (Scribner, 1980), won the British Crime Writers' Association John Creasey Award for Best First Novel. *Bucket Nut* won the Silver Dagger Award from the Crime Writers' Association.

Gillian Slovo, Anabel Donald, and Sarah Dunant also write novels set in London with hard-boiled investigators Kate Baeier, Alex Tanner, and Hannah Wolfe, while Val McDermid uses Manchester as a backdrop.

Cohen, Janet. See **Neel, Janet.**

Coker, Carolyn. Coker writes light, intelligent mysteries with art history backgrounds. Her continuing heroine is art restorer Andrea Perkins. The series begins with *The Other David* (Dodd, Mead, 1984), with Andrea on leave from her job at Harvard to work at the Galleria Dell' Accademia in Florence, Italy. An elderly priest gives her an old painting that has been in his family for a long time. Is it a Michelangelo portrait of the biblical David or is it a forgery? Coker mixes technical details of the craft of art restoration and the chemical analysis and dating of paintings into her beguiling tales of murder. *The Vines of Ferrara* (Dodd, Mead, 1986) is set in Ferrara at a fictional castle of Lucrezia Borgia. Andrea is now a freelance art restorer, specializing in the Italian Renaissance, and she is doing jobs all over Europe. The castle has its own vineyard, and it seems that the tradition of Borgia poisonings has resurfaced and there may be poison in some of the bottles of wine from the vineyard. Coker provides a stirring backdrop of Italy and its multitude of art masterpieces. She continues this theme in an English setting in *The Balmoral Nude* (St. Martin's Press, 1990). Andrea is asked by an old friend and his wife to restore some rather scandalous nineteenth-century drawings done by an prominent artist who killed his mistress and was hanged for it. This involves her in a case of art theft and authentication.

Magdalen Nabb sets her mysteries in Florence, and Sarah Caudwell and Mickey Friedman have each set a crime novel there as well. Marcia Muller (in her Elena Oliverez series), Earlene Fowler, Carol Clemeau, Cecil Dawkins, and Elizabeth Peters (in the Vicky Bliss novels) have created protagonists who are art historians or museum curators. Jane Langton's unusual mysteries capture something of the same spirit of art as a living force.

Comfort, B. A portrait and landscape painter, Barbara Comfort divides her time between New York City and Landgrove, Vermont. She chose Vermont as the setting for her mystery novels, having published books about two different main characters.

The first two books, *The Vermont Village Murder* (Landgrove Press, 1982) and *Green Mountain Murder* (Landgrove Press, 1984), feature young artist Liz Bell, who has returned to Vermont in search of her roots. In the first book, she finds some of those roots in a town called Bellsville, where she also finds a sinister conspiracy involving uranium mining and murder. In the second book, she has moved to Lofton, and though she has the same name, some of the events of the first novel seem never to have happened.

With *Phoebe's Knee* (Foul Play, 1994; reprint of a 1986 publication), Comfort began a new series, starring the elderly and irascible painter Tish McWhinny. With her dear friend, octogenarian Hilary Oats, and her pug Lulu, Tish investigates mysterious happenings and murders in and around Lofton. Comfort draws an entertaining portrait of an older woman character, proud and independent, and an affectionate landscape painting of beautiful Vermont, under siege from those who would develop away all of its pristine rural charm.

Those acquainted with Comfort's work might also enjoy the work of B. J. Morison, Corinne Holt Sawyer, Stefanie Matteson, and Margot Arnold.

Conant, Susan. All those dog lovers tired of seeing cats get all the cover art in pet-centered mysteries found a welcome new voice in Conant. Her series detective is Holly Winter, columnist for the magazine *Dog's Life* and malamute enthusiast. In between writing her column and training her malamute Rowdy, Holly stumbles upon crimes, usually involving dogs in some way, in and around Cambridge, Massachusetts. Sparked by a sense of humor with a strong streak of irony, Holly has a pithy narrative voice and little patience for those who fail to treat animals with respect. In addition to giving man's and woman's best friend a share of the spotlight, Conant also manages to raise the consciousness of her readers with her plots, which often involve issues relating to animal welfare. These issues sometimes make the books perhaps less cozy than some readers might prefer, but Conant, like Nancy Pickard, has the knack of blending trenchant social comment with an entertaining story. The series begins with *A New Leash on Death* (Berkley, 1990).

Dogs are still in the minority when it comes to appearances in mystery novels, but Melissa Cleary has recently debuted with a new series of dog lovers' mysteries with *A Tail of Two Murders* (Berkley, 1992). Joan Hess's novel, *Roll Over and Play Dead* (St. Martin's Press, 1991), is a strong comment on some of the same issues that concern Conant. Barbara Moore wrote two books about a crime-solving veterinarian, and both Susan Kelly and Kathryn Lasky Knight write about Cambridge and its environs in their series.

Cooper, Natasha. Cooper is a pseudonym for British author Daphne Wright. Under this name, she writes romantic mysteries featuring Willow King, a civil servant who leads a double life as a romance novelist. Willow works three days a week in the Department of Old Age Pensions as an administrator and lives in a scruffy south London flat on a tight budget. But in her second life as Cressida Woodruffe, she spends Friday through Monday writing romance novels and living in a lavishly decorated apartment with a gourmet cook–housekeeper. The success of this strange existence is threatened when she encounters murderous events. In *A Common Death* (Crown, 1990), the Minister of State in charge of Willow's department is killed, she meets Chief Inspector Tom Worth, who is investigating the murder, and she is threatened by an attacker who burglarizes and befouls her luxurious Cressida Woodruffe flat. Cooper establishes Willow as a person who possesses great self-control and personal fortitude but who also has built an emotional wall around herself. As the series progresses, that personal armor slowly breaks down, and she begins to admit other people behind her defenses. For example, she comes at once to the aid of a former lover accused of murder in *Bloody Roses* (Crown, 1992). Cooper's novels are entertaining, light reading; the improbable double life plot twist becomes less important as Willow develops into a sympathetic and three-dimensional character.

Janet Neel and Ruth Dudley Edwards also use the British civil service system as a backdrop for their mysteries. Dorothy Cannell, Elizabeth Peters, and Nancy Atherton have written romantic mysteries.

Cooper, Susan Rogers.   A writer who describes herself as half fifth-generation Texan and half Yankee, Cooper has let the Texas half prevail in her two series set in the Southwest.

The first series features chief deputy Milt Kovak of the Prophesy County, Oklahoma, Sheriff's Department. In his first recorded case, *The Man in the Green Chevy* (St. Martin's Press, 1988), Milt has to deal with a rapist and murderer of little old ladies, and the whole county is horrified. Cooper describes her territory well, and she manages to convey the atmosphere of rural and small-town Oklahoma with the ease of a veteran. She also makes Milt Kovak sound like a completely believable, somewhat irascible, forty-eight-year-old man. In a voice that is wry, reflective, and occasionally raunchy, Milt narrates these tales of murder and misbehavior with a definite Southwestern inflection.

These same strong qualities carry over into Cooper's second series, which features housewife and romance novelist, E. J. (Eloise Janine) Pugh. Debuting in *One, Two, What Did Daddy Do?* (St. Martin's Press, 1992), E. J. and her husband Willis, residents of the small community of Black Cat Ridge, Texas, solve the murders of their next-door neighbors.

Cooper has also begun a third series with *Funny as a Dead Comic* (St. Martin's Press, 1993), starring stand-up comic Kimmey Kruse. In her first appearance, Kimmey looks like a good chief suspect when another comic, a former lover, is murdered. Kimmey fights an attraction to the Chicago homicide cop, Sal Pucci, who is assigned to the case. He even seems to dog her steps when she encounters murder among her Cajun relatives in Port Arthur, Texas, in *Funny as a Dead Relative* (St. Martin's Press, 1994). Kimmey is funny, vulnerable, and very appealing.

Cooper demonstrates her versatility with three distinctive and engaging series.

Those readers for whom the Southwestern setting has an appeal might try the two Texas Panhandle series of D. R. Meredith, the Oklahoma series of Jean Hager and Eve K. Sandstrom, or B. J. Oliphant's series about a Colorado rancher, Shirley McClintock.

Cornwell, Patricia D.   Having spent a number of years working as a computer analyst in the office of the chief medical examiner of the Commonwealth of Virginia, Cornwell uses her knowledge of forensic pathology and the methods of contemporary crime-solving to give her fiction a compelling realism. The main character in the series is Dr. Kay Scarpetta, Virginia's chief medical examiner. Tough and intense, Scarpetta makes an effective centerpiece for the series. She develops a strong working relationship with Richmond homicide cop Pete Marino, who complements the prickly Scarpetta well. The settings of the series are Richmond and its environs. Cornwell has a strong sense of pace; the action rarely lags in her work. She also has a knack for explaining the complexities of forensic pathology to the ignorant. She sometimes includes details that the squeamish might quickly skim over, but, for the most part, Cornwell treats matter-of-factly the details that some novelists tend to sensationalize for mere effect. Cornwell understands that the commonplace or ordinary can become quite sinister in the hands or mind of a killer. For example, when Scarpetta comes to understand the link among the victims of the serial killers in *Postmortem* (Scribner, 1990) and *Body of Evidence* (Scribner, 1991), the reader will never again take some relatively mundane things for granted. The first novel in the series, *Postmortem*, has won a host of prestigious awards for first novels, including the Edgar, the Creasey, the Macavity, and the Anthony. Cornwell's combination of suspense and unusual professional setting for her protagonist has propelled her rapidly onto the best-seller lists.

D. J. Donaldson currently writes a series featuring a medical examiner who works in New Orleans. Susan Dunlap's Kiernan O'Shaughnessy is a former medical examiner turned private investigator. Readers looking for other fast-paced series with tough-minded main characters should try the work of Sue Grafton, J. A. Jance, T. J. MacGregor, and Sara Paretsky.

Craig, Alisa. See **MacLeod, Charlotte.**

Crane, Caroline. Agatha Christie knew that one secret of writing a good mystery novel was seeking out the sinister in the commonplace. Crane makes good use of this technique in her low-key novels of suspense, which generally involve ordinary people in difficult situations beyond their control. For example, in *Woman Vanishes* (Dodd, Mead, 1984), a young wife and mother finds herself on the run from a vicious loan shark when her husband disappears after defaulting on his loan. How will she save herself and her young daughter from harm? In another novel, *Someone at the Door* (Dodd, Mead, 1985), Crane takes an intriguing premise and spins it into a good yarn. A pregnant woman in labor calls her sister to come look after her young autistic son while she drives herself to the hospital. The pregnant woman interrupts the conversation, saying there's someone at the door. When the sister arrives at the house later, the door is open, and her pregnant sister is missing. She never turned up at the hospital, and the police at first can find no trace of her. The answer to this puzzle is a chilling one. Readers looking for quietly effective tales of suspense will find pleasure with Caroline Crane's work. Crane has written a number of novels for children and young adults. Her first adult novel was *Summer Girl* (Dodd, Mead, 1979).

Those who have enjoyed Crane might try Mary Higgins Clark, Velda Johnston, and Phyllis A. Whitney. Valerie Wolzien and Katherine Hall Page also write engagingly about the suburban Northeast.

Crane, Hamilton. See **Mason, Sarah J.**

Crespi, Trella/Crespi, Camilla T. Simona Griffo is the protagonist in Crespi's series of The Trouble With . . . mysteries. Simona has emigrated from Italy to New York in search of a new life after a difficult divorce; now she works as an art buyer in an advertising agency. Simona loves to cook and to eat. The books are full of descriptions of food, especially Italian food (and the author does give recipes). Simona also likes, as she says, to stick her Roman nose into trouble, which naturally turns out to be murder. In the series, she is confronted with crimes on a film set with an Italian director, in her own advertising office, and at Club Med in Guadaloupe. Simona is not a completely independent woman; she is aware that, for her, happiness depends on having a man around. However, she is curious, emotional, talkative, and an interesting personality study.

The first Simona Griffo novel is *The Trouble with a Small Raise* (Zebra, 1991). *The Trouble with Thin Ice* (HarperCollins, 1993) is the first book published under the Camilla T. Crespi name.

Readers also may like Carole Berry's Bonnie Indermill novels. Other mystery writers who are adept at descriptions of gustatory delights include Virginia Rich, Janet Laurence, and Diane Mott Davidson. For mysteries set in ad agencies, try *Strangle Hold* (Harper, 1951) by Mary McMullen and *Murder Must Advertise* (Harcourt Brace, 1933) by Dorothy L. Sayers.

Crombie, Deborah.   Native Texan Crombie is following somewhat in the footsteps of fellow American writers Elizabeth George and Martha Grimes in that she is writing a series of mysteries set in England, featuring English police detectives. Otherwise, Crombie's books are quite different from those of George and Grimes. Crombie's main characters are Superintendent Duncan Kincaid and Detective Sergeant Gemma James. Kincaid, in his mid-thirties, is a little younger than most men of his rank, but his intelligence and skill in his job have brought him promotion early. Gemma James is a young, divorced mother of a toddler named Toby; she is bright, somewhat impulsive in her thinking, but altogether an appealing character. Kincaid is cast in the mold of the sensitive, thinking detective, like Adam Dalgliesh and Thomas Lynley, but Kincaid is not constantly riven by soul-wrenching angst as are his peers. Kincaid and James make an effective and interesting duo. Their first appearance is *A Share in Death* (Scribner, 1993), which was nominated for the Agatha Award for Best First Novel. Crombie has taken the conventional English detective story and updated it pleasantly; fans of the traditional English mystery will find much to enjoy here.

Readers who have already encountered the work of Crombie

might try as well the series of Anthea Fraser, Susan B. Kelly, Elizabeth Lemarchand, Susannah Stacey, Medora Sale, and Clare Curzon.

Cross, Amanda. When she made her debut on the mystery scene in 1964, Columbia English professor Carolyn G. Heilbrun masked her identity with the pseudonym Amanda Cross to safeguard her academic reputation. The choice of the first name for her pseudonym turned out to be a propitious one, for Cross has become a well-loved writer, and her detective, English professor Kate Fansler, is the epitome of the feminist sleuth. Kate comes from a wealthy and socially prominent New York family, but she finds her values much at odds with those of the rest of her family, with one or two exceptions. Having invested Kate Fansler with her own academic, if not her social and financial, background, Cross has made her detective the most literate and literary since Dorothy L. Sayers's Lord Peter Wimsey. In a career that has spanned nearly thirty years, Kate has solved several crimes with a literary bent, such as *The James Joyce Murder* (Macmillan, 1967) or *The Players Come Again* (Random House, 1990). Acclaimed by her fans and critics alike for the richness of her dialogue, Amanda Cross always provides a veritable feast for the lover of the English language. Perhaps her most interesting novel is *Death in a Tenured Position* (Dutton, 1981), which involves Kate in the murder of the only woman to have received tenure in the Harvard English department. First in the series is *In the Last Analysis* (Macmillan, 1964).

Like Cross, Sara Paretsky also brings a distinct moral and political stance to her fiction, though Paretsky's V. I. Warshawski and Kate Fansler come from very different social and economic backgrounds. B. J. Oliphant's series character, Shirley McClintock, holds very strong opinions as well, and she is not shy about sharing them with those around her. For enjoyable academic mysteries, Dorothy L. Sayers's *Gaudy Night* (Harcourt Brace, 1936) is the epitome. Readers should also try the works of Nora Kelly and Sophie Belfort.

Curzon, Clare. After writing a series of mysteries in the 1960s under the name of Rhona Petrie, Curzon turned away from crime for a while, until the publication of *A Leaven of Malice* (Collins Crime Club, 1979). Eight Curzon novels were published in England before the ninth, *Three-Core Lead* (Doubleday, 1990), was published in the United States. Most of the Curzon novels feature the Thames Valley Serious Crimes Squad under the direction of Detective-Superintendent Mike Yeadings. Yeadings much of the time is the central character in this series, but in true police procedural fashion, Curzon aims her spotlight on various members of the team, like Detective Inspector Angus Mott, Yeadings's right-hand man, throughout the books. Curzon weaves authentic details of ordinary police procedure into her tales, which feature solid plotting and engaging series characters as well. Curzon's world of the Thames Valley Serious Crime Squad is very much contemporary England, but occasionally there are echoes of the England of the classic detective novel. Curzon's work is an effective and entertaining blend of both, as demonstrated in the recent *First Wife, Twice Removed* (St. Martin's Press, 1993).

Other writers of contemporary British police procedurals similar to Curzon are Susannah Stacey, Anthea Fraser, Marjorie Eccles, Deborah Crombie, and Jill McGown.

Daheim, Mary.   A Seattle native who is an award-winning writer of historical romances, Daheim has recently added two mystery series to her repertoire.

The first series features Judith McMonigle, who has turned her family home into a bed-and-breakfast named Hillside Manor Inn. The city that serves as the setting in this series is never named but is otherwise a thinly veiled Seattle. Judith, a widow with one college-age son, operates the bed-and-breakfast despite the ill-natured interference of her mother, Gertrude, who lives with her. In the first of the series, *Just Desserts* (Avon, 1991), a fortune-teller meets an unforeseen end at Hillside Manor Inn. Aided by her cousin Renie, Judith solves the mystery.

In Daheim's second series, which begins with *The Alpine Advocate* (Ballantine, 1992), the main character is Emma Lord, journalist turned newspaper owner, in the small town of Alpine, Washington, in the foothills of the Cascade Mountains.

Both series characters have much in common, including troubled relationships with old lovers who reappear to complicate their lives. While one series is written in third person (Judith) and the other in the first person (Emma), Daheim's voice in both series is wry, occasionally ribald, and often sarcastic. Both series have a pleasant, cozy feel, and readers looking for conventional mystery reading will find good entertainment value with Daheim.

Like Mary Daheim, Joan Hess writes humorously of the tribulations of single-parenthood in her Claire Malloy series. Otherwise, readers might try the work of Jill Churchill, Celestine Sibley, Joyce Christmas, Gloria Dank, and Katherine Hall Page. Readers looking for Seattle and Pacific Northwest settings might try the work of J. A. Jance and Janet L. Smith, though both writers are somewhat harder-edged than Daheim.

Dain, Catherine/Garwood, Judith. Her first mystery, *Make Friends with Murder* (St. Martin's Press, 1992), was published under her own name, Judith Garwood. Garwood tells the story of Morgan Reeves, a writer of magazine articles and former television newscaster, who finds murder in a winery near Santa Barbara.

Garwood's later mysteries appear under the pseudonym of Catherine Dain. Her series stars Freddie O'Neal, a Reno private investigator. Freddie is a hard-boiled private eye and licensed pilot who carries a gun in her cowboy boot and can disarm a knife-wielding attacker by kicking him where it hurts the most. She is a loner who has grown up in Reno, and the sense of place in the stories is strong. Freddie is addicted to playing keno in the casinos, and she pals around with Deke, a retired cop who is now a casino security guard. In the first book, *Lay It on the Line* (Jove, 1992), Freddie takes on a simple stolen car recovery that turns into a case involving drug sales and multiple murder. *Sing a Song of Death* (Jove, 1993), is set mostly in Lake Tahoe, where Freddie takes a job as a bodyguard to Vince Marina, a charming alcoholic singer. When Vince is killed, everyone except Freddie assumes the obvious suspect, his ex-wife, is the murderer.

Readers also may enjoy the hard-boiled stories of Sue Grafton, Judith Van Gieson, Janet Dawson, and Karen Kijewski. Deborah Valentine has written a mystery series set in Lake Tahoe.

D'Amato, Barbara. D'Amato has created freelance Chicago reporter Cat Marsala, who often investigates social problems like gambling and prostitution. The first Cat Marsala novel is *Hardball* (Scribner, 1990). In each of the novels, Cat's research for her current assignment leads her into a murderous situation. D'Amato obviously researches each topic extensively herself. In *Hard Tack* (Scribner, 1991), for example, she manages to fit into the story just about everything anyone could want to know about sailing on the

Great Lakes. *Hard Women* (Scribner, 1993) uses the device of Cat doing research for her television assignment on the lives of hookers to bring the reader into the everyday worlds of different kinds of prostitutes, from street hookers to high-priced call girls. Cat investigates the crimes she encounters as carefully as she does her basic research; her interviewing techniques help get the story plus solve the murder. The part of each book that is strictly mystery plot is tightly constructed and well-planned, and a small group of suspects is typically identified and analyzed wittily.

Before she began the Cat Marsala series, D'Amato also wrote two puzzlers in the classic mode: *The Hands of Healing Murder* (Charter, 1980) and *The Eyes on Utopia Murder* (Ace, 1981). D'Amato also has written the Anthony Award–nominated *On My Honor* (Windsor, 1989) under the pseudonym of Malacai Black, and the true crime story *The Doctor, the Murder, the Mystery* (Noble, 1992), which won Agatha and Anthony Awards.

D'Amato's Chicago settings are somewhat cheerier than Sara Paretsky's. Other resourceful reporters and writers appear in Sarah Shankman's amusing Samantha Adams books, and in Mickey Friedman's Georgia Lee Maxwell stories.

Davidson, Diane Mott. The biographical information included on the dust jacket of her first book claimed that Davidson is "addicted to cooking." If that be the case, Davidson has put her addiction to good use in her series of culinary crimes featuring caterer Gertrude "Goldy" Bear. In the first novel, punningly titled *Catering to Nobody* (St. Martin's Press, 1990), Goldy is catering a wake for her eleven-year-old son's favorite teacher. Her ex-father-in-law almost dies from something he ate at the wake, and Goldy scrambles to redeem her reputation as a caterer and to save herself from jail. Along the way she has to cope with her physically abusive husband, a nastily charming doctor prominent in their Aspen Meadow, Colorado, hometown. Davidson mixes mouth-watering recipes and descriptions of food with complex plotting. In addition, she explores the life of a single mother who is trying to rear her son while fending off the psychotic behavior of an ex-husband. Goldy is a courageous character, whose offbeat sense of humor and compassionate heart carry her through. *Catering to Nobody* was nominated for the Agatha, Anthony, and Macavity Awards for Best First Novel.

The late Virginia Rich laced her plots with recipes, and Amy

Myers includes descriptions of Victorian dishes in her series. Janet Laurence writes a series about an Englishwoman who is a gourmet cook.

Davis, Dorothy Salisbury. Davis was awarded the Grand Master Award by the Mystery Writers of America in 1984, and she has received multiple Edgar nominations for her books. Davis is known for creating a mean streets atmosphere in her psychological mysteries, many of which are set in New York City. *A Gentle Murderer* (Scribner, 1951) uses a parallel construction, with a young priest, Father Duffy, and Detective Sergeant Goldsmith of the New York City police each searching separately for the same murderer. The murderer has confessed anonymously to Duffy, and the priest wants to find him in order to save his soul. The background and psychology of the killer is slowly revealed as Goldsmith and Father Duffy each talk to the people they find in their searches. Davis also uses a Catholic priest as a main character in *Where the Dark Streets Go* (Scribner, 1969), and many of her mysteries have a decidedly Irish-American atmosphere.

Davis has written several mysteries with series characters Mrs. Norris and Jasper Tully. The first is *Death of an Old Sinner* (Scribner, 1957), which tells the story of the mysterious death of a retired general who has gotten mixed up with New York gangsters. Mrs. Norris is his Scottish housekeeper; Jasper Tully is an investigator for the District Attorney's office.

Davis's newest series character is Julie Hayes. The first mystery in this series is *A Death in the Life* (Scribner, 1976). Julie is married to an older man who travels a great deal, and she finds herself insecure and at loose ends. On impulse, she sets up a storefront fortune-telling establishment and bills herself as Friend Julie. She encounters crime and hostility in the seedy neighborhood, but also discovers that she can investigate murder successfully. In the later novels in the series, Julie grows and changes as she gains confidence and skills, and even a paying job.

Davis's first novel was *The Judas Cat* (Scribner, 1949).

Readers looking for psychological mysteries and suspense novels might try Elizabeth George, Celia Fremlin, Patricia Highsmith, and B. M. Gill. Dorothy Uhnak and Lillian O'Donnell write effectively of the New York underworld, while the late Mary McMullen added a distinctly Irish atmosphere to her mysteries.

Davis, Lindsey.   Davis has taken the world of first-century A.D. Rome and made it her own. Her series character, public informer Marcus Didius Falco (pun most definitely intended, *falco* being the Latin for *falcon*), is the ancient Roman ancestor of Philip Marlowe and Sam Spade. Falco's voice makes the first novel in the series, *Silver Pigs* (Crown, 1990), seem almost anachronistic in the early pages, but then the reader watches the streets and the people of ancient Rome come vividly alive and forgets about the modern world. The plebeian Falco is an ardent republican in the days of the Flavian emperors, and, to his own disgust, he often finds himself working for the emperor Vespasian or his son, Titus. In *Silver Pigs*, Falco meets the patrician Helena Justina, and the sparks fly between them, for Helena Justina is just as strong-willed as Falco. These lovers' paths to each other is difficult, for the barriers of social class and wealth are difficult ones to breach, but Davis makes the struggle an enjoyable and involving one. Davis is a fine historical novelist, and she's no mean mystery writer, either. Davis stands alongside Ellis Peters and Anne Perry, other writers who make their respective historical periods lively and unforgettable.

Other authors who write mysteries set in ancient Rome are Steven Saylor, whose fine debut, *Roman Blood* (St. Martin's Press, 1991), is a worthy peer of Davis's work, Joan O'Hagan, John Madox Roberts, and Ron Burns.

Dawson, Janet.   Dawson, a former naval officer, writes hard-boiled mysteries set in Oakland, California, and the Bay Area. Her first mystery, *Kindred Crimes* (St. Martin's Press, 1990), introduces Jeri Howard, an Oakland private eye. Jeri is hired to find a woman who has abandoned her child and disappeared. As she is fired and rehired by various clients in the same family, Jeri begins to peel away layers of deception and abuse that hide the true story of an old crime. In *Till the Old Men Die* (Fawcett, 1993), a Filipino history professor has been murdered, and Jeri's father asks her to look into the circumstances behind his friend's death. Jeri's investigations draw her into the local Filipino-American community, and she learns a great deal about the politics and recent history of the Philippines. In *Take a Number* (Fawcett, 1993), Jeri becomes involved with the personnel from a local navy base as she searches for money that an abusive husband has hidden from his estranged wife. Dawson provides richly detailed urban landscapes for her novels, and Jeri Howard is a persistent and courageous investigator.

Kindred Crimes won the St. Martin's/PWA Contest for first private eye novels, and was nominated for the Shamus Award.

Marcia Muller, Linda Grant, Elizabeth Pincus, and Margaret Lucke write mysteries with women private eyes that are set in the Bay Area.

Day, Marele. Australian writer Day sets her series of hard-boiled private eye mysteries in an atmospheric Sydney. The action in Day's mysteries is sharp and quick, with eccentric characters and slangy dialogue. The series begins with *The Life and Crimes of Harry Lavender* (Allen and Unwin, 1988). The protagonist is private investigator Claudia Valentine, who lives in a flat above a bar in a seedy area of Sydney. She has children who live with her ex-husband and come to visit her for school vacations. Her father is a wino who may be dead for all she knows, and her mother is a former exotic dancer who refuses to spend her elderly years sitting in front of the television. Her lover is a pacemaker technician and former phone company employee, whose knowledge of computers and phone taps comes in handy in this first novel. Claudia takes on a job in the Chinese community in Sydney in *The Case of the Chinese Boxes* (Allen & Unwin, 1990). She is asked to find a key that was taken from a safe-deposit box during a big bank robbery. Her obnoxious client, a restaurant owner and influential presence in the local community, tries to keep as much information as possible from Claudia about the key and its importance. Claudia is curious about the real purpose of the key, and she is persistent, even when she is no longer working for the person who hired her. Day won the Shamus Award for Best Paperback Original for her next work, *The Last Tango of Dolores Delgado* (Allen & Unwin, 1992). Claudia is out of work, so she takes a job as a bodyguard to a professional tango dancer, Dolores Delgado. Claudia is intrigued by Dolores's stories of an impossibly exotic life, and when Dolores dies onstage, Claudia feels compelled to dig into her past. Claudia dyes her hair and turns herself into a Dolores look-alike to fool people into thinking Dolores is still alive, while she investigates. Claudia rather enjoys being Dolores at first, and she buys Dolores-type clothes and uses her company credit card. But she finds that Dolores has many layers of secrets in her past, and Claudia peels away the layers like an onion. Day is particularly good at character development in this novel, and the feisty, rather melancholy Claudia is a memorable portrayal.

Other Australian writers include Susan Geason, Kerry Greenwood, Claire McNab, and Jennifer Rowe; of these, Susan Geason's mysteries are perhaps closest in spirit to Marele Day's novels.

Dentinger, Jane.   Not only has Dentinger worked as an actor, director, and mystery bookstore manager, she also has written a series of mysteries featuring Jocelyn (Josh) O'Roarke, a New York actress. Dentinger's novels are traditional in form, with a lively theatrical ambience and a wealth of backstage detail. In the first novel, *Murder on Cue* (Doubleday, 1983), Josh meets and is attracted to NYPD Detective Phillip Gerrard during a murder investigation. Their relationship, however, is far from easy, and Josh values her independence and her career. In *Death Mask* (Scribner, 1988), Josh directs a revival of Shaw's *Major Barbara* to raise money and save an old theater; crime, of course, interferes with the production. *Dead Pan* (Viking, 1992) is set in Los Angeles, as Josh goes west to work in television with her old friend, writer Austin Frost. Josh is knowledgeable and wise about the craft of acting and the turbulent lives of actors. She also is garrulous, and the novels are replete with quotes from classic plays. Josh's lively observations and her friendships with eccentric secondary characters make these mysteries entertaining experiences.

Readers may also appreciate the theatrical mysteries of Ngaio Marsh, Anne Morice, Dorian Yeager, Annette Meyers, and Barbara Paul, the Maggie Ryan series of P. M. Carlson, and the Michael Spraggue mysteries by Linda Barnes.

Dewhurst, Eileen.   An Oxford-educated playwright and journalist, Dewhurst has penned a number of crime novels, several of them featuring the suavely attractive Scotland Yard detective Neil Carter. Handsome, young, with more charm than is sometimes good for him, Neil has quite a way with the women suspects in his cases. In addition to his physical assets, he has a keen mind and a good grasp of the quirks of human behavior. One of Carter's most interesting cases occurs in *Trio in Three Flats* (Doubleday Crime Club, 1981), when divorcée Hilary Fielding moves into Neil's building. The alluring Hilary sets Neil several interesting problems, not the least of which is the murder of her husband. One of Neil's neighbors, Cathy McVeigh, provides the third piece of the trio, and Neil soon finds that his feelings for Cathy are an added complication. Besides the Neil Carter books, the first of which was apparently *Curtain Fall* (Doubleday Crime Club, 1982; originally published in England in 1977), Dewhurst has also written several nonseries mysteries.

In *Dear Mr. Right* (Doubleday Crime Club, 1990), a widower looking for a second wife is arrested for the murder of a woman he met through a personals ad. Did he kill her, or has he been framed?

Readers looking for similar English police procedurals should try the work of Marjorie Eccles, Anthea Fraser, and Clare Curzon. Other suggestions are the works of Anna Clarke, Celia Fremlin, and E. X. Ferrars.

Dominic, R. B. See **Lathen, Emma.**

Donald, Anabel. Donald is a headmistress in an English girls' school, who became well-known in Britain with the publication of her first novel, *Hannah at Thirty-five* (London: Hodder & Stoughton, 1984). Hannah's husband leaves her on her birthday, and she spends the next year trying to become a fully independent person. It's a men-are-scum novel, but Donald's wit and sense of the absurd saves it from being preachy. Donald then published two other novels about women with crippling emotional handicaps who must learn how to make their own way through life's crises. Donald imbues all of these mainstream novels with wry, sophisticated humor and an acute observation of character.

Donald's first mystery novel was *An Uncommon Murder* (St. Martin's Press, 1992). The heroine is Alex Tanner, who is a part-time private investigator and part-time freelance TV researcher. Alex is a self-reliant and fiercely independent loner who always wanted to be a private eye like the ones in the classic hard-boiled mysteries that she reads. She was shuttled around to various foster homes as a child, had to grow up early and go out on her own to earn money, and now has trouble with long-term relationships. She is uncomfortable with the aristocracy, although in this first novel she must investigate an old murder, never solved, in an upper-class household. She is also hired by a former governess to find a troubled adolescent girl who is missing from school. Alex is hired to find out why a wealthy teenager died in a boarding school swimming pool in the next novel, *In at the Deep End* (St. Martin's Press, 1994). In a rather unusual twist, she is asked to find out what the boy's state of mind was before the seemingly accidental death. Alex takes on a teenage assistant who wants to learn the business, and she begins to get more work as a detective. A homeless, possibly crazy woman calling herself the "Womun in a Balaclava Helmet" asks Alex to take on a case in *The Glass Ceiling* (London: Macmillan, 1994). Four feminists who were in a group together at Oxford University are being threatened. A new teenage assistant who has emotional problems and has been homeless helps Alex out, as does her friend and occasional employer, documentary producer Barty O'Neill. In the Alex Tanner mysteries, Donald reiterates her thematic interests in the psychological development of women and the emotional issues of troubled teenagers.

Readers may also enjoy hard-boiled British mysteries by Denise Danks, Val McDermid, Sarah Dunant, Gillian Slovo, and Liza Cody, and their Australian counterparts, Marele Day and Susan Geason.

Douglas, Carole Nelson. Two very different series of mysteries are emerging from the talented pen of Carole Nelson Douglas, in addition to her romance and science fiction novels.

Douglas has bravely taken on the task of adding to the Sherlock Holmes canon by writing stories from the point of view of Irene Adler ("THE woman" for Holmes). The novels are Holmesian in their technique and storytelling, with beautifully re-created Victorian backgrounds. They are narrated by Penelope (Nell) Huxleigh, a typist and impecunious parson's daughter, who functions as Adler's Dr. Watson. The first book, *Good Night, Mr. Holmes* (Tor, 1990), is an expanded version of Doyle's story, "A Scandal in Bohemia." *Good Morning, Irene* (Tor, 1991), the second novel, continues the adventures of Irene and Nell in Paris and Monte Carlo. In each book, Irene, Nell, and Godfrey Norton match wits with Sherlock Holmes himself in their investigations.

Douglas has begun a second series of mystery novels with *Catnap* (Tor, 1992), a light romp told by Temple Barr, a Las Vegas publicist, and Midnight Louie, a large Runyonesque black cat. The feline narrative of Midnight Louie is in the hard-boiled tradition (somewhat reminiscent of Archy the cockroach's observations in the Archy

& Mehitabel stories of Don Marquis). Both of Douglas's series are fun to read and well worth the time of mystery lovers.

Readers who relish the Victorian atmosphere of the Irene Adler novels may want to try Anne Perry's series of novels. Laurie R. King, L. B. Greenwood, and Marian J. A. Jackson have written mysteries that make use of the Sherlock Holmes tradition. Elizabeth Peters has written an outstanding series of Victorian mysteries with the unforgettable Egyptologist Amelia Peabody. Amy Myers has also written a series of Victoriana. For fans of the Midnight Louie stories, Lilian Jackson Braun's The Cat Who . . . novels and Rita Mae Brown's tales of Mrs. Murphy are enjoyable feline mysteries.

Douglas, Lauren Wright.   Douglas writes about the adventures of lesbian detective Caitlin Reece. Caitlin is a private eye on Vancouver Island in Canada, and she is especially concerned with solving crimes committed against women, children, and animals. She is strong, courageous, and very certain that she knows what is wrong and what is right. Douglas has created a group of clearly drawn secondary characters to help Caitlin with her sleuthing. They include Maggie, a doctor who had her license lifted for doing an abortion when they were illegal; Gray Ng, a mysterious Vietnamese woman who is an animal psychologist; Sandy the cop; Lester the electronics expert; and Francis the Ferret. *The Always Anonymous Beast* (Naiad, 1987) is the first book in the series. Two lesbians are being blackmailed and Caitlin is called in to investigate. In *Ninth Life* (Naiad, 1989), animal rights activists hire Caitlin to look into a murder and a cosmetics company that is supposedly cruelty-free, but secretly conducts gruesome tests on cats and rabbits. Douglas's mysteries feature good writing, a strong social agenda, and violent denouements. They are action-filled, with contemplative moments in which Caitlin reflects on her life and her Celtic heritage.

Elisabeth Bowers has a series of private eye novels set in Vancouver, British Columbia. Other writers about lesbian private investigators include Sandra Scoppettone and Ellen Hart.

Drake, Alison.   See **MacGregor, T. J.**

Dreher, Sarah.   Offbeat humor and quirky characters highlight the series of mysteries written by Dreher. Her detective is Stoner McTavish, a travel agent in the Boston area. In her debut, *Stoner*

McTavish (New Victoria, 1985), Stoner gets hooked into investigating a strange situation by her eccentric Aunt Hermione, a psychic. Raised by emotionally distant parents, Stoner fled her home as a teenager when her parents couldn't cope with her attraction to other girls. Aunt Hermione gave her a home and the emotional support she needed, though Stoner, now in her thirties, continues to battle with the demons raised by her parents' neglect. Besides Aunt Hermione, Stoner has the love and support of her straight partner in the travel agency, Marylou, who'd rather eat than travel. In her first outing, Stoner encounters love and danger in Grand Teton National Park as she tries to prevent a murder. Subsequent adventures take Stoner on unconventional paths, through a story redolent of Hopi mysticism in *Gray Magic* (New Victoria, 1987) and even into the nineteenth century in *A Captive in Time* (New Victoria, 1990).

Unconventional is a good word to describe Dreher's work and her characters. Dreher experiments with the conventional forms of the mystery novel, and she provides unusual entertainment with her efforts.

Those looking for other lesbian detectives might try the work of Ellen Hart, Barbara Wilson, Vicki P. McConnell, and Val McDermid.

Dunant, Peter. See **Dunant, Sarah.**

Dunant, Sarah. British television journalist Dunant writes literate, reflective novels. Her first two books, *Exterminating Angels* (London: Deutsch, 1983) and the medical thriller *Intensive Care* (London: Deutsch, 1986), were written in partnership with Peter Busby under the pseudonym of Peter Dunant.

Sarah Dunant's first novel under her own name was *Snowstorms in a Hot Climate* (Random House, 1988), which is not so much a mystery as a novel of the chase. Marla Masterson, a British professor of Anglo-Saxon literature, comes to America in response to a message from her friend Elly, to find Elly mentally and physically in thrall to her slick drug-dealer lover. The novel centers around the cocaine culture and trade and follows the drug trail from Colombia to New York to California to Scotland. Dunant provides sharp renditions of the seduction of the drug and the maneuverings of the dealers. She shows each character's version of the truth about Elly, and each character's self-interest and weakness.

In *Birth Marks* (Doubleday, 1992), Dunant begins a series of mysteries with sleuth Hannah Wolfe, who does contract work for a London private eye agency. The victim, a missing ballet dancer, is clearly and sympathetically drawn. Dunant makes references (both literal and metaphorical) to Raymond Chandler's novel *The Big Sleep* (Knopf, 1939); most of the Chandler influence, however, is in the language and attitude of her detective, with little of Chandler's violence. Much of the book also discusses aspects of parenthood and child-parent relations. *Fatlands* (Otto Penzler, 1994), which won the Silver Dagger Award, takes Hannah into an investigation centered around animal experimentation. During the course of her investigation, Hannah must face the personal issue of how devastated she is by the emotional and physical aftermath of violence. In *Under My Skin* (Scribner, 1995), Dunant tells a strong story set in a cosmetic surgery clinic and examines why women feel the need to alter their bodies.

Other British private eyes appear in the works of Liza Cody, Lesley Grant-Adamson, Val McDermid, Anabel Donald, and Gillian Slovo.

Dunlap, Susan.   Sue Dunlap has written three sets of novels featuring female sleuths Vejay Haskell, Jill Smith, and Kiernan O'Shaughnessy. In the first series, Haskell is an executive dropout turned meter-reader in Russian River, California. *The Last Annual Slugfest* (St. Martin's Press, 1986) is one of Dunlap's best, with its vivid descriptions of the small settlements among the redwoods in northern California.

The second series features Berkeley homicide detective Jill Smith. Smith is cool and persistent, determined to solve crimes in spite of departmental constraints and sexism. The unique and slightly crazed nature of the city of Berkeley and its inhabitants creates suitably oddball crimes for Jill to investigate, such as the murder of a guru in *Karma* (Raven, 1981). *Death and Taxes* (Delacorte, 1992) is a sharp, funny story of the murder of an IRS agent and Jill Smith's investigation of his many enemies and financial victims.

Dunlap's newest protagonist, Kiernan O'Shaughnessy, is a former (read: fired) medical examiner and gymnast, now a private eye. She specializes in cases with medical oddities, charges enormous fees, and lives an unashamedly opulent life with a young male housekeeper in a beach house in La Jolla.

Dunlap's style is spare and humorous; her protagonists are curious, bright women with a cynical eye for the absurdities of the large corporate entities with which their lives are intertwined.

If possible, readers may want to read these series in order. The first Vejay Haskell is *An Equal Opportunity Death* (St. Martin's Press, 1984); the first Jill Smith is *Karma*; the first Kiernan O'Shaughnessy is *Pious Deception* (Villard, 1989).

Readers who like Dunlap may enjoy Margaret Maron's police procedurals with Lt. Sigrid Harald; Marcia Muller; Patricia Cornwell; L. V. Sims; or Jaqueline Girdner's stories of New Age life in Marin County, California.

Dunnett, Dorothy.   Scottish writer and painter Dorothy Dunnett began to contribute a female voice to the overwhelmingly male world of espionage novels in the late 1960s. Her thrillers center around two continuing elements: the portrait painter and British agent Johnson Johnson, and his yacht, the *Dolly*. The first Johnson Johnson novel was *The Photogenic Soprano* (Houghton Mifflin, 1968), also published with the author's name as Dorothy Halliday and the title as *Dolly and the Singing Bird* (London: Cassell, 1968). In each book, the narration is provided by a different woman (the "bird" of the titles) who becomes involved in a crime. Each woman has a distinct personality and career of her own, and is a vibrant character in contrast to the bland and shadowy Johnson. The imperious and strong-willed Madame Tina Rossi of *The Photogenic Soprano*, for example, is a very different character study from Sarah Cassells, the impecunious but blue-blooded young caterer of *Murder in the Round* (Houghton Mifflin, 1970), also published as *Dolly and the Cookie Bird* (Cassell, 1970). Dunnett's stories often unfold at a leisurely pace, with an abundance of descriptive prose about the novel's location (Scotland, Ibiza, the Bahamas, and other picturesque locales). *Send a Fax to the Kasbah* (Harcourt Brace Jovanovich, 1992), however, sends its players in the game of multinational business intrigues through the souks and mountains of Morocco at a fast clip.

Dunnett also has become famous for her lengthy historical novels, including the Francis Crawford of Lymond cycle and the House of Niccolo series.

Readers also may enjoy the thrillers of Susan Moody, Janice Law, Dorothy Gilman, and Jessica Mann.

Early, Jack. See **Scoppettone, Sandra.**

Eccles, Marjorie. Eccles wrote a number of romance novels in her native England before turning to a life of crime, and the mystery lover's gain may well be the romance world's loss. Her series features Detective Chief Inspector Gil Mayo, a Yorkshireman now transplanted farther south. In the first of the series, *Cast a Cold Eye* (Doubleday, 1988), Mayo investigates the death of a prominent architect. In the five novels in the series published thus far, Eccles demonstrates a quietly effective hand with both plot and character. The focus in each novel is the cast of characters whom the murder most directly affects; Mayo and his supporting cast from the police are developed slowly as the series progresses. Working within the classic traditions of the British mystery, Eccles takes an old form and makes it both contemporary and entertaining. A standout in the series is the recent *More Deaths Than One* (Doubleday, 1991), which easily puts Eccles on a par with such favorites as Dorothy Simpson and June Thomson.

Other good "village" English police procedural writers are Anthea Fraser, Clare Curzon, Catherine Aird, Susan B. Kelly, and Erica Quest (whose lead character is a woman).

Edwards, Ruth Dudley. Edwards is an Irish writer living in London, and a former civil servant. In her first mystery, *Corridors of*

Death (St. Martin's Press, 1982), a much-disliked senior civil servant is murdered. Police Superintendent James Milton uses Robert Amiss as his mole in the affected department, in order to get information on the suspects. Although he is only a very junior civil servant, Amiss's inside knowledge eventually solves the crime. As with several of Edwards's books, the mystery is set against a backdrop of incompetence and mismanagement in the British civil service system. *St. Valentine's Day Murders* (St. Martin's Press, 1985) begins hilariously with Amiss temporarily seconded to a purchasing department, which is a corporate Siberia for fallen bureaucrats. These bureaucrats scheme against each other endlessly and their intrigues inevitably escalate into murder. In *Clubbed to Death* (St. Martin's Press, 1992), Amiss finally has left the civil service in disgust. Superintendent Milton asks him to go undercover as a waiter at an old-fashioned London gentlemen's club, the ffeatherstonehaugh Club (pronounced *fanshaw*). The club secretary has been killed, and further deaths follow while Amiss works there. The members are unrepentantly racist and sexist and the club atmosphere exudes the worst kind of English snobbishness, so Amiss is even worse off than he had been in the civil service.

In *Matricide at St. Martha's* (London: HarperCollins, 1994), Edwards takes on the latest fad in academia: political correctness. St. Martha's is an obscure and old-fashioned Cambridge college that has suffered an influx of American-style radical lesbian activists who no longer want to teach the works of DWEMs (dead white European males). Edwards has great fun with the sacred cows of academia and current events. In all of her mystery novels, Edwards has brought a bitingly satirical view of English institutions to the traditional mystery format.

Janet Neel and Natasha Cooper have provided other views of the British civil service system in their mysteries. Sarah Caudwell's crime novels about barristers are slyly witty. M. C. Beaton, Nancy Livingston, and Marian Babson write gently humorous mysteries.

Egan, Lesley.   See **Linington, Elizabeth.**

Elrod, P. N.   Not many detectives get the chance to solve their own murders, but in *Bloodlist* (Ace, 1990), reporter Jack Fleming gets to do just that. Fleming wakes up one night to discover that he has been murdered, and he is now a vampire. Putting his investigative skills to work, and trying to cope with his initiation into the world of the living dead, Jack sets out to discover who killed him. Patricia Elrod has set her series of vampire detective novels in the Depression era, and the 1930s background helps give the books a suitably hard-boiled feel. Fleming finds a friend in actor Charles Escott, who becomes his Watson. In the course of the series, Fleming also makes the acquaintance of one Jonathan Barrett, also a vampire, and Elrod is writing a series of historical novels, with some mysterious twists, starring Barrett. The first of these is *Red Death* (Ace, 1993) and is set during the Revolutionary War period.

Tanya Huff and Mercedes Lackey both write books that blend multiple genres. Barbara Hambly has also written a couple of vampire mysteries.

Eyre, Elizabeth.   See **Stacey, Susannah.**

Fallon, Ann C.   Fallon has taken the traditional English mystery and given it an agreeable Irish brogue with a series of novels about young Dublin solicitor James Fleming. A bachelor with a comfortable income, an upper-middle-class background, and a passion for railways all over the world, James Fleming makes an attractive character for a series set in contemporary Ireland. Through his law practice, James encounters some odd cases that call for using his skills as a lawyer in more creative ways. In *Dead Ends* (Pocket, 1992), James goes to a beautiful country inn near Sligo to draw up a will for the inn's owner, an old friend of a colleague. A mysterious death occurs at the inn while James is there, and soon he finds himself working to solve the puzzle to save the owner of the inn from arrest. Fallon's writing style is leisurely, spinning out the thread of the narrative in the fashion of mysteries from the Golden Age. While the pace is not fast, the plot is usually neatly and fairly constructed. The series begins with *Blood Is Thicker* (Pocket, 1990).

Other writers who have set their work in Ireland are Eilis Dillon and Nigel Fitzgerald. Readers who enjoy lawyers as sleuths might also try the work of Sara Woods, Frances Fyfield, M. R. D. Meek, or E. X. Giroux.

Fawcett, Quinn.   See **Yarbro, Chelsea Quinn.**

Fennelly, Tony. With a past as colorful as any of her novels, Fennelly has made use of her background in her mysteries set in New Orleans. Her first novel, *The Glory Hole Murders* (Carroll & Graf, 1985), nominated for an Edgar, introduced Matthew Sinclair. Son of a prominent Crescent City family, Matty is a gay, thirtyish antique dealer. A Tulane Law School graduate, he gave up his career as a prosecutor in the district attorney's office and now sells furniture to the high-and-mighty of New Orleans society. He lives with his young lover, Robin Fearing, but he has an occasional liaison with a woman. In his first appearance, Matty helps a friend in the police department, homicide detective Frank Washington, with the murder of a local businessman with political ambitions. The method of murder in this book is one guaranteed to make any male reader squirm. Matty continues sticking his nose into crime in *The Closet Hanging* (Carroll & Graf, 1987). These two books have been reprinted together as *Murder with a Twist* (Carroll & Graf).

Recently, Fennelly published a book about a female character, former stripper turned society wife, Margo Fortier. In *The Hippie in the Wall* (St. Martin's Press, 1994), Margo digs into her own past when the body of a hippie is found stuffed in the wall of a topless bar where she once worked. Married to the gay son of a prominent New Orleans family, Margo works as a gossip/society columnist for the paper, but she hungers for bigger stories. Full of New Orleans atmosphere, with a decidedly gay twist, Fennelly's work offers a fascinating look at the life of one of America's most individual cities.

Julie Smith, Chris Wiltz, and J. M. Redmann also use New Orleans to good effect in their works. Readers looking for other gay male protagonists should try the work of Joseph Hansen and Michael Nava.

Ferrars, E. X. Known in her native England as Elizabeth Ferrars, this grande dame of the English mystery novel steadily produced a novel or two a year for fifty-five years, until her death in March of 1995. Her first few novels, with series detective Toby Dyke, followed closely in the classic tradition of the upper-class, gentleman sleuth. Dyke first appeared in *Give a Corpse a Bad Name* (Hodder and Stoughton, 1940). These books are adequate representations of the genteel English mystery, but it was not until Ferrars abandoned Dyke that she found a better and fresher voice. Ferrars writes convincingly about civilized people faced with that most uncivilized of crimes, and each novel unfolds like a small but elegantly presented movie.

In recent years, Ferrars adopted two sets of series characters. One series features Virginia Freer and her estranged, but not-quite-divorced husband Felix, who has a gift for staying on the right side of the law—just barely. They appear first in *Last Will and Testament* (Doubleday, 1978). The other series features Andrew Basnett, retired professor of botany (supposedly modeled upon Ms. Ferrars's husband). Basnett, who debuts in *Something Wicked* (Doubleday, 1984), serves as an effective tool for Ferrars to write simply and affectingly about life in old age. Ferrars is a special vintage, one that connoisseurs of the English mystery will always enjoy.

Like Ferrars, Anna Clarke until recent years eschewed a series character, and her novels of mystery are much in the Ferrars vein, as are the works of Celia Fremlin. American Corinne Holt Sawyer writes an entertaining series about two elderly women sleuths. Other entertaining English cozy writers are Sarah J. Mason and Catherine Aird.

Forrest, Katherine V.   Forrest has written a series of police procedurals with protagonist Kate Delafield, a detective in the Los Angeles Police Department. Kate is a lesbian in an occupation notable for its homophobia, so she has kept her private life a secret from her coworkers. Her partner is Ed Taylor, an older man who seems to exemplify the prejudices of many LAPD officers in the novels. Kate is a good police officer: thoughtful, sensitive, and scrupulous about the details of her work. Above all, she has integrity. She deals fairly with suspects in interviews and is painstakingly careful in her examinations of crime scenes. Forrest writes extensively about the details of murder investigations, and the scenes in which Kate questions suspects are especially effective. There usually is an explicit sex scene or two per novel. The first mystery in the series is *Amateur City* (Naiad, 1984), a story of murder in an office design firm in Los Angeles. Kate has lost her lover of many years a few months earlier in a car wreck; she meets a woman here who reminds her of her dead lover and who is a witness to the murder. *Murder at the Nightwood Bar* (Naiad, 1987) revolves around the murder of a young woman at a lesbian bar who is a bisexual hooker. A gay-bashing murder occurs in *Murder by Tradition* (Naiad, 1991) and Forrest follows it from Kate's investigation through the trial.

Other writers of effective police procedurals include Lillian O'Donnell, Faye Kellerman, Teri White, and Susan Dunlap. Other mystery writers with lesbian protagonists are Claire McNab, Sandra Scoppettone, Barbara Wilson, Mary Wings, Ellen Hart, Deborah Powell, Lauren Wright Douglas, and Sarah Dreher.

Fowler, Earlene. Fowler's mysteries in the Benni Harper series all have a quilting theme, and each one has marvelous cover art that shows the quilt pattern for which the book is named. In the first, *Fool's Puzzle* (Berkley, 1994), Benni is a widow and the curator of a folk art museum on the central California coast. She is still in mourning for her husband Jack, who was killed a few months earlier in a car accident. Benni is organizing an exhibit of quilts at the museum when she stumbles over a murder victim one night. When she meets acting police chief Gabriel Ortiz, she withholds evidence from him, and so begins a lively, contentious relationship between two strong-willed characters. As Benni noses around her town, looking for clues to the murder, she also is going through the stages of mourning, and Fowler treats this process sensitively and articulately. In addition, Fowler's memorable setting and characters remind the reader that ranches, cowboys, and cowgirls (like Benni) still exist in California, and that many Californians like Benni and her grandmother Dove come from a mixture of Southern and Western heritages. *Fool's Puzzle* was nominated for an Agatha Award for Best First Novel. In *Irish Chain* (Berkley, 1995), two elderly residents of a nursing home are murdered. Benni is teaching a quilting class there, and she finds the bodies. As she digs further into the past of the victims, she discovers the fascinating possibility of an old, secret crime that is part of her hometown's history. Benni and Gabe Ortiz still don't trust each other, and they continue to spar over their growing relationship and their individual habits of secrecy and privacy. The issue of trust between partners crops up again in *Kansas Troubles* (Berkley, 1996), when Benni and Gabe, who are newly married, go to Kansas to meet Gabe's family. While they are at a welcoming party, a young woman from an Amish family is murdered. She has left the Amish community, in spite of their condemnation, to become a country and western singer. Benni goes with her sister-in-law to visit the local Amish community, and she is drawn into the murder probe through her knowledge of quilts. This novel not only has an entertaining murder plot but a lively backdrop of Kansas and its ever-changing weather, its Amish farms, and its tradition of Midwestern quilting. Fowler's writing has matured throughout her first three books, and she does an excellent job of developing her characters into multidimensional people. Benni still has a smart mouth, Gabe is still stubborn and reticent, but increasingly we understand how their personalities were formed and how they are trying to change. Fowler also provides wise and witty insights into the difficulties a second marriage can have when the couple are over thirty and set in their ways.

Other mystery writers who use strongly Western backdrops include Catherine Dain, Margaret Coel, and Sandra West Prowell.

Frankel, Valerie.   Frankel, an editor at *Mademoiselle* magazine, writes a series with New York City private eye Wanda Mallory. Wanda is as hard-boiled as it gets, with a perpetual craving for sex, violence, cigarettes, and designer clothes. Her debut adventure, *A Deadline for Murder* (Pocket, 1991), concerns the murder of Belle, a soft-core porn magazine editor, who was Wanda's first client and sometime friend. Wanda and her sidekick Alex Beaudine have an on-again, off-again relationship, and they do plenty of bantering while on the case. This first book is rather raunchy, like a female equivalent of a Mickey Spillane novel. In *Murder on Wheels* (Pocket, 1992), Wanda is hired by the leader of a biker gang to look for some missing money that he owes a loan shark. Wanda is supposed to replace a missing roulette dealer at the gang's illicit gambling den as part of her investigation, when the dealer turns up very messily murdered. Wanda is on the rebound from a failed relationship, and she falls in lust with the biker leader and even dyes her red hair black for him. *Prime Time for Murder* (Pocket, 1994) finds Wanda in the process of messing up yet another romantic relationship and trying to quit smoking. The hostess of a TV dating show has hired Wanda to protect her after she gets a series of ever more mutilated tarantulas in her fan mail. One of the show's contestants is murdered onscreen and Wanda and Alex switch from doing a protection job to an active investigation. Wanda is a smart-mouthed, amoral, rather self-destructive heroine in this series of tough, bawdy escapades.

Denise Danks's protagonist, Georgina Powers, is also a Generation X detective with self-destructive tendencies. Other Manhattan private eyes include Blaine Stewart in mysteries by Sharon Zukowski, Gwenn Ramadge in the series by Lillian O'Donnell, and Lauren Laurano in novels by Sandra Scoppettone.

Fraser, Anthea. She began her writing career with short stories and had her first novel published in 1970, going in turn to romantic fiction to paranormal fiction to crime fiction. With *A Necessary End* (Walker, 1986) and *A Shroud for Delilah* (Doubleday, 1986), Fraser commenced a series of police detective mysteries starring Inspector David Webb. The viewpoint of several of the early novels is a young woman character, different in each book, of course, but nevertheless similar in some respects. Often estranged from her husband or family, the young woman is in a vulnerable position in which murder threatens. In the more recent books, however, Fraser has shifted toward the telling of her stories mostly from the viewpoint of Webb, and this has added considerable strength and variety to her plotting. With *The Nine Bright Shiners* (Doubleday, 1988), Fraser began taking her titles from the old folk tune "Green Grow the Rushes-O." One of the strongest in the series is *Six Proud Walkers* (Doubleday, 1989). Fraser's work falls well within the conventions of the contemporary British police procedural: engaging characters, deftly constructed plots, and regional English settings.

Readers of Fraser would also enjoy the work of Dorothy Simpson, Clare Curzon, June Thomson, and Susan B. Kelly, all of whom expertly use the various regions of England as their settings, proving that London is not the only setting for good police procedural work.

Fraser, Antonia. Well-known for her popular biographies of British historical figures, Antonia Fraser also writes mysteries. Her series character is Jemima Shore, a television journalist. Jemima does documentaries on social problems, and she is known to the public as Jemima Shore, Investigator. Her primary attribute is curiosity; she is also elegant and wry. Fraser's first Jemima Shore novel was *Quiet as a Nun* (Viking, 1977). A young nun from a wealthy family dies mysteriously in the convent where Jemima was educated, and the Reverend Mother calls in Jemima to investigate. *The Wild Island* (Norton, 1978) is set in the Highlands of Scotland, where Jemima has rented a cottage on an island for a month of quiet away from her frenetic career. She becomes involved, willy-nilly, in the batty activities of a group of islanders who think the local laird is the legitimate descendant of Bonnie Prince Charlie and the rightful king of Scotland. *A Splash of Red* (Norton, 1982) is set in the Bloomsbury section of London, where Jemima's old friend Chloe has disappeared after lending Jemima her penthouse flat. Most of the characters in Fraser's novels are affluent professionals or aristocrats, and the settings are generally affluent ones as well.

Fraser also has written two volumes of short stories about Jemima Shore, *Jemima Shore's First Case* (Norton, 1986) and *Jemima Shore at the Sunny Grave* (Bantam, 1991).

Fraser's biographical works include the well-received *Mary, Queen of Scots* (Delacorte, 1969) and *The Wives of Henry VIII* (Knopf, 1992).

Readers also may enjoy the works of British crime novelists Lesley Grant-Adamson and Joan Smith.

Frazer, Margaret. See **Pulver, Mary Monica.**

Fremlin, Celia. English novelist Fremlin struck gold her first time out, winning the Edgar for Best Novel with *The Hours Before Dawn* (Lippincott, 1959). This tale of suspense exhibits many of the qualities that inform Fremlin's later work. A young housewife and mother, trying her best to tend to a husband, two small daughters, and a constantly crying infant son, thinks there is something odd about their new lodger. But, then again, maybe she's just groggy from lack of sleep. Fremlin takes these very ordinary circumstances and turns them into a fascinating tale of suspense. This knack for taking ordinary, domestic details, weaving them in with the oddities and frailties of ordinary human beings, and producing quietly suspenseful tales makes Fremlin rather unusual among her peers. Novels such as *The Long Shadow* (Doubleday, 1976) and *The Parasite Person* (Doubleday, 1982) are excellent examples of her work. If there may be said to be a cozy psychological suspense novel, then Fremlin is its premiere practitioner.

Those who have enjoyed Fremlin's work might try the novels of Margaret Yorke, Anna Clarke, Barbara Vine/Ruth Rendell, Dorothy Salisbury Davis, E. X. Ferrars, Sheila Radley, or Frances Hegarty.

Friedman, Mickey. Friedman's first novel, *Hurricane Season* (Dutton, 1983), is not only a mystery but a fine evocation of the people and landscape of a small Florida fishing town in the early

1950s. She draws the reader completely into a world dominated by moonshining, local politics, and the ever-present heat and humidity. This is not the Florida tourists see; it is rural, redneck, and poverty-stricken swampland. Friedman also sets a later suspense novel, *Riptide* (St. Martin's Press, 1994), in rural Florida, with a contemporary setting. *Venetian Mask* (Scribner, 1987) offers a detailed look at Venice during Carnival. A game that turns to murder occurs among a group of self-absorbed acquaintances. The story is dark, brooding, and full of sexual tensions.

Friedman also has written a series of books with protagonist Georgia Lee Maxwell, an expatriate journalist in Paris. Her cases involve stories that she starts to research and write that then turn into mysteries. Georgia Lee wants the story, and she must investigate the murder to get it. Friedman's writing in these books is lucid and suspenseful. Georgia Lee is a believable, rounded character, especially in the first series novel, *The Magic Mirror* (Viking, 1988).

Investigative journalists who also solve mysteries include Jessica James, created by Meg O'Brien; Cat Marsala, invented by Barbara D'Amato; and Chris Martin, created by Annette Roome.

Fyfield, Frances/Hegarty, Frances.   Hailed as a star already in the tradition of her fellow Englishwomen P. D. James and Ruth Rendell, Fyfield uses her own extensive background as a solicitor specializing in the criminal law to lend authenticity to her writing. In an Edgar- and Agatha-nominated debut, *A Question of Guilt* (Pocket, 1989), Fyfield's series characters, Crown Prosecutor Helen West and Detective Superintendent Geoffrey Bailey, demonstrate with quiet effect the often opposing goals of the law courts and the police. Fyfield's great strength as a writer comes from the assurance with which she delineates character. Her plots are always meticulous in their construction, but her ability to conjure fully fleshed and compelling characters makes for powerful reading. Fyfield also possesses the saving grace of a sense of humor, realizing—unlike some of her peers—that her characters need not be relentlessly morose to be believable.

Fyfield has also written, thus far, two books about solicitor Sarah Fortune; the first is *Shadows on the Mirror* (Pocket, 1990). After the death of her unfaithful husband, Sarah chooses to share her affections with men who appear to warrant her special gifts. In her first appearance, she encounters two men with very different needs, and one of them just might be a psychopath.

As Frances Hegarty (her real name), Fyfield has followed the lead of Ruth Rendell and Rendell's alter ego Barbara Vine by writing a somewhat different kind of novel. In *The Playroom* (Pocket, 1991), Hegarty demonstrates considerable skill with the type of psychological novel that Rendell/Vine regularly produces, proving herself a worthy peer of the better-known writer.

Those who enjoy Fyfield's work should try Jill McGown, whose strengths are also those of character and plot; other suggestions are Ruth Rendell's long series of novels about Inspector Wexford, M. R. D. Meek's series about lawyer Lennox Kemp, and Sheila Radley's series about policeman Douglas Quantrill. For the more psychological side, readers might try the work of Minette Walters, Margaret Yorke, or Margaret Millar.

Gallison, Kate. Gallison has written a series of books featuring Nick Magaracz ("rhymes with pots"), an investigator in Trenton, New Jersey. Nick is an average guy, a Korean War veteran who knows everybody in his hometown and yearns to be a hotshot private eye. In the first book, *Unbalanced Accounts* (Little, Brown, 1986), Nick goes undercover as a state worker to investigate the theft of state-issued checks and a subsequent murder. Nick quickly becomes absorbed into the daily routine of a civil service office, portrayed with sardonic humor by Gallison. In *The Death Tape* (Little, Brown, 1987), Nick has stayed on as a state employee, and he is now at the Bureau of Tax Enforcement. A militant antitaxation right-wing group has taken over a sleepy ethnic social club to use as a front for their illegal activities, and Nick must track them down. *The Jersey Monkey* (St. Martin's Press, 1992) is perhaps the most savagely humorous of the series; it concerns corporate graft and the testing of drugs on animals.

Gallison has started a new series about Mother Lavinia (Vinnie) Grey, an Episcopalian priest in an almost moribund New Jersey parish. The lively and absorbing *Bury the Bishop* (Dell, 1995) is the first book in the series. The Bishop of New Jersey is unfortunately murdered at a diocesan conference in Trenton. Vinnie and the lay delegates from her parish are all suspects, since the Bishop had been trying to eliminate their church, St. Bede's. Vinnie has an active social conscience and she is particularly concerned here with the issue of homelessness in her parish, but she is also a conscientious and devout priest.

Readers looking for other mysteries set in New Jersey should try Janet Evanovich's *One for the Money* (Scribner, 1994) and Valerie Wilson Wesley's *When Death Comes Stealing* (Putnam, 1994). Ruth Dudley Edwards and Janet Neel have written crime novels with civil service settings. Isabelle Holland and D. M. Greenwood write mysteries featuring women clergy.

Garwood, Judith. See **Dain, Catherine.**

Geason, Susan. Australian writer Susan Geason is a freelance writer and a former journalist. Her first mystery, *Shaved Fish* (Allen & Unwin, 1990), is a collection of short stories about Sydney private eye Syd Fish. Syd appears to be a macho guy, but he is easily diverted by tales of woe and kids in difficult situations. Indeed, several of the stories concern runaway children. Syd was press secretary to a corrupt politician and disliked it intensely; he became a private eye after being fired for helping the politician's abused wife. He has a galaxy of eccentric friends and girlfriends of all sorts, and he likes to meet attractive women in the course of his investigations. Syd is a funny, shambling, laid-back private eye, with a sardonic and politically incorrect wit; he makes plenty of mistakes and spends quite a bit of his time pub-crawling. In *Dogfish* (Allen & Unwin, 1991), Syd is hired by a transvestite hooker who is the head of the Sex Workers' Union in Sydney. S/he turns out to be an old classmate of Syd's from Catholic boys' school. Syd quickly becomes embroiled in a very weird, convoluted series of events involving land development, the gay and yuppie communities, and urban corruption. The comic aspect of Syd's investigations and the people he meets comes to the fore here, and the reader is in for a wild ride. *Sharkbait* (Allen & Unwin, 1993) has Syd investigating the disappearance of an elderly ex-jockey. Geason has fun with lurid descriptions of chop shops, biker gangs, horse-racing scams, and all kinds of criminal activities in Kings Cross, a rather seedy neighborhood. She gives us a lively tour of criminal Sydney, lots of zingy remarks, and the amusing spectacle of caffeine-addicted Syd trying to give up drinking coffee while his best friend gives up smoking. Geason's tales of incidents in bloodbath pubs, rorts, hoons, and other idiosyncracies of Australian life and language are consistently entertaining.

Other Australian women crime writers include Marele Day, Kerry Greenwood, Jennifer Rowe, Jean Bedford, Anne Infante, and the team of Catherine Lewis and Judith Guerin.

George, Elizabeth. George is a novelist from Southern California who is, nevertheless, clearly at home writing classic mysteries set in Great Britain. In a distinguished series of novels, George charts the emotional lives of her detectives as well as those of the murder victims and suspects. She has created a memorable group of continuing characters: Scotland Yard Inspector Thomas Lynley, the eighth earl of Asherton; his unflinchingly working-class partner, Sergeant Barbara Havers; forensic pathologist Simon Allcourt-St. James and his wife Deborah, a photographer; and Lady Helen Clyde, St. James's laboratory assistant. The lives of Lynley, Simon, Deborah, and Lady Helen have been intertwined for years; they carry with them emotional baggage from the past that affects their current investigations. Each novel then becomes a chapter in the ongoing saga of the investigators' personal lives; each murder case moves the relationships onward and causes the characters to reflect on some part of their emotional makeup. A recurring theme in the books is living with a physical difference or disability. This theme is personified by St. James, who is partially disabled after a car crash (inevitably, the car was driven by a drunken Lynley, St. James's best friend), and the theme is central to the plot of *For the Sake of Elena* (Bantam, 1992), in which the murder victim is deaf. George's style is psychological and intense, with vividly detailed settings and many strands of plot artfully pulled together in the end. She uses traditional English mystery formats, like the locked-room mystery in *Payment in Blood* (Bantam, 1989), and brings new life and power to the genre.

George's first novel was *A Great Deliverance* (Bantam, 1988), which won both the Anthony and the Agatha Awards for Best First Novel. *A Suitable Vengeance* (Bantam, 1991), although published later, tells of events in the lives of George's characters that occur before the time of *A Great Deliverance*.

Readers who admire George's writing may also like P. D. James, Dorothy L. Sayers, Deborah Crombie, and Ruth Rendell. American novelists who also may prove enjoyable for readers include Faye

Kellerman, Audrey Peterson, and Julie Smith (especially Smith's Skip Langdon mysteries).

Gill, B. M.   Gill is a pseudonym for Welsh novelist Barbara M. Trimble; before beginning her career as a mystery novelist, she wrote romantic thrillers under the name of Margaret Blake and romance novels as Barbara Gilmour. Gill is expert at providing grim psychological motivations for her characters. Her dark tales revolve around the motivations and reactions of people in a crisis: during a criminal trial, the breakup of a marriage, or the addition of foster children to a family, for example. Gill won the Gold Dagger for *The Twelfth Juror* (Scribner, 1984), a strong exploration of the characters of a juror and a defendant in a murder trial, whose lives cross in and out of the courtroom. *Seminar for Murder* (Scribner, 1986) and *The Fifth Rapunzel* (Scribner, 1991) feature a rather detached but observant police inspector, Tom Maybridge. *Dying to Meet You* (Doubleday, 1990) is a somber view of a doomed romantic triangle. *Time and Time Again* (Scribner, 1990) is a story of a middle-class woman who is jailed after inadvertently injuring a policeman during a peace demonstration. Jail changes her so completely that, on her release, she cannot fit back into her comfortable marriage and home. Like many of Gill's novels, this one is as much a character study as a mystery. *Nursery Crimes* (Scribner, 1987) is an Edgar-nominated tour de force psychological novel about the crimes of a psychopathic child during and after World War II.

Other writers of psychological crime novels include Ruth Rendell, P. D. James, Elizabeth George, Patricia Highsmith, S. T. Haymon, and L. R. Wright.

Gilman, Dorothy.   Gilman is known best for her tales of Mrs. Emily Pollifax who, bored with widowhood and retirement, decided to apply one day for a job with the CIA, in *The Unexpected Mrs. Pollifax* (Doubleday, 1966). After initial demurs, the CIA hires Mrs. Pollifax under the assumption that no one would *ever* suspect such a grandmotherly figure of being a spy. Mrs. Pollifax has trotted around the globe on various errands for the CIA, all of them proving highly dangerous of course, anywhere from Mexico to Albania to Switzerland to Africa. In more recent years, with the cooling down of the Cold War, Mrs. Pollifax has had several adventure in the Orient. Whatever the reader's reservations about the plausibility of Mrs. Pollifax as a spy, the novels provide terrific escape to various exotic locales.

In addition to the Pollifax novels, Gilman has written a number of other very entertaining works, including two recent adventure/ suspense novels, *Incident at Badamya* (Doubleday, 1989) and *Caravan* (Doubleday, 1992). One of her most popular nonseries novels is the suspense tale, *The Tightrope Walker* (Doubleday, 1979); another is *A Nun in the Closet* (Doubleday, 1975). Gilman has also written numerous children's books.

The recent novel by Serita Stevens and Rayanne Moore, *Red Sea, Dead Sea* (St. Martin's Press, 1991), features a character, Jewish grandmother Fanny Zindel, who has much in common with Emily Pollifax. Other entertaining elderly sleuths can be found in the work of Corinne Holt Sawyer, Eleanor Boylan, Margot Arnold, Gallagher Gray, and Kate Morgan.

Girdner, Jaqueline.   The heroine of Girdner's mystery series is Kate Jasper, who lives in Marin County, California. Kate owns Jest Gifts, a company that makes humorous mail-order gifts such as shark ties for lawyers. Kate is also a fanatic vegetarian, non-dairy, non-caffeine, non-sugar, non-everything person. Her friends in Mill Valley are psychics, software developers, artists, trendy restaurateurs, and other yuppie entrepreneurs. A former drug dealer is murdered at the office of Kate's chiropractor in *Adjusted to Death* (Diamond, 1991), the first book in the series. Everyone in the office at the time, including Kate, is a suspect. *The Last Resort* (Diamond, 1991) is set in Southern California in a spa that is being restored. The girlfriend of Kate's ex-husband, Craig Jasper, is killed, and Craig asks Kate to help prove that he didn't do it. *Murder Most Mellow* (Diamond, 1992) is set in Marin County, where a computer programmer and robot designer, who is also a member of Kate's study group, is killed. Girdner's plots are developed as her characters take part in typically New Age, Marin County kinds of activities: sitting in hot tubs, eating tofu, designing robots, and talking about their chakras.

Detectives created by Kate Green, Shelley Singer, and Susan Dunlap also find crime among California's New Age populace.

Giroux, E. X.   Canadian novelist Doris Shannon adopted the Giroux pseudonym for a series of English mysteries featuring barrister Robert Forsythe and his secretary, Abigail Sanderson. The first novel in the series, *A Death for Adonis* (St. Martin's Press, 1984), offers a complex plot that smacks of Agatha Christie in its construction, if not in its subject matter. Throughout the series, Forsythe and Sandy, as she is affectionately called, have shared almost equal billing, and in at least two of the novels, *A Death for a Doctor* (St. Martin's Press, 1986) and *A Death for a Dietitian* (St. Martin's Press, 1988), Sandy does most of the detecting herself. The warm relationship between Forsythe and Sandy, who is almost old enough to be, and indeed often seems like, Forsythe's mother, adds a charming touch to a series notable for the cleverness of the plots. On a recent case, *A Death for a Dancing Doll* (St. Martin's Press 1991), the intrepid duo leaves England for British Columbia, Giroux's home turf. Readers who still enjoy puzzles constructed in the classic vein will find much that appeals in Giroux's work.

Other English legal detectives of interest include Sara Woods's long-running series about barrister Antony Maitland, Ann Fallon's series about Irish solicitor James Fleming, and M. R. D. Meek's series about Lennox Kemp.

Godfrey, Ellen. Godfrey was born in America, but she lives in Canada and sets her books there. She founded a small publishing company and has owned a computer software company. Her first two mysteries, *The Case of the Cold Murderer* (Don Mills, Ontario: Musson, 1976) and *Murder among the Well-to-Do* (Erin, Ontario: Press Porcepic, 1977), feature Rebecca Rosenthal, an elderly Toronto anthropologist. Rebecca is an interesting character, capable of admitting her flaws, and her musings reveal how her background formed her personality. She escaped a pogrom in Poland in 1914 and brought her four siblings through war-torn Europe to Canada. Since then, family concerns have been highly important to her, and she wants to help and protect her niece and grandson in the first novel, and her brother in the second one. Each novel is a detailed look at a group of characters, including many of Rebecca's relatives.

In Godfrey's second series, the protagonist is Jane Tregar, a corporate headhunter in Toronto. She works for an openly sexist boss who keeps waiting for her to make mistakes. Jane suffers many crises of confidence but must project total control and professionalism, which is hard because she's a physically small woman who needs to be a powerful presence. In *Murder Behind Locked Doors*

(St. Martin's Press, 1988), Jane investigates murder at a computer software company. The company is about to do a big joint-marketing deal with an American company when their financial expert is killed in a locked computer room to which only a few people had the key. In *Georgia Disappeared* (Markham, Ontario: Viking, 1991), Jane investigates the disappearance of her friend Georgia, an executive at another software company. Georgia has left behind an acrimonious research and development team and a revolutionary new product that was just about to be released. Godfrey creates good workplace settings and portrays high-tech and high-stress occupations with smart, devious suspects.

Godfrey also wrote a true crime book, *By Reason of Doubt* (Clarke, 1982) about the Belshaw case, and it won a special Edgar Award.

Other writers who use Toronto settings include Medora Sale, Margaret Millar, Alison Gordon, and Eve Zaremba. Linda Grant and Sharon Gwyn Short write computer-oriented mysteries, and Annette Meyers has a series about executive headhunters.

Gordon, Alison. Gordon was the first woman journalist to cover major league baseball. It seems inevitable, then, that her mysteries are set in that world, with Toronto sports writer Kate Henry as Gordon's protagonist. Kate covers the fictional Toronto Titans, much as Gordon covered the Toronto Blue Jays in her newspaper career. Kate is a completely professional, mature woman, with the inquisitive bent of a reporter and an amateur sleuth. As one would expect, Gordon gives the reader an insider's view of baseball and the experience of touring with a team. She has a crisp, journalistic style and creates distinctive Toronto settings. Her first novel was *The Dead Pull Hitter* (St. Martin's Press, 1989). Two players are murdered and Kate finds herself involved in the crimes as she covers the story. She meets Staff Sergeant Andy Munro of Homicide, who is in charge of the case, and they begin a relationship. In *Safe at Home* (St. Martin's Press, 1990), young boys are being murdered by a serial killer. There is an interesting subplot about the difficulties encountered by a ballplayer who decides to come out of the closet with the news of his homosexuality. Gordon depicts the homophobia present in major league sports. *Night Game* (St. Martin's Press, 1993) is set in Florida at the Titans' spring training camp. A sexy woman journalist is killed on the beach, and Kate investigates.

In all of her mysteries, Gordon provides a principled, positive view of the media, and she shows how a working journalist gets her daily stories and works with her sources.

Other novelists who use Canadian settings include L. R. Wright, Alisa Craig, Medora Sale, Elisabeth Bowers, and Lauren Wright Douglas. Linda Mariz and Julie Robitaille write sports mysteries.

Gosling, Paula. American born and bred, Gosling moved to England permanently in 1964, and in 1979, she launched a full-time writing career after *Fair Game* (Coward, McCann, 1978; English title, *A Running Duck*, Macmillan, 1978) was published and received the Crime Writers' Association John Creasey Award for Best First Novel. In this first novel, set in San Francisco, Gosling offered an entertaining variation on the woman-in-jeopardy novel. Other action-packed suspense novels followed, like *Solo Blue* (Coward, McCann, 1980; English title, *Loser's Blues*, Macmillan, 1980), about a musician named Johnny Cosatelli, whose involvement with the wrong woman leads to a deadly situation.

With *Monkey Puzzle* (Doubleday, 1985), which won the CWA Gold Dagger, Gosling launched her first series. This combination academic mystery and police procedural is set in the American Midwestern city of Grantham, and the main characters are homicide cop Jack Stryker and English professor Kate Trevorne. They appear as supporting characters in the hilarious *Hoodwink* (Doubleday, 1988), which demonstrates Gosling's knack for writing deliciously funny physical comedy scenes. Two further novels have featured Stryker and Trevorne as central characters. In *The Wychford Murders* (Doubleday, 1986), Gosling introduced English cop Luke Abbott, who reappeared in a supporting role in *Death Penalties* (Mysterious, 1991). Gosling creates strong, likable characters. Her wicked sense of humor is an important element in many of the novels, and she has a knack for writing vivid and believable action scenes.

Readers who have enjoyed Gosling's crime novels might try the humorous suspense novels of Elizabeth Peters, the Sigrid Harald novels of Margaret Maron, the Tamara Hoyland novels of Jessica Mann, or the British police mysteries of Cynthia Harrod-Eagles, Caroline Graham, Susan B. Kelly, and Jill McGown.

Grafton, Sue. The daughter of the late lawyer and mystery novelist C. W. Grafton, Sue Grafton has written numerous screenplays in addition to two novels and her series of best-selling mysteries starring Kinsey Millhone. In the decade since her debut (in *"A" is for Alibi*; Holt, Rinehart, Winston, 1982), private eye Kinsey Millhone has become one of the most popular characters in current mystery fiction. In her early thirties, Kinsey is something of a loner. Twice-divorced, she lives in a small apartment with few possessions and even fewer emotional attachments. One of Kinsey's most important emotional ties, however, is to her octogenarian landlord, Henry Pitts, a retired baker who supplements his income by devising crossword puzzles. Henry serves as something of a father figure and emotional anchor for Kinsey. Tough, stubborn, but with a healthy sense of humor as a saving grace, Kinsey is definitely a descendant of the wisecracking, hard-boiled male private eye who has been a staple of American detective fiction for seventy years. The fictional California town of Santa Teresa, where Kinsey lives and works, is a thinly veiled Santa Barbara, home to one of Grafton's important influences, the writer Ross MacDonald. Though she is part of an established tradition, Kinsey nevertheless remains an individual. Grafton's style, which moves easily between action and introspection, from grim reality to humorous aside, demonstrates the range of an author well in command of her voice. Kinsey's yearly progress toward the end of the alphabet is usually a much-anticipated event for mystery fans.

Grafton fans unacquainted with the work of Ross MacDonald might enjoy these older works which are, in many ways, the epitome of Southern California detective fiction. Otherwise, readers might try the work of Marcia Muller, Linda Barnes, Patricia D. Cornwell, or Janet Dawson.

Graham, Caroline. With her first novel published in the United States, the Agatha-nominated *The Killings at Badger's Drift* (Adler & Adler, 1988), Graham quickly became a favorite among English mystery fans. Her traditional style harks back to the Golden Age classics, but her subject matter and the frank treatment she gives it make her work thoroughly contemporary. Those who love the work of James and Rendell will appreciate the psychological acuity with which Graham delineates her characters and the flashes of wit with which she leavens the mixture. Her detective, Chief Inspector Barnaby, is a likable and intelligent figure in his two appearances to date; the second is the theatrical mystery, *Death of a*

Hollow Man (Morrow, 1990). Here the author uses her own experience with theater and television to construct a complex and engaging story.

Graham's third novel, the funny *Murder at Madingley Grange* (Morrow, 1991), offers a contemporary twist on the classic country-house scenario. Powerful and compelling at her best, Graham is a fine new voice in the English mystery tradition.

Readers of Graham might also enjoy the Inspector Bone mysteries of Susannah Stacey, the work of Frances Fyfield, Paula Gosling, P. D. James, Patricia Moyes, Janet Neel, or the American writer of English mysteries, Martha Grimes.

Granger, Ann.   Like her heroine, Meredith Mitchell, Granger has worked in the diplomatic service in various parts of the world. In the first novel of the series, *Say it with Poison* (St. Martin's Press, 1991), Meredith is visiting her glamorous actress cousin, Eve, on the night before Eve's daughter's wedding. Weddings are always an occasion for drama, but soon Meredith finds herself mixed up with murder and blackmail and a certain divorced Chief Inspector Alan Markby. Markby, an avid gardener, is drawn to the aloof but appealing Meredith, and as he investigates the crime, the two of them edge toward some sort of relationship. Meredith uses her diplomatic skills to help in the investigation. Granger uses the Cotswolds and the village atmosphere to advantage in this series. The relationship between Meredith and Markby is the cornerstone of the series. Meredith is prickly and uncertain, while Markby definitely knows that he wants to get married. Will Meredith give up her career for domestic life leavened with crime-solving? Readers who enjoy the English village whodunit will find an able practitioner in Granger, who handles characters, plots, and settings with consistent skill.

Other enjoyable English village cozy series are those of June Thomson, Susan B. Kelly, Ann Cleeves, Hazel Holt, Elizabeth Lemarchand, and Kay Mitchell.

Grant, Linda.   Catherine Sayler, Grant's protagonist in a series of mysteries, is a private investigator in San Francisco. Catherine has her own firm (with a partner in later books), and she specializes in financial crime. She deliberately has tried to avoid taking cases where she might have to deal with violent and habitual criminals;

she prefers to work only with white-collar crime. Somehow, Catherine's cases aren't always as straightforward as she would like, as in *Blind Trust* (Scribner, 1990), and she is forced into dangerous and volatile confrontations. Catherine is, however, adept at aikido, and she uses her skills in some physical showdowns. One character who brings a somewhat different perspective to this series is Catherine's assistant, Jesse, an African-American computer whiz who eventually becomes her partner in the firm. Grant's novels portray Catherine as an independent and thoughtful woman, and she has given readers a welcome addition to the ranks of female private eyes.

The first Catherine Sayler novel is *Random Access Murder* (Avon, 1988).

Admirers of Grant's novels also may enjoy Janet Dawson, Catherine Dain, and Sarah Dunant. Other contemporary mysteries set in San Francisco have been written by Margaret Lucke, Marcia Muller, Lia Matera, Gloria White, and Elizabeth Atwood Taylor.

Grant-Adamson, Lesley. A veteran British journalist, Grant-Adamson has written several different kinds of crime novels. She has explored the psychological mystery in *The Face of Death* (Scribner, 1985) and the cozy English village mystery in *Death on Widow's Walk* (Scribner, 1985). London gossip columnist Rain Morgan is Grant-Adamson's protagonist in many of the mysteries. Rain is curious and persistent, with an instinct for discovering an oddity that may turn into a good story for her newspaper column. The first Rain Morgan novel is *Death on Widow's Walk*, which was published in the United Kingdom under the title *Patterns in the Dust* (Faber, 1985). It is a fairly typical English village mystery, updated to the 1980s with new technology as an essential part of the plot element. *Wild Justice* (St. Martin's Press, 1987) is set in the offices of the fictional London *Post*, and Grant-Adamson provides an insider's view of how a megalomaniacal businessman might run a British newspaper.

The female private eye genre is explored by Grant-Adamson in *Too Many Questions* (St. Martin's Press, 1991), which was published in Great Britain as *Flynn* (Faber and Faber, 1991). Laura Flynn comes from a large Irish family and grew up in a close-knit Irish community in London. She is a sardonic, single, and persistent investigator.

The latest series for Grant-Adamson features Jim Rush, an amoral and charming con man. The series begins with *A Life of Adventure* (Faber and Faber, 1992). Grant-Adamson creates literate, compelling, well-crafted plots and effective settings in her varied mysteries.

Readers may also enjoy mysteries by Minette Walters, Liza Cody, Sarah Dunant, Anabel Donald, Antonia Fraser, B. M. Gill, and Joan Smith. Annette Roome and Gillian Slovo write about British journalist-sleuths, and Patricia Highsmith's Ripley series features classic tales of an intriguing rogue.

Gray, Gallagher. The morning after he has retired as personnel manager of a prestigious Wall Street bank, T. S. Hubbert receives a telephone call, seeking his help in solving the murder of one of the bank's partners. With the people skills honed from thirty years in personnel selection and management, T. S. wades into the fray, assisted by his octogenarian aunt, Lillian Hubbert. Auntie Lil, as she is affectionately called, spent over sixty years in the fashion industry, and she has a flair for the dramatic Bette Davis would have envied. Together, T. S. and Auntie Lil make a formidable detective duo. As the series progresses, they gain assistance from secondary characters, such as Herbert Wong, a retired messenger for T. S.'s old firm, and Lilah Cheswick, the widow of the murder victim in the first book. The pseudonymous Gray, who is in reality Katy Munger, has created vivid and interesting characters for her series. Readers will enjoy the books as much for keeping up with the exploits of Auntie Lil as they will for solving the intricately designed puzzles of whodunit that Gray has created. The first book in the series is *Hubbert & Lil: Partners in Crime* (Donald I. Fine, 1991).

Readers acquainted with Hubbert and Lil might also try the series by Emma Lathen and Annette Meyers, both of whom use the Wall Street and New York City milieu to great effect. Readers looking for other sleuths of retirement age might try the work of Eleanor Boylan, Stefanie Matteson, M. K. Lorens, and Corinne Holt Sawyer.

Green, Christine. Her varied experiences in nursing have given Green the background knowledge for one of two series she is currently writing. Her first series character is Kate Kinsella, a nurse who is also a private detective. Her initial appearance is in

Deadly Errand (Walker, 1992). A young nurse is found dead on the grounds of a local hospital; the police believe it was a random killing, but the victim's aunt employs Kate to find the culprit. In each investigation, Kate receives the aid, often unsolicited, of her landlord and would-be sidekick, Hubert Humberstone, who owns the funeral home and the building that houses Kate's office. A quirky character with a foot fetish, Hubert nevertheless turns out to be a good friend to Kate. The books in the series generally have some medical connection, thanks to Kate's dual professions.

With *Death in the Country* (London: Macmillan, 1993; Bantam 1995), Green began a series of police procedurals featuring Chief Inspector Connor O'Neill and Detective Sergeant Fran Wilson. This is Fran's first day on a new job and her first homicide. She is also saddled with a troubled boss; will she be able to cope with an enigmatic Irishman as well as the rigors of being a female in the very male-oriented world of the English police?

Readers who like medically oriented mysteries should also try Mary Kittredge and Stella Shepherd. Those interested in English police procedural series like Green's should try the work of Susan B. Kelly, Anthea Fraser, and Marjorie Eccles.

Green, Kate.   Green writes suspense novels that often contain elements of the occult. Her first book was the Edgar-nominated *Shattered Moon* (Dell, 1986). It introduces Theresa Fortunato, a California psychic who keeps seeing visions of horrible killings; she then helps the police find victims of a serial murderer. The positive (if New Age) orientation of the psychic is counterpointed by the madness of the killer in the narrative, and both characters are well-depicted by Green. Theresa continues to work with LAPD detective Oliver Jardine in the hauntingly effective *Black Dreams* (HarperCollins, 1993).

In *Night Angel* (Delacorte, 1989), Green portrays a group of old friends who lived together in Berkeley in the 1960s and are reunited after a mysterious death within the circle. Maggie Shea, now a psychologist in Minneapolis, returns to California, and the surviving friends try to come to terms with the unexpected death. The setting is atmospheric and nostalgic (especially for readers of the '60s generation), but not overly sentimental.

Green's *Shooting Star* (HarperCollins, 1992), is about an actress who thinks she's being stalked by a crazed admirer. Violent events in the scripts of her films are duplicated in her real life, and Green keeps the level of suspense high and the inside look at filmmaking absorbing.

Other suspense writers of interest to the reader may include Mary Higgins Clark and T. J. MacGregor (who also writes as Alison Drake and Trish Janeshutz). Authors who have created characters who are psychics include Mignon Warner, Jaqueline Girdner, and Dorothy Gilman in her novel *The Clairvoyant Countess* (Doubleday, 1975).

Greenwood, D. M. The author describes herself as an ecclesiastical civil servant, and she uses to her advantage knowledge of the workings of the hierarchy and institutions of the Church of England in her series of ecclesiastical mysteries. Her series character is Deaconess Theodora Braithwaite, who stands over six feet tall and comes from a distinguished English clerical family. In her first appearance, in *Clerical Errors* (St. Martin's Press, 1991), the deaconess delves into a murder that takes place within the precincts of Medewich Cathedral. In *Unholy Ghosts* (St. Martin's Press, 1992), Theodora is on holiday in a Norfolk village when the mysterious death of the parish priest once again involves her in murder. Greenwood observes with a keen eye the lives of those whose vocation is the care of souls, and she writes novels that are bound to interest those who enjoy mysteries with clerical settings. The politics of cloister and cathedral can be no less vicious than those of statehouse or university, and Greenwood ably employs Theodora Braithwaite, committed but clear-eyed in her vocation, to sort out the trouble.

Fans of mysteries with clerical settings might try the Claire Aldington novels of Isabelle Holland, the series by Veronica Black, Sister Carol Anne O'Marie, Kate Charles, Mollie Hardwick, and Barbara Whitehead. Those looking for clerical mysteries with a different twist might try Ellis Peters's tales of her twelfth-century Benedictine sleuth, Brother Cadfael.

Greenwood, Kerry. Australia in the 1920s is the setting for a series of amusing and fast-paced stories about a flapper sleuth named Phryne Fisher by Melbourne native Greenwood. The Honourable Miss Fisher, the daughter of an earl, grew up in an impoverished family until the day her father succeeded to the title, and the family's fortunes changed forever. Phryne never forgot the privations of her childhood, however, and now that she has the money to live the way she wishes, she indulges her own whims by helping those less fortunate than she. Phryne's spirit of charity often leads her into danger, but dauntlessly she perseveres until right triumphs (albeit with a few kicks to the backside by the Honourable Miss Fisher). The first novel in the series, *Death by Misadventure* (Fawcett, 1991; entitled *Cocaine Blues* when first published in Australia in 1989), has Phryne investigating the desperate straits of a well-bred young woman who seems to be at the mercy of a scoundrel husband. Or is she?

Life in the Jazz Age Down Under is great fun with Phryne Fisher. Another light-hearted series featuring a flapper sleuth are the Iris Cooper books of American writer K. K. Beck. Carola Dunn is also writing a new series about a young Englishwoman of the 1920s who solves mysteries.

Grimes, Martha. Her debut novel, *The Man with a Load of Mischief* (Little, Brown, 1981), was greeted by American fans of the traditional English mystery with a warm reception. Grimes's next two novels, *The Old Fox Deceiv'd* (Little, Brown, 1982) and *The Ano dyne Necklace* (Little, Brown, 1983), followed in much the same vein: Agatha Christie and Dorothy L. Sayers blended with early P. D. James. Subsequent books began to take on something of a different flavor and demonstrated, perhaps, the crossbreeding of an American, albeit a devout Anglophile, writing the traditional British mystery. Critics, particularly the English ones, have taken Grimes to task for elementary errors of fact, such as having trains leaving London from the wrong station. Most fans have been willing to overlook such details for the rich rewards of character and setting. Grimes's moodiness and flair for the eccentric have made her chief characters, the policeman Richard Jury and the aristocrat Melrose Plant, an unusual and somewhat unlikely duo. Grimes is also possessed of a wicked sense of humor, which surfaces in many of the books, perhaps most notably in *I Am the Only Running Footman* (Little, Brown, 1986), with the creation of the Warboys family, a dangerously inept crew running a country pub. In *The Horse You Came in On* (Knopf, 1993), Grimes aims her guns at literary theft with humorously entertaining results. The intensity of her plots and the emotional appeal of her characters have made Grimes a great favorite with the American reading public, who have put Grimes onto the best-sellers' list. The recent *The End of the Pier* (Knopf, 1992), set in America, shows Grimes putting aside the mystery for a more mainstream novel. The titles of all the Jury books are taken from the names of English pubs.

Like Grimes, the American writer Elizabeth George is also writing English mysteries, though George is much more British of the two, closer to P. D. James or Ruth Rendell than is Grimes. Grimes fans might also enjoy the work of Frances Fyfield, Caroline Graham, and Deborah Crombie.

Gunning, Sally. The central character in Gunning's series is Peter Bartholomew, who is owner of a business called Factotum. Pete and his partner, Rita Peck, and their changing cast of employees literally do just about anything in their setting of the Cape Hook island of Nashtoba, Massachusetts. In addition to the run-of-the-mill odd jobs that anybody would need doing, Pete often finds himself playing detective because murders just seem to keep happening in this small community. Pete, who's in his mid-thirties and comfortable with his job and his island, is an amiable, attractive character, and Gunning renders the small-town setting well. The reappearing cast of minor characters is reminiscent of the denizens of television's Cabot's Cove, Maine (on *Murder, She Wrote*); there's a special flavor to the Down East type of murder, which Gunning seems to have captured. Complicating Pete's life is the return of his ex-wife Connie, and their tortured rapprochement serves as a subplot through the books in the series published thus far. The first in the series is *Hot Water* (Pocket, 1990); subsequent entries in the series also have *water* in their titles.

Readers looking for other New England series might try the work of J. S. Borthwick, Susan Kenney, Charlotte MacLeod, B. J. Morison, and the work of an older writer, Phoebe Atwood Taylor, whose Asey Mayo might be considered something of a literary grandfather to Pete Bartholomew.

Gur, Batya. A best-selling novelist in her native Israel, Gur is a teacher of literature in Jeruslem. Her series of police procedurals star Moroccan-born Michael Ohayon, who has the rank of chief inspector in the first novel, *The Saturday Morning Murder* (HarperCollins, 1992). In his first appearance, subtitled *A Psychoanalytic Case*, Ohayon is investigating the death of a well-known psychoanalyst in Jerusalem. Gur creates richly detailed backgrounds for each of her tales of murder, examining a particular community in thorough fashion. In *The Saturday Morning Murder*, the setting is a psychoanalytic institute; in the second book, *Literary Murder* (HarperCollins, 1993), the setting is the Literature Department at the Hebrew University. Ohayon is a well-educated, intense professional who has considerable gifts of sensitivity and intuition. Sculpted in the mold of detectives like Adam Dalgliesh and Reginald Wexford, Ohayon is definitely a "cousin" of the main characters in the best of the English police procedural school. Gur has successfully taken the form of the English detective story and transposed it to Israel. The novels offer a fascinating look at a complex society, a blend of both East and West.

Those who have enjoyed the work of Batya Gur should also read P. D. James, Ruth Rendell, Elizabeth George, and the late Dorothy L. Sayers. Robert Rosenberg has recently begun a series also set chiefly in Israel.

Haddam, Jane/Papazoglou, Orania. Under her own name, Papazoglou has written a series of mysteries featuring writer Patience (Pay) Campbell McKenna. In the first novel, *Sweet, Savage Death* (Doubleday, 1984), Pay is a writer of respectable articles in national magazines, but she also writes category romance novels (under a pseudonym, of course). Some of the major figures in romance publishing are murdered, and Pay and her friend and fellow novelist Phoebe investigate the crimes. Papazoglou provides plenty of satire on the romance publishing business. In the succeeding books in the series, Pay is writing true-crime books for a living. Papazoglou also has written a psychological suspense novel, *Charisma* (Crown, 1992), about a succession of killings of former nuns in New Haven, Connecticut.

For another series of mysteries, Papazoglou adopted the pseudonym of Jane Haddam. Her protagonist is Gregor Demarkian, a retired FBI agent, and the series is set around the celebration of holidays. The novels are strongly imbued with the atmosphere of the Armenian-American community of Philadelphia, and Demarkian eventually becomes famous for his sleuthing and known as the Armenian-American Hercule Poirot. The series begins with a Christmas mystery, *Not a Creature Was Stirring* (Bantam, 1990), set in Philadelphia and its wealthy Main Line suburbs. Gregor is assisted in his cases by Father Tibor Kasparian, an Armenian Orthodox priest, and by Bennis Hannaford, a rich and intelligent writer of fantasy novels. Demarkian is an expert in poisons and the behavioral analysis of serial killers, and the crimes he solves are traditional cozy puzzle mysteries.

Readers who enjoy the Patience McKenna novels should try Elizabeth Peters's *Die for Love* (Congdon & Weed, 1984) and the Ben and Carrie Porter mysteries by Elizabeth Travis. Aficionados of the Demarkian series might want to look for books by Agatha Christie, Carolyn G. Hart, Jennifer Rowe, Dorothy Sucher, and Betty Rowlands. Gillian Roberts also gives her mysteries a Philadelphia backdrop.

Hadley, Joan. See **Hess, Joan.**

Hager, Jean. Hager has written three series of mysteries, as well as writing romances under the pseudonyms of Leah Crane and Jeanne Stephens. The books in Hager's first mystery series are police procedurals, with a background of Cherokee lore and medicine. They are set in Oklahoma, with a continuing protagonist in Police Chief Mitch Bushyhead. Bushyhead is one-half Cherokee, but he is an outsider to the tribe since he was raised as a white man and married a white woman. His wife is dead, and now he has to cope with raising a teenage daughter by himself. Another continuing character in the books is Crying Wolf, a Cherokee medicine man. Bushyhead dispenses the white man's justice; Crying Wolf uses his medicine to work problems out in the historic Cherokee way. The first novel in the series is *The Grandfather Medicine* (St. Martin's Press, 1989).

Hager's second series begins with *Ravenmocker* (Mysterious, 1992), in which the heroine is Molly Bearpaw, an investigator for the Native American Advocacy League. Molly works out of Tahlequah, Oklahoma, and deals with cases in which members of the Cherokee tribe may have been denied their civil rights. In *Seven Black Stones* (Mysterious, 1995), Molly investigates two mysterious deaths that seem to have no link except for the presence of seven black stones found near the bodies.

The quintessentially cozy mystery *Blooming Murder* (Avon, 1994) is the first entry in a third series by Hager. Set in a small town in Missouri, these novels revolve around a bed-and-breakfast, Iris House, run by Tess Darcy. Tess has inherited the Victorian house from an aunt who grew irises, and murder occurs during the annual iris-growers' convention. Members of the local garden club are all suspects, and the story is embellished with gardening lore.

Eve K. Sandstrom, D. R. Meredith, Mary Willis Walker, Anne Wingate, Barbara Burnett Smith, and Susan Rogers Cooper also write mysteries set in Oklahoma and Texas. Dana Stabenow, Margaret Coel, Cecil Dawkins, and Chelsea Quinn Yarbro write series with Native American investigators.

Hall, Patricia. British writer Patricia Hall writes mysteries set in a Yorkshire town that is struggling with the social ills of modern England. In *The Poison Pool* (St. Martin's Press, 1993), policeman Alex Sinclair and social worker Kate Weston investigate murder at a run-down public housing project. When a retarded boy is accused of the crime, Kate hears about the situation through her daily interactions with the residents, while the traditional methods of inquiry by the police meet with hostility. This is not a traditional English country house murder mystery, but a fine and unsparing view of life and death amid the poverty and bleakness of council housing. With *The Coldness of Killers* (London: Crime Club, 1992), Hall explores race relations in a comprehensive school in Bradfield. When an Asian ex-student is found dead in the boys' showers, the town is consumed by race riots, drug scares, and municipal corruption. Hall details the daily conflicts faced by Asian students, especially girls, between a westernized lifestyle and their Islamic beliefs. *Death by Election* (St. Martin's Press, 1994) begins a series of mysteries that feature reporter Laura Ackroyd and police inspector Michael Thackeray. Laura dislikes being assigned to write features for the women's pages and would leave Yorkshire if it weren't for her elderly grandmother, a feisty Labour Party stalwart who lives surrounded by urban decay. Thackeray has recently been transferred into Bradfield, and he is battling his own alcoholism and despair. They meet when the local Member of Parliament dies. A by-election is scheduled amid rumors of scandal and unrest, particularly in the local gay community. In *Dying Fall* (London:Little, Brown, 1994), Laura and Thackeray meet again. In the housing projects, teenagers are stealing cars and joyriding on hot summer nights; when the police chase them, a crash results in death and simmering anger among the residents. Tensions are close to explosion when, in an echo of the Birmingham Six and Guildford Four cases, an old child murder resurfaces, and allegations emerge of police brutality and wrongful conviction. In her mysteries, Hall provides a devastating picture of how high-rise, low-income housing can breed crime and despair in its tenants.

Gillian Slovo, Liza Cody, and Sara Paretsky write about urban problems. Peter Robinson and Barbara Whitehead set their mysteries in Yorkshire.

Hardwick, Mollie.   Hardwick's mysteries are quintessential English cozies, with a spot of evil spreading through each book. The heroine is Doran Fairweather, who owns an antique business and lives in a beautiful old house in the village of Abbotsbourne in Kent. In the first book, *Malice Domestic* (St. Martin's Press, 1986), Doran begins a close personal and investigative relationship with the local vicar, Rodney Chelmarsh. At the beginning of the series, Doran is an uncertain, vulnerable young woman; she matures into an interesting, thoughtful woman with a group of loyal friends and family. A strong vein of religion and literature runs through all of Hardwick's mysteries. Crimes take place against the backgrounds of the antique trade, the art world, and the Anglican church. Hardwick's writing is charmingly erudite and chock-full of quotes; she will often use an individual English artist or writer for a thematic background—including Keats, Lewis Carroll, Gilbert and Sullivan, and Dante Gabriel Rossetti.

Hardwick has also written many historical novels, and she is perhaps best-known for writing the Upstairs, Downstairs series of books.

Those interested in mysteries with an Episcopalian or Anglican church setting may enjoy Isabelle Holland, Kate Charles, D. M. Greenwood, and Barbara Whitehead.

Harris, Charlaine.   For the setting of her first mystery novel, *Sweet and Deadly* (Houghton Mifflin, 1981), Harris used her native Mississippi Delta and the fictional town of Lowfield. The heroine of this novel, Catherine Linton, has the characteristics that are hallmarks of Harris's creations. Catherine, like Nickie Callahan of *A Secret Rage* (Houghton Mifflin, 1984), is intelligent, independent, and attractive. Catherine Linton is delving into the mysterious deaths of her parents while working as a society editor for the Lowfield *Gazette*. Nickie is a former New York model who has tired of the glamorous life and has returned to the South for a college education. The small town of Knolls, Tennessee, is being terrorized by a rapist, and Nickie falls prey to him. Writing with sensitivity and compassion, Harris handles a difficult subject well.

Lately, Harris has begun a series starring Aurora "Roe" Teagarden, a diminutive librarian with a sassy tongue and an affinity for true crime. In the Agatha-nominated *Real Murders* (Walker, 1990), Roe finds herself investigating the murders of fellow members of her real murders club. All the victims have died in a way reminiscent of some famous true crime. Roe's adventures continue in *A Bone to Pick* (Walker, 1992). Wit, humor, intelligence, and Southern settings grace Harris's accomplished work.

Readers who have enjoyed the work of Harris should try Sharyn McCrumb, Margaret Maron, Carolyn G. Hart, and Sarah Shankman. Those looking for other librarian detectives may seek out the Jacqueline Kirby novels of Elizabeth Peters.

Harris, Lee. This series of mystery novels features Christine Bennett, a young woman who has recently left the convent to resume a secular life. She inherited a house from her aunt and teaches part-time at a nearby college in a small town not far from New York City. In the first book in the series, *The Good Friday Murder* (Fawcett, 1992), Christine becomes involved in investigating a forty-year-old murder. This murder was apparently perpetrated by a pair of autistic twins on their mother, and the two boys were institutionalized separately after the murder. Now one of them, whom Christine has met, is being moved into a group home in Christine's small town, and furor erupts. As she investigates, Christine realizes that the twins could not have killed their mother. She is aided in her efforts at uncovering the truth by an attractive policeman, Jack Brooks, who becomes her romantic interest as the series develops. Harris devises interesting and unusual scenarios, and her main character is sympathetically drawn. Motivated in part by her own spiritual and religious values, Christine perseveres in search of the truth so that justice might be served. *The Good Friday Murder* was nominated for the Edgar Award for Best Paperback Original Mystery.

Readers who have encountered Lee Harris might try as well the work of Veronica Black and Sister Carol Anne O'Marie, both of whom have nuns as series characters.

Harrod-Eagles, Cynthia. The prolific Harrod-Eagles penned over thirty historical and fantasy novels before turning to the crime novel with *Orchestrated Death* (Scribner, 1992), which introduced London policeman Bill Slider. Slider is a detective inspector, and he is content with his rank, though his wife keeps nagging him to work for promotion. Promotion, however, would take Slider away from the work of detection into the world of administration, and he fights against it, though it could cost him his marriage. In *Orchestrated Death*, Slider is investigating the case of a murdered female, left naked and unidentifiable, the only clues at the scene a priceless Stradivarius and a giant tin of olive oil. From this, Harrod-Eagles fashions a complex and engaging police procedural novel. Her London cops are earthy, often ribald, and tough when necessary. Readers who have watched the "Prime Suspect" dramas aired on *Mystery!* on PBS will identify easily with the characters in this series, though there is no highly ranking female detective in the series.

Readers who enjoy English police procedurals might try the work of Paula Gosling, Jennie Melville, P. D. James, the Wexford novels of Ruth Rendell, the private eye series of Sarah Dunant, and the Canadian police procedural series of Medora Sale.

Hart, Carolyn G. Hart writes tightly plotted mysteries in the classic tradition. Her first series features Annie Laurance, and the initial novel is *Death on Demand* (Bantam, 1987). Annie owns Death on Demand, a mystery bookstore on Broward's Rock Island, off the coast of South Carolina. Annie has an encyclopedic knowledge of crime novels and a strong bent for detection. She is assisted in her sleuthing by Max Darling, with whom she has a relationship that develops throughout the series. Hart shows particular strength in her creation of memorable secondary characters like Max's dotty mother, Laurel, who enjoys a succession of dubious enthusiasms, and Henny Brawley, a bookstore customer who knows even more about mysteries than Annie and never lets her forget it. *The Christie Caper* (Bantam, 1991), one of Hart's best works, is a classic puzzle novel set at a convention in honor of the one hundredth birthday of Agatha Christie. Hart pays homage in her novels to other honored mystery writers, especially those from the Golden Age of crime fiction. In *A Little Class on Murder* (Doubleday, 1989), for example, Annie teaches a class on three of the great women mystery writers:

Agatha Christie, Dorothy Sayers, and Mary Roberts Rinehart. Hart also builds upon the traditional styles of mysteries for her books. *Southern Ghost* (Bantam, 1992), to cite one instance, uses many of the conventions of the Southern Gothic suspense novel, but in a fresh and noteworthy fashion. Hart is especially good in this novel at chronicling the family traditions and emotional baggage with which a contemporary generation of Southerners feels burdened.

Hart has started a new series of mysteries whose heroine is Oklahoma journalist Henrietta (Henrie O) O'Dwyer Collins. The first novel in the series is *Dead Man's Island* (Bantam, 1993), which won an Agatha Award for Best Novel and was made into a television movie.

Hart has won both the Agatha and the Anthony Awards for Best Novel for *Something Wicked* (Bantam, 1988), an Anthony Award for *Honeymoon with Murder* (Bantam, 1988), and a Macavity Award for Best Novel for *A Little Class on Murder*.

Fans of Hart should try the mysteries of Agatha Christie, Jill Churchill, Dorothy Cannell, Jennifer Rowe, and Betty Rowlands. The adventures of other bookseller-sleuths have been chronicled by Joan Hess, M. K. Wren, and Sheila Simonson.

Hart, Ellen. The main character in Hart's first series, set in Minneapolis, is lesbian restaurant owner Jane Lawless, who is in her mid-thirties and is recovering from the death of her longtime lover a few years before the series begins. Jane's restaurant, The Lyme House, reflects part of Jane's heritage: her mother was English, and Jane spent a considerable part of her childhood and adolescence in England. Jane's father, Raymond Lawless, is a well-known criminal lawyer in Minneapolis, and he and Jane have an uneasy relationship that grows and changes as the series progresses. Jane's "Watson" in the series is her old college friend, Cordelia Thorn, who is artistic director of a well-known theater in St. Paul. Cordelia, also a lesbian, has a deliciously theatrical manner that contrasts humorously with the much more sober and self-effacing character of Jane. Together, the two make an enjoyable detective duo in the time-honored tradition of Holmes and Watson, but with a decidedly feminist twist. Hart follows the format of the traditional mystery closely, and she weaves in her feminism as integral and understated parts of her plots. The first in the series is *Hallowed Murder* (Seal

Press, 1989), in which Jane becomes involved with the murder of a member of her old college sorority.

Recently, Hart has begun a second series, starring food critic Sophie Greenway. In the first book, *This Little Piggy Went to Murder* (Ballantine, 1994), Sophie and her husband, Bram Baldric, a Minneapolis radio talk show host, become involved in the political campaign of an old family friend. When the campaign turns deadly, Sophie turns her reporting skills to good use as an amateur sleuth.

Seal Press founder Barbara Wilson is currently writing two series about lesbian amateur detectives; those acquainted with Hart's work will find Wilson's books of great interest. Other lesbian mystery writers include Katherine V. Forrest, Claire McNab, Sandra Scoppettone, and Sarah Dreher. Those who have enjoyed the Sophie Greenway books might read Katherine Hall Page and Janet Laurence.

Haymon, S. T. Haymon's first mystery novel has perhaps one of the most distinctive and curious titles in contemporary mystery fiction. *Death and the Pregnant Virgin* (St. Martin's Press, 1980), besides introducing policeman Benjamin Jurnet, Norwich-born and bred, to modern detective fiction, signals the author's taste for the Baroque. The characters and relationships in Haymon's work are never commonplace. Her central character sets the tone of the series. Somewhat in the mold of P. D. James's Adam Dalgliesh, Jurnet is introspective, often moody, and Haymon uses the setting of Norwich and Norfolk effectively to reinforce her characterizations. In addition to solving crimes, Jurnet also pursues the love of Miriam, a beautiful Jewish woman who refuses to marry outside her faith. Jurnet therefore determines to convert to Judaism, and thus the reader is often witness to Jurnet's struggles of faith and conscience as well as to his methods of detection. Haymon does not flinch to present human behavior at its nastiest or most depraved, although her prose, as stylish as that of James or Rendell, does not sensationalize the subject matter. Although very much a part of the modern school of British psychological detective fiction, Haymon nevertheless is a distinctive, if sometimes disturbing, voice.

Readers who appreciate the psychological acuity of Haymon's work might also try the works of P. D. James, Gwendoline Butler, Minette Walters, Ruth Rendell, Frances Fyfield/Frances Hegarty, Sheila Radley, B. M. Gill, and Margaret Yorke.

Hegarty, Frances. See **Fyfield, Frances.**

Henry, Sue. Henry's *Murder on the Iditarod Trail* (Atlantic Monthly Press, 1991) won both the Macavity and the Anthony Awards for Best First Mystery. It's a striking tale set in Alaska during the Iditarod Trail sled dog race from Anchorage to Nome. The main characters are dogsledder Jessie Arnold and Alaska state trooper Sergeant Alex Jensen, who meet during the race. Henry provides a stirring account of the race, along with detailed descriptions about how racers and their dogs survive the bitter cold and endure the pace of a 1,000-mile-long, grueling race. As the race progresses, contestants are dying mysteriously, and Jessie and Alex struggle to discover a killer. Henry's second novel, *Termination Dust* (Morrow, 1995), is a worthy sequel to this tour de force. A canoer on the Yukon River in Canada finds a journal and the bones of a man who died during the Klondike gold rush. As he reads the Klondiker's tale of an old betrayal and murder, more murders occur on the river and the canoer himself becomes a suspect. Alex Jensen and a friend who is a Mountie are sent to investigate the modern crimes. Henry's descriptions of the Yukon and its history are detailed and fascinating, and the plot is satisfyingly complex.

Readers may want to look for Dana Stabenow's mysteries, which are also set in Alaska.

Hess, Joan/Hadley, Joan. Hess currently is writing two series of books under her own name. One series, known as the Ozarks murder mysteries, is set in the small town of Maggody, Arkansas, with protagonist Police Chief Arly Hanks. Arly has returned to her childhood hometown reluctantly, after a bitter divorce in New York. Somehow, she manages to keep her sanity in the eccentric, rural community, while surrounded by bizarre townsfolk. For example, there's Arly's mother Rubella Belinda, who runs Ruby Bee's Bar & Grill and tries to solve crimes while swapping rumors with her buddy, beautician Estelle Oppers. Then there's Brother Verber, the pastor of the Voice of the Almighty Lord Assembly Hall and a busy reader of pornography, and upright (if a trifle crooked) citizens like Hizzoner Mayor Jim Bob and his sanctimonious wife Mrs. Jim Bob (Mizzoner). And the county is full of members of the inbred, illiterate Buchanon clan (like good ol' boy Raz Buchanon, who likes to watch TV with his pig, Marjorie). The first Maggody novel is *Malice in Maggody* (St. Martin's Press, 1987).

Hess's other series is set in a college town in Arkansas, and its continuing characters are amateur sleuth and bookstore owner Claire Malloy and her obnoxious teenage daughter Caron. Claire persists doggedly in her sleuthing on local crimes despite the constant hindrance of Caron, her pimply friend Inez, and attractive (if jaded) local cop Peter Rosen. The first Claire Malloy mystery is *Strangled Prose* (St. Martin's Press, 1986).

Hess also wrote two novels under the name of Joan Hadley. The protagonist in these is Theo Bloomer, a retiree who loves plants and has exotic adventures in crime. The first Theo Bloomer book is *The Night-Blooming Cereus* (St. Martin's Press, 1986).

The tone of Hess's work is sarcastic, biting, and hilarious. The Maggody series especially is pretty much off the wall. Readers will enjoy these novels if they like slapstick humor, strong regional description, eccentric Southern writing, or redneck satire. Hess is a winner of the American Mystery Award for *A Diet to Die For* (St. Martin's Press, 1989).

Readers who like Joan Hess also may enjoy Carole Berry, whose sleuth, Bonnie Indermill, has an ironic and sharp mind; Charlotte MacLeod, whose humor is gentler; Dorothy Cannell; Taylor McCafferty; and Sharyn McCrumb. Annette Roome's Chris Martin novels should be fun to read for admirers of the Claire Malloy books.

Highsmith, Patricia. The late Patricia Highsmith was American by birth but lived for most of her life in Europe, where many of her novels are set. Her first work was *Strangers on a Train* (Harper, 1950), which Alfred Hitchcock filmed, though in altering the ending, he deprived the story of much of its punch. In *Strangers on a Train*, two seemingly normal people meet accidentally; one is quickly revealed to be corrupt, and the other withdraws, only to be caught up in the other's criminality in spite of himself. Highsmith's leading characters are often the criminals, and their victims come across as frightening and villainous. Robert Forester, in *The Cry of the Owl* (Harper, 1962), is a Peeping Tom who is caught by the young woman he's been watching through her window. He introduces himself, makes friends, and steals her from her fiancé, who comes after Robert with murderous intent. Robert ruins lives and families from beginning to end, yet somehow the reader sides with him and against the people he harms. Highsmith's stories usually include a strong dose of paranoia, complex relationships, and sexual ambiguity; her lead characters are usually men drawn into criminal difficulties by their failure to take advantage of potential ways out that are apparent to the reader.

Highsmith's best-regarded crime novels are the series involving Tom Ripley, beginning with *The Talented Mr. Ripley* (Coward, 1955) and continuing through to *Ripley Under Water* (Knopf, 1992). Tom Ripley is a young man, fired from his job and supporting himself through minor forgery, who's commissioned by a concerned father to go to Europe and persuade the man's expatriate son, with whom Tom is slightly acquainted, to return to America and the family business. Seeing a chance for a free vacation, Tom goes to Italy, looks up the son, and makes himself a part of his life. Eventually, he assumes the son's identity, his income, even his clothing. When the man's friends start to question events, he can think of no solution other than to murder them. Through the Ripley series, Tom forges, impersonates, murders, and yet lives an increasingly luxurious life, free of guilt and penalty, improvising his escapes from the police who are always suspicious of his lengthening list of dead associates, yet never quite smart enough to pin anything on him.

Highsmith also wrote *The Price of Salt* (Coward-McCann, 1952), a novel about a lesbian relationship, under the pseudonym of Claire Morgan.

Highsmith received the Silver Dagger Award in 1964 for *The Two Faces of January* (Doubleday, 1964).

The mix of comedy and killing in Highsmith's books; the mood darkening from an initial everyday calm into terror; and the amoral acceptance by characters of their and others' crimes, may remind readers of the noir writer Jim Thompson. Joyce Carol Oates writes psychological suspense novels under the pseudonym of Rosamond Smith, and Barbara Paul writes mysteries that are noted for their strong vein of black comedy and memorable villains.

Hightower, Lynn S. Born in Tennessee but currently hailing from Kentucky, Hightower began her career with a series of futuristic police procedurals somewhat reminiscent of the popular film *Alien Nation.* The first of Hightower's series is *Alien Blues* (Ace, 1992), and the setting is Saigo City about half a century in the future. The main character is homicide detective David Silver, who works with his partner and brother-in-law, Mel Burnett, to track down murderers in this dark and disturbing future world. A group of slightly superior aliens, the Elaki, have come to Earth to help the Earthlings sort out some of their serious problems, but the mix of Elaki and Earthling is an uneasy one. The Elaki resemble extremely large manta rays, and David and Mel are forced to work with an Elaki, with the Earth name of String, on their investigations. Hightower offers a compelling picture of a world of the future in which the old problems of prejudice and violence have not been solved but have merely mutated into slightly new forms.

Recently, however, Hightower has begun developing two different series set in the present. *Satan's Lambs* (Walker, 1993), which won the Shamus Award for Best First Private Eye Novel, introduced private detective Lena Padgett, who works out of Lexington, Kentucky. In this first case, Lena is on the trail of her brother-in-law, Jeff Hayes, recently released from jail after serving his sentences for murdering Lena's pregnant sister and her young nephew. Hayes grew up in a family of practicing Satanists, and the group is threatening Lena and the life of a kidnapped child. With *Flashpoint* (HarperCollins, 1995), Hightower introduces another new character, Cincinnati homicide detective Sonora Blair. In her debut, Sonora is on the trail of a vicious serial killer. Both Lena Padgett and Sonora Blair are well-drawn characters: intelligent, passionate, and all too human. Hightower creates high-octane suspense, and readers can feel the impact long after the book has been put away.

Readers who have enjoyed Hightower's Alien series might also try the robot mysteries of Isaac Asimov and the fantasy mysteries of Mercedes Lackey. Otherwise, readers might try Sue Grafton, Marcia Muller, Patricia Cornwell, and Linda Barnes.

Holland, Isabelle. Holland has written both romantic suspense novels and mysteries. Her investigator in a series of mysteries is the Reverend Claire Aldington, an assistant rector of St. Anselm's Episcopal Church in Manhattan. Claire's position is somewhat anomalous, as she is a psychologist as well as a priest. Throughout the series, she often has to justify her work in the church to others, especially those who don't think churches should offer psychological assistance. Claire's private life is troubled as well; she is a widow with a difficult teenage stepdaughter. Holland provides the reader with plenty of insider details about the running of a parish and

Episcopal Church traditions. St. Anselm's is an inner-city church, but one with wealthy white parishioners; the church members and the clergy (including Claire) struggle with the ever-present urban issues of racism, homelessness, and alcoholism. The first Claire Aldington book is *A Death at St. Anselm's* (Doubleday, 1984).

Holland has also written *Bump in the Night* (Doubleday, 1988), not a series book, but a suspense novel dealing with the problems of alcoholism and missing children. It was filmed for a television movie.

Mollie Hardwick, Kate Charles, Barbara Whitehead, and Veronica Black write clerical mysteries. D. M. Greenwood has a series with protagonist Deaconess Theodora Braithwaite. Annette Meyers uses interesting New York City settings, similar to Holland's.

Holt, Hazel. Known before her forays into crime fiction as the friend and literary executor of English novelist Barbara Pym, Holt is now becoming known as the creator of Sheila Malory, writer of literary criticism and occasional amateur sleuth. The widowed Sheila Malory lives in the seaside village of Taviscombe, England, and this is where her first case occurs, in *Mrs. Malory Investigates* (St. Martin's Press, 1989; entitled *Gone Away* in England). A brash young woman is marrying an old friend of Sheila's, and the whole village whispers that she is marrying him for his money. Though Sheila secretly agrees, she cannot fail to help her old friend when his fiancée disappears. In her second outing, Sheila is in Oxford, doing research at the Bodleian Library in *The Cruellest Month* (St. Martin's Press, 1991). Who murdered the blackmailing spinster librarian in the stacks of the Bodleian? Sheila Malory makes an engaging narrator, and Holt keeps her busy with puzzles in the traditional vein.

Those who have read Holt might try the work of Ann Granger, Betty Rowlands, Mollie Hardwick, Kay Mitchell, the Paula Glenning novels of Anna Clarke, E. X. Ferrars, and Nora Kelly.

Hornsby, Wendy. The first two mysteries written by Hornsby featured Southern California policeman Roger Tejeda and professor Kate Teague. Tejeda and Teague meet in *No Harm* (Dodd, Mead, 1987) and investigate the murder of Teague's uncle; their relationship and the results of the earlier investigation continue in *Half a Mind* (New American Library, 1990). These are hard-boiled police procedurals with a fair amount of violence and strong Orange County coastal settings. Tejeda and Teague are an interesting study in contrasts: Tejeda comes from a middle-class Latino background, while Teague is an heiress from an old-money family.

Hornsby's more recent series begins with *Telling Lies* (Dutton, 1992). Maggie MacGowen, a documentary filmmaker from San Francisco, is the protagonist. Maggie comes to Los Angeles in response to an urgent message from her sister, a physician and former radical, only to find her in a coma from a gunshot wound. As she investigates this shooting, Maggie meets and becomes involved with homicide detective Mike Flint. She returns to L.A. and Mike in the gripping *Midnight Baby* (Dutton, 1993), a story about the murder of a young girl who runs away from home. Hornsby is good at building suspense and describing the dark underside of Los Angeles, and her plot twists keep the reader engrossed until the very end. This series is perhaps most notable for the realistic details and vibrant storytelling skills that Hornsby brings to her tales of police officers and their families.

Readers looking for Los Angeles and Orange County settings should try Faye Kellerman, Rochelle Majer Krich, A. E. Maxwell, and Maxine O'Callaghan.

Huff, Tanya.   Fantasy writer Huff has created a series of four (to date) novels about a Toronto cop turned private eye with an unusual line in investigation. Vicki Nelson, nicknamed Victory for her track record in Toronto's police department, left the force when her deteriorating eyesight threatened to end her career. Now out on her own, late one night Vicki witnesses the attack of a deadly force that soon has Toronto terrorized, in *Blood Price* (DAW Books, 1991). In the course of investigating, Vicki meets the enigmatic Henry Fitzroy, who makes his living writing historical romance novels as Elizabeth Fitzroy. Henry is also a vampire, the illegitimate son of Henry VIII (he is supposedly Henry, Duke of Richmond, who died young under odd circumstances). Drawn to Henry, Vicki discovers that she needs an otherworldly ally in a case straight out of a horror movie. Complicating the scenario is Vicki's old partner and on-again, off-again flame, Mike Celluci, who is very suspicious of Henry. In the second book, *Blood Trail* (DAW Books, 1992), Vicki and Henry aid a family of werewolves in London, Ontario, who are being murdered one by one. Huff blends aspects of the detective novel with the horror genre for an unusual but entertaining mix.

Readers looking for other genre-bending mysteries should try the work of Mercedes Lackey, P. N. Elrod, and Lynn S. Hightower.

Isaacs, Susan. Best-selling novelist Isaacs has penned several mystery and suspense novels, and several of her works have been turned into successful movies. Her first novel, *Compromising Positions* (Times Books, 1978), became a hit starring Susan Sarandon and the late Raul Julia. This book tells the story of suburban Long Island housewife Judith Singer, who becomes fascinated with the murder of a local orthodontist, Dr. Bruce Fleckstein. Isaacs uses the frame of the mystery plot to satirize the oddities of upper-middle-class families, and her wit is never better than in *After All These Years* (HarperCollins, 1993). Returning to Shorehaven, the setting for her first novel, Isaacs tells the story of Rosie Meyers, who gets a very unpleasant surprise on her twenty-fifth wedding anniversary. Her husband, Richie, wants a divorce. Some time later, Richie Meyers winds up dead, and Rosie is the chief suspect. Suburbia was never so deadly—nor so funny—than in the hands of this consummate storyteller.

Readers who have enjoyed the work of Isaacs might try the suburban sleuths created by Valerie Wolzien and Jill Churchill. Those looking for witty satire might try the works of Sarah Shankman and Sharyn McCrumb.

Jackson, Marian J. A. Miss Abigail Patience Danforth is an American heiress with considerable strength of mind and of purpose. Spurred on by the example of the exploits of Sherlock Holmes, Miss Danforth vows to become the world's first female consulting detective in this series set circa 1900. In her debut, *The Punjat's Ruby* (Pinnacle, 1990), Miss Danforth goes so far as to inveigle a meeting with Sir Arthur Conan Doyle to ask his advice. Not dampened by Conan Doyle's discouraging response, Miss Danforth takes on the case of the Punjat's missing ruby, all the while keeping a titled English suitor at bay. The action moves from England back to Abigail's native New York, where the story is resolved. From there, Abigail journeys west across America with her new companion, Maude Cunningham, and the two find themselves in a real Western adventure with *The Arabian Pearl* (Pinnacle, 1990). Jackson's stories about her turn-of-the-century detective are a mixture of adventure, mystery, and a dash of romance.

Those who have read Jackson might try the Irene Adler novels of Carole Nelson Douglas, which are even more Holmesian in flavor than Jackson's.

Jacobs, Nancy Baker. Jacobs is one of the few writers of private eye novels who actually has been a private investigator herself. Her series with Devon MacDonald, a private eye in Minneapolis, thus has the detail and feel of authenticity. Jacobs's first novel in the series, *The Turquoise Tattoo* (Putnam, 1991), is an engrossing story about a boy dying of leukemia who needs a bone marrow transplant. His natural father, a Jewish doctor, also donated his sperm many years ago to a sperm bank. Devon finds the half-brother conceived from that donation, but the adoptive father is an Aryan supremacist. Devon and her partner Sam Sherman investigate the inevitable murder. Devon has lost a child of her own to a drunk driver, and this case engages her emotions as well as her skills. The second Devon MacDonald novel, *A Slash of Scarlet* (Putnam, 1992), is about a middle-aged Lothario who courts and then robs gullible women.

As well as her series mysteries, Jacobs also has written suspense novels. *Deadly Companion* (Dell, 1986) tells the story of a twisted nurse who murders elderly patients and steals their possessions. *See Mommy Run* (Penguin, 1992) is a particularly strong tale of a mother on the run with her preschool daughter, who has been sexually abused by her father. There are interesting descriptions of an underground network that helps abuse victims, and the book details how the mother gets a new identity and stays ahead of the police and private detectives. In her novels, Jacobs is clearly engaged with social issues that affect women and children, and she uses these concerns as effective elements in her well-constructed plots.

Readers also may want to try private eye mysteries by Maxine O'Callaghan, Karen Kijewski, and Liza Cody. Sara Paretsky's investigator, V. I. Warshawski, is often involved with social problems, as is lawyer Neil Hamel in Judith Van Gieson's series of crime novels. Other suspense writers include Mary Higgins Clark and Judith Kelman.

James, P. D. In private life, she is Phyllis Dorothy White, who worked as a civil servant for many years. In 1991, she was awarded a life peerage as Baroness James of Holland Park, and she now sits in the House of Lords. James is considered by many critics and readers to be one of the best crime writers of her generation. Her protagonists in two different series are Commander Adam Dalgliesh of the Metropolitan Police, and private investigator Cordelia Gray. James's first novel was *Cover Her Face* (Scribner, 1966). The format is that of a typical English village cozy, but with some Jamesian trademarks: acutely observed characters, an atmosphere of menace, medical details, and a loving attention to architectural details. The detective here is Dalgliesh, who is a poet as well as a policeman. Dalgliesh is rather an omniscient and morose detective, known for his exactitude and objectivity. In 1972, James created a female private eye, Cordelia Gray, thus predating a comparable trend by American crime writers. Cordelia has been trained as a private investigator by Bernie Pryde, who commits suicide at the beginning of *An Unsuitable Job for a Woman* (Scribner, 1972), leaving Cordelia his agency and his gun. Cordelia is less confident and controlled a detective than Dalgliesh. James is known for her extensive use of literary quotations and symbolism as well as for her adroit plotting. For example, *The Skull Beneath the Skin* (Scribner, 1982) has many allusions to Shakespeare and the Jacobean revenge playwrights. In both this novel and *A Taste for Death* (Knopf, 1986), James's skill in using detailed architectural and interior descriptions of houses and churches to further her plot and character analysis is fully realized. Both novels are rather Gothic and brooding, with the crimes deftly foreshadowed and each character carefully delineated. These novels show James at the height of her powers. Her elegant prose and psychological acuity lift her work far above the standard crime novel.

James also has written nonseries books, including *Innocent Blood* (Scribner, 1980), a suspense novel. It is the macabre and sensational story of a young girl, Philippa Palfrey, who gains access to her adoption records and discovers that her birth parents were a rapist and a murderer. With *The Children of Men* (Knopf, 1993), James produced a science fiction novel, set in the year 2021. No children have been born in the world for twenty-five years, and society is in decline. James returned, however, to the mystery field, with the publication of a Dalgliesh novel, *Original Sin* (Knopf, 1995).

James won Silver Dagger Awards for both *The Black Tower* (Scribner, 1975) and *Shroud for a Nightingale* (Scribner, 1971). She won a Macavity Award for Best Novel and a Silver Dagger Award for *A Taste for Death*. She won a Diamond Dagger Award for lifetime achievement from the Crime Writers' Association in 1986, and was awarded the Order of the British Empire by the Queen in 1983.

Readers who admire James also may enjoy the works of Minette Walters, Elizabeth George, Laurie R. King, Ruth Rendell, B. M. Gill, and Jennifer Rowe.

Jance, J. A.   The author has established a large following for her series of novels featuring Seattle homicide cop J. P. Beaumont. Beau, as he is known to his friends, is a bit of a maverick, lover of junk food and booze, in the best tradition of the free-wheeling cop of mystery fiction. In the first book of the series, *Until Proven Guilty* (Avon, 1985), Beau's on the trail of a child killer with his new partner, Detective Ron Peters. During the course of the investigation, Beau meets and falls for a mysterious, wealthy woman, whom he marries. Police procedurals by form, the series is fast-paced and generally full of action. Beau, though stubborn and irascible, demonstrates that he's capable of change as the series progresses. He's willing to rethink some of his prejudices and ideas, though he remains steadfast in others. The Seattle setting is an important component of the books, and Jance makes the city a living entity, much in the way Sara Paretsky makes Chicago integral to her work or Julie Smith makes New Orleans in her Skip Langdon books.

Recently, Jance has begun a new series with a female character in *Desert Heat* (Avon, 1993). Joanna Brady is the widow of a sheriff's deputy in Cochise County, Arizona. Like the Beaumont books, this series promises fast action and a tough yet appealing central character.

Jance has, in addition, penned one novel of psychological suspense, *Hour of the Hunter* (Morrow, 1991).

Those who have enjoyed the Beaumont series might try the work of Anne Wingate who writes also as Lee Martin and Martha G. Webb, M. J. Adamson, the Skip Langdon books of Julie Smith, and the many novels of Elizabeth Linington who wrote also as Lesley Egan and Dell Shannon.

Janeshutz, Trish.   See **MacGregor, T. J.**

Johnston, Velda.   A veteran suspense novelist with more than thirty novels to her credit, Johnston began her work in the heyday of romantic suspense with *Along a Dark Path* (Dodd, Mead, 1968). Though Johnston's work features most of the characteristics of the romantic suspense or Gothic novel as it was called then, Johnston is so skilled at the suspense half of the recipe that many readers quite often forget that they are reading a Gothic. The heroines of Johnston's fiction, whether contemporary or nineteenth-century, are independent, often stubborn, resourceful, and intelligent. Two

119

of Johnston's early period settings, *The Late Mrs. Fonsell* (Dodd, Mead, 1972) and *Masquerade in Venice* (Dodd, Mead, 1973), rank alongside the best work of Victoria Holt and Phyllis A. Whitney. A more recent work, *The House on Bostwick Square* (Dodd, Mead, 1987), shows Johnston's skill at blending unusual and suspenseful elements into a not-so-traditional romantic suspense novel. *The Etruscan Smile* (Dodd, Mead, 1977), with its vividly etched foreign setting and intriguing plot, is one of the author's best contemporary suspense novels.

Readers acquainted with the work of Johnston will also enjoy the work of Barbara Michaels and her alter ego Elizabeth Peters, Phyllis A. Whitney, Caroline Crane, D. F. Mills, and Jane Aiken Hodge.

K

Kallen, Lucille.   Kallen was a writer for such television comedies as Sid Caesar's classic *Your Show of Shows* before she began writing novels. Her first effort was *Outside There, Somewhere—!* (Macmillan, 1964), a comic feminist novel. She then turned to writing mysteries, and her first effort was *Introducing C. B. Greenfield* (Crown, 1979). It was a popular success and was nominated for The American Book Award (TABA). Kallen's series sleuths are Maggie Rome, a weekly newspaper reporter, and C. B. (Charlie) Greenfield, her editor and publisher. Their newspaper is the Sloan's Ford *Reporter*, and most of the books are located in the affluent suburban town of Sloan's Ford, Connecticut. The novels are narrated by Maggie, and she plays the Archie Goodwin role to Greenfield's Nero Wolfe. Maggie is the legman for Charlie; he is the grouchy, acerbic man of ideas. Inevitably, they argue a lot, and their version of the war of the sexes becomes an important part of the plot in each book. Classical music is also important to these characters, for C. B. and Maggie play together in a chamber music group. *C. B. Greenfield: The Tanglewood Murder* (Wyndham, 1980), for example, is set at the Tanglewood Music Festival in the Berkshires. Kallen does take Maggie and Charlie out of Sloan's Ford occasionally. *C. B. Greenfield: The Piano Bird* (Random House, 1984) is set on a Florida island, and *C. B. Greenfield: A Little Madness* (Random House, 1986) is set in a women's peace camp and has a political bent. Kallen's novels are classic American puzzle mysteries with strong lead characters.

Readers also may enjoy Diane K. Shah's Paris Chandler series (Paris is another newspaper legman) and Annette Roome's Chris Martin books. Gloria Dank, Melodie Johnson Howe, and Dorothy Sucher have created other amusing teams of investigators.

Kellerman, Faye. Kellerman's crime novels are both exciting police procedurals and windows into the little-known world of Orthodox Judaism. The protagonists are Rina Lazarus and Peter Decker. Rina is a widow with young sons; Peter is an LAPD cop in the Foothill Division. They meet in the first novel, *The Ritual Bath* (Arbor House, 1986), and their relationship deepens throughout the series. Peter discovers and learns about Judaism after being raised as a Baptist by his adoptive parents. Rina is Orthodox; each book in the series, especially *The Ritual Bath* and *Day of Atonement* (Morrow, 1991), gives details of the customs and rites of the Orthodox community. The murders Peter investigates, and Rina assists him with, are often gory and emotionally disturbing. There is quite a bit of graphic realism in these police stories, and it is contrasted with the security, faith, and love that Rina offers to her family.

Kellerman has also written a historical mystery, *The Quality of Mercy* (Morrow, 1989), about Rebecca Lopez, a Jewish woman who lives in sixteenth-century London and becomes the model for Shakespeare's Dark Lady in his sonnets. The novel is particularly good at creating the atmosphere of converso life in England for the hidden Jewish community.

Kellerman won a Macavity Award for Best First Novel for *The Ritual Bath*.

Wendy Hornsby and Teri White also write hard-boiled, gritty tales of Los Angeles cops. Rochelle Majer Krich, the team of Serita Stevens and Rayanne Moore, and S. T. Haymon also have written mysteries with backgrounds of Jewish culture.

Kelly, Mary Anne. Though Kelly does not write mysteries with a culinary theme, her work could easily be described as a rich and varied stew, with a fascinating mixture of ingredients, meaty and satisfying. The heart of this somewhat eccentric series is Claire Breslinsky, who has come back to her loving and sometimes irascible family in the Richmond Hill neighborhood of Queens, New York, after wandering in Europe and Asia for ten years. Fleeing her family and her grief after the murder of her twin brother Michael, a rookie cop, Claire has practiced her profession of photography far afield. Eventually, she decides to return to the fold, and she lives with her parents, the Irish Mary and the Polish Stan, and her oldest sister Carmela, in the family home. Another sister, Zinnie, is a cop with a young son, Michaelaen, and Zinnie's ex-husband, Freddie, is a gay restaurateur and former football star. In the first of the series, *Park Lane South, Queens* (St. Martin's Press, 1990), someone discovers the body of a murdered child in the neighborhood, and Claire is an unwitting witness to some key information in the crime. Johnny Benedetto is the cop assigned to the case, and he and Claire fight an unwilling attraction to each other. By the second book of the series, *Foxglove* (St. Martin's Press, 1992), they are married and the parents of a toddler, Anthony. Claire's family and the marvelous denizens of the neighborhood are fascinating characters. Kelly offers a special blend of mystery and drama, drawing upon the inspiration of a quirky and engaging neighborhood.

P. M. Carlson writes a lively series about an engaging family in her Maggie Ryan books, and M. K. Lorens has a lovably eccentric cast of characters in her Winnie Sherman books. Readers looking for New York atmosphere might also try the works of Gallagher Gray and Joyce Christmas.

Kelly, Nora. A historian in real life, Kelly has given her profession to her series sleuth, Gillian Adams, who ably demonstrates that the disciplined academic mind is well-suited to the rigors of mystery-solving. In the first novel, *In the Shadow of King's* (St. Martin's Press, 1984), Gillian is on sabbatical in Cambridge, where she took her doctorate fifteen years earlier. The regius professor of modern history is murdered, and Gillian, along with the policeman assigned to the case, Edward Gisborne of Scotland Yard, solves the case. Kelly describes the atmosphere of Cambridge in lucid, evocative prose. In its way, her first novel does for Cambridge what Dorothy L. Sayers's classic *Gaudy Night* (Harcourt Brace, 1936) did for the Oxford of half a century ago. In the second novel, *My Sister's Keeper* (St. Martin's Press, 1992), the setting is the University of the Pacific Northwest in Vancouver, British Columbia. Feminism and the university's backwardness in women's rights issues are central to the plot of the book, and Kelly fashions a literate and compelling story from the mix.

Like Kelly, Amanda Cross and Sophie Belfort write literate and thought-provoking series of academic mysteries. Fans of Kelly might also try the work of English feminist Joan Smith. Hazel Holt's Sheila Malory is an enjoyable academic-type sleuth as well.

Kelly, Susan. Kelly is a college English professor with a Ph.D. in medieval literature. She has created an ongoing series of mysteries with the attractive heroine Liz Connors. Liz is a tall, red-headed former English professor, now a freelance writer who often concentrates on true-crime stories. Her lover in the series is Jack Lingemann, a homicide detective. Liz is humorous, independent, and literate, while Jack is sensitive, thoughtful, and realistic about the violence he sees every day. Kelly provides Connors with finely detailed Cambridge, Massachusetts, surroundings, and the crimes she encounters often are based on recent events. Thus, the first Liz Connors mystery, *The Gemini Man* (Walker, 1985), is the story of a serial killer and singles bars, and *Summertime Soldiers* (Walker, 1986), brings back old sixties radical terrorists, who resurface and begin to kill people they associate with the present high-tech military-industrial complex. An especially memorable novel in the series is *Out of the Darkness* (Villard, 1992), in which Connors assists a famous true-crime writer in his research on a brutal serial killer, while events in her own life go awry. Kelly is particularly good at building suspense from a quiet recounting of the daily events in her protagonist's life.

Kathryn Lasky Knight also uses a Cambridge setting for her mysteries. Readers of Kelly may enjoy Julie Smith's Paul McDonald books, in which the main character is a freelance writer.

Kelly, Susan B. The American publisher has added the initial *B* to this Susan Kelly's name to distinguish her from the American writer Susan Kelly. Susan Kelly the English author is writing a series of police detective mysteries set in the Hop Valley. In the first novel, *Hope against Hope* (Scribner, 1991), rich, intelligent, and attractive businesswoman Alison Hope moves her computer software business from London to the remote Hop Valley, where she soon encounters Detective Inspector Nick Trevellyan of the Hopbridge CID. When Alison's cousin and former business partner turns up dead, Alison becomes a prime suspect, and Nick has to fight a growing attraction to her in order to solve the case. The second novel in the series, *Time of Hope* (Scribner, 1992), chronicles further developments in the relationship of Nick and Alison. Kelly has created likable, realistic characters as the focus of her series. The plots are neatly constructed and should give pleasure to those looking for good whodunits. This is an attractive series that should build a strong following.

Other writers of English police detective series whom readers of Kelly might like are June Thomson, Dorothy Simpson, Clare Curzon, Marjorie Eccles, Cynthia Harrod-Eagles, and Anthea Fraser.

Kelman, Judith. Kelman writes chilling novels of psychological suspense, with plots involving women and particularly children in jeopardy from crazed serial killers. The psychology of the murderer is explored as he stalks his victims through their daily lives. The books are often set in the suburbs, and the graphic violence and horror of a madman pursuing innocent children is contrasted with their ostensibly safe surroundings. *The House on the Hill* (Bantam, 1992) for example, has a maniacal sociopath, a missing child, and an attractive woman parole officer as key elements in an archetypal suspense story. In *Someone's Watching* (Bantam, 1991), the villain commits hit-and-run attacks, as well as kidnapping and killing neighborhood kids. In *Where Shadows Fall* (Berkley, 1987), Kelman tells the story of a mother investigating her son's alleged suicide at a distinguished university. As with other Kelman novels, it is notable for her effective scene-setting, research, and an atmosphere of lurking evil.

Kelman's first novel was *Prime Evil* (Berkley, 1986).

Readers also may want to try the novels of Mary Higgins Clark, T. J. MacGregor, D. F. Mills, and Nancy Baker Jacobs's *See Mommy Run*.

Kelner, Toni L. P. Herself a daughter of the South somehow transplanted north of the Mason-Dixon Line, Kelner writes a series of traditional mysteries with a heroine who has some things in common with her creator. Laura Fleming left her native Byerly, North Carolina, to attend college at MIT, and with job prospects beckoning in Massachusetts, she stayed there after finishing her degree, with a husband to boot. Now, however, a tragic family accident has brought her home to find out what's going on in the first in the series, *Down Home Murder* (Zebra, 1993). Someone has tried to kill Laura's beloved grandfather, Paw, and Laura is determined to find out which of her relatives is cold-blooded enough to kill. In *Dead Ringer* (Zebra, 1994), Laura comes home to Byerly once again, this time to encounter the murder of a stranger who looks like the owner of the old town mill. What family secrets have brought on murder this time around? Kelner's stories of Southern murder and mayhem highlight the author's affection for the area where she was reared, and fans of the traditional mystery will find much to enjoy in the quiet humor of eccentric relatives, nosy aunts and cousins, and the occasional murdering black sheep.

Patricia H. Sprinkle, Sarah Shankman, Kathy Hogan Trocheck, and Celestine Sibley all write mysteries with Southern settings. Readers might also enjoy Sharyn McCrumb's series of novels about Elizabeth MacPherson, with Elizabeth's funny observations about Southern life and customs.

Kenney, Susan.   Novelist and college professor Kenney has created a series of mysteries about Roz Howard, professor of English, whose specialties are medieval literature and women's studies. In her first appearance, *Garden of Malice* (Scribner, 1983), Roz is in England to work on the papers of Lady Viola Montfort-Snow, a well-known gardener and writer. While staying at Montfort Abbey, Roz encounters murder and mystery about Lady Viola's work, and she also meets Alan Stewart, an attractive and wealthy man of many talents, with whom she becomes romantically involved. In the second novel, *Graves in Academe* (Viking, 1985), Roz is teaching at Canterbury College in Maine, where someone has begun murdering faculty in ways straight out of the classics of English literature. *One Fell Sloop* (Viking, 1990) finds Roz and Alan at odds in their relationship while on a sailing vacation on the Maine coast. Murder intervenes, and they put aside their differences to focus on the solution of the crime. Kenney writes literate and leisurely mysteries that have much to offer to the fan of the traditional mystery and of the academic mystery novel. Roz Howard is a modern woman trying to balance the demands of a career where women have to work much harder to compete and of a relationship with a man who sometimes seems to have just too much to offer.

If readers find Kenney's work appealing, they might try the work of J. S. Borthwick, Amanda Cross, Sally Gunning, Sophie Belfort, and Jane Langton.

Kijewski, Karen. The sleuth in this series is Kat Colorado, PI, who operates out of Sacramento. Kijewski's writing is conversational and colloquial, with plenty of snappy dialogue. The secondary characters in the series—Kat's adopted grandmother, her best friend Charity, and her lover Hank—have their own well-developed styles and idiosyncrasies. Kat is a tough, smart woman, but clients can appeal to her vulnerabilities, especially kids, the elderly, and people who apparently have nowhere else to turn. In many ways, Kat's persona follows the model of the hard-boiled detective, but she brings a female perspective to these conventions: for example, she and her friends don't drink a lot of whiskey, but they certainly do eat, especially desserts. Kat is a former bartender (as is Kijewski), and this skill comes in handy when she goes undercover in *Copy Kat* (Doubleday, 1992). Kat takes her own risks, gets herself out of dangerous situations, and resents men in her life who try to protect her.

The first book in the series is *Katwalk* (St. Martin's Press, 1989), which won the Best First Private Eye Novel Award (the Shamus) from the Private Eye Writers of America.

Creators of other hard-boiled women private eyes include Janet Dawson, Catherine Dain, and Linda Barnes. Another view of Sacramento is given in Mary Bowen Hall's novels about Emma Chizzit. Marcia Muller also sets scenes from some of her Sharon McCone novels in the area.

King, Laurie R. The creator of two very distinctive series of mysteries with strong women characters, King made quite a splash in the mystery world by winning the Edgar for Best First Novel with *A Grave Talent* (St. Martin's Press, 1993). This book introduced San Francisco homicide detective Kate Martinelli, a woman with some secrets of her own to hide as she works hard with her new partner, Al Hawkin, to solve the sensational murders of two young girls. King's second novel, *The Beekeeper's Apprentice* (St. Martin's Press, 1994), an Agatha nominee for Best Novel, introduced the extraordinary Mary Russell, who is fifteen years old when, in the spring of 1915, she literally stumbles across Sherlock Holmes on the Sussex Downs. Thus begins an unusual partnership as Holmes takes on the orphaned young American girl as his protégée. Mary Russell proves more than a match for the great detective, however. In both series, intelligent, vital women demonstrate very capably that they need take a backseat to no one when it comes to solving crimes. King, who has a master's degree in theology, examines the effects of a crime upon those involved, and her themes are among some of the most unusual and original in contemporary mystery fiction.

Readers acquainted with the work of King might also try the work of Jo Bannister, Frances Fyfield, and the late Margaret Millar. Those looking for another series set in the early years of this century might try the Nell Bray series of Gillian Linscott.

Kingsbury, Kate. Kingsbury has assembled an engaging cast of characters for her series set in Edwardian England. The main character, Cecily Sinclair, is a widow who is running a resort hotel in the seaside town of Badgers End, ably aided by the hotel manager, Baxter. Two of Mrs. Sinclair's friends, the vicar's mother and the local herbalist, occasionally lend a hand with entertainments and floral arrangements to make the Pennyfoot Hotel a highly desirable vacation spot for England's upper crust. Working behind the scenes are the servants, such as Mrs. Chubb, the housekeeper, and Gertie Brown, one of the housemaids. No matter how smoothly the Pennyfoot runs, murder keeps turning up as an uninvited guest, but Cecily Sinclair quietly perseveres to restore order and protect the reputation of her hotel. Baxter, the manager, often protests what he sees as Madam's unladylike interests in matters of crime, but he comes up to scratch when he has to help. Over the course of the series, the relationship between Cecily and Baxter grows warmer, and events in the lives of the servants become just as interesting as the mystery plots that Kingsbury devises. The charm of the ensemble and its two leading players make this a delightful series for the dedicated reader of cozies. First in the series is *Do Not Disturb* (Berkley, 1993).

Fans of Kingsbury might also try the work of Emily Brightwell and Claudia Bishop (who writes a contemporary series also set in an inn). Gillian Linscott also writes a series set in Edwardian England.

Kittredge, Mary. Creator of two series of mysteries, Kittredge is a former respiratory therapist for a major urban hospital.

Her first series features freelance writer Charlotte Kent. In *Murder in Mendocino* (Walker, 1988), Kent is living in California, teaching a writing class in a small town and writing how-to books. She becomes involved with a troubled adolescent, whom she later adopts, and the two move to New Haven, Connecticut, when the adopted son, Joey Rosen, develops medical problems. This also allows Kent to be near her lover, surgeon Rob Solli.

Kittredge's second series is also set in New Haven, often connected with the Chelsea Memorial Hospital, which figures in the other series. Edwina Crusoe, R. N., comes from a wealthy family and has a private income, which means she works only because she wants to. Her debut is *Fatal Diagnosis* (St. Martin's Press, 1990). At the end of the book, she decides to leave the hospital and open her own agency for a combination of private nursing and medical investigation. Her boyfriend is Martin McIntyre, a cop whom she meets in the first book; his official status and expertise are often helpful. Both women characters are strong-willed and independent, and the medical backgrounds in the Crusoe books are vividly detailed.

Fans of mysteries with medical settings might try the work of English writers Stella Shepherd and Christine Green or the best-selling thrillers of Robin Cook. P. D. James has several times used a medical or scientific research background to excellent effect.

Knight, Alanna.   A historical novelist and an expert on Robert Louis Stevenson, Knight has recently turned her talents to a series of mystery novels set in Victorian Edinburgh. Knight's series character is Detective Inspector Jeremy Faro, a widower with two young daughters (who live in Orkney with their grandmother) and a grown stepson, Dr. Vincent Laurie. Vince often provides unofficial assistance to Faro in his cases. In the first of the series, *Enter Second Murderer* (St. Martin's Press, 1988), Faro investigates a gruesome murder in which one murderer has already been tried, convicted, and hanged. Faro believes, however, that another murderer is still at large. Knight's Victorian Edinburgh is an intriguing place, and the period detail makes an effective backdrop for the puzzles that Knight devises. Her writing style is somewhat lush, in the good Victorian manner, so readers might sometimes think they are reading actual Victorian prose. Faro and his stepson Vince are likable characters, serving as well-drawn centerpieces for a good historical mystery series.

Readers with a taste for Victorian murder and mayhem might

try the two series of Anne Perry, the work of Amy Myers, or the American Victorian mysteries of Marian J. A. Jackson.

Knight, Kathryn Lasky. Calista Jacobs, a successful children's book illustrator, is the unusual heroine of Knight's series. Calista is earthy, bright, and imaginative, with an active sense of humor. She is widowed in the first book and begins her sleuthing career by discovering who killed her husband. Calista has able assistants in her investigations: her son Charley, who is precocious and enthralled by computers, and Archie Baldwin, an archaeologist for the Smithsonian. The books are set primarily in Cambridge, Massachusetts, although *Mumbo Jumbo* (Summit, 1991) is set in the Southwest at an archaeological site. The qualities that make Knight's books fun to read are the finely drawn characters of Calista and Charley, the absorbing descriptions of Calista's work as an illustrator, and the use of current issues like creationism and New Age cults as plot elements.

Knight has written many children's books under the name Kathryn Lasky. Her first adult mystery novel is *Trace Elements* (Norton, 1986).

Readers also might enjoy Susan Kelly and Jane Langton, who also have used Cambridge, Massachusetts, as a setting for mysteries. Judith Van Gieson sets her mysteries in the Southwest, with close attention to current social issues.

Kraft, Gabrielle. Screwball comedy-mysteries, like their film counterparts, flourished in the 1930s and 40s. This classic American form returns in Kraft's series of novels starring Beverly Hills lawyer Jerry Zalman and his girlfriend Marie Thrasher. Diminutive, cigar-chomping Jerry somehow always gets clients with nutty problems that escalate into bizarre murders. A great deal of Kraft's writing is snappy, smart dialogue, filled with sarcastic remarks about Southern California and its strange denizens. A zany atmosphere and loony characters abound in these novels. In *Let's Rob Roy* (Pocket, 1989), for example, a heavy metal rock musician is being blackmailed by a psychic. The rock star's manager (Jerry's sister) is convinced that the singer will lose all his teenage fans if the psychic reveals that her client is really a mild-mannered English lad who likes to bake cakes and do needlepoint, rather than a Satan-worshipping headbanger. Naturally, Jerry tries to concoct a scheme to avert disaster; naturally, disaster strikes anyway.

The first Jerry Zalman novel, *Bullshot* (Pocket, 1987), was nominated for an Edgar Award.

Kraft also has written *Hollywood Hills* (Pocket, 1993), a novel about an actress and agent that spans fifty years of her Hollywood career.

Craig Rice's John J. Malone novels are classics of screwball humor. Joan Hess, Marissa Piesman, and Meg O'Brien write humorous mysteries.

Krich, Rochelle Majer.   Krich's first book, *Where's Mommy Now* (Windsor, 1990), which won an Anthony Award and was made into a film, is a suspense novel about a young woman who has inherited millions. She has two children from her first marriage, and is now happily married to a doctor. Her comfortable life begins to unravel with the arrival in her household of an au pair baby-sitter from Switzerland.

Krich's second book, *Till Death Do Us Part* (Avon, 1992), is a very different mystery about an Orthodox Jewish woman, Deena Vogler, whose ex-husband will not give her a religious divorce (a *get*). Without the *get*, Deena cannot marry again and resume a normal life. Krich sets her story of frustration and murder in an affluent neighborhood of Los Angeles, and she provides an in-depth look at Orthodox life and customs.

Fair Game (Mysterious, 1993), which was nominated for an Agatha Award for Best Novel, is a taut, chilling tale of a search for a serial killer in Los Angeles. The police, including detective Jessie Drake, cannot discover how the killer is picking his victims, and much of the book concerns their attempts to deduce his methodology and thus anticipate his plans.

Jessie Drake returns in the Agatha Award-nominated *Angel of Death* (Mysterious, 1994).

With *Nowhere to Run* (Avon, 1994), Krich gives us a compulsively readable story of a woman whose marriage to a widower with two children puts her and her unborn child in jeopardy from a jealous woman.

Faye Kellerman's series of mysteries with Peter Decker and Rina

Lazarus gives another view of Orthodox Judaism in a Los Angeles setting. Writers of suspense novels include Nancy Baker Jacobs, Meg O'Brien, Judith Kelman, and Susan Moody in *Hush-a-bye* (London: Macdonald, 1991).

Lacey, Sarah. See **Mitchell, Kay.**

Lackey, Mercedes. Lackey is best-known for her very popular series of fantasy novels, some written in collaboration with such luminaries of the science fiction/fantasy world as Andre Norton and Anne McCaffrey. She has also written several entertaining novels that blend aspects of the detective novel with the fantasy genre.

In *Sacred Ground* (Tor, 1994), Jennifer Talldeer is a private detective of Osage and Cherokee heritage who successfully combines her gifts as a shaman with her skills as a detective. Her grandfather, Mooncrow, a revered shaman, is her teacher and guide to the matters of the spirit. In this case, Jennifer is trying to figure out just who is behind the mysterious events at a construction site in Tulsa, when fragments from an ancient Native American burial site are unearthed.

In a series of three novels to date, practicing witch and psychic Diana Tregarde solves mysteries that involve some otherworldly criminals. *Burning Water* (Tor, 1989), the first published of the series, finds Diana in Dallas, helping an old friend who is now a cop try to stop a series of increasingly savage ritual murders. In *Children of the Night* (Tor, 1990), chronologically the first of the series, set in New York City in the early 1970s, Diana helps track down a mys-

133

terious group of vampirelike creatures who feed off violent human emotion rather than human blood.

Lackey's inimitable blend of spiritualism, fantasy, and detective fiction can provide great entertainment for the adventurous mystery reader.

Readers looking for other mysteries that blur genre lines might try the work of Tanya Huff, Lynn S. Hightower, and P. N. Elrod. Readers interested in the blending of Native American culture and history with mystery might read Jean Hager, Margaret Coel, and Tony Hillerman.

Landreth, Marsha. The author of a Western and a biography of Civil War general William T. Sherman, Landreth has also penned a series of novels about pathologist Samantha Turner. The young and beautiful widow of a much older man, Sam Turner lives in Sheridan, Wyoming, on a buffalo ranch. She races back and forth between her ranch and the town, where she works at the local hospital and also serves as the county coroner. In her first appearance, *The Holiday Murders* (Walker, 1992), Sam is faced with continuing opposition from the local good old boys in her efforts to unmask a murderer who kills only on holidays. A complication in her life is the sudden appearance of her former husband's son, Derek, whom she has never before met, since her husband's children had refused to have anything to do with her. Derek claims to be a journalist interested in a story on her buffalo ranch; in reality, he's a CIA agent interested in one of the victims of the holiday killer. The romantic spark between Samantha and Derek grows through the series, resulting in their marriage in the second book of the series, *A Clinic for Murder* (Walker, 1993). Sam Turner is strong-willed, intelligent, and passionate about her work, willing sometimes to go to great lengths to see that justice is done. Details of forensic pathology spice the narrative throughout each book.

Patricia Cornwell and Susan Dunlap also write series about women who are medical examiners. Readers looking for books with Western settings might try the work of B. J. Oliphant/A. J. Orde, J. A. Jance, and Judith Van Gieson.

Langton, Jane. Langton is a unique talent in the mystery world. Her lyrical, exuberant novels are more imaginative than puzzling, and she illustrates her books with witty pen-and-ink drawings.

The reader generally knows all along who did the crime; the mystery lies in how and when justice will be done. Justice is not necessarily dispensed by human means; retribution is sometimes achieved through the vast impersonal workings of the universe. Homer Kelly, a Thoreau scholar and former lawyer and policeman, appears in most of Langton's novels. Homer worships at the shrine of New England transcendentalism, and his admiration is mirrored in many of the books. Most of these poetic, charming novels are set in historic Concord and Boston, and Langton brings the past, especially the nineteenth-century literary giants of Thoreau, Emerson, and Dickinson, to vibrant life. Langton's books also make excursions into the worlds of natural history, art, and music. Langton's descriptions of the natural world are graceful and memorable, especially in *Natural Enemy* (Ticknor & Fields, 1982) and *God in Concord* (Viking, 1992). Langton also writes jewel-like books for young adults.

The first Homer Kelly novel is *The Transcendental Murder* (Harper, 1964), also published as *The Minuteman Murder* (Dell, 1976).

For other strong senses of place and environmental concern, readers may enjoy Nevada Barr, Janet LaPierre, Judith Van Gieson, and M. K. Wren. For settings in Cambridge and Massachusetts, try Kathryn Lasky Knight, Irene Allen, Susan Kelly, and Charlotte MacLeod. For elegance of writing, wisdom, and wit, read Sarah Caudwell, Laurie R. King, Mary Stewart, and Sharyn McCrumb.

LaPierre, Janet.　The setting for LaPierre's novels is Port Silva, California, a fictional town based on the real Fort Bragg on the Mendocino coast. Meg Halloran, a local teacher, and Vince Gutierrez, the Port Silva chief of police, are featured characters in the mysteries. The Port Silva novels begin with *Unquiet Grave* (St. Martin's Press, 1987); the second book in the series, *Children's Games* (Scribner, 1989), is a prequel that introduces Meg Halloran and her daughter. *The Cruel Mother* (Scribner, 1990) centers around Vince's bratty teenage niece and Meg, who become kidnap victims.

In *Grandmother's House* (Scribner, 1991), LaPierre shifts her focus to protagonists Charlotte Birdsong and her precocious son Petey, along with their tenant, Police Officer Val Kuisma. LaPierre is particularly good at depicting the parent-child relationship, especially with children who are smart and protective of their mothers. Other strengths include good psychological analyses of the main characters and a realistic North Coast atmosphere. The sense of threat and danger lurking in a small town is very well done. As much suspense novels as mysteries, these books are clearly and precisely rendered.

Readers of LaPierre may enjoy M. K. Wren's atmospheric North Coast novels, and the mysteries of Kathryn Lasky Knight, P. M. Carlson, and Isabelle Holland, all of whom write convincingly about mothers and children.

Lathen, Emma/Dominic, R. B. Since 1961, Mary Latsis and Martha Henissart have been publishing mystery novels under two pseudonyms: Emma Lathen and R. B. Dominic. Mysteries written under the Lathen name predominate; there have been more than twenty Lathen novels and eight Dominic novels as of this time. Latsis and Henissart guard their privacy, but it is known that they are, respectively, an economist and a lawyer, both living in Massachusetts. Under the Lathen name, they write financial and banking mysteries; under the Dominic name, they write political mysteries.

In the Lathen books, the amateur sleuth is John Putnam Thatcher, senior vice president of the Sloan Guaranty Trust in New York. Thatcher has a lively team to assist him in his sleuthing: Miss Corsa, his loyal secretary, and fellow bankers Everett Gabler and Charlie Trinkham. The authors have a distinctive talent for writing clearly and entertainingly about complicated financial intrigues, for combining these business matters with current events, and for creating tightly plotted mysteries that produces fascinating and civilized novels. The first Lathen novel was *Banking on Death* (Macmillan, 1961).

The Dominic mysteries feature Ben Safford, a Democratic congressman from Ohio. As in the Lathen novels, the authors have created detailed and realistic backdrops for each book and have surrounded Safford with a spirited group of professional colleagues and crime-solvers. The first Dominic novel was *Murder, Sunny Side Up* (Abelard-Schuman, 1968).

The authors were awarded the Gold Dagger Award in 1967 for *Murder Against the Grain* (Macmillan, 1967), and the Silver Dagger for *Accounting for Murder* (Macmillan, 1964). They also received the Mystery Writers of America Ellery Queen Award in 1982.

Fans of financial mysteries may enjoy Annette Meyers's Smith and Wetzon books, Dianne Pugh's Iris Thorne series, and Margaret

Logan's *A Killing in Venture Capital* (Walker, 1989). Readers of the Dominic mysteries may want to try the political crime novels of Margaret Truman.

Laurence, Janet. Making excellent use of her own background as a cooking instructor and contributor to cooking columns in English newspapers, Laurence has created as the heroine of her mystery series Darina Lisle, an expert cook. In her first outing, *A Deepe Coffyn* (Doubleday, 1990), Darina is assisting her detestable cousin Digby Cary, the golden boy of British gourmets, with the cooking for a meeting of the Society of Historical Gastronomes. Soon, Darina is investigating Digby's murder to prove her own innocence. Amid mouth-watering descriptions—but no recipes, alas!—of elaborate medieval dishes, Laurence presents an engaging murder mystery. Darina also becomes acquainted with police sergeant William Pigram, an attractive man of good family, who appears in subsequent books trying to woo the staunchly independent Darina while also trying in vain to keep Darina out of harm's way. Though Laurence presents no recipes, she provides enough descriptions of good food to set the reader's mouth watering. She also delivers good entertainment in a time-honored form, the traditional British mystery.

The late Virginia Rich added many a recipe to her fiction, and newcomer Diane Mott Davidson is following well in her footsteps. Amy Myers writes a series about a Victorian master chef, and Katherine Hall Page's main character is also a caterer by profession. Claudia Bishop's mysteries about the Hemlock Falls Inn also include a recipe in each book.

Law, Janice. After writing nonfiction, Law turned to the suspense novel, and her first, *The Big Payoff* (Houghton Mifflin, 1976), received an Edgar nomination for Best First Novel. This book introduced Anna Peters, research assistant to an executive high in the ranks of New World Oil. At the age of thirty, Anna had come somewhat to terms with some of the demons of her past life, including a brief but lucrative career as a blackmailer. When she suspects that her boss is part of a plot to sabotage profitable oil company dealings in the North Sea, Anna reluctantly becomes involved, and the results almost cost her her life and that of her boyfriend, Harry Radford. In subsequent books, Anna undertakes various missions for New World Oil, all of which require her skills as an intelligent and resourceful investigator. In *The Shadow of the Palms* (Houghton Mifflin, 1980), Anna has left New World Oil and has opened her own agency, Executive Security. After a lengthy hiatus, the series has continued with *Time Lapse* (Walker, 1992). Anna Peters has much in common with many of her peers as a private eye. She is tough, undaunted in the face of physical danger, and Law has involved her in plenty of hair-raising situations that are fast-paced and suspenseful.

In addition to the series, Law has penned one other suspense novel, *Infected Be the Air* (Walker, 1991), and several historical novels.

Those familiar with Law and Anna Peters might try the work of Dorothy Dunnett, whose heroines also get involved in similar situations, the Tamara Hoyland novels of Jessica Mann, and the Mrs. Pollifax novels of Dorothy Gilman.

Lemarchand, Elizabeth. After retiring from a career as a school headmistress in England, Lemarchand embarked upon a second career as a crime writer. Her series of mysteries featuring Inspector Tom Pollard and Sergeant Gregory Toye of Scotland Yard began with the publication of *Death of an Old Girl* (London: Hart Davis, 1967; Walker, 1985). In this debut, Lemarchand made excellent use of her considerable expertise in crafting an entertaining whodunit about the murder of an obnoxious old girl, or alumna, of the Meldon School for Girls. Subsequent novels demonstrate a similar pattern; the two Yard men are called to various parts of England to take on cases somewhat beyond the ken of the local constabulary. *The Affacombe Affair* (London: Hart Davis, 1968; Walker, 1985) takes Pollard and Toye to a West Country village, and *Death on Doomsday* (London: Hart Davis, 1971; Walker, 1975) to the county of Midshire and murder in a stately home. Puzzles constructed in the classic Golden Age vein are a hallmark of Lemarchand's work, and Pollard and Toye make an effective and engaging detective team, reminiscent in some ways of the team of Alleyn and Fox, created by the late Dame Ngaio Marsh.

Fans of Lemarchand might try the work of Ngaio Marsh, Catherine Aird, Marjorie Eccles, Patricia Moyes, and June Thomson.

Leon, Donna. Leon is an American who has lived for more than fifteen years in Venice, where she has taught English for the

University of Maryland extension campus at a U.S. Air Force base. The setting of Leon's series of novels about policeman Guido Brunetti is the intriguing city of Venice, which Leon has woven so thoroughly into her novels that the city is as much a character in the books as are any of the people. Guido Brunetti is a principled, intelligent, and caring man who has to steer his way carefully through the maze of Italian politics in order to see justice done. His wife comes from a very wealthy and prestigious Venetian family, and her connections are sometimes a hindrance, sometimes a help. In the first novel, *Death at la Fenice* (HarperCollins, 1992), which won Japan's prestigious Suntory Prize as Best Suspense Novel of 1991, Brunetti is called to the renowned opera house, the Teatro la Fenice, to investigate the death of world-famous conductor-director Helmut Wellauer. In the second novel, *Death in a Strange Country* (HarperCollins, 1993), Brunetti is in charge of the investigation of the seemingly random murder of a young American from the nearby U.S. Air Force base. Leon uses the American military installation near Venice to give readers a glimpse of a setting rarely ever seen in most fiction.

Readers looking for other series with Italian settings should try the work of Magdalen Nabb, whose series is set in Florence. Other series that make effective use of setting are the York mysteries by Barbara Whitehead, the London series by Cynthia Harrod-Eagles, and the Australian books of Jennifer Rowe.

Linington, Elizabeth. With her various pseudonyms and numerous series of mysteries, the late Elizabeth Linington has legions of fans for her police procedurals. Under her own name, Linington, she began a series about policeman Ivor Maddox in *Greenmask!* (Harper & Row, 1964). The policemen in this series work out of the Hollywood section of the Los Angeles police force.

As Lesley Egan, she created two series. The first Egan book, *A Case for Appeal* (Harper & Row, 1961), features policeman Vic Varallo and lawyer Jesse Falkenstein; both men went on to have their own separate series in subsequent books.

Linington may be best known, though, under her pseudonym Dell Shannon, for the series featuring Lieutenant Luis Mendoza of the LAPD. Mendoza debuted in *Case Pending* (Harper & Row, 1960).

Most of the books that Linington wrote share certain characteristics. She had rather an idealized view of the police; they were always the good guys. Readers won't find corruption in the LAPD in her novels. Also, Linington's cops do not get divorced, nor do they suffer from alcoholism, two fates that seem to befall many cops in the grittier police procedurals now in fashion. Despite this, Linington created characters whom readers came to know and care about, so that each new Linington, Egan, or Shannon promised further revelations about the lives of old and dear friends.

In addition to her mysteries, Linington published a Gothic suspense novel, *Nightmare* (Harper & Row, 1961), under the name Anne Blaisdell. A number of her books were published under the Blaisdell name in England. She also published several historical novels under various of her names.

Readers of the prolific Linington's series might find enjoyment with American writers J. A. Jance and Anne Wingate, who writes also as Lee Martin and Martha G. Webb, in addition to a number of the English writers of police procedurals, such as Dorothy Simpson, Marjorie Eccles, Clare Curzon, and Anthea Fraser.

Linscott, Gillian. Once a Parliamentary reporter for the BBC, Linscott now writes full-time. Her first mystery novel, *A Health Body* (St. Martin's Press, 1984), introduced ex-policeman Birdie Linnet, whose wife has left him for another man, one who can afford to take Birdie's former wife and his daughter on a trip to a holiday camp in France. Birdie follows them, and to his dismay, he discovers the camp is for nudists. Furthermore, he discovers his rival dead on the beach, and he must solve the murder to save his own skin. He appears in two further novels.

With *Murder, I Presume* (St. Martin's Press, 1990), Linscott penned her first historical mystery, revolving around British explorations in Africa after the death of David Livingstone.

In *Sister Beneath the Sheet* (St. Martin's Press, 1991), Linscott introduced Edwardian suffragette Nell Bray in an intriguing story about the murder of a fashionable courtesan in the resort town of Biarritz. Nell appears again in *Hanging on the Wire* (St. Martin's Press, 1992), set in an unusual military hospital during the height of World War I. Linscott has a fine touch with setting, character, and plot. Nell Bray is perhaps her strongest creation, and Nell's political beliefs and the historical background against which she is portrayed are convincingly drawn.

Readers looking for mysteries set in the Victorian and Edwardian periods should try the works of Anne Perry, Carole Nelson Douglas, and Amy Myers. Those who have enjoyed Linscott's novels with contemporary settings might try the work of Paula Gosling or Lesley Grant-Adamson.

Livingston, Nancy. Connossieurs of the humorous British mystery novel may place the late Nancy Livingston high on their must-read lists. Her series detective, retired tax inspector G. D. H. Pringle, on first glance seems a mild and singularly ineffective character. But those who have been on the receiving end of Mr. Pringle's expertise with both tax laws and crime know better. Along with his lady love, Mrs. Mavis Bignell, Mr. Pringle has ferreted out crime in numerous places, including England, Greece, Australia, and the United States. Mr. Pringle first appeared in *The Trouble at Aquitaine* (St. Martin's Press, 1985). Two of his funniest adventures are *Death in a Distant Land* (St. Martin's Press, 1989), which won an award for humor from the British Crime Writers' Association, and *Mayhem in Parva* (St. Martin's Press, 1991), somewhat reminiscent of Colin Watson's devilishly offbeat novels. With *Death in Close-Up* (St. Martin's Press, 1989), Livingston uses her own experiences as a production assistant in television land to offer a quirkily entertaining look at soap opera making, English style. Besides her mysteries, Livingston has written several historical novels.

Heron Carvic's Miss Seeton is another character who provides some of the funniest detection in crime fiction, and the series has been continued by Sarah J. Mason under the name Hamilton Crane. Less competent but no less funny than Mr. Pringle is the late Joyce Porter's delightfully awful Inspector Dover. Readers might also enjoy the humor of Ruth Dudley Edwards and Gloria Dank.

Llewellyn, Caroline. After the heyday of romantic suspense in the 1960s and 1970s, few besides the long-established practitioners (e.g., Victoria Holt, Mary Stewart, Phyllis A. Whitney, Barbara Michaels/Elizabeth Peters) are still writing in the genre. Llewellyn is an outstanding newcomer to the fold, and her two novels demonstrate a knack for suspense and an eye for setting that are reminiscent of Mary Stewart. Llewellyn's heroines are intelligent professional women who find themselves in dangerous circumstances through no fault of their own. Though they may have the assistance of an attractive male in extricating themselves from danger, they do so with courage, wit, and resourcefulness. *The Masks of Rome* (Scribner, 1988) is set in Rome during Carnival time, and *The Lady of the Labyrinth* (Scribner, 1990) is set in Sicily. Her latest novel, *Life Blood* (Scribner, 1993) is set in England. In all her work, Llewellyn makes effective use of setting.

Those who have read Llewellyn but who are unfamiliar with Mary Stewart's early work should look for such gems as *My Brother Michael* (Morrow, 1959) and *Nine Coaches Waiting* (Morrow, 1958). Also recommended are Velda Johnston, Elizabeth Peters, and Phyllis A. Whitney.

Logan, Margaret.   In each of her mysteries, Logan satirizes her characters' social and work settings. The first book, *Deathampton Summer* (Walker, 1988), is set on Long Island, with an elderly amateur sleuth, Tersh Trowbridge, investigating murder among his high-society friends. Backbiting, adultery, gossip, and social climbing abound in this wealthy WASP enclave, along with sudden death by poison.

In Logan's second book, *A Killing in Venture Capital* (Walker, 1989), Drew Lispenard, a venture capitalist, looks into the murder of his cousin's gay lover, a financial director of a biotechnology company. The setting is Boston, and Logan has created a high-tech, high-finance backdrop for her puzzle.

Logan's third mystery, *C.A.T. Caper* (Walker, 1990), also takes place in Boston and its suburbs. This time she sets her mystery among troublesome teenagers and a group of English teachers who are responsible for correcting the College Aptitude Tests (obviously the SAT exams in disguise). The sleuth is high school English teacher Dodge Hackett, who tends to be sexist and politically incorrect. The victim is a shrill and ugly feminist who is universally disliked. Logan's novels have a strongly sardonic tone, and she takes aim at the contemporary icons of money, social status, and education.

Readers also may enjoy Barbara Paul, Annette Meyers, and Emma Lathen.

Lorens, M. K. Lorens's debut novel, *Sweet Narcissus* (Bantam, 1990), introduces one of the most eccentric and oddly likable casts of characters in current detective fiction. The centerpiece is Shakespeare professor Winston Marlowe Sherman, who writes mysteries of the Gilded Age under the pseudonym Henrietta Slocum about a character named Winchester Hyde. Winnie's longtime companion is Sarah Cromwell, a famous concert pianist, with whom he lives in Sarah's ancestral mansion in a small town not far from New York City. Sarah's younger brother David, much like a son to Winnie and Sarah, is a famous actor. Also part of the ménage is Winnie's retired colleague, Edward Merriman, who lives in one wing of the Cromwell mansion. Lorens's plots are generally complex, much in the traditional vein, but readers who adore unusual characters in their mystery novels will find much to fascinate them in the adventures of Winnie Sherman and crew. The intensity of the emotions among the central characters in this series make them seem startlingly real sometimes, eccentric though they be.

Readers who like the intense and eccentric characters of Lorens should try the work of P. M. Carlson, B. J. Oliphant (who also writes as A. J. Orde), Gallagher Gray, Mary Monica Pulver, Mary Anne Kelly, and Kate Wilhelm, whose characters, though certainly less eccentric, are nevertheless intense and intriguing.

MacGregor, T. J. Janeshutz, Trish/Drake, Alison.   Under three different names, this author has written three separate series of suspense thrillers set in South Florida.

She began with two titles published under her unmarried name of Trish Janeshutz. In the first Janeshutz book, *In Shadow* (Ballantine, 1985), a killer stalks women on a Florida college campus, and this plot device is echoed in the recent MacGregor novel, *Spree* (Ballantine, 1992). As with other novels by this author, the occult is an integral plot element: the murder victim has developed a hallucinogenic drug that facilitates mind-reading.

The second series of books, written under the name Alison Drake, stars police detective Aline Scott. *Tango Key* (Ballantine, 1988), for example, is a lurid, brutal story of murder and smuggling set in the Florida Keys.

The third and most extensive series is written under the name T. J. MacGregor. In these books the sleuths are Quin St. James and Mike McCleary, who are married and partners in their own private eye firm. The novels are psychological suspense stories with New Age and supernatural elements. *Death Flats* (Ballantine, 1991), depicts the murder of a psychologist who specializes in near-death experiences. A killer is stalking the widow, who is accused by the police of murdering her husband. The first MacGregor book is *Dark Fields* (Ballantine, 1986).

144

Other writers who may be of interest include Mary Higgins Clark, Wendy Hornsby, and Soledad Santiago.

MacLeod, Charlotte/Craig, Alisa.   Under her own name, Mac-Leod writes two series of novels. One is set in Boston, with amateur sleuth Sarah Kelling and investigator Max Bittersohn, and the entire blue-blooded, eccentric Kelling clan as a supporting cast. The second series is set in rural Balaclava County, Massachusetts, with a set of oddball academics from Balaclava Agricultural College, led by Professor Peter Shandy and his librarian wife Helen Marsh Shandy. MacLeod's work is humorous, often gently satirical, and imaginative. Her strong points are character development, a fondness for the stranger byways of the English language, and a charming New England setting. A few of the novels incorporate fantasy elements into their settings; the most unearthly of these is *Curse of the Giant Hogweed* (Doubleday, 1985).

MacLeod also writes two series of Canadian mysteries under the pseudonym of Alisa Craig. The Grub-and-Stakers series recounts the dizzy adventures of the Grub-and-Stake Gardening and Roving Club, in Lobelia Falls, Ontario. The chief characters include homemaker Dittany Henbit Monk, her husband Osbert Monk, a writer of Westerns, and his aunt, Arethusa, a writer of swashbuckling romances. The second series of mysteries focuses on Royal Canadian Mounted Police officer Madoc Rhys, his wife Janet, and the eccentric, Welsh, and musical Rhys family.

The Family Vault (Doubleday, 1979) is the first Sarah Kelling book; *Rest You Merry* (Doubleday, 1978), one of the funniest-ever Christmas mysteries, is the first Peter Shandy novel. The opening Grub-and-Stakers novel is *The Grub-and-Stakers Move a Mountain* (Doubleday, 1981); the first Madoc Rhys book is *A Pint of Murder* (Doubleday, 1980). *The Corpse in Oozak's Pond* (Mysterious, 1987), a Peter Shandy mystery, was nominated for an Edgar Award in 1987. MacLeod has also recently written a biography of Mary Roberts Rinehart, *Had She But Known* (Mysterious, 1994), which was nominated for an Agatha Award for Best Non-Fiction work.

Readers who like Charlotte MacLeod also may enjoy Jane Langton, whose style is more literary but equally charming; Dorothy Cannell; Nancy Pickard's New England stories with Jenny Cain; Carolyn G. Hart; and Phoebe Atwood Taylor's Asey Mayo mysteries set on Cape Cod.

Maiman, Jaye. Robin Miller is a lesbian who writes very successful straight romance novels as well as travel articles, and she is living a comfortable, if lonely, life in New York City when she is notified that an old lover has died in San Francisco. In the first novel of the series, *I Left My Heart* (Naiad, 1991), investigative reporter Mary Oswell supposedly died from an allergic reaction, according to the police, but Robin knows better. In San Francisco, Robin confronts the police as well as Mary's old friends in her search for the truth. As she slowly works her way toward the solution of the mystery, Robin also uncovers some uncomfortable truths about her own relationship with Mary. In the second book, *Crazy for Loving* (Naiad, 1992), Robin is back in New York City, working as a private detective as she struggles to deal with old ghosts from her past. Robin is stubborn, intelligent, and passionate, and she fits comfortably into the mold of the strong female private investigator. The occasional explicit love scene adds some spice to the narrative.

Readers looking for other lesbian private eyes should read J. M. Redmann, Lauren Wright Douglas, and Sandra Scoppettone.

Mann, Jessica. With degrees in archaeology and Anglo-Saxon from Cambridge University, Mann made both her women series characters archaeologists as well. The first of these is Professor Thea Crawford, who debuts in *Troublecross* (McKay Washburn, 1972; as *The Only Security* in England). Thea Crawford and her journalist husband Sylvester appear as the main characters in one other novel, and thereafter they often appear as minor characters in novels featuring Mann's second series detective, Tamara Hoyland, who was once one of Thea's students. Tamara first appears as a minor character in *Funeral Sites* (Doubleday, 1982), in which she aids a woman running from a vicious brother-in-law with political ambitions. Later, Tamara is recruited to work in the mysterious Department E as a spy, though she continues her work as an archaeologist for the Royal Commission on Historical Monuments as a cover. The plots often involve archaeology, English history, and politics. Tamara Hoyland is intelligent, tough, and efficient; she does not hesitate to kill in the line of duty. The stories featuring her are fast-paced, believable, and suspenseful.

In addition to her crime novels, Mann has also written a valuable critical study, *Deadlier Than the Male* (Macmillan, 1981), which

146

examines the work of English writers Margery Allingham, Agatha Christie, Ngaio Marsh, Dorothy L. Sayers, and Josephine Tey.

Fans of Jessica Mann might also enjoy the exploits of Dorothy Gilman's Mrs. Pollifax, an American spy, though there are considerable attitudinal and age differences. Otherwise, readers might try the works of Margot Arnold, Dorothy Dunnett, Paula Gosling, Liza Cody, and Susan Moody.

Maron, Margaret. Maron has two series characters, cop Sigrid Harald and lawyer Deborah Knott. Harald, Maron's first character, features in a series of police procedurals in the traditional vein set in New York City; her debut was in the novel *One Coffee With* (Raven House/Worldwide, 1981). Knott's first novel-length appearance is in *Bootlegger's Daughter* (Mysterious, 1992), which made history in the mystery world by sweeping all four of the major mystery awards for best novel: the Edgar, the Agatha, the Macavity, and the Anthony. Deborah Knott lives and works in North Carolina, Maron's own home ground. Sigrid Harald is a tightly sealed character, efficient and seemingly emotionless, as the series opens, but as the books progress, Sigrid slowly becomes more involved with those around her, largely thanks to a relationship with a character introduced in the first book of the series. This is a textbook example of how a writer can use a series for a natural and interesting development of a character who continues to grow and change.

With Deborah Knott, Maron uses a different voice, writing in the first person, and through Deborah, Maron achieves perhaps her best work to date. The Southern setting seems effortlessly realized, and the dialogue is pitch-perfect. Maron won an Agatha Award for the story "Deborah's Judgment" in the collection *A Woman's Eye* (Delacorte, 1991), Deborah's debut.

For other series female police officers, try Lillian O'Donnell's novels about Norah Mulcahany; Erica Quest's novels about DCI Kate Maddox, Jennie Melville's long-running series about Charmian Daniels, or Susan Dunlap's funny series about Berkeley cop, Jill Smith. Other writers of Southern mysteries are Sharyn McCrumb, Charlaine Harris, and Celestine Sibley.

Martin, Lee. See **Wingate, Anne.**

Mason, Sarah J. At the moment, Mason is perhaps better known by her pseudonym of Hamilton Crane, under which she has been continuing the Miss Seeton novels of the late Heron Carvic. Before his death in 1980, Carvic penned five novels about the English spinster Emily Dorothea Seeton, retired teacher of art and slightly unworldly catalyst of crime-solving. Hampton Charles wrote three novels more in the series before Mason took the helm as Hamilton Crane, and the series continues apace. Crane's first is *Miss Seeton Cracks the Case* (Berkley, 1991). The small village of Plummergen, with its eccentricities and gossip-mongering, much of it revolving around poor Miss Seeton, lives on, and Miss Seeton continues to be involved in humorous criminous escapades. With her umbrella firmly in hand, the Battling Brolly crosses paths with criminals, never quite realizing just how lethal a secret weapon she continues to be in the unorthodox arsenal of Chief Superintendent Delphick of Scotland Yard. Mason's sprightly style, with its attention to the oddities and quirks of the language, is well-suited to the unusual Miss Seeton.

Under her own name, Mason wrote *Let's Talk of Wills* (St. Martin's Press, 1985), a mystery in the traditional English vein. Starting with *Murder in the Maze* (Berkley, 1993), Mason begins a second series featuring Detective Superintendent Trewley and Sergeant Stone of the Allingham constabulary. Many of the same qualities that are present in the Seeton books are present in this new series as well. Those with a taste for the eccentric English mystery novel will find Mason/Crane just their cup of tea.

Those who have enjoyed Mason's Miss Seeton novels might try the work of the late Gladys Mitchell, whose Dame Beatrice Bradley remains one of the most eccentric of all English detectives. Other suggestions are the work of writers like Catherine Aird, Marian Babson, Marjorie Eccles, Ann Cleeves, Anthea Fraser, or Nancy Livingston, whose Mr. Pringle books also feature that special brand of English humor.

Matera, Lia.   Matera writes two series: one featuring Willa Jansson and one featuring Laura Di Palma, both of whom are San Francisco attorneys.

Willa is the mixed-up daughter of aging leftist protesters who are still going strong, and she continues to live and work in her parents' milieu. She has a clear voice of her own, full of sardonic remarks about the political posturings of both left and right. We follow her through law school, her first job, and then subsequent jobs, in all of which she becomes involved with murder. (Willa starts to worry about being Homicide Mary, as she is on the scene of so many killings.) The murders are investigated by Lt. Don Surgelato of the San Francisco Police Department, with whom Willa spars verbally.

Laura Di Palma is another kettle of fish: she is a high-powered defense attorney with a barracuda courtroom style. Di Palma can be an unlikable character, especially when she seems to be mired in materialism and the demands of her career. But her moments of self-awareness and honesty, coupled with her legal expertise, bring her alive for the reader. Matera is wonderful at skewering pretension and presenting '80s and '90s lifestyles with a strong, dry wit.

The first Willa Jansson novel is *Where Lawyers Fear to Tread* (Bantam, 1987); the first Laura Di Palma book is *The Smart Money* (Bantam, 1988). Matera was nominated for Edgar Awards for *A Radical Departure* (Bantam, 1988) and *Prior Convictions* (Simon & Schuster, 1991).

Another wry look at the legal profession (British style) is offered by Sarah Caudwell. Readers may also enjoy Susan Wolfe's San Francisco legal mystery, *The Last Billable Hour* (St. Martin's Press, 1989), and the legal mysteries written by Carolyn Wheat, Chelsea Quinn Yarbro, Lisa Scottoline, and Janet L. Smith.

Matteson, Stefanie. Matteson has written a series of traditional mysteries starring Charlotte Graham, a noted Oscar-winning film and stage actress who lives in New York City. Charlotte is a finely detailed character who may remind the reader of Katharine Hepburn or Bette Davis. As well as being intelligent and observant in her sleuthing, Charlotte is a movie star of the old school: elegant, aristocratic, and strong-willed. The first book, *Murder at the Spa* (Charter/Diamond, 1990), is set at a chic spa in Upstate New York, where a client is murdered during treatment. Matteson provides a detailed background of the operations of a health spa, and she recounts the history of American spas as part of her scene-setting. *Murder at Teatime* (Diamond, 1991) is set on a secluded island off the coast of Maine; this novel includes plenty of herbal lore and information on rare books, especially early herbals. *Murder on the Cliff* (Diamond, 1991) takes place in Newport, Rhode Island, and

Murder on the Silk Road (Diamond, 1992) takes Charlotte to China for further adventures. These novels are notable for the research that Matteson has done to provide detailed backgrounds for each, and her skill in weaving her research into lively, interesting backdrops for her classic plots.

Other writers who portray active elderly sleuths include Kate Morgan, Virginia Rich, Dorothy Gilman, and Mary Bowen Hall.

Maxwell, A. E. (Ann and Evan). The Maxwells write fast, witty, and sharp suspense/action novels with philosophical undertones. The setting is Southern California; the heroes are Fiddler and his brilliant ex-wife Fiora Flynn, an investment banker. They are assisted by Benny Speidel, Fiddler's buddy from Vietnam days, who is a wheelchair-bound electronics genius and setter of fiendish traps for bad guys. Fiddler is independently wealthy, so he is able to help people in trouble for free—but mostly for the excitement of the hunt and the violence. Fiora, of course, knows all the money angles and scams used by con men and international criminals. Fiddler got his wealth from a steamer trunk of used drug money left by his Uncle Jake, a drug runner; he says he got his taste for "the adrenaline life, the outlaw life" from him, too. The action in these novels zooms along as fast as Fiddler's Shelby Cobra sports car. The first Fiddler and Fiora novel is *Just Another Day in Paradise* (Doubleday, 1985).

Science fiction and romantic suspense novels appear under the name of Ann Maxwell, and Ann publishes romance novels under the pseudonym of Elizabeth Lowell.

The landscape and people of Orange County, California, are also evoked in the mysteries of Jean Femling, Wendy Hornsby, and Maxine O'Callaghan.

McCafferty, Taylor/Tierney McClellan. The small town of Pigeon Fork, Kentucky, is the venue for McCafferty's series of novels about Haskell Blevins, private eye. Though some residents of the town insist rather rudely that Haskell reminds them of Howdy Doody, Haskell himself can't see the resemblance, despite his red hair and freckles. Haskell grew up in Pigeon Fork, spent eight years as a cop in Louisville, then returned home after a divorce and job burnout to become a private eye in this town of about eleven hundred. In between cases, Haskell helps out his brother Elmo in his drugstore in return for office space above the drugstore. Haskell does a lot of this, since Pigeon Fork often seems not to have a pressing need for a private eye. The series begins with *Pet Peeves* (Pocket, 1990), in which Haskell investigates the problem of who killed an elderly lady, along with her parakeet and her cat. Delving into the case, Haskell discovers just how many secrets a small town can try to hide. McCafferty handles her small-town setting with ease and skill and describes her characters with affectionate humor. Haskell narrates his doings in a style reminiscent of his harder-boiled brethren, but overall, the feel of this series is much cozier than the series of male PI writers. After all, a guy who has a dog with a phobia about stairs can't be all that hard-boiled.

With *Heir Condition* (Signet, 1995), McCafferty, writing as McClellan, has begun a series set in Louisville, Kentucky, featuring real estate agent Schuyler Ridgway. Divorced, with two sons, Schuyler finds herself in deep trouble in her first outing when a wealthy Louisville businessman names her as an heir in his will. Everyone assumes that Schuyler was having an affair with him, and she soon finds herself the chief suspect in his murder.

Readers who have enjoyed McCafferty/McClellan and her Southern settings might try the work of Deborah Adams, Kay Hooper, Sharyn McCrumb, or Mignon F. Ballard.

McClellan, Tierney.   See McCafferty, Taylor.

McCrumb, Sharyn.   McCrumb is a wise and witty voice in contemporary mystery writing. She writes a series of books about forensic anthropologist Elizabeth MacPherson, and a series of Appalachian novels.

The MacPherson books are the lightest in tone; although Elizabeth solves murders with her forensic knowledge, she also can succumb to imbecility in the expectation of attending a Royal garden party in *The Windsor Knot* (Ballantine, 1990). *Missing Susan* (Ballantine, 1991) is a funny tale of an accident-plagued bus trip through England, during which the guide keeps trying to kill an obnoxious tourist—and missing her. The first Elizabeth MacPherson novel is *Sick of Shadows* (Avon, 1984).

McCrumb also has written two mystery–science fiction novels featuring professor and writer Jay Omega and his sidekick Marion Farley. The Edgar Award–winning *Bimbos of the Death Sun* (TSR,

1988) is a bitingly hilarious satire of science fiction conventions; its sequel, *Zombies of the Gene Pool* (Simon & Schuster, 1992), is a more sober and thoughtful exploration of science fiction fans and their self-enclosed world.

In recent years, McCrumb has concentrated increasingly on presenting acutely observed Appalachian backgrounds in her novels. *If Ever I Return, Pretty Peggy-O* (Scribner, 1990) begins her explorations of Appalachian life and mythology, and it is a splendid expansion of McCrumb's strength as a writer. *The Hangman's Beautiful Daughter* (Scribner, 1992) and *She Walks These Hills* (Scribner, 1994), which won the Agatha, Macavity, and Anthony Awards for Best Novel, both showcase McCrumb's full force as an elegant and powerful writer. In all of her mysteries, McCrumb makes trenchant observations on human behavior and thought patterns. Her writing is perceptive and lyrical; she has certainly grown and matured into a fine writer.

Other mystery writers that readers may enjoy include Joan Hess (for humor), Nevada Barr, Nancy Pickard, Margaret Maron, Deborah Adams, and Elizabeth Peters. Peters's novel, *Naked Once More* (Warner, 1989), is set in a sympathetically rendered Appalachia.

McDermid, Val. English journalist McDermid has created two separate series of mysteries. The first features journalist Lindsay Gordon, who, in her own words, is "a cynical socialist lesbian feminist." In her debut, *Report for Murder* (St. Martin's Press, 1990), Lindsay finds herself embroiled in a murder in just the type of setting she despises, a girls' school, a bastion of privilege. But Lindsay needs the work of writing a feature article about the school, so she goes for a weekend. Murder occurs, an old friend of Lindsay's is arrested, and Lindsay solves the crime. Lindsay reappears in *Open and Shut* (St. Martin's Press, 1991), which is set in Glasgow. Lindsay is much as she describes herself, and McDermid weaves the politics of feminism and alternative lifestyles into her novels compellingly.

With *Dead Beat* (St. Martin's Press, 1993), McDermid introduces Manchester-based private eye Kate Brannigan. Kate lives next door to her lover, rock music journalist Richard Barclay. When a rock star, an old friend of Richard's, asks Kate to find an important person from his past, Kate has little idea that murder will be the result. Kate, like Lindsay, is intelligent, resourceful, and independent. Readers looking for strong women characters will find McDermid of great interest.

Other writers of series with lesbian detectives include Katherine V. Forrest, Sandra Scoppettone, Vicki P. McConnell (whose character Nyla Wade is also a journalist), Barbara Wilson, J. M. Redmann, and Pat Welch. Readers interested in other journalist detectives might try the series of Sarah Shankman, Lesley Grant-Adamson, and Annette Roome.

McGiffin, Janet. Fortyish Dr. Maxene St. Clair is the heroine in the series of medical mysteries penned by McGiffin. Dr. St. Clair has recently left the research laboratory at the Medical College of Wisconsin at Marquette University, following the breakup of her marriage, to get back into the clinical side of medicine. Working as an emergency room physician at an inner city hospital, St. Agnes's, Maxene gets as much hands-on clinical experience as as she could want. In the first novel of the series, *Emergency Murder* (Fawcett, 1992), the wife of a prominent surgeon appears in the emergency room, dressed as a prostitute. The woman dies shortly thereafter, and Maxene suspects that she was murdered. When it turns out that she was poisoned by a rare substance from Maxene's old lab at the medical college, Maxene turns sleuth to save her own hide. The cop on the case is Detective Joseph Grabowksi, and he and Maxene have an on-again, off-again romantic relationship. Maxene St. Clair is stubborn, dedicated, and intelligent, an appealing series sleuth. Her relationship with Grabowski adds an enjoyable, lightly romantic twist to the stories. The medical background is described well, but it is not overly graphic.

Patricia Cornwell, Mary Kittredge, Christine Green, and Stella Shepherd all write series with medical backgrounds of varying depth of detail.

McGown, Jill/Elizabeth Chaplin. Thanks to her standout police procedurals, McGown is fast earning an excellent critical reputation. Beginning with the enjoyable *A Perfect Match* (St. Martin's Press, 1983), McGown has written, to date, five novels featuring the police detectives Lloyd (who maddeningly refuses to divulge his first name) and Judy Hill, his partner and lover. The relationship of Lloyd and Hill serves in these novels as an interesting counterpoint to the mystery plots, and McGown handles the relationship with skill, avoiding the clichés that some writers fall into with their series characters. The mystery plots of McGown's novels, moreover, are a marvelous fusion of the intricately knitted classic English school and the fully fleshed character novels of contemporary mystery fiction. For example, *Gone to Her Death* (St. Martin's Press, 1990; *Death of a Dancer* in England) utilizes the setting of an English public school to great effect. McGown takes the conventions of the traditional English mystery and gives them a thoroughly modern interpretation.

In addition to the Lloyd and Hill series, McGown has produced a number of suspense novels with memorable characters and settings, such as *The Stalking Horse* (St. Martin's Press, 1988). These works feature excellent puzzles as well.

McGown has recently published a novel as Elizabeth Chaplin, titled *Hostage to Fortune* (Mysterious, 1993), which is much like her nonseries novels as Jill McGown.

Those who have sampled McGown and liked her work should also consider the work of Frances Fyfield, Susan B. Kelly, Cynthia Harrod-Eagles, Jennie Melville, Sheila Radley, and Paula Gosling.

McKenna, Bridget. McKenna's first mystery, *Murder Beach* (Diamond, 1993), is set in a beach town in Southern California. Caley Burke is a newly fledged private investigator who tries to help out an old friend from high school. A courtly elderly painter is the prime suspect in the murder of a well-liked local entrepreneur and developer. This is Caley's first case on her own, and she is emotionally vulnerable around her old friends, but she carefully and systematically unwinds the motives of the victim's associates and relatives. The affluent beach setting is a memorable one, and this first effort is a light, enjoyable read. McKenna's writing and plotting continues to mature with *Dead Ahead* (Berkley, 1994), which was nominated for a Shamus Award for Best Paperback Original Private Eye Novel. Family friends hire Caley to investigate a suspicious car crash that occurred just after the victim had a well-publicized argument with some white supremacists. The setting is a small town in the California gold rush country, and the backdrop is a detailed, well-realized one. Caley dislikes violence but uses a gun to defend her life, and she reflects quite a bit about death after killing a villain in a previous case. In *Caught Dead* (Berkley, 1995), she is still battling the emotional repercussions of being caught up in violence.

Her boss insists that she take vacation time and go to see a psychiatrist. Although she stays at home (in the fictional Northern California town of Cascade), she cannot refuse a request from a teenage boy to help him find out who his father is. She is caught up again in a murder case, only this one is in her own town.

California is fertile ground for fictional private eyes, and memorable tales have been written by Maxine O'Callaghan, Karen Kijewski, Linda Grant, Marcia Muller, Janet Dawson, Elizabeth Pincus, Gloria White, and of course Sue Grafton.

McNab, Claire. McNab writes a series that features Detective Inspector Carol Ashton and is set in Sydney, Australia. Ashton is a blond, beautiful lesbian who is divorced and has a son. In the first mystery, *Lessons in Murder* (Naiad, 1988), a high school shop teacher has been killed by a Black & Decker drill driven through his skull. Carol is in charge of the investigation, and she falls in love with a suspect, Sybil Quade, who has always been heterosexual. *Cop Out* (Naiad, 1991) finds Ashton investigating the murder of Bryce Darcy, a member of an influential and wealthy local family. It is generally assumed that his sister, Charlotte, killed him. But Charlotte's confession is suspect because she is hooked on amphetamines. Ashton and Detective Sergeant Mark Bourke uncover family secrets and hidden animosities in their search for the truth. McNab's mysteries are mixtures of police procedurals and classic cozies, with some graphic sex scenes as well.

Katherine V. Forrest, Mary Wings, Lauren Wright Douglas, and Sandra Scoppettone write about lesbian detectives. Jennifer Rowe and Kerry Greenwood also set mysteries in Australia.

McQuillan, Karin. The mysterious land of Kenya and its endangered fauna are the canvas for McQuillan's series of mystery novels starring Jazz Jasper, an American running a safari business. Herself a former Peace Corps volunteer in Africa and an ardent naturalist, McQuillan has evidently endowed her series character with her own enthusiasm for these subjects. The first novel in the series, *Deadly Safari* (St. Martin's Press, 1990), finds Jazz, newly divorced and struggling to make it on her own, leading a safari that is ripe for violence. Two wealthy businessmen, each with wife in tow, along with a tall, beautiful model named Candy, spell trouble for the future of Jazz's venture when people start getting murdered.

Complicating the situation are two men to whom Jazz is strongly attracted: Dan Striker, a reporter, and Inspector Omondi, with whom Jazz always argues about getting involved in the murders that keep happening around her. McQuillan paints the Kenyan setting vividly, and her concerns for the animals of Africa are well to the fore. Particularly affecting in *Elephants' Graveyard* (Ballantine, 1993) is a scene in which poachers massacre an entire herd of elephants.

Readers who have enjoyed McQuillan's mix of mystery and conservancy should also read Susan Conant's animal-centered mysteries and Nevada Barr's series, which is set in the nation's national parks.

Meek, M. R. D.   A retired solicitor, Meek brings her knowledge of the law and the legal life to a series starring lawyer Lennox Kemp. In his American debut, *Hang the Consequences* (Scribner, 1985), Kemp is disbarred and working for McCready's Detective Agency. (An earlier novel, *With Flowers That Fell* [Hale, 1983], not published in the United States, apparently tells the story behind Kemp's disbarment.) In the next book in the series, however, Kemp has been reinstated at the bar, and the murders with which he becomes involved thereafter generally begin somehow with one of his legal cases. Meek, though British, displays an obvious affection for American detective fiction in her work, for the wry and cynical Kemp often has more in common with Archie Goodwin or Lew Archer than with Peter Wimsey or Hercule Poriot. Meek's prose is spare yet often elegant, and her observations of the human character are penetrating and compassionate. This is a series rich in character—a special treat for those who value characterization—as well as clever puzzles, and Meek handles both with dexterity.

Like Meek, Frances Fyfield uses her legal expertise to create an authentic background for her characters. Hannah Wakefield has recently begun a new series about a woman lawyer in London. Readers looking for other enjoyable English legal mysteries might try the work of the late Sara Woods or the series by E. X. Giroux. Also try Janet L. Smith's series, which is set in Seattle, or the funny and cleverly plotted novels by the late Anthony Gilbert, starring the unforgettable Cockney lawyer, Arthur Crook.

Melville, Jennie.   See **Butler, Gwendoline.**

Meredith, D. R. The *D* stands for Doris. Meredith, a former librarian and bookseller, lives in Amarillo, Texas, and she has claimed the Texas Panhandle as her own in two mystery series.

The first features Sheriff Charles Matthews of mythical Crawford County, Texas. In *The Sheriff and the Panhandle Murders* (Walker, 1984), Matthews investigates the case of a good ol' boy and a beautiful young Hispanic woman. Matthews is honest and courageous, a good man to have on your side.

Meredith's second series is set in the real town of Canadian, Texas, near Amarillo, but her characters are fictional. The star of the series is lawyer John Lloyd Branson, a forceful, intense, and intelligent man who is a little like a Peter Wimsey in a bolo tie. Branson's assistant is Lydia Fairchild, a law student from Southern Methodist University in Dallas. Amid the solving of crimes, as in *Murder by Impulse* (Ballantine, 1987), the first in the series, John Lloyd and Lydia fight a wary but insistent attraction to each other. John Lloyd is a true Texas-style character, slightly outrageous in everything he does. Meredith has a grand time inviting the reader to have a sly laugh along with her as she involves John Lloyd and Lydia in intriguing and cleverly constructed plots. Meredith depicts with a loving eye her corner of the world, and between them, Charles Matthews and John Lloyd Branson do their best to keep the Panhandle a law-abiding area.

Readers who like their mysteries Southwestern style might try the work of Susan Rogers Cooper, Lee Martin, and Mary Willis Walker. Jean Hager and Eve K. Sandstrom also use the Southwest, namely Oklahoma, to good effect in their series.

Mertz, Barbara. See **Peters, Elizabeth.**

Meyers, Annette/Meyers, Maan. Annette Meyers writes a series of novels with Wall Street headhunters Xenia Smith and Leslie Wetzon. Smith is a shallow, greedy, manipulative yuppie; Wetzon is a former chorus dancer and is warm, caring, and loyal. Wetzon is an amateur sleuth and the real star of the stories, and the reader (along with Wetzon herself) continually wonders why she puts up with Smith. As well as creating memorable characters in her mismatched duo, Meyers has devised vibrant settings in the diverse neighborhoods of New York City for her mysteries. The first Smith and Wetzon novel is *The Big Killing* (Bantam, 1989). The plots of the mysteries revolve around stockbroking and financial malfeasance, and Meyers brings an insider's view to her accounts of white-collar crime in the '80s and '90s. In the well-received *Murder: the Musical* (Doubleday, 1993), Meyers draws upon her own experience in the theater to tell a story of murder on Broadway.

Annette Meyers and her husband, Martin Meyers, also have written a series of historical mysteries under the name of Maan Meyers. The series begins with *The Dutchman* (Doubleday, 1992), featuring Pieter Tonneman, the *schout,* or sheriff, for the community of New Amsterdam in 1664. In *The Kingsbridge Plot* (Doubleday, 1993), Pieter's descendant John Tonneman is a London-trained physician who returns to New York in time to witness the political upheavals of 1775 and give his help in solving a series of murders.

Readers who appreciate Meyers might like Emma Lathen, the dean of financial mystery writers: A. E. Maxwell, who writes knowledgeably about banker Fiora Flynn: Margaret Logan; and Ellen Godfrey. Barbara Paul, Dorian Yeager, Jane Dentinger, and P. M. Carlson write theatrical mysteries set in New York.

Meyers, Maan.   See **Meyers, Annette.**

Michaels, Barbara.   See **Peters, Elizabeth.**

Millar, Margaret.   The Canadian-born Millar grew up to become half of one of the world's most famous husband-and-wife teams. The late Kenneth Millar, perhaps better known as Ross MacDonald, actually turned to writing crime fiction after seeing the success of his wife. Margaret Millar began her career with three novels in the conventional detective vein featuring psychiatrist Dr. Paul Prye (beginning with *The Invisible Worm,* Doubleday, 1941). Prye's whimsical name is evidence of his creator's sense of humor, which is an underlying element in even the most hair-raising of her novels. Soon, however, Millar abandoned the detective story and concentrated on the mystery novel, and with such tales she found her greatest success. A prime example is the Edgar-winning *Beast in View* (Random House, 1955), often imitated, but never with the level of skill Millar brings to her work. Millar starts with some unusual event—a disappearance, a murder, a crime of some sort—then weaves a subtle tale of menace and suspense. Often the reader is never quite certain whodunit or whydunit until the last line of the novel. *The Listening Walls* (Random House, 1959) demonstrates this powerful technique beautifully. Late in her career, Millar created a new series character, the young Chicano lawyer Tom Aragon, who debuted in *Ask for Me Tomorrow* (Random House, 1976). Intelligent, compassionate, with a strong streak of unconventional humor, Aragon is an appealing sleuth. Standouts among the Millar oeuvre are *The Murder of Miranda* (Random House, 1979), *Beyond This Point Are Monsters* (Random House, 1970), and *How Like an Angel* (Random House, 1962). For her continued excellence in the field, the late Millar was named a Grand Master by the Mystery Writers of America in 1983.

Those who have enjoyed the work of Margaret Millar might try the psychological suspense novels of Ruth Rendell/Barbara Vine, Margaret Yorke, Rosamond Smith, Minette Walters, Anna Clarke, and Frances Hegarty.

Millhiser, Marlys. Millhiser began her writing career with the romantic suspense novel *Michael's Wife* (Putnam, 1972). A young woman finds herself alone in the Arizona desert with no memory of who she is or how she got there. This is a story rich in the antiwar tensions and concerns of the late '60s and early '70s. As with all of Millhiser's books, there is an emphasis on mood, a vividly portrayed setting, and a strong narrative. *Nella Waits* (Putnam, 1974) is a memorably creepy ghost story set in Iowa. Lynette Stewart returns to her hometown and falls in love with Jay Van Fleet, who has returned to inherit the family estate. The house is haunted by the ghost of his mother, Nella, who wants only to keep Jay single and with her in the house. *The Mirror* (Putnam, 1978) is a splendid time-travel book with female main characters. An antique mirror is intrinsically evil, and it is given to Brandy McCabe in turn-of-the-century Colorado as a wedding present, and then passed down to Brandy's granddaughter Shay. On the night before Shay's wedding, she looks into it and becomes her grandmother Brandy. The two women are unforgettable characters, and the historical details are fascinating. Time travel occurs in *The Threshold* (Putnam, 1984) as well, and this time Millhiser sets her novel in the mining town of Telluride, Colorado. Millhiser brings her characters and settings to vivid life so that the reader is caught up in the story of both a young girl striving to survive amid the labor struggles and miserable living conditions, and her modern counterpart.

Millhiser returned to print with a series of lively, eccentric mysteries featuring Charlie Greene, a literary agent in Hollywood. Charlie became an unwed mother at the age of sixteen; now she has a gorgeous teenage daughter about whom she worries constantly. The series begins with *Murder at Moot Point* (Doubleday, 1992), set in a small beach town in Oregon. Charlie is visiting one of her clients when a local woman is found dead under the wheels of Charlie's car. The town is full of old hippies, all suspects in the murder. Millhiser creates quixotic and amusing secondary characters in an atmospheric, small-town setting. *Death of the Office Witch* (Otto Penzler, 1993) is a smart, funny look at life and death in contemporary Los Angeles. Charlie works in the entertainment business, and there is plenty of Beverly Hills ambience. Her office receptionist is murdered, and Charlie may even be psychic, since she keeps hearing the dead woman whispering to her from a trash can near the office. Charlie returns to investigate murder in the Canyonlands of Utah in *Murder in a Hot Flash* (Otto Penzler, 1995), along with her unconventional mother Edwina, who is serving as an adviser on an environmental documentary. A trashy science fiction movie about giant rats invading the earth is filming at the same location, and when the director is murdered, the sheriff thinks Edwina did it. After all, she's going through menopause, and everyone thinks she's acting a bit odd. But Millhiser turns stereotypes and conventions on their heads with this amusing tale of mayhem, romance, and oddities.

Readers may also enjoy mysteries with an occult bent by Kate Green, Mignon Warner, Trish Janeshutz, and Barbara Michaels.

Mills, D. F. Mills writes compelling novels of suspense that would have been called, once upon a time, romantic suspense. But in Mills's case, the emphasis in her work is definitely on the suspense, with romance only a small part of the entire picture. Mills takes women, often with some great difficulty to overcome, puts them into trying and terrifying situations, and lets the reader sweat to see how things will turn out. In *Deadline* (Diamond, 1991), the heroine is a writer, Tess Alexander, who is becoming well-known for her true-crime works. She is asked by a former governor of Texas to write the true story of his innocence in the arson deaths of his wife, daughter, and grandchild. Tess agrees to write the book—on her own terms, though—and soon she is plunged into a terrifying situation that forces her to confront long-buried secrets in her own past. Another novel, *Freefall* (Diamond, 1992), offers an intriguing twist on the heroine-with-amnesia convention. Mills creates believable and often scary situations in her novels, which most readers will want to devour in a single sitting. Her first novel was *Darkroom* (Charter/Diamond, 1990).

Fans of the suspense novel are certainly acquainted with the current American queen of suspense, Mary Higgins Clark. Other suspense novelists of interest are Barbara Michaels, Phyllis A. Whitney, Judith Kelman, Mary Willis Walker, and Velda Johnston.

Mitchell, Kay/Lacey, Sarah.   A former nurse and health visitor in England, Mitchell has lately turned her talents to the writing of crime fiction. Her series character is Chief Inspector John Morrissey of Malminster CID. In the first novel of the series, *A Lively Form of Death* (St. Martin's Press, 1991), Morrissey investigates a death by poisoning in the nearby village of Little Henge, which is rife with secrets and seething passions. Mitchell's territory is in many ways the conventional English village of the traditional crime story, but though her work might appear cozy from a cursory look, the novels have thus far included crimes that were beyond the pale in the Golden Age. Mitchell has updated the cozy, old-fashioned English murder mystery in an effective and entertaining way. Her second novel, *In Stony Places* (St. Martin's Press, 1992), demonstrates that a serial-killer book need not be gory and nasty to be suspenseful. Along with a number of other Englishwomen writing today, Mitchell shows that there is considerable life in a venerable form of entertainment.

Writing as Sarah Lacey, Mitchell has begun a second series. Her character is twenty-five-year-old Leah Hunter, a tax inspector. Unabashedly nosy, Leah loves delving into the puzzles of people's lives. In her first outing, *File Under: Deceased* (St. Martin's Press, 1993), a handsome man falls dead into her arms, and she uses her authority as a tax inspector to investigate him and figure out why someone wanted him dead. Leah's nosiness, coupled with a brash taste for danger, make her adventures lively ones, and her sense of humor should please those who like their crime novels leavened with clever quips.

Readers who have enjoyed Mitchell might try the work of Pat Burden, Ann Granger, Susan B. Kelly, and Erica Quest. Fans of the Lacey novels might enjoy the Tamara Hoyland novels of Jessica

Mann, Susan Moody's Penny Wanawake and Cassandra Swann novels, and Val McDermid's Kate Brannigan series.

Moffat, Gwen. Landscape is an important component in the work of Moffat, for her series character, Miss Melinda Pink, is a dedicated mountaineer. Since her debut in *Lady with a Cool Eye* (Gollancz, 1973), Miss Pink has combined climbing with sleuthing in twelve novels, about half of which have been published in the United States. In addition to her mountain climbing, Miss Pink also finds the time to serve as a magistrate and to write novels. The settings of the books always involve mountain regions, either in Great Britain or the United States. In a number of her more recent works, such as *The Stone Hawk* (St. Martin's Press, 1989) and *Rage* (St. Martin's Press, 1990), Miss Pink has visited Utah canyon country and California, respectively. Miss Pink faces physical danger and harsh conditions with great equanimity, and she offers the reader her opinions, as a matter of course, on many issues regarding the environment. Moffat is a distinctive writer with a woman series character not quite like any other in mystery fiction.

Those acquainted with Miss Pink might enjoy the work of Judith Van Gieson, for whom environmental concerns form an important thread in her books. Otherwise, readers might look for the out-of-print works by Glyn Carr, whose character, Sir Abercrombie Lewker, is also a climber of distinction.

Monfredo, Miriam Grace. A writer and former librarian who lives in western New York State, Monfredo has utilized her interest in the history of her area to produce an unusual series set in nineteenth-century New York State. The central character of the series is Glynis Tryon, librarian in the city of Seneca Falls. Determining early on that she wasn't too keen on the yoke of marriage, Glynis sets her sights on having a career at a time when very few women had such ideas. Her budding feminist ideas get her involved with Elizabeth Cady Stanton and the meeting on women's rights that was held in Seneca Falls in 1848. Around this historic occasion, Monfredo has fashioned an entertaining murder mystery with *Seneca Falls Inheritance* (St. Martin's Press, 1992), which was an Agatha and Macavity nominee for Best First Novel. By the time of the second novel in the series, *North Star Conspiracy* (St. Martin's Press, 1993), the time is 1854, and Monfredo wraps her tale around the story of the Underground Railroad. Though Glynis is determined to remain independent, the town constable, Cullen Stuart, has set his sights on making Glynis his wife, and their relationship adds emotional depth to an intriguing series. Readers looking for a satisfying blend of historical fiction and mystery novel will find Monfredo a welcome discovery.

Those acquainted with Glynis Tryon should try the work of Anne Perry and Amy Myers, who write about England of the nineteenth century. Also, readers might find Gillian Linscott's novels about Edwardian suffragette Nell Bray of interest because of the interest in women's rights. The other librarian detectives are all twentieth-century, in the Jacqueline Kirby novels of Elizabeth Peters, the work of Kate Morgan, Charlaine Harris, and L. R. Wright.

Moody, Susan. British writer Susan Moody has created a series of mysteries starring Penny Wanawake, a black amateur investigator. Penny is the daughter of an African ambassador and a titled Englishwoman; she is six feet tall, outspoken, and a talented photographer. She and her lover, Barnaby Midas, an antique dealer and jewelry thief, have set up a scam in which he steals jewels from the rich, and they give the proceeds to feed famine victims in Africa. Penny is beautiful and flippant, with an active sex life in these novels. In the first book in the series, *Penny Black* (Fawcett, 1984), Penny's school friend, Marfa Lund, is murdered in a bathroom at Los Angeles Airport. *Penny Dreadful* (Ballantine, 1986) is set in Canterbury, England, and revolves around the killing of an obnoxious thriller writer. The Penny Wanawake books are tongue in cheek and lively, with a distinctly wry wit.

A new series for Moody features Cassandra Swann, a professional bridge instructor and amateur sleuth. The series begins with *Death Takes a Hand* (Otto Penzler, 1994). Cassandra is a witty and humorous detective, and the books provide plenty of scenes at the bridge tables.

Moody also has written a romantic suspense novel, *Mosaic* (Delacorte, 1991), and a thriller about the kidnapping of a baby, *Hush-a-bye* (London: Macdonald, 1991).

Readers who enjoy flippant heroines may want to try mysteries by Carole Berry, Liza Cody, Dorothy Dunnett, Marissa Piesman, and Natasha Cooper. Kerry Tucker writes a series of crime novels with a photographer character, Libby Kincaid.

Morgan, Kate. Morgan is a pseudonym for Ann Hamilton Whitman. Her cozy mysteries, published as paperback originals, feature Dewey James as an amateur sleuth. Dewey is an elderly librarian who is the widow of a police chief. She is known in her home town of Hamilton as an eccentric who quotes endlessly from literary classics. The setting for most of the novels is a typical small town, and Dewey is an updated American version of Miss Marple, with a fund of sharp observations on local behavior. In the first book in the series, *A Slay at the Races* (Berkley, 1992), Dewey, in a neighbor's stable, finds a dead banker under the hooves of a racehorse. In *Days of Crime and Roses* (Berkley, 1992), she goes to New York City to visit an old friend. There she inevitably finds murder at an arts foundation, where her friend is on the board. Dewey's investigations often involve her old friend and suitor George Farnham, and the current Hamilton police captain Fielding Booker. Morgan gives her readers cozy mysteries with time-honored elements like the traditional denouement where suspects are gathered together in one room to establish who's guilty.

Stefanie Matteson, D. B. Borton, Elizabeth Daniels Squire, Mary Bowen Hall, and Corinne Holt Sawyer write American cozies with elderly sleuths.

Morice, Anne. The late Felicity Shaw, who wrote crime novels as Ann Morice, was a playwright, and her skill with dialogue and dramatic pacing is evident in the long-running series about actress Theresa (Tessa) Crichton. In the first of the series, *Death in the Grand Manor* (London: Macmillan, 1970), Tessa is still in the early stages of her career when she encounters her first murder. Morice here introduces several of the characters who are regulars in the series: Tessa's eccentric cousin Toby Crichton, a well-known playwright; Toby's daughter, Ellen; and Robin Price, a detective inspector who has become Tessa's husband by the second book, *Murder in Married Life* (London: Macmillan, 1971). The novels are narrated in the first person by Tessa, and the dialogue as well as Tessa's observations, can be sharp, witty, and insightful. Tessa's career generally offers the situations in which she encounters murders; an excellent example of this is *Death in the Round* (St. Martin's Press, 1980), where murder occurs in a repertory company Tessa has briefly joined. Witty and elegant in style, Morice and her creations are enjoyable reading for those who like their murders mixed with the performing arts. Two of Morice's last three novels, *Design for Dying* (St. Martin's Press, 1988) and *Planning for Murder* (St. Martin's Press, 1990), do not feature Tessa.

Fans of Anne Morice might try the Charles Paris novels of Simon Brett and the series by American writer Jane Dentinger, as well as the theatrical mysteries of the late Dame Ngaio Marsh. P. M. Carlson has often made use of theatrical settings in her Maggie Ryan series.

Morison, B. J. Maine native Morison has created one of the more unusual series characters to grace the pages of an adult mystery novel. Elizabeth Lamb Worthington, the star of these books, is eight years old when the series begins with *Champagne and a Gardener* (Thorndike Press, 1982); the time is the early 1970s, for Nixon is still President. Elizabeth Lamb (as she is called by her family) and her mother have come to Mount Desert Island, off the coast of Maine, after living for a number of years in Europe, while her father, scion of an old Maine family, was off in South America trying to revive his fortunes. Her Continental experiences, along with her own natural intelligence, have combined to give Elizabeth Lamb a perspicacity unnerving, even downright terrifying, to many of the adults around her. Through the course of the series, Elizabeth Lamb has aged to thirteen in the latest installment, *The Martini Effect* (North Country Press, 1992). Morison has penned a distinctive series that is as much modern comedy of manners as murder mystery, for she delights in skewering the pretensions of the rich. The series is chock-full of information about the history and society of the inhabitants of Mount Desert Island and Bar Harbor.

Readers looking for more murder Down East should try the work of J. S. Borthwick and Susan Kenney. For more general New England settings, Sally Gunning, Charlotte MacLeod, and Phoebe Atwood Taylor all have series set in Massachusetts.

Moyes, Patricia. An accident while on a skiing holiday led Moyes to write her first mystery novel, and though Moyes may not have spent her holiday entirely as planned, this fortuitous accident witnessed the birth of a distinguished career in the mystery field. This first novel, titled, aptly enough, *Dead Men Don't Ski* (Rinehart, 1960), introduced Scotland Yard Inspector Henry Tibbett and his good-natured wife Emmy, who are on a skiing holiday in the Italian

Alps. For more than three decades now Moyes has delighted fans of the traditional English mystery with her dazzling combination of razor-sharp wit, complex plots, and the knack for describing unusual settings vividly. Henry Tibbett is one of those who has a true nose for crime, and he has learned never to ignore his hunches, which have brought him success and recognition at Scotland Yard. Moyes also has a keen sense of humor, a talent for picking out the unusual, as evidenced by the engaging Manciple family, the centerpiece of two novels, *Murder Fantastical* (Holt, Rinehart, Winston, 1987) and *A Six-Letter Word for Death* (Holt, Rinehart, Winston, 1983). In *Johnny under Ground* (Holt, Rinehart, Winston, 1965), Moyes tells a poignant tale of Emmy's reunion with some of her World War II Air Force buddies, and the easygoing Emmy proves as engaging a character as her husband. The Moyes books also offer a variety of settings, from Switzerland, Holland, Washington, D.C., and the Caribbean, where Moyes now lives with her husband.

Those who enjoy the classic touch of Moyes might try the work of Marian Babson and Sarah Caudwell, both of whom infuse their works with their highly individual senses of humor. Readers looking for police detectives might try the work of Clare Curzon, Martha Grimes, June Thomson, Dorothy Simpson, or the early Dalgliesh novels of P. D. James.

Muller, Marcia. Her female private eye Sharon McCone debuted in *Edwin of the Iron Shoes* (McKay Washburn, 1977) five years before her best-selling peers, Sue Grafton and Sara Paretsky, published their first novels in their private eye series. Muller has been called by Grafton (as quoted on the dust jackets of Muller's recent novels) the "founding 'mother' of the contemporary female hard-boiled private eye." Based in San Francisco and working chiefly for a legal cooperative, All Souls, McCone is tough and independent, certainly an engaging epitome for the characters who have come after her. The early McCone novels have a softer-boiled feel to them, but with more recent works, such as the standouts *The Shape of Dread* (Mysterious, 1989) and *Wolf in the Shadows* (Mysterious, 1993), which won an Anthony for Best Novel, Muller displays a strong, reflective, and hard-edged voice that makes her work equal the best of Grafton and Paretsky, for whom she opened the door.

Muller has also written two other enjoyable but short-lived series. One featured Chicana museum curator Elena Oliverez, beginning with *The Tree of Death* (Walker, 1983), and the other starred art security expert Joanna Stark, who first appeared in *The Cavalier in White* (St. Martin's Press, 1986).

Fans of Sharon McCone generally enjoy Sue Grafton's Kinsey Millhone novels, though McCone is a little older and more consciously political than Kinsey. Linda Grant, Maxine O'Callaghan, and Janet Dawson also have created enjoyable, California-based female private eyes.

Myers, Amy. Myers mixes history with cooking to dish up an entertaining series that features maître chef Auguste Didier as detective par excellence in late Victorian England. Half-English and half-French, Didier was trained by the maître Escoffier himself, and the pages of Didier's adventures are peppered with the names of mouthwatering dishes (sadly, no recipes are given). In his first appearance, *Murder in Pug's Parlour* (Headline, 1986; Avon, 1992), Didier is chef at Stockbery Towers, rural seat of the Duke of Stockbery. He becomes the chief suspect when the duke's much-hated steward is murdered, and Didier turns sleuth to save himself. Scotland Yard soon appears, in the guise of Inspector Egbert Rose, and a new "detective duo" is born. In the second book, *Murder in the Limelight* (Headline, 1987; Avon, 1992), Didier is in London, chef of the café at the famed Galaxy Theatre. As always, Didier's nose for crime is equaled only by his skills as a chef. Myers has a light touch, endowing Didier with charm despite his healthy ego. The plots are neatly constructed, and the period detail adds an excellent flavor to the mélange.

Readers who enjoy the Victorian period might try the work of Anne Perry, Alanna Knight, L. B. Greenwood, Carole Nelson Douglas, the Amelia Peabody Emerson series of Elizabeth Peters, or Gillian Linscott's novels about Edwardian sleuth Nell Bray. Contemporary series with a culinary twist include the works of Janet Laurence, Diane Mott Davidson, and Katherine Hall Page.

Nabb, Magdalen. An Englishwoman long resident in Florence, Italy, Nabb as a neophyte mystery writer could hardly have asked for higher praise than that which greeted her first novel, *Death of an Englishman* (Scribner, 1982), and from no less a writer than the late Georges Simenon. Writing about her adopted city, Nabb has created a superb series of novels starring a humane and very human character, Marshal Salvatore Guarnaccia. Sicilian by birth, the marshal finds himself posted to Florence, where he learns to cope with the often mysterious ways of Northern Italy and its people. Florence itself is an important character in these novels, but it is the marshal, working slowly and steadily in each case, persisting against the stultifying pace of Italian bureaucracy, persevering in the name of justice, who makes the series so appealing. *Death of a Dutchman* (Scribner, 1983) and *The Marshal and the Madwoman* (Scribner, 1988) are excellent examples of Nabb's skill with plotting and characterization.

Readers longing to visit other parts of contemporary Italy might try Donna Leon's series set in Venice, and the works of Edward Sklepowich and Michael Dibdin, who also write about Venice. Those who enjoy the character of Guarnaccia might try the work of M. R. D. Meek and the late Georges Simenon. For the lighter side, there is always wickedly funny Sarah Caudwell's *Thus Was Adonis Murdered* (Scribner, 1981).

Neel, Janet. British novelist Neel (aka **Janet Cohen**) has written a well-received series of books with protagonists Detective Inspector John McLeish of the London Metropolitan Police and Francesca Wilson, a civil servant in the Department of Trade and Industry. The books are an engrossing mixture of police procedural and the British psychological crime novel. John and Francesca meet in the first book, *Death's Bright Angel* (St. Martin's Press, 1988), and they begin a stormy relationship against a backdrop of police work and financial malfeasance. Francesca has a fast-lane career, as well as four younger brothers whom she mothers and overprotects. Several of the brothers are brilliant singers, and Neel's creation of an eccentric family and their musical obsessions is well-done. In her novels, Neel also has written an insider's description of the workings of the British civil service system. In *Death Among the Dons* (St. Martin's Press, 1994), Neel moves her story to the insular and financially troubled world of a women's college. Francesca has a temporary assignment as college bursar when an intruder begins attacking students. The setting reminds the reader of Dorothy L. Sayers's classic *Gaudy Night* (Harcourt, 1936). The suspense is potent and the writing strong in this worthy English series.

Death's Bright Angel won the John Creasey First Novel Award from the Crime Writers' Association. *The Highest Bidder* (London: Michael Joseph, 1992), a financial thriller, has been published under the author's own name of Janet Cohen.

Other novelists that readers may enjoy include P. D. James, Emma Lathen, and Annette Meyers. Ruth Dudley Edwards and Natasha Cooper also write about the British civil service.

Neely, Barbara. Neely has brought to life one of the most original voices in contemporary mystery fiction. In her first appearance, *Blanche on the Lam* (St. Martin's Press, 1992), African-American Blanche White is a domestic in a small town in North Carolina. Called up before the local judge for yet another bad check, Blanche panics in the courthouse, and when she sees an opportunity to escape from a certain jail sentence, she runs. She ends up taking refuge out in the country with a very eccentric white family. Blanche soon realizes that something very strange is going on, and she turns sleuth. Blanche is a very strong character, and her voice is distinctive. Throughout the books, Blanche ruminates on what it is like to be female and black in contemporary American society. In the second book, *Blanche among the Talented Tenth* (St. Martin's Press, 1994), Neely places Blanche temporarily in an exclusive all-black resort on the coast of Maine, where the shade of one's skin color is a very important social issue. The mystery plots of the novels fall comfortably into the traditional cozy mold, and the presence of Blanche assures the reader of a provocative take on the world.

Readers interested in series with other African-American heroines should try the work of Valerie Wilson Wesley, Eleanor Taylor Bland, and Nikki Baker.

Newman, Sharan.   The author of a trilogy of historical novels about the Arthurian legends and of a novel for children, Newman recently turned her scholarly interest in the European Middle Ages to a fascinating series of mysteries set in twelfth-century France. The first novel, *Death Comes as Epiphany* (Tor, 1993), introduced Catherine LeVendeur, a young novice in the Convent of the Paraclete, presided over by the famous Abbess Heloise. Because of her notorious relationship with the theologian Abelard, Heloise and her convent were often the target of intrigue, and in this first novel, Newman spins a deadly tale of murder and mischief directed against the convent. Heloise sends Catherine, one of her brightest novices, on a mission to the great abbey of St. Denis outside Paris to discover who has tampered with a prayer book prepared by the nuns of the Paraclete in an attempt to discredit Heloise. Along the way to the solution of the mystery, Catherine meets a mysterious young stonemason named Edgar and uncovers disturbing secrets about her own wealthy Parisian mercantile family. In *The Devil's Door* (Forge, 1994), Catherine is horrified by the brutal attack on a noblewoman, who has sought the peace of the Convent of the Paraclete for her final days, as she slowly dies from the aftermath of the assault. Investigating the motives behind the attack proves dangerous for Catherine, as she reconsiders her decision to leave the world of the cloister. Full of the sights and sounds and smells of the medieval world, this series provides rich and rewarding reading for the lover of the historical mystery novel. *Death Comes as Epiphany* was nominated for the Agatha and Anthony Awards for Best First Novel and won the Macavity Award in that category.

Readers interested in the medieval world of mystery have no doubt already read Ellis Peters; other recommendations are the works of Kate Sedley and Candace M. Robb. Other excellent historical mystery writers are Anne Perry and Kate Ross.

O'Brien, Meg. O'Brien's journalist/sleuth, Jessica James (inevitably nicknamed Jesse) fights a recurring attraction toward criminality and irresponsibility. But Jesse is also an award-winning journalist, a recovering alcoholic, and a wisecracking, impetuous, and persistent investigator. She falls off the wagon, suffers bouts of self-recrimination, and possesses all the human failings needed to keep the reader fascinated. Jesse has an on-again, off-again relationship with a sexy, upscale Mafioso, Marcus Andrelli. Andrelli, his bodyguard Tark, and the teenage Genesee Three help Jesse investigate crimes that involve her family and friends. The Rochester, New York, setting is unusual and memorable, and Jesse's first-person narrative is smart, quick, and profane. It helps to read the Jesse James mysteries sequentially; the first title in the series is *The Daphne Decisions* (Bantam, 1990).

More recently, O'Brien has turned to writing suspense novels with women protagonists, including *The Keeper* (Doubleday, 1992), about a mother's search for her kidnapped daughter, and *Thin Ice* (Doubleday, 1993), a tale of the mysterious death of a medical researcher.

Other writers with journalist sleuths include Sarah Shankman, Alison Gordon, Annette Roome, Mickey Friedman, and Barbara D'Amato. Readers also might want to try Liza Cody, whose private eye Anna Lee is equally prone to personal failure. A classic predecessor of O'Brien's is the screwball comedy-mystery writer Craig Rice; Gabrielle Kraft is writing contemporary screwball mysteries.

O'Callaghan, Maxine. Delilah West, the heroine of O'Callaghan's mysteries, was one of the first modern American female private eyes in fiction. Delilah and her husband, Jack West, jointly operated a detective agency, West & West, in Orange County, California. Jack is killed in the first book in the series, *Death is Forever* (Raven, 1980), and of course Delilah must go after her husband's murderer. She won't give up and she keeps the agency going by herself. In *Hit & Run* (St. Martin's Press, 1989), Delilah is reduced to doing small-time work, like serving subpoenas and delivering legal papers. Even with a second job, she has little money, so she uses a sleeping bag in her office and showers at friends' houses. She has little self-confidence, and she is still grieving for her dead husband. In *Set-Up* (St. Martin's Press, 1991), Delilah is doing better financially, largely due to the help of a wealthy developer friend, Erik Lundgren. Delilah, however, loses some of her hard-won affluence by taking on the case of an antidevelopment activist accused of murder. In the tradition of California hard-boiled detectives, Delilah must fend off violent attacks during her investigations.

O'Callaghan also writes horror novels such as *Dark Time* (Diamond, 1992).

Other mystery novelists who set books in Orange County are Wendy Hornsby, Jean Femling, and A. E. Maxwell. Authors who write about Western private eyes include Sue Grafton, Karen Kijewski, Janet Dawson, Catherine Dain, Linda Grant, and Margaret Lucke.

O'Connell, Carol. Media attention and glowing reviews, as well as an Edgar nomination for Best First Novel, greeted O'Connell's debut, *Mallory's Oracle* (Putnam, 1994), and readers have responded in kind. Kathleen Mallory, the heroine of O'Connell's work, is one of the most original and compelling characters to come along in many a year. At the age of ten or eleven, street kid Kathy Mallory was trying to break into a Jaguar when homicide cop Louis Markowitz stopped her. Instead of turning her over to the juvenile authorities, Markowitz took Kathy home to his wife Helen, a gentle but fiercely protective woman who did her best to humanize this savage child of the streets. At the beginning of *Mallory's*

Oracle, Helen Markowitz has been dead of cancer for a year or so and Louis Markowitz has been found murdered at the scene of another murder, perpetrated by the serial killer known to the Big Apple as the Invisible Man. Sergeant Kathy Mallory, though she is suspended from the force, works on the case with the aid of Charles Butler, who had been exhorted by Markowitz to look after her, and Markowitz's friends in homicide. Mallory's genius with computers and her skill in hacking into practically any database are an integral part of each investigation. Kathy Mallory is enigmatic, seemingly conscienceless, and ruthless. Having met her once, readers will find it difficult to forget her.

Those who have encountered Mallory might also enjoy the work of Minette Walters, Lynn S. Hightower, and Rosamond Smith.

O'Donnell, Lillian. O'Donnell has written several series of mysteries. She began her best-known series, the Norah Mulcahaney mysteries, with *The Phone Calls* (Putnam, 1972). In the story, young widows receive threatening anonymous phone calls and are driven to commit suicide. Norah is a young policewoman with good instincts who gets a chance to prove herself on the case. Norah starts at the bottom of the New York City police force, and eventually she is promoted into homicide. She is a perceptive, honest cop who is devoted to what she calls The Job. Norah grows and changes in her personal life, as well as her career, over the years depicted in the books. She always works in homicide, except in *Leisure Dying* (Putnam, 1976), where she sets up a Senior Citizens Task Force within the police department. Norah is one of the first strong policewomen who care deeply about their careers to be depicted in mystery fiction. The Norah Mulcahaney books are well-done, methodical, detailed police procedurals. O'Donnell often uses contemporary news items, like the stories of mugging victims who shoot their assailants, or a teacher who hires teenagers to kill her husband, to add verisimilitude to her books. She also creates realistic New York City settings for her crime novels.

O'Donnell also is writing a series featuring Mici Anhalt, a compassionate young caseworker for the Crime Victims Compensation Board. The first novel in this series is *Aftershock* (Putnam, 1977). Again, O'Donnell creates vibrant New York backgrounds to go with her detailed exposition of Anhalt's daily workload.

O'Donnell's newest mystery series features New York private eye

Gwenn Ramadge, who is somewhat reminiscent of P. D. James's character, Cordelia Gray. The first book in the series is *A Wreath for the Bride* (Putnam, 1990).

Readers also may want to try Sue Dunlap's Jill Smith novels; Margaret Maron's Lt. Sigrid Harald novels; L. V. Sims's Dixie Struthers mysteries; and the police procedurals of Dorothy Uhnak and Katherine V. Forrest. For a view of a very different police-woman, try Julie Smith's Skip Langdon books.

Oleksiw, Susan. Oleksiw writes quintessentially cozy New England mysteries. *Murder in Mellingham* (Scribner, 1993) begins the series and introduces Oleksiw's protagonist, police chief Joe Silva of Mellingham, Massachusetts. He is in his late forties, a thoughtful, sensitive police officer who appreciates the slow pace and atmosphere of a small town. Mellingham has many wealthy citizens, and murder occurs in this first novel at a party in a rich couple's home. The victim is hated by everyone at the party, and they all have secrets to hide from the police. Oleksiw develops the motives and opportunity of each suspect in a leisurely and time-honored fashion. *Double Take* (Scribner, 1994) concerns the murder of an unpopular work-study student at the local art college. Oleksiw carefully establishes the daily life of the college and its students and faculty, and shows how they fit into the life of Mellingham. Then only when murder occurs does Joe Silva come into the picture to solve the mystery. In *Family Album* (Scribner, 1995), a retired man who volunteered his time at a local history museum is murdered. Oleksiw furnishes her book with rich particulars of the heirloom furniture and paintings that may be handed down in old Yankee families, and the handworked lace made in many Portuguese immigrant families. In addition, she paints a detailed picture of a small New England town and how the local residents—the rich, the poor, and the middle class—live there.

Other mysteries with a traditional New England flavor have been written by Nancy Pickard, Sally Gunning, B. Comfort, Leslie Meier, Dorian Yeager, and Charlotte MacLeod. Phoebe Atwood Taylor's Cape Cod mysteries are classics from an earlier era.

Oliphant, B. J./Orde, A. J. Oliphant is a pseudonym for science fiction writer Sheri S. Tepper, who writes a second mystery series under the pseudonym A. J. Orde.

Oliphant's series character is crusty and intrepid Colorado rancher Shirley McClintock, who debuted in *Dead in the Scrub* (Fawcett, 1990), which was an Edgar nominee for Best Paperback Original. After spending a number of years in Washington, D.C., in an influential position, the fifty-something, six-foot-two Shirley has returned to the ranch her parents left her. Intolerant of fools, with a razor-sharp mind, Shirley is a natural when it comes to ferreting out the truth behind mysterious deaths. Shirley also has strong opinions on many subjects, and she gives these opinions free rein in each book.

Oliphant/Orde's other series character, Jason Lynx, is much the same in this regard. Writing as Orde, the author has created another complex and intriguing character. Mysteriously orphaned, Lynx was taken in as an adolescent by a well-to-do Jewish businessman, who has turned his interior design business over to Jason when the series begins with *A Little Neighborhood Murder* (Doubleday, 1990). In the third book of the series, *Death for Old Times' Sake* (Doubleday, 1992), Orde finally reveals the secret of Lynx's past. Literate and thought-provoking, both these series offer rewarding reading.

Those who've enjoyed the work of Oliphant/Orde might try the series written by M. K. Lorens, Mary Monica Pulver, and P. M. Carlson. In addition to hiding behind initials, these authors also specialize in complex and intense characters with strongly held opinions. Readers looking for mysteries with Colorado settings should try the work of Diane Mott Davidson and Yvonne Montgomery.

O'Marie, Sister Carol Anne. Perhaps the only nun actively publishing crime fiction, Sister Carol Anne has created a popular character in her nun detective, Sister Mary Helen. At seventy-five, Sister Mary Helen is nominally retired, but in her first appearance, *A Novena for Murder* (Scribner, 1984), the good sister is anything but retired, as she pokes her nose into the murder of a history professor at Mount St. Francis College for Women in San Francisco. With the wisdom and wit that has come from fifty years of service to her order, Sister Mary Helen and her cohorts, the other nuns and San Francisco homicide detectives Kate Murphy and Dennis Gallagher, solve the murder. Sister Mary Helen, who loves murder mysteries and disguises them with her prayerbook cover, is a charming character. Like other older women sleuths, the good sister proves that age does not necessarily diminish one's capacities, and in this case, certainly, age has provided a thorough understanding of human nature and its many foibles and follies.

Ralph McInerny, creator of the Father Dowling series, writes a series of mysteries featuring Sister M. T. Dempsey under the pen name Monica Quill. English writer Veronica Black is currently writing a series with a nun as the detective. Other clerical mysteries of interest are the series of D. M. Greenwood and Kate Charles. Readers looking for active, older women sleuths might try the works of Virginia Rich and Stefanie Matteson.

Orde, A. J.   See **Oliphant, B. J.**

P

Padgett, Abigail. Padgett is a former court investigator who writes mysteries about children in danger. Her protagonist, Bo Bradley, is a child abuse investigator, and she suffers from a manic-depressive illness. Bo is a strongly evoked character who speaks in a voice unique in mystery fiction. The series begins with *Child of Silence* (Mysterious, 1993), an eerie story about child abuse. A child is found abandoned in a ruined house on an Indian reservation outside San Diego. Bo is assigned to his case, and she recognizes that the child is deaf. The killers who are after the child come after Bo, too. Bo recognizes the signs of an impending manic attack, and tries to stave it off until she can get the child to safety and find his attacker. This is a highly unusual story and heroine, and Padgett's tale is rendered lyrically and suspensefully. It was nominated for an Agatha Award for Best First Novel. Padgett's second novel, *Strawgirl* (Mysterious, 1994), was on the Los Angeles *Times*'s list of the ten best mysteries of 1994. A small girl is raped and dies, and Bo is sent to take the older sister into protective custody. The police assume that the mother's boyfriend, who is a member of a cult, must have done it. Bo is joined in her investigation by Dr. Andrew LaMarche, a Cajun pediatric surgeon who often treats abused children. Bo makes a good sleuth; her illness makes her so aware of the details of her surroundings that she picks up very quickly on small impressions and nonverbal cues. She is delicately poised and alert to people's nuances. In *Turtle Baby* (Mysterious, 1995), a Mayan baby who has been poisoned is brought to a San Diego hospital. Bo finds that the mother is living in Mexico and boarding the baby in the U.S. As she digs deeper into the case, she learns more about Mayan life, and she struggles with the beliefs of a culture very different from her own. The Bo Bradley novels are very intense books, hard to read lightly, but well worth the effort.

Carol O'Connell and Nancy Pickard write movingly of mental illness. Julie Robitaille and Janice Steinberg write mysteries with San Diego settings.

Page, Katherine Hall. Winner of the Agatha for Best First Novel for *The Body in the Belfry* (St. Martin's Press, 1990), Page has quickly become a favorite with readers of the traditional mystery. Page's series character is Faith Sibley Fairchild, the daughter of a minister and now married to a minister and living in the small Massachusetts town of Aleford. Before her marriage, Faith had been an exclusive caterer in Manhattan. She's making an adjustment to life in a small town with her husband Tom and their small son Ben. Something of a food snob, Faith is nevertheless a charming character as she comments inwardly on the food habits of her fellow townspeople and other amusing information about small-town life. Page handles the conventions of the traditional mystery novel, with its enclosed setting and relatively small cast of characters, very well. The atmosphere of the small town is an effective backdrop for the series, though Page often takes her characters farther afield: to Maine in *The Body in the Kelp* (St. Martin's Press, 1991) and to France in *The Body in the Vestibule* (St. Martin's Press, 1992). Page has recently begun a series of juvenile mysteries, also set in Aleford, with a trio of young girls who solve mysteries. First in the series is *Christie & Company* (Avon, 1996).

Another mystery series with culinary associations is the work of the late Virginia Rich. Janet Laurence, Diane Mott Davidson, and Joanne Pence all write series whose main characters are caterers or cooks. For small-town New England or suburban Northeastern flavor, readers might try Sally Gunning, B. J. Morison, or Valerie Wolzien.

Paige, Robin. See **Albert, Susan Wittig.**

Papazoglou, Orania. See **Haddam, Jane.**

Paretsky, Sara. Along with Sue Grafton, Paretsky is one of the few American women mystery writers who consistently receives serious critical attention and acclaim for her novels. She has revolutionized the genre with her creation of the independent private eye, V. I. Warshawski, and her bleak settings in corrupt and grimy industrial Chicago. One does not read Paretsky for an escape into a Christie-style intellectual puzzle; the reader instead is grabbed by the throat in the first chapter and dragged into Warshawski's world of injustice, pollution, and vicious urban politicking. V. I., like her male counterparts in hard-boiled novels, follows the tradition of packing a gun, drinking whiskey neat, and operating as a lone wolf to right wrongs. But she transcends the stereotypes by virtue of being a fully rounded character with her own failings, idiosyncrasies, and strengths. The crimes she solves are generally not simple individual antisocial acts; each book reflects a social problem about which Warshawski can exercise her legendary anger and frustration.

The first Warshawski book is *Indemnity Only* (Dial Press, 1982). Paretsky worked in the insurance industry for many years, and she began her series of mysteries by telling a strong story of insurance fraud. In later novels, Warshawski investigates arson, environmental offenses, and medical crimes.

Blood Shot (Delacorte, 1988), published in Great Britain as *Toxic Shock* (London: Gollancz, 1988), won the British Crime Writers' Association Silver Dagger Award in 1988. Paretsky founded and was the first president of the Sisters in Crime organization. She has edited the short story anthology *A Woman's Eye* (Delacorte, 1991), and has written her own volume of short stories featuring V. I. in *Windy City Blues* (Delacorte, 1995).

Admirers of Paretsky should certainly try the works of Sue Grafton. Other writers of interest are Marcia Muller, the originator of the hard-boiled female private eye genre; Linda Barnes, whose protagonist Carlotta Carlyle is a remarkable creation; Karen Kijewski; Catherine Dain; Gloria White; and Liza Cody and Gillian Slovo for a view of hard-boiled British PIs.

Paul, Barbara. Paul is a former English and drama teacher who has directed plays as well. Many of her mysteries have theatrical backgrounds, including her series of three opera mysteries with En-

179

rico Caruso and Geraldine Farrar as amateur sleuths. They are *A Cadenza for Caruso* (St. Martin's Press, 1984), *Prima Donna at Large* (St. Martin's Press, 1985), and *Chorus of Detectives* (St. Martin's Press, 1987). These mysteries share New York City historical backgrounds, memorable characterizations of celebrities, and an operatic back-stage ambience.

In *The Renewable Virgin* (Scribner, 1985), Paul writes about a series of crimes that entangle three very different women. The char-acters of Marian Larch, a police detective; Kelly Ingram, a television actress; and Fiona Benedict, a history professor, are drawn clearly through their first-person reflections on the crimes. Paul is now writing a continuing series with Marian Larch, in which her career grows and changes.

In her later books, Paul often creates plots that feature manip-ulative, Machiavellian characters. She is excellent at characterizing the sort of fiendishly self-obsessed people among whom murder seems liable to brew. *He Huffed and He Puffed* (Scribner, 1989) has no positive characters, just crafty connivers deceiving each other and outwitting each others' complex plans. A. J. Strode is attempt-ing to buy shares from three people so he can close down a business competitor. He tries to blackmail them when he discovers that each of the three has gotten away with murder. His victims get together and conceive a detailed plan to murder him. The novel is funny and wonderfully nasty, just like its characters. Paul has a distinct talent for creating vivid villains.

Other musical mysteries include the works of Janet Neel, Lucille Kallen, and Audrey Peterson. Marian Babson writes cozy mysteries with amusing, distinctive characters, and Sarah Caudwell's humor-ous mysteries are memorable.

Pence, Joanne. Native San Franciscan Pence, who holds a mas-ter's degree in journalism from the University of California at Berkeley, is the creator of sassy culinary sleuth Angelina Amalfi. The youngest daughter of a wealthy San Francisco Italian family, Angie is charming, impulsive, and a little too rich for her own good. In her first appearance, *Something's Cooking* (HarperPaperbacks, 1993), Angie is writing a food column for a Bay Area weekly paper when one of her contributors turns up dead. Plus, someone is trying to do some very nasty things to Angie. Enter handsome, enigmatic homicide cop Paavo Smith, and the recipe is just right for romance *and* suspense. As Angie and Paavo warily get to know each other, they find themselves butting heads over the solving of the crime. Their relationship continues in *Too Many Cooks* (HarperPaperbacks, 1994), when Angie is working for a chef who has a local radio show. The murders in this series are spiced with the prickly romance between Angie and Paavo.

Readers who enjoy a mixture of romance and suspense might also try the works of Sherryl Woods and Kay Hooper. Those looking for a culinary twist should read Camilla T. Crespi/Trella Crespi, Katherine Hall Page, and Diane Mott Davidson.

Perry, Anne. The Victorian era offers a rich vein of subject matter for the writer, and Perry brings her novelist's imagination and sensitivity to two series of novels set in this fascinating and complex period of English history. The longer-running series, set during the mid- to late 1880s, features Inspector Thomas Pitt and his wife Charlotte, who has come down in the world by marrying a humble policeman. Having forsaken her comfortable upper-middle-class lifestyle after the first novel in the series, *The Cater Street Hangman* (St. Martin's Press, 1979), the intelligent and socially conscious Charlotte aids her educated and sensitive husband in all his cases. Using her own family connections as an entrée to the homes of the wealthy and powerful, Charlotte, often assisted by her sister Emily (who married as far up the social scale as Charlotte married down), pokes her nose into the secrets of the Victorian upper crust. In the second series, set in the mid-1850s after the end of the Crimean War, the main characters are Inspector William Monk and nurse Hester Latterly. In the brilliant debut of this series, the Agatha-nominated *The Face of a Stranger* (Fawcett Columbine, 1990), Monk awakes in hospital having no memory of who he is. Confronted by a brutal murder case and a superior who would enjoy his disgrace, Monk struggles to solve the mystery of his own identity along with the murder. In both series, Perry takes a keen sense of social justice and unsparingly lays bare all the hypocrisy and injustice of Victorian England, when a minute percentage of the population literally held the power of life and death over the vast majority. Perry's later works, such as *Belgrave Square* (Fawcett Columbine, 1992) and *A Dangerous Mourning* (Fawcett Columbine, 1992), are particularly compelling. In Perry's hands, the joining of social commentary, mystery plot, and historical novel means compelling reading.

Other novelists who use the Victorian era as a setting are Amy Myers and Carole Nelson Douglas. Taking a slightly different part of the realm for her series, Alanna Knight writes an unusual series set in Victorian Edinburgh. Gillian Linscott, in her series about suffragette Nell Bray, writes about Edwardian England.

Peters, Elizabeth/Michaels, Barbara. The legendary and prolific Barbara Mertz uses two pseudonyms for her books: Elizabeth Peters and Barbara Michaels. She has also written nonfiction books on Egyptology under her own name.

Under the Peters name, Mertz has created the series characters of Vicky Bliss, art historian; Jacqueline Kirby, librarian; and Amelia Peabody, Victorian archaeologist and adventurer. The Peters books are generally humorous and lively, with strong-willed and appealing heroines who find mysteries in exotic locations. Peters's first novel was *The Jackal's Head* (Meredith, 1968).

The first Jacqueline Kirby book is *The Seventh Sinner* (Dodd, Mead, 1972). Kirby is a middle-aged woman who thoroughly enjoys her forays into adventure and mystery. In *Die for Love* (Congdon & Weed, 1984), for example, she decides to make money by writing a swashbuckling romance novel and ends up at a romance convention by way of doing research. A hilarious satire on the excesses of the genre ensues, as does murder and a bit of romance for Jacqueline herself.

The first Vicky Bliss novel is *Borrower of the Night* (Dodd, Mead, 1973). Vicky is tall, voluptuous, and smart; she works in a museum in Germany and has occasional adventures with the mysterious Sir John Smythe, a charming rogue and art forger. Vicky appears for an Egyptian adventure in the Agatha Award–nominated *Night Train to Memphis* (Warner, 1994).

The first appearance of Amelia Peabody is in *Crocodile on the Sandbank* (Dodd, Mead, 1975). These novels are particularly noteworthy for the characterizations of the intelligent and adventurous Peabody, her irascible husband, Egyptologist Radcliffe Emerson, and their precocious son Ramses.

Under the Michaels name, Mertz writes suspense novels, often with a touch of the supernatural (more than a touch in the earlier novels). The first novel that appeared under this name was *The*

Master of Blacktower (Appleton Century Crofts, 1966). The Michaels novels are often set in Maryland or Virginia. Sometimes there is a tinge of the occult, and sometimes these are full-blooded ghost stories. Especially notable are *Ammie, Come Home* (Meredith, 1968) and *Shattered Silk* (Atheneum, 1986), which are set in the same historic house in Georgetown. In their setting, they are matched bookends, yet these quite different novels show Mertz's growth as a writer and are reflective of their times: the late 1960s and the mid-1980s. Books published under the Michaels name are known for their intriguing characters and vivid settings.

Naked Once More (Warner, 1989) won the Agatha Award for Best Novel in 1990.

Other writers who may appeal to the legions of Michaels/Peters admirers include Dorothy Cannell, Sharyn McCrumb, Kathryn Lasky Knight, Margot Arnold, and Charlotte MacLeod.

Peters, Ellis. Novelist Edith Pargeter launched her mystery-writing career in the early 1950s with the novel *Fallen into the Pit* (Heinemann, 1951; Mysterious, 1994). But Pargeter fans, who were used to the author's historical novels and general fiction, were somewhat confused by the switch in genres, and thus the Peters pseudonym was born. For nearly thirty years, Ellis Peters produced excellent novels of mystery and suspense with contemporary settings, many of them featuring the Felse family. The Felses, consisting of father George, a policeman, mother Bunty, a retired opera singer, and son Dominic, star in several outstanding novels, including the Edgar Award–winning *Death and the Joyful Woman* (Doubleday, 1962). In many of her contemporary novels, Peters effectively uses her interest in music, such as in *Mourning Raga* (Morrow, 1970) or *The Horn of Roland* (Morrow, 1974).

In 1978, Peters wrote what was to be a single excursion into the historical mystery with *A Morbid Taste for Bones* (Morrow), which was based on the story of St. Winifred and the Abbey of St. Peter and St. Paul in Shrewsbury. Once the story was finished, however, the main character, the Welsh Benedictine monk Cadfael, refused to let go of his creator, and thus was born one of the most beloved of current mystery series. Weaving the actual historical events of the period, beginning in the late 1130s, through the plots of the mystery novels, Peters gives her readers a tantalizing glimpse of the medieval past. Peters does not, however, impose modern characters and modern psychology upon the period; her characters are distinctly medieval. Her long experience as a historical novelist has given Peters an unusual understanding of the complexities of medieval life, and her people are medieval to the core. The novels in the series often revolve, for example, around concepts that are peculiarly medieval, such as *The Sanctuary Sparrow* (Morrow, 1983), *The Pilgrim of Hate* (Morrow, 1984), or *The Potter's Field* (Mysterious, 1990). Peters's vivid prose, like that of Anne Perry and Lindsey Davis, conjures up the past and makes it almost tangible.

Both Kate Sedley and Margaret Frazer have recently begun series set in late-fifteenth-century England, while Candace M. Robb writes about late-fourteenth-century York, and Elizabeth Eyre has claimed Renaissance Italy with a new series. Sharan Newman writes a marvelous series set in twelfth-century France. P. C. Doherty, who writes also as Michael Clynes, Paul Harding, and C. L. Grace, offers several series set in varying periods in medieval English history.

Peterson, Audrey. Peterson is a Californian who writes traditional cozy mysteries set in England with American protagonists. In her first series, her sleuths are Jane Winfield and Andrew Quentin. Jane is an American scholar of music history, and Andrew is a professor and Jane's thesis adviser. In *Nocturne Murder* (Arbor House, 1987), Jane is in London working on a graduate fellowship in music history. She has an affair with a music critic who turns up dead in her room, and she is accused of his murder. In *Elegy in a Country Graveyard* (Pocket, 1990), Jane is writing a biography of an eminent pianist who died of AIDS. Her aunt dies suspiciously, and a long-lost cousin reappears to claim an inheritance. The settings are London and Yorkshire, and Peterson provides plenty of references to the Brontës. In her Winfield and Quentin series, Peterson has created entertaining, likable characters, including a gallery of eccentric musicians.

Peterson has started a new mystery series with *Dartmoor Burial* (Pocket, 1992). The heroine is Claire Camden, an English literature professor at a California university. Claire has commuted between California and England for the many years of her marriage to an Englishman. She is now divorced but still lives part of the year in London. In the first novel of the series, Claire is visiting her ex-mother-in-law in a small Dartmoor town where a body is found floating in a bog. Claire becomes friendly with the police inspector who is investigating the case. *Dartmoor Burial* is an atmospheric mystery with strong parallels to the plot of a Victorian novel that Claire is researching.

Readers may want to try the musically oriented mysteries of Janet Neel, Lucille Kallen, and Barbara Paul. Elizabeth George, Marian Babson, and Martha Grimes are other American writers who set their mysteries in contemporary Great Britain.

Pickard, Nancy.   Jenny Cain is the lively, thoughtful protagonist created by Pickard in her series of mysteries. Jenny's family once owned the biggest business in Port Frederick, Massachusetts (a town known locally as Poor Fred), until they closed it down in bankruptcy, throwing many out of work. Jenny is the director of a local philanthropic foundation, and many of the crimes she becomes involved with are linked to her work in evaluating and disbursing foundation grants. Her dysfunctional family haunts her, especially her mentally ill mother and her irresponsible father. Jenny marries a policeman, Geof Bushfield, and he tries with little success to protect her from the grim realities of life and crime. The mysteries are generally set in the fictional New England seaport of Port Frederick, although Jenny goes to Kansas on a case in *Bum Steer* (Pocket, 1990). *I.O.U.* (Pocket, 1991) is Pickard's most mature work to date. In this novel, Jenny tries to come to grips with the death of her mother and with the cause of her mother's long-term mental illness. It is a wise and caring book; it is also emotionally grueling but probably rewarding for readers who have experienced the death of a parent.

Pickard also has written *The 27 Ingredient Chili con Carne Murders* (Delacorte, 1993), which is based on a manuscript left by Virginia Rich at the time of her death. It is a noteworthy blending of the writing styles of Pickard and Rich, with Rich's series protagonist, 'Genia Potter, finding murder on her Arizona ranch.

Pickard won an Agatha Award for Best Novel for *Bum Steer*, both Agatha and Anthony Awards for Best Novel for *I.O.U.*, and she won a Macavity Award for *Marriage Is Murder* (Scribner, 1987). *I.O.U.* was also nominated for an Edgar Award.

The first Jenny Cain novel is *Generous Death* (Avon, 1984).

American cozy mystery writers include Carolyn G. Hart, Gillian Roberts, Virginia Rich, Sharyn McCrumb, Jane Langton, and Charlotte MacLeod.

Piesman, Marissa. Piesman's lively amateur sleuth is Nina Fischman, who is ably assisted in her snooping by her elderly and equally spirited mother, Ida Fischman. Nina is an attorney for the New York Legal Services Project for Seniors. She is thirtyish, single, and increasingly dubious about her career and her single state. Nina maintains a constant flow of humor about New York City, men, clothing, religion, money, and the obsessions of her generation. Actually, Nina can obsess neurotically about almost anything. She was a red-diaper baby (a child of two left-wing social activists) and she continually tries to reconcile her upbringing with the practices of the greedy 1980s. The first book in the series, *Unorthodox Practices* (Pocket, 1989), deals with the cutthroat New York City real estate market in affordable Manhattan apartments. In *Personal Effects* (Pocket, 1991), Nina's best friend is murdered after answering a personal ad; naturally Nina needs to find out what happened to her and who could be such a murderous date. In *Heading Uptown* (Delacorte, 1993), Nina is named the executor of the estate of her mother's best friend. The dead woman's son recently has been killed in a suspicious car crash, and Nina assumes his wife must have murdered him, since she turns up at her mother-in-law's funeral wearing a black leather miniskirt and high heels. Anyone that tacky certainly could be a murderer, Nina theorizes. Nina analyzes endlessly, and she's interested in everything around her. Nina's humor, kvetching, and self-deprecation are beautifully brought out by Piesman. A funny, observant sleuth and a strong sense of place make Piesman's books memorable.

Sparkle Hayter, Janet Evanovich, Gabrielle Kraft, and Joan Hess write humorous mysteries. The heroines of both Lia Matera's and Linda Barnes's mysteries, like Nina, were red-diaper babies and now muse humorously on their radical backgrounds. Serita Stevens and Rayanne Moore have written two mysteries featuring an elderly Jewish woman who is active and smart, like Ida Fischman.

Pincus, Elizabeth. Pincus is a former private eye who has written a series of mysteries featuring Nell Fury, a lesbian private eye in San Francisco. In *The Two-bit Tango* (Spinsters Ink, 1992), a woman comes up to San Francisco from Los Angeles to look for her missing twin sister. Since the sister is a lesbian, she wants to hire a lesbian private eye and chooses Nell. Nell is on her own now after working for an agency, and she treks determinedly through colorful San Francisco locations, looking for the sister and then her client, when she disappears as well. In this classic, almost Chandleresque plot, the twins get mixed up in an elaborate swindle, with murder, arson, a prostitution ring, organized crime, and crooked politicians all involved. In *The Solitary Twist* (Spinsters Ink, 1993), Nell gets another job looking for a woman who has disappeared. When it seems that the missing woman has been kidnapped, the search intensifies, although Nell finds both her client and the missing woman's fiancé to be highly suspicious. When Nell isn't chasing criminals, she drinks root beer, goes to a lot of movies, lives in the Mission District, and has an active sex life. She has a teenage daughter, Pinky, who lives part of the year in England and part with Nell. Nell is physically courageous and disdains the use of a gun. She is very concerned about political issues that affect lesbians and gays, and she has strong political principles. The Nell Fury novels contain fairly graphic sex and violence.

Sandra Scoppettone's Lauren Laurano mysteries are set in New York and have a protagonist who is a lesbian private eye. Other private eye novels set in San Francisco include those of Gloria White, Margaret Lucke, Marcia Muller, and Linda Grant.

Prowell, Sandra West. Prowell writes a series of mysteries with Billings, Montana, private eye Phoebe Siegel. Phoebe is a tough, stubborn, and strongly individual investigator with a troubled family past that she must confront in the impressive debut novel, *By Evil Means* (Walker, 1993). Her father was Jewish, her mother a devout Catholic, and one of her brothers is a priest. Family and religion are topics much discussed in Prowell's mysteries. Another of Phoebe's brothers was a police officer who apparently committed suicide, and when a client comes to her with a case that is connected to her dead brother, Phoebe cannot resist looking for the truth, even when it may mean more pain for her family. The client's daughter is a drug addict who seems to have gotten worse, rather than better, after treatment in a secretive facility run by a doctor who seems to keep his patients locked away from all outside influence. *By Evil Means*, which was nominated for the North American Hammett Prize, is a compulsively readable, dramatic, fast-paced mystery with a memorable heroine. Prowell's second mystery was *The Killing of Monday Brown* (Walker, 1994), and it was nominated for a Shamus Award for Best Private Eye Novel. Monday Brown is a collector and seller of Indian artifacts who is suspected of becoming a grave-robber in his zeal to find more valuable items to sell. Monday disappears, and the police think he has been killed by a local man from the Crow reservation near Billings. Sheriff's deputy Kyle Old Wolf, a friend of Phoebe's, hires her to clear his cousin of suspicion. Prowell provides good local color and an interesting view of Indian-white relations and hostility. The spiritual practices of the Crow tribe are integral to the plot, and Prowell's explanations and descriptions of the religion are fascinating. Each of the mysteries is set against a vivid Montana backdrop.

Christine Andreae and Lise McClendon set their mysteries in Montana, and Jamie Harrison's *The Edge of the Crazies* (Hyperion, 1995) and Judith Van Gieson's *Raptor* (Harper & Row, 1990) are set there as well.

Pugh, Dianne G. Pugh's mystery series is set in the fast-paced world of corporate Los Angeles, and her heroine is investment counselor Iris Thorne. Iris is an expert at making cold calls to prospective financial clients on the telephone, and she is highly successful at her job. She works every day, however, in a daunting atmosphere of sexual harassment, and she is the only professional woman in the office. In the series opener, *Cold Call* (Pocket, 1993), Iris is shocked by the murder of Alley, a deaf man who worked as a courier in her firm. Iris worked as a teacher with the deaf before getting her MBA, and she liked and understood Alley. The ambitious, uncaring yuppies in her office ignored and disdained him, but Iris noticed oddities in Alley's behavior, and she begins to poke around into curious events in the office. In *Slow Squeeze* (Pocket, 1994), Iris has achieved minor fame for her part in uncovering corporate scandals. As a result, she gets a new client, Barbie Stringfellow, a nouveau riche transplanted Southerner. Somehow, Barbie manages to become an integral part of Iris's personal and professional life, and a labyrinthine plot is set in motion. The events in this taut, suspenseful novel take place in the same time frame as the Rodney King–LAPD beating trial, and Pugh's depiction of a steadily increasing tension in the city and in her life mirrors the progress of the historic trial. The book's explosive denouement takes place on the first night of the Los Angeles riots.

A. E. Maxwell and Emma Lathen write persuasive financial mysteries, and Faye Kellerman, Teri White, and Wendy Hornsby depict gritty Los Angeles settings.

Pulver, Mary Monica/Frazer, Margaret.   A member of the Society for Creative Anachronism, which is devoted to the study of the European Middle Ages and whose members spend time in activities such as medieval tournaments and wars, Pulver has endowed her series characters with her own interests. In the first published novel of the series, *Murder at the War* (St. Martin's Press, 1987), policeman Peter Brichter and his wife Kori are traveling with friends to a field in the Pennsylvania countryside where they and fellow SCA members will hold a battle, medieval-style. In the midst of the mock battle, however, one death turns out to be real, and Peter uses his detective skills to solve the crime. The second published novel, *The Unforgiving Minutes* (St. Martin's Press, 1988), is actually the first chronologically in the series. In this novel, readers learn the true story of Katherine "Kori" Price and how she came to know Peter Brichter, and a riveting story it is. This novel demonstrates one of Pulver's strengths: the ability to create compelling and likable characters. Later novels in the series show the developing relationship between Kori and Peter. *Original Sin* (Walker, 1991) is an excellent variation on the snowbound, country-house mystery.

Recently, Pulver and a friend, Gail Bacon, have collaborated on a medieval mystery, *The Novice's Tale* (Berkley Diamond, 1992) as Margaret Frazer. This series features fifteenth-century English nun Dame Frevisse as detective. The period detail is nicely handled, and Dame Frevisse has promise to be a worthy series character.

Readers who have enjoyed Pulver might try writers like P. M. Carlson, M. K. Lorens, Kate Wilhelm, B. J. Oliphant/A. J. Orde, or Kathryn Lasky Knight, who all write series with distinctive and interesting series characters quite unlike anyone else's. Those who have read Pulver as Frazer might try the work of Ellis Peters, Kate Sedley, and Sharan Newman.

Radley, Sheila.　Her first novel, *Death in the Morning* (Scribner, 1979), marked Radley as a writer to watch develop. This novel, featuring English police detective Douglas Quantrill, set the tone for much of Radley's work to follow: fairly traditional mysteries in their framework, but with a blending of the psychological style in the vein of Rendell and James. Radley at some point worked for the postal service in a village, and her experience there has come through in her writing. Her keen eye for characters and their motivations never fail to make her novels interesting, and her ability with characterization has allowed her to experiment successfully with the traditional form of the English detective story. *A Talent for Destruction* (Scribner, 1982) is more a psychological study than a tale of detection, and the recent *This Way Out* (Scribner, 1990), though it again features Inspector Quantrill, offers an intriguing variation on Patricia Highsmith's *Strangers on a Train* (Harper, 1950). The blend of psychology and detection that is such a prominent feature of contemporary English mystery fiction at its best is a staple with Sheila Radley.

　　Those who like Radley and her village settings might also try the Wexford novels of Ruth Rendell, the work of June Thomson, who also handles the village setting with considerable skill, Caroline Graham, Jill McGown, or the novels of Lin Summerfield and Minette Walters. Both of these last writers offer intriguing variations on the English village mystery.

Redmann, J. M. This series about tough private eye Michele "Micky" Knight is set in New Orleans and its environs, and, as always, the Crescent City lends its distinctive flavor to the books. Micky, who is described as a hard-hitting, tough-talking dyke detective, conforms to this description, at least on the surface. In the course of her first appearance, *Death by the Riverside* (New Victoria, 1990), Micky must confront the demons of her own past in order to solve the case, and readers come to understand just what the tough talk serves to protect. Micky physically endures beatings that would convince many others to seek other employment, but her dedication to her work and her own pursuit of justice make her indomitable. Redmann spices the detective story with some explicit sex scenes, offbeat characters, and humor to create a mixture just right for readers looking for a Cajun surprise.

Other writers with New Orleans area settings readers might try are Julie Smith and Chris Wiltz. Readers interested in other lesbian detectives should try the work of Katherine V. Forrest, Claire McNab, and Sandra Scoppettone.

Rendell, Ruth/Vine, Barbara. She has been hailed by some critics as the best mystery writer in the English language anywhere in the world, and she is generally mentioned in the same breath as her peer and countrywoman, P. D. James, as one of the leading lights of the modern crime novel. Rendell's career began, modestly enough, in the mid-1960s, with two novels that were to set some of the patterns of her career. *From Doon with Death* (Doubleday, 1965) introduced Reginald Wexford, her popular policeman detective, and *To Fear a Painted Devil* (Doubleday, 1965) introduced readers to the psychological Rendell, one for whom the abnormal and unusual exerts a powerful fascination. Many books of both types, and many awards and laudatory reviews later, Rendell is one of the most celebrated of current crime writers. The Wexford novels in the early years followed the fairly traditional pattern of the English police detective mystery, but Rendell's skill in characterization and puzzle-making has lifted the Wexford books far above the ordinary. These same skills, plus her interest in the why of crime, have made her psychological novels, such as *A Judgment in Stone* (Doubleday, 1978), some of the most original in contemporary mystery fiction. These latter also make uncomfortable reading for some crime fiction fans who don't wish to know so much about the abnormal psychology of the criminal mind.

Lately, Rendell has written several novels under the pseudonym of Barbara Vine. These works have also attracted their share of awards and critical praise, such as *A Dark-Adapted Eye* (Bantam, 1986) and *King Solomon's Carpet* (Harmony Books, 1992). Though darker and certainly more psychological than the Wexford books, the Vine novels are often more approachable for crime fiction fans than the psychological Rendell novels. Whatever the reader's choice, Rendell has much to offer crime fiction aficionados.

Fans of the Wexford novels generally also enjoy the Adam Dalgliesh series of P. D. James. American writer Elizabeth George has a powerful appeal for English mystery lovers with her novels of English policeman Thomas Lynley. Other recommendations are the series of Cynthia Harrod-Eagles, Gwendoline Butler, Jennie Melville, Sheila Radley, and Magdalen Nabb. Those who prefer the psychological approach might try the work of Margaret Millar, Frances Hegarty, Patricia Highsmith, Rosamond Smith, Minette Walters, or Margaret Yorke.

Rich, Virginia.   The late Virginia Rich wrote only three novels, but she achieved a reputation for well-crafted classic mysteries, and her books have remained popular. Her sleuth, 'Genia Potter, is a widow and a good cook who lives part of the time in Arizona and part of the time in New England. Rich's first novel, *The Cooking School Murders* (Dutton, 1982), is set in Mrs. Potter's old hometown in Iowa. 'Genia is charmingly unassuming and warm, with a large and eccentric group of friends and neighbors. Rich writes Christie-like puzzles; she introduces the suspects in the first chapter, then sets up a murder, and she gives further details on each suspect gradually as the plot unfolds. There are plenty of cooking details and dinner parties in each story, and the plots are worked out meticulously. Another popular writer of cozy mysteries, Nancy Pickard, was commissioned to write a new 'Genia Potter book, *The 27-Ingredient Chili con Carne Murders* (Delacorte, 1993), based on a story and notes left by Virginia Rich at the time of her death.

Readers inclined toward culinary mysteries may want to sample the offerings of Diane Mott Davidson and Trella Crespi. Susan Dunlap has written a mystery set around a trendy restaurant in Berkeley, *A Dinner to Die For* (St. Martin's Press, 1987). And then, of course, there's *A Diet to Die For* (St. Martin's Press, 1989) by Joan Hess, and even *The Thin Woman,* by Dorothy Cannell.

Robb, Candace M. Fourteenth-century York is the setting for this fine series of historical mysteries from the pen of Seattle medievalist Robb. The main character in the series is the Welsh Owen Archer, once captain of the king's archers. A wartime injury, however, left Owen blind in one eye, and he chose to retire from his post. For a while, he served as a spy for the wily Duke of Lancaster, John of Gaunt, but upon Gaunt's death, Owen passed into the service of the Lord Chancellor and Archbishop of York, John Thoresby. In Thoresby's service, Owen goes to York to discover the truth behind the death of one of the archbishop's wards. The hapless victim died from a potion made by the apothecary Nicholas Wilton, and Owen goes undercover as an apprentice to Wilton in order to ferret out the truth. Wilton's lovely young wife, Lucie, herself an apothecary, soon presents Owen with a dilemma. Could he be falling in love with a murderess?

The first novel in the series is *The Apothecary Rose* (St. Martin's Press 1993). Robb offers a richly detailed background with her portrait of late medieval York, and her portrayal of Owen Archer as a passionate, intelligent, and honorable man will likely win her many fans.

Those looking for other medieval mysteries should try the works of Ellis Peters, Sharan Newman, Kate Sedley, and Margaret Frazer.

Roberts, Gillian. Judith Greber has adopted the pen name of Gillian Roberts for her series of mysteries about thirtyish Philadelphia schoolteacher Amanda Pepper. The author is a former high school English teacher, and her mysteries are full of amusing stories about the horrors of teaching English to adolescents. In the series, Amanda teaches English at Philly Prep, a school for rich, underachieving kids. Amanda is a lively and funny character, with a group of meddlesome acquaintances and family. She has something going (she's never sure exactly what) with the reticent C. K. Mackenzie, a Philadelphia cop. A recurring joke in the books is the spate of phone calls from Amanda's mother in Florida, who keeps trying to contrive ways to get her daughter married off. The first book in the series is *Caught Dead in Philadelphia* (Scribner, 1987), which won an Anthony Award for Best First Novel in 1987. *I'd Rather Be in Phila-*

delphia (Ballantine, 1992) is about wife-beating and is the most serious and harrowing book so far in the series. Its structure is that of the average person who finds evidence that a crime will be committed, but doesn't know the identity of either the criminal or the victim, as in the classic *Warrant for X* (Doubleday, 1938) by Philip MacDonald.

Other distinctive character studies may be found in the works of Nancy Pickard, Janet LaPierre, Meg O'Brien, Jane Dentinger, and Marissa Piesman. Jane Haddam, Donna Huston Murray, and Lisa Scottoline use Philadelphia settings in many of their mysteries.

Roberts, Lora/Smith, Lora R. Her first book, *Revolting Development* (Perseverance Press, 1988), was written under her own name of Lora Roberts Smith. It is set in Palo Alto, and the protagonist is Bridget (Biddy) Montrose, a young mother and aspiring writer. She finds a body one day in a dumpster outside a new real estate development and becomes involved willy-nilly in murder. Officially on the case is policeman Paul Drake, who is attracted to Bridget. Bridget appears as a secondary character in later books by this author, as does Claudia, her friend and mentor.

Deciding that there were too many mystery writers named Smith, Lora Roberts abbreviated her name for her new series, also set in Palo Alto. This features Liz Sullivan, a freelance writer and avid gardener, who is homeless in the first novel, *Murder in a Nice Neighborhood* (Fawcett, 1994). Liz lives on the edge of respectability in her old VW bus, eats minimally, and buys her few clothes at thrift shops. One day she wakes up to find the body of a homeless man under her VW bus. She immediately becomes a suspect, especially when the police discover that she has already spent time in prison for an assault on her ex-husband (who had been assaulting her for years). Roberts gives readers an absorbing view of the life of the homeless. In *Murder in the Marketplace* (Fawcett, 1995), Liz's fortunes have improved somewhat, but she is still very poor. To supplement her income from writing, she takes on temp jobs and works part-time for the Census Bureau. When she is walking door-to-door for the census, she finds the body of a woman she knows from her temporary data entry job. To further complicate her life, her runaway teenage niece comes to live with her. Roberts portrays Liz's daily life as an abstemious but interesting one, with an active mental existence and many material choices forced by poverty.

D. B. Borton often deals with the issue of homelessness in her series of mysteries, and Carole Berry's books feature a protagonist who works at temporary jobs and solves crimes.

Robinson, Lynda S.   She writes award-winning historical romances as Suzanne Robinson, but for her series of historical mysteries set in ancient Egypt, she chose to write as Lynda. Robinson earned a Ph.D. in anthropology, with a concentration in archaeology, from the University of Texas at Austin. The first novel in the series is *Murder in the Place of Anubis* (Walker, 1994), and the main character is the Lord Meren, an adviser to young Pharaoh Tutankhamen in the Egypt of the Eighteenth Dynasty. Lord Meren holds the title The Eyes and Ears of the King, and, as such, he serves as a chief of intelligence, rooting out palace conspiracies that could topple the reign of the young king. In the first novel, the murder of a scribe offers Lord Meren a complicated puzzle to solve. Not only does he have to find out whodunit, Lord Meren has to keep his job, for there are many who would like to see him disgraced. The series is full of the color and panoply of ancient Egypt, and readers looking for enjoyable historical mysteries will find much to entertain them here.

Readers interested in other works set in ancient Egypt might look for the works of writers Pauline Gedge and Anton Gill; Agatha Christie wrote one mystery set in ancient Egypt, *Death Comes as the End*. Otherwise, readers might try the works of Lindsey Davis and Steven Saylor, both of whom use Roman history as the backdrop for their series.

Rosenberg, Nancy Taylor.   Rosenberg is a former police investigator and probation officer who now writes legal thrillers. Her first, *Mitigating Circumstances* (Dutton, 1993), stars Lily Forrester, a workaholic assistant district attorney in Ventura County in Southern California. She has a young daughter, a disintegrating marriage, and a new promotion to be head of the sex crimes division. When she begins to have an affair with a colleague, her husband throws her out. Lily moves into a new house, and the first night she and her daughter stay there turns into a night of unmitigated terror. Rosenberg creates an atmosphere of menace for the average person, and near chaos in the criminal justice system.

This sense of the imminent breakdown of order and the escalation of violence in society also permeates her second suspense novel, *Interest of Justice* (Dutton, 1993). The life of Judge Lara Sanderstone, the protagonist, is changed completely when her sister and brother-in-law are killed brutally. She takes in her nephew and tries to find her sister's killer. Her sister had been working as a hooker with her husband as her pimp, and the mystery seems to revolve around some photographs that they had been using to blackmail someone who could be a major figure in the court system.

Rosenberg switches gears a bit with *First Offense* (Dutton, 1994). Ann Carlisle is a tough probation officer and former police officer who is attacked one day on the street for no apparent reason. She has an emotionally troubled son, and her husband, a highway patrolman, has been missing for four years. This novel, like the others, does contain graphic sex and violence.

Darian North, Lisa Scottoline, and Mimi Lavenda Latt have written popular legal thrillers.

Ross, Kate. Regency dandy Julian Kestrel is the hero in this series of historical mysteries by Boston trial lawyer Ross. A genteel, impoverished man-about-town in London society in the early nineteenth century, Kestrel is a young man of keen intelligence and mysterious background. In his first appearance, *Cut to the Quick* (Viking, 1993), Kestrel rescues young Hugh Fontclair from a sticky situation in a gaming house, and Fontclair asks him to be best man at his wedding. The families of bride and groom, however, are at loggerheads, and soon murder disrupts the festivities. Aided by his Cockney manservant, Dipper, a reformed pickpocket, Kestrel solves the mystery. In *A Broken Vessel* (Viking, 1994), Dipper's sister Sally, a prostitute, is the link among suspects in a very puzzling case, and Kestrel finds Sally an intriguing riddle in herself. Ross has a keen sense of the period, both in her exquisitely wrought backgrounds and in her well-drawn characters. The rough-and-tumble world of Regency society, in all its glamour and its squalor, provides Ross a delightful canvas for her work. Readers of historical fiction who lament the passing of the late, great Georgette Heyer need look no further than Kate Ross for a worthy successor.

Readers who have enjoyed Ross's work should also read the novels of Anne Perry, Alanna Knight, Miriam Grace Monfredo, and Amy Myers for their nineteenth-century flavor.

Rothenberg, Rebecca. Rothenberg's mysteries feature botanist and amateur sleuth Claire Sharples. *The Bulrush Murders* (Carroll & Graf, 1991) was nominated for both Agatha and Anthony Awards for Best First Novel, and its unusual use of local color and deft characterizations make it a memorable mystery. Claire moves to the rural San Joaquin Valley of Central California from the Boston area, and she suffers severe culture shock. She had a purely theoretical laboratory job at MIT, and now she is catapulted abruptly into practical fieldwork at a University of California agricultural extension station. She learns firsthand about the effects of pesticides on farmworkers and can see what real agricultural problems are like and what applications may come of her research work. She meets Sam Cooper, the local expert on stone fruit, and it takes her a while to see beyond his nerdy exterior to the possibility of a relationship. Claire learns about rural valley life and becomes interested in its native plants, knowledge that comes in handy when she becomes involved in murder. In *The Dandelion Murders* (Mysterious, 1994), Claire is having troubles in her relationship with Sam. She moves into a cheap motel room in the barrio where a murder victim had been staying. As she lives there and talks to locals about the murder, she learns more about the lives of Mexican farmworkers and about the personal effects of the use of pesticides on crops. Rothenberg provides an appealing look at the daily life of a scientist, lively characters, and fascinating botanical details in her mysteries.

John Sherwood writes a series of botanical mysteries featuring nursery owner Celia Grant. Claire's interior monologues about the state of her personal life are echoed in the works of Dianne G. Pugh, Lisa Scottoline, and Marissa Piesman.

Rowe, Jennifer. Editor of *The Australian Women's Weekly,* Rowe has made murder Down Under increasingly popular with her series of clever mysteries set in Australia. The first novel in the series, *Grim Pickings* (Bantam, 1991), which has already been a miniseries in Australia, is cast in the traditional mold. There is a good-sized cast of characters in an enclosed setting—in this case, an apple farm. The Tender family, along with various friends, has gathered to help elderly Aunt Alice gather in her crop, and immediately the tensions begin to surface. On the scene is Verity Birdwood, known as Birdie, researcher for one of the television networks, and her nimble mind makes her a natural as an amateur detective. Birdie is a prickly, difficult character. She hides her feelings, even from her best friend, Kate Delaney, who also appears throughout the series, along with her husband and daughter. The Australian setting makes a pleasing change from the usual venue of the traditional mystery, and Rowe's skill in devising intricate plots makes her work delightfully reminiscent of the best of the Golden Age detective stories. *Murder by the Book* (Bantam, 1992) offers murder in a publishing house, and the recent *Death in Store* (Doubleday, 1993), a collection of short stories featuring Birdie, demonstrates that Rowe is very much at home with the short form as well.

Readers looking for Australian settings might try the work of Arthur W. Upfield and Jon Cleary. Otherwise, writers with qualities similar to Rowe's are Jill McGown, Carolyn G. Hart, Betty Rowlands, and Paula Gosling. They all write mysteries in the traditional vein, but with decidedly modern themes.

Rowlands, Betty.   Rowlands writes traditional cozy English mysteries in her Melissa Craig series of novels. Melissa is a famous crime writer who has bought a cottage in the Cotswolds. Her next-door neighbor and friend is Iris Ash, an artist and textile designer. In the first book in the series, *A Little Gentle Sleuthing* (Walker, 1990), Melissa is learning to live independently in the countryside. Iris finds a body in the woods, and Melissa's curiosity impels her to investigate. *Over the Edge* (Walker, 1993) is set at an adult school in the south of France. A German visitor is found at the bottom of a cliff at the beginning of the novel. Was he pushed by a disturbed former member of the French Resistance who hates Germans, or by an unknown enemy with contemporary problems? Rowlands evokes the fascinating medieval and World War II history of the area as an essential element of her plot. Rowlands's mysteries are peopled with eccentric characters, and she strews her red herrings adroitly.

Readers who enjoy Rowlands should look for cozy mysteries by Carolyn G. Hart, Audrey Peterson, Hazel Holt, Kay Mitchell, Caroline Graham, and Pat Burden.

Sale, Medora. This Canadian author has a Ph.D. in medieval studies from the University of Toronto, but when she turned to a life of crime-writing, she chose as her setting contemporary Toronto. Her first novel, *Murder on the Run* (Paperjacks, 1986), won the Arthur Ellis Award for Best First Novel from the Crime Writers of Canada and introduced Inspector John Sanders of the Toronto police. In her second novel, *Murder in Focus* (Scribner, 1989), Sale introduced Sanders's companion-in-crime, architectural photographer Harriet Jeffries. The slowly developing relationship between Sanders and Jeffries, both of whom are definitely wary of emotional entanglements, is one of the chief appeals of this series. Sale handles the emotional topography of the relationship with restraint and insight. Above this, however, Sale also provides entertaining plots and an intriguing cast of secondary characters, some of whom sometimes take the lead role in the novels. An excellent example of this is *Sleep of the Innocent* (Scribner, 1991), in which Sergeant Rob Lucas investigates a murder involving an attractive young rock singer, while John and Harriet are on a disastrous vacation. This is a good, solid series that builds on the author's various strengths with each new book.

Writers looking for crime in Canada might try the work of Eric Wright, whose series of novels about Toronto cop Charlie Salter have won considerable critical acclaim, or the sports mysteries of

Canadian sports writer Alison Gordon. Edgar-winner L. R. Wright sets her mysteries on the opposite side of the country. An excellent English series is that of Cynthia Harrod-Eagles.

Sandstrom, Eve K.   A columnist and former award-winning reporter for the Lawton, Oklahoma, *Constitution*, Sandstrom uses her reporter's eye for detail to create soundly constructed puzzles as the basis for her Down Home series set in southwestern Oklahoma. Sandstrom's detectives are husband and wife Sam and Nicky Titus. Sam is an officer in the Army's Criminal Investigation Division, and Nicky is the daughter of a general. In their debut, *Death Down Home* (Scribner, 1990), the newlyweds are just moving into their new quarters in Frankfurt, Germany, when they get a call from Sam's brother, telling them that Sam's father, Big Sam, lies critically ill from a mysterious accident. Sam and Nicky immediately return to Holton, Oklahoma, to help out the family. As they make adjustments to the ranch and to small-town life, Sam and Nicky delve further into the mystery. Sam uses his skill as an army investigator, and Nicky uses hers as a photojournalist. Sandstrom writes convincingly about her people and her places, and the second novel, *The Devil Down Home* (Scribner, 1991) is an effective and entertaining tale of small-town murder and mayhem.

Another Oklahoma writer who uses the small-town setting to good advantage is Jean Hager, currently writing two series. Otherwise, readers might try the works of Carolyn G. Hart, Susan Rogers Cooper, and D. R. Meredith.

Sawyer, Corinne Holt.   Little old lady detectives have been a staple of mystery fiction almost from the beginning, and Sawyer has taken a stock character and added an enjoyable spin. Her series, set in a posh retirement community in Southern California, features not one, but two little old ladies who are nothing like stereotypes. One of the main characters is the peppery and often irritating Angela Benbow, widow of an admiral. Though she might look like a small, delicate blossom, Angela is just about as tough as old boots. Her boon companion is Caledonia Wingate, also the widow of an admiral, but physically the opposite of Angela. Tall, imposing, and never afraid to throw her considerable weight around, Caledonia serves as an effective damper on Angela's sometimes ill-conceived plans. When murder strikes their exclusive retirement community in *The J. Alfred Prufrock Murders* (Donald I. Fine, 1988), Angela, Caledonia, and a small circle of their friends decide to investigate. Eventually, the officer in charge of the case, suave and attractive—but young—Lieutenant Martinez, allows them to "help." Sawyer writes with clear eyes and no false sentimentality about the elderly. Her characters are engaging and believe, her plots solidly constructed, and her humor restrained but effectively employed. The first novel in the series was an Agatha nominee for Best First Malice Domestic Mystery Novel.

Like Sawyer, Margot Arnold, Mary Bowen Hall, E. X. Ferrars, Eleanor Boylan, and Gallagher Gray write about the elderly, proving that the skills for detecting crimes don't necessarily diminish with age. Readers who enjoy little old lady detectives might also try two of the classics, Agatha Christie's Miss Marple and Patricia Wentworth's Miss Silver.

Scoppettone, Sandra/Early, Jack. Under the pseudonym of Jack Early, Scoppettone has written three hard-boiled mysteries, which now have been reprinted under her own name. The first was *A Creative Kind of Killer* (Franklin Watts, 1984). It features Fortune Fanelli, a private eye who lives in the SoHo area of New York City. A teenager from the New Jersey suburbs is killed across the street from his apartment, and the girl's uncle hires him to investigate. Fortune is a single father of two teenagers, and is a sympathetic, charming character. As in her later novels, the author creates vivid scenes of Italian-American family life in New York. *Donato & Daughter* (Dutton, 1988) is a darkly dramatic suspense novel about a series of killings of nuns. Police lieutenant Dina Donato heads up a crime team set up for these cases and her father, Sergeant Michael Donato, assists her.

Under her own name, Scoppettone now is writing a series of mysteries with lesbian private eye Lauren Laurano. The first Lauren Laurano novel is *Everything You Have Is Mine* (Little, Brown, 1991). Lauren is a bright and observant character, and she shares her life with her long-term lover Kip, a psychotherapist. These novels are fairly hard-boiled mysteries, with humorous observations by Lauren on the foibles of humanity. They are atmospheric, with settings primarily in Greenwich Village. Lauren likes to compare herself to fictional sleuths; she often asks herself, "What would Kinsey Millhone [or another fictional detective] do?" *I'll Be Leaving You Always*

(Little, Brown, 1993) is a darker novel, with an exploration of the nature of friendship and the eternal possibility of betrayal. Scoppettone creates well-realized New York City backdrops for her stories.

Sue Grafton, J. M. Redmann, Linda Grant, Sara Paretsky, Liza Cody, and other writers have created feisty women who are private eyes. Lillian O'Donnell, Dorothy Uhnak, and Dorothy Salisbury Davis use vivid New York settings.

Scottoline, Lisa.   Like her protagonists, Scottoline is a lawyer who lives in the Philadelphia area. Her first novel, *Everywhere That Mary Went* (Harper, 1993), was nominated for an Edgar Award for Best Paperback Original. The heroine is Mary DiNunzio, a widowed lawyer. She is trying to become a partner in her law firm and the decision is imminent when she realizes that someone is harassing and stalking her. She cannot call the police and have them investigate her colleagues or she will lose her job. Scottoline's expert version of the woman-in-jeopardy novel is professional, funny, and yet emotionally complex. In *Final Appeal* (Harper, 1994), the protagonist is Grace Rossi, a part-time assistant to a chief appeals court judge, who is murdered early on in the novel. This suspenseful, well-written novel has a smart, appealing protagonist and crisp, amusing details of the working lives of legal assistants. *Final Appeal* won an Edgar Award for Best Paperback Original. Scottoline's gift for vivid characterizations appears again in *Running from the Law* (HarperCollins, 1995). Rita Morrone is an assertive, tough lawyer who will do practically anything to win, and she plays at the edge with her ethics and honesty. Her father, Vito, and his old friends have taught her to play poker avidly, too, and Rita treats her legal arguments as though they are poker games. But one day she chooses to represent her lover's father, a judge, in a sexual harassment case, and discovers that someone, perhaps the chess-playing judge, is setting her up for a fall. Scottoline creates marvelous secondary characters in the three old men who are poker buddies with her and her father, and who are anxious to help Rita play the ultimate game of outwitting a murderer.

Readers may want to try legal mysteries by Lia Matera, Carolyn Wheat, Janet L. Smith, Mimi Lavenda Latt, Marissa Piesman, and Darian North. Gillian Roberts, Mary McMullen, Donna Huston

Murray, and Jane Haddam have written mysteries set in Philadelphia.

Sedley, Kate. Medieval England is becoming increasingly popular as a setting for mystery fiction, and Sedley's new series takes as its time frame a particularly turbulent era of English history, the Wars of the Roses. This period of political strife affords the author excellent opportunity to weave tales of murder into the fabric of history, as Ellis Peters does with her series set just over three centuries earlier. Sedley's detective is Roger the Chapman, a young man who had been sent as a novice to the Benedictine monastery at Glastonbury by his widowed mother. But Roger felt the call of the world outside the abbey, so he left the cloisters and eventually ended up as a chapman, or peddler. Following this trade, Roger can travel around England as he pleases. In the first of the series, *Death and the Chapman* (St. Martin's Press, 1992), the year is 1471. While the York-Lancaster war rages on, Roger agrees to look for a wealthy young man who disappeared in London. Along the way, Roger becomes acquainted with Richard, Duke of Gloucester, the future Richard III, and does the duke a service. The duke calls upon Roger for help in the second book, *The Plymouth Cloak* (St. Martin's Press, 1993), and thus Sedley establishes a strong link for her detective with the troubled figure of Richard III. Sedley handles the period detail with ease, and her sleuth, Roger, is an amiable and intelligent protagonist.

Fans of the medieval mystery are certainly acquainted with Brother Cadfael and his creator, Ellis Peters. Other writers of medieval mysteries are Elizabeth Eyre, Margaret Frazer, Sharan Newman and P. C. Doherty, who writes under three additional names, Michael Clynes, C. L. Grace, and Paul Harding.

Shankman, Sarah. She began her life in crime as Alice Storey, to separate the criminous Storey from the mainstream fiction-writing Shankman, at an editor's insistence. Thus the first two novels in her Samantha Adams series, *First Kill All the Lawyers* (Pocket, 1988) and *Then Hang All the Liars* (Pocket, 1989), were published under the Storey name. Sam Adams is a journalist, born and bred in Atlanta. After the death of her policeman lover in San Francisco, the formerly hard-drinking Sam has returned to her native Atlanta, where she now works for the *Constitution*. The two Storey novels are thoroughly enjoyable stories with a nicely realized setting and interesting characters. But with the switch back to her real name with the third novel of the series, *Now Let's Talk of Graves* (Pocket, 1990), Shankman's full voice unleashed itself, and the result was a wickedly funny novel. Set in New Orleans during Mardi Gras, *Graves* is a veritable feast of eccentric characters, pitch-perfect Southern dialogue, and a rollicking plot that keeps the reader gasping with laughter and guessing till the end. The fourth novel, *She Walks in Beauty* (Pocket, 1991), peeks behind the scenes at the Miss America pageant, and Atlantic City will never be the same. Shankman gives the reader an unusual combination of unsparingly satiric humor and a keen eye for the often absurd contradictions of the contemporary South. Her work is evolving into her own unique style of crime novel.

Like Shankman, Joan Hess has a satiric eye and pen with her Maggody series. Those who enjoy the Atlanta setting should try the works of Celestine Sibley and Kathy Hogan Trocheck. Meg O'Brien writes a series about another hard-edged journalist. Readers who have enjoyed Shankman's view of the modern South might try the New Orleans series of Julie Smith and Chris Wiltz as well, though they are much harder-edged than Shankman.

Shannon, Dell. See **Linington, Elizabeth.**

Shepherd, Stella. Before turning full-time to writing, Shepherd studied medicine and worked as a doctor specializing in radiotherapy. She brings her knowledge of medicine to her series of mysteries featuring Inspector Richard Montgomery of Nottingham CID. In the first book, *Black Justice* (Doubleday, 1989), the action is centered around the murder of a young doctor, which occurs during a weekend meeting of the Medieval Circle. This society is made up of mostly amateurs interested in the Middle Ages, and some of the amateurs are colleagues at a Nottingham hospital. The action in the second book, *Murderous Remedy* (Doubleday, 1990), takes place in a Nottingham teaching hospital, but in the third book, *Thinner Than Blood* (Doubleday, 1992), Shepherd has moved out of the hospital into the village. Shepherd's medical knowledge plays a strong role in the methods of murder; various drugs are used in devious and effective ways, and Shepherd paints an interesting picture of medical life and culture in England. She reveals bits and pieces of the life of her main character and his subordinates as the series unfolds, in time-honored English police procedural fashion.

Readers looking for the combination of the medical world and the mystery should try P. D. James, whose own work in hospitals has given her extensive knowledge of the milieu, and the two series of American writer Mary Kittredge. Other good English traditional mystery writers in much the same vein as Shepherd are E. X. Ferrars, Anthea Fraser, and Ann Cleeves (with her series about Inspector Ramsay).

Sibley, Celestine.   The veteran Atlanta reporter Sibley may well hold the record for the number of years between debut and second appearance of a mystery series character. Sibley's first murder mystery was *The Malignant Heart* (Doubleday, 1958), which featured as its detective a young reporter, Katherine "Katy" Kincaid. Someone has murdered a powerful woman columnist at Katy's paper, and Katy is a suspect. The policeman investigating the crime is Katy's childhood chum, Lieutenant Benjamin Mulcay, and muted sparks fly between them until the crime is solved. When Katy makes her second appearance, it is as the widowed Kate Mulcay in *Ah, Sweet Mystery* (HarperCollins; 1991). In the thirty-three years between her appearances, Kate has married and lost her beloved Benjy. She is still a reporter, writing a thrice-weekly column for an Atlanta newspaper and living in a log cabin in a tranquil and sparsely populated suburb of Atlanta. Then one of Kate's neighbors, a beloved elderly woman friend, confesses to the murder of her own obnoxious stepson, and Kate becomes involved in sorting out the mess. Kate is sensible, albeit stubborn, altogether an attractive character. Sibley's depiction of the modern South is adroit, and fans of the regional crime story will find much to enjoy.

Other reporter-detectives whom readers might enjoy are Samantha Adams (created by Sarah Shankman), Kate Henry (created by sports journalist Alison Gordon), and Henrietta O. Collins (the new series character created by Carolyn G. Hart). Readers looking for an Atlanta setting might try some of the works of Patricia H. Sprinkle, Kay Hooper, and Kathy Hogan Trocheck.

Simonson, Sheila.   Simonson, a college teacher, wrote Regency romances before publishing her first mystery, *Larkspur* (St. Martin's Press, 1990). Her series protagonist, Lark Dailey, owns a bookstore in a small town in Northern California. Lark is a former Olympic-level basketball player who coaches basketball part-time. Lark's mother is a poet, and in the first novel, Lark and her friend Jay Dodge go to a Fourth of July gathering at the country house of a legendary poet. Murder ensues, and Jay, a policeman, investigates with Lark's help. *Skylark* (St. Martin's Press, 1992) takes place in 1989, and it reflects dramatic political events of the time like terrorism, glasnost, and the threats against Salman Rushdie. Lark has gone to London for a booksellers' convention. A Czech dissident is attacked on the Underground, and Lark and her friend end up with some of his crucial papers. Murder ensues in their building, and they are inevitably involved. Lark has married Jay, who has left the police force to become a community college instructor, and he joins them in London. Simonson offers an intelligent, literate American tourist's view of London, and hints of international intrigue. In *Mudlark* (St. Martin's Press, 1993), Jay is on sabbatical and is setting up police training courses at a community college while Lark takes a year off to try to get pregnant. They have moved to a small town on the coast in Washington, and the descriptions of life in a northwestern beach town are detailed and evocative. A woman is found dead on the beach, and police suspect her ex-husband, who is Lark's neighbor. Simonson has created appealing characters in Lark and Jay, and her charming settings add to the appeal of these cozy, entertaining novels.

Joan Hess (in her Claire Malloy series), Carolyn G. Hart (in her Annie Laurance books), and M. K. Wren have bookseller protagonists.

Simpson, Dorothy. Her first novel, *Harbingers of Fear* (London: Macdonald, 1977), was suspense; her second, *The Night She Died* (Scribner, 1981), was an English police procedural in the traditional vein. With this traditional series, starring policeman Luke Thanet, however, Simpson found a special place in contemporary mystery fiction. Thanet is an ordinary family man with a wife and two children. As the series begins, Thanet's wife Joan is at home with two young children, and as the series progresses, the reader watches the natural growth and evolution of the Thanet family. This core of ordinariness, with a series character grappling with the common problems of daily life, offers a center to Simpson's fiction that is, actually, rather unusual in contemporary mystery fiction. The

Kent town of Sturrenden and its environs serve as the setting for the series. Simpson delineates her area with a loving eye and brings to her writing an excellent understanding of English urban life in the latter decades of the twentieth century. The excellent *Last Seen Alive* (Scribner, 1985) won the Silver Dagger from the British Crime Writers' Association.

Those who like their mysteries set in England's villages and smaller urban areas should try also the work of Marjorie Eccles, June Thomson, and Anthea Fraser. Pat Burden, Patricia Moyes, and Susan B. Kelly also write police procedural series in the traditional vein.

Singer, Shelley.   A former journalist and editor, Singer uses the Bay Area, where she herself lives, as the setting for her two series of mysteries.

The first series features Jake Samson, who debuted in *Samson's Deal* (St. Martin's Press, 1983). Once a cop in his native Chicago, Jake found his enthusiasm for his job waning in the wake of the 1968 riots, and he left the Midwest for California. Eventually, after several moves and several career changes, Jake settled in Oakland, where he lives off the income from a trust fund and from some rental property he owns. In the first book, Jake helps out the friend of a friend with a problem, which turns out to be solving the murder of the man's wife. Jake doesn't have a license for private investigation, but he does have a friend who's an editor for an investigative magazine who gives him press credentials so that he can nose around. Helping Jake in his investigations is his tenant, Rosie Vicente, a woman given to wearing cowboy boots and Gertrude Stein T-shirts. She also has a standard poodle named Alice B. Toklas. Jake himself is a cat lover. This series, like Jake, is pretty mellow, with the feel of somewhat other-worldly Northern California.

Recently, Singer created a new series, starring Barrett Lake, high school history teacher, who decides she'd rather become a private eye instead. Her debut is *Following Jane* (Signet, 1993).

Singer uses the Bay Area settings effectively. Her characters are genial, and the plots are engaging puzzles.

Readers who have enjoyed Singer might try the work of other Bay Area writers, like Marilyn Wallace, Susan Dunlap, Linda Grant, or Marcia Muller.

Slovo, Gillian. Slovo is an expatriate South African novelist and journalist. Her mysteries are hard-boiled stories with journalist and private eye Kate Baeier. Kate is Portuguese, plays the saxophone, and lives in a racially diverse area of London. Her politics are decidedly left-wing and her cases generally have political overtones. In the first book, *Morbid Symptoms* (Dembner, 1984), she is asked to look into the death of a fellow writer who has been doing research on South Africa. In her first three novels, Slovo provides absorbing portraits of a London full of left-wing students, squatters, poor immigrants, street markets, and high-minded communes of argumentative intellectuals.

After writing three mysteries, Slovo wrote two novels about South Africa, *Ties of Blood* (Morrow, 1990) and *The Betrayal* (London: Michael Joseph, 1991). *Facade* (London: Michael Joseph, 1993) is a novel of psychological suspense in which Laura Weber, an actor, uncovers the shadowy pasts of both her parents.

Slovo then returned to the Kate Baeier series with *Catnap* (London: Michael Joseph, 1994). Slovo's writing has matured, and her characterizations have deepened in this tale of Kate's return to London after five years as a war reporter. The vibrant London of the earlier novels has vanished; the settings and criminal activities portrayed in this novel are much darker and more violent.

Liza Cody, Sarah Dunant, and Anabel Donald also write hard-boiled tales of women detectives in London, while Val McDermid's gritty crime novels are set in Glasgow and Manchester.

Smith, Evelyn E. Smith has created, in Miss Susan Melville, perhaps the only gently bred assassin in contemporary mystery fiction. Miss Melville, descendant of a long line of Melvilles, whose family fortunes were begun by a Caribbean pirate, has fallen on hard times in the first book of the series, *Miss Melville Regrets* (Donald I. Fine, 1986). When the genteel New York school at which she teaches art must close, Miss Melville begins a downward spiral, at the nadir of which she decides to kill herself at a society function as something of a political protest. At the last moment, however, she decides to kill the speaker, an obnoxious and morally corrupt man who is the son of an old family friend. What Miss Melville didn't know was that her victim was already the target of a highly secret organization in the assassination business. Soon Miss Melville has a lucrative new career, as a highly paid assassin in New York

City, but she insists that her hits must be for persons who, for moral reasons, deserve to die. Through the eyes of Miss Melville, Smith offers mordant and humorous observations of life in contemporary New York City, with particular attention given to the foibles of the rich and pretentious. Miss Melville's life changes considerably during the course of the series, but Smith wisely makes her focus the character of Miss Melville herself. This is an unusual series, but those looking for an uncommon heroine will enjoy it.

Like Evelyn E. Smith, Joyce Christmas also sets her novels among society in the Big Apple. Other entertaining series with New York settings are those by Gallagher Gray, Jane Dentinger, Annette Meyers, and Margaret Maron.

Smith, Janet L. Smith's series character, Annie MacPherson, is, like Smith, a lawyer in Seattle. In the first book, *Sea of Troubles* (Perseverance Press, 1990), Annie and her partner Joel Feinstein have their own firm. Annie travels to a resort hotel in the San Juan islands to look into its sale for a client. The buyer's girlfriend is kidnapped, and all negotiations are halted until the case is solved. Annie learns about kayaking and whale watching while investigating the kidnapping and multiple murders. At the beginning of *Practice to Deceive* (Fawcett, 1992), Annie is returning to work from an extended leave of absence. Her partnership is merging with a much larger and more prestigious law firm, and she goes to work for the powerful and sexist Gordon Barclay. He is planning to secede from the company and take his clients with him. Smith provides plenty of back-stabbing and office politics in her insider's view of law firms. Annie is a smart, interesting character, and the legal backgrounds are as well-described as the Northwestern scenery.

Readers also may enjoy Susan Wolfe's *The Last Billable Hour*, another novel of murder and mayhem in a West Coast legal firm. Lia Matera, Carolyn Wheat, Judith Van Gieson, and Julie Smith have female series characters who are lawyers. J. A. Jance, Barbara Wilson, and Mary Daheim use Seattle settings for their crime novels, and Dana Stabenow writes about a lawyer turned investigator in Alaska.

Smith, Joan. British novelist Smith has written a series of mysteries about Loretta Lawson, a professor of English at the University of London. Loretta is a thoughtful, analytic sleuth, as well as an active feminist theoretician. The first book, *A Masculine Ending* (Scribner, 1988), involves the murder of a deconstructionist English literature professor in Paris. Loretta, assisted by her Oxford friend Bridget Bennett, looks into this murder as a matter of self-defense, since she found the body and might be a suspect. *Why Aren't They Screaming?* (Scribner, 1989) is set in Oxfordshire, where Loretta has taken a country cottage in which to recuperate from an illness. Unfortunately, she finds that the owner has turned the back garden over to a women's peace camp. Loretta gets little peace and quiet, especially when her landlady is killed. In *Don't Leave Me This Way* (Scribner, 1990), a woman Loretta knew years ago shows up on Christmas Eve in need of a place to sleep. She disappears, however, on New Year's Eve. Loretta finds out later that she's been killed in a suspicious car crash on that same night. Loretta's curiosity impels her to look into this mystery, and she is subsequently threatened and injured while engaged in her search. Smith's novels are densely written academic mysteries, and her protagonist Loretta is a deliberative, mature scholar.

Readers in search of other academic mysteries might turn to Amanda Cross, Susan Kenney, Nora Kelly, and Edith Skom. Maggie Elliott, in the mysteries of Elizabeth Atwood Taylor, is another self-reflective, intense character.

Smith, Julie.   The first Edgar Award for Best Novel given to an American woman since 1956 was awarded to Smith for *New Orleans Mourning* (St. Martin's Press, 1990).

Smith started her writing career as a journalist, then began to write mysteries with a series that featured San Francisco lawyer Rebecca Schwartz. The first Rebecca Schwartz book is *Death Turns a Trick* (Walker, 1982). Rebecca, who identifies herself as a Jewish feminist lawyer, matures in her personal approach to life and in her career throughout the series. The Schwartz novels are generally light, amusing fare, although *Dead in the Water* (Ivy, 1991) is more harrowing and violent than the earlier books.

Smith's second series of mysteries set in the Bay Area stars Paul McDonald, freelance writer and former journalist. There are two Paul McDonald novels to date; these are humorous, hard-boiled private eye novels. The first is *True-Life Adventure* (Mysterious, 1985); the second is *Huckleberry Fiend* (Mysterious, 1987).

Julie Smith's most recent crime series chronicles the adventures of Skip Langdon, a policewoman in New Orleans. Smith hit her stride as a mature writer with these novels. The first, *New Orleans Mourning*, gives the reader an insider's view of Mardi Gras and particularly its high-society participants. Skip Langdon is a fully rounded, believable character; readers learn about her neuroses, weaknesses, and insecurities, as well as her talent as an investigator. She is confident and skilled in her job, but she feels awkward about almost everything else. The Garden District social background that Skip grew up in has been of assistance in her crime-solving, even though she felt out of place there and has abandoned that life to become a cop. The second Skip Langdon novel is *The Axeman's Jazz* (St. Martin's Press, 1991); it's another excellent examination of New Orleans murders. This time a serial killer is repeating the modus operandi of a legendary killer from earlier in the century. Smith brings a vivid, bawdy, drunken, and hedonistic New Orleans to life in her novels, but she also captures the inner lives and motives of the natives of this city as well as other Southerners.

Other San Francisco lawyers appear in the works of Lia Matera and Chelsea Quinn Yarbro. Mysteries set in New Orleans include Sarah Shankman's *Now Let's Talk of Graves* (Pocket, 1990) and the novels of Chris Wiltz. Lillian O'Donnell's Norah Mulcahaney novels and Margaret Maron's Sigrid Harald novels portray the lives of policewoman, and Elizabeth George's mysteries give us psychological insights into the minds of investigators.

Smith, Lora R. See **Roberts, Lora.**

Smith, Rosamond. One of the premiere names in American belles lettres, Joyce Carol Oates, has adopted the Smith pseudonym to pen her masterful novels of psychological suspense. Like Ruth Rendell, Smith writes about disturbed personalities or about how a crime can affect the people concerned with it. In her first novel, *Lives of the Twins* (Simon & Schuster, 1987), Molly Marks finds herself intrigued with a puzzle from her lover's past. When she and her lover, a psychotherapist, move in together, he tells her that he has an identical twin brother with whom he no longer has any contact. Molly, for reasons she can't understand, seeks out her lover's twin and becomes enmeshed in a relationship with him as well. How will she get herself out of this increasingly difficult dilemma?

Another Smith novel, *Nemesis* (Dutton, 1990), probes the aftermath of an accusation of rape brought by a male graduate student against a world-famous male composer at a select New England school of music. Eventually, a murder complicates the situation, and Smith unravels the mystery with great skill. The complexities of human behavior are fertile ground for Rosamond Smith, whose work is very much in the tradition of writers like Margaret Millar and the aforementioned Ruth Rendell.

In addition to Millar and Rendell, those who have read Rosamond Smith might enjoy the suspense novels of Frances Hegarty, Patricia Highsmith, and Minette Walters.

Sprinkle, Patricia H.   The star of this series, Sheila Travis, is recently widowed when the series begins with *Murder at Markham* (St. Martin's Press, 1988). Sheila's husband, an abusive and controlling man, had been a diplomat in Japan, and Sheila's experience as a diplomatic wife wins her a job at the Markham Institute of International Studies in Chicago, which trains students for the diplomatic corps. Sheila's sleuthing skills quickly come to the fore, however, when an uneasy situation erupts into murder. Aided by her wealthy and charming elderly Aunt Mary, Sheila sorts out the situation. Subsequent books find Sheila moving back to her native South. In *Murder in the Charleston Manner* (St. Martin's Press, 1990), Sheila goes to South Carolina to aid an old school friend of Aunt Mary's. Recent books find Sheila, who grew up in Japan, living and working in Atlanta for a large Japanese corporation. Sprinkle writes about the Southern setting and her mostly Southern characters with warmth and understanding. The mood of the stories is definitely cozy, but Sprinkle has a keen eye for the often odd contrasts of life in the modern South, and she uses them to good effect.

Other Southern series of interest are the works of Mignon F. Ballard, Charlaine Harris, Toni L. P. Kelner, Taylor McCafferty, and Sharyn McCrumb. Those looking specifically for the Atlanta setting might try the work of Celestine Sibley, Kathy Hogan Trocheck, and the first two books of Sarah Shankman.

Squire, Elizabeth Daniels.   Squire is a newspaperwoman from North Carolina, and she uses her journalism background in her mysteries. Her first novel, *Kill the Messenger* (St. Martin's Press, 1990), is set at a small newspaper where the owner-editor has been poisoned just as a major conglomerate makes a buyout bid. In the traditional mode, everyone around the victim is a suspect and has a secret to hide. Since the victim is not only a well-known local figure but an arrogant, self-satisfied womanizer, he has plenty of enemies for the police and his son to investigate.

With *Who Killed What's-Her-Name?* (Berkley, 1994), Squire began a series of mysteries with Peaches Dann, a forgetful amateur sleuth. Peaches has never had a good memory, and now that she's in her fifties she is collecting all the coping mechanisms she has learned over the years and putting them into a book called *How to Survive Without a Memory.* Her eighty-three-year-old father, although a strong-willed personality, is forgetful as well, and he has bad days when he is convinced there are burglars on his roof. His fears may be all too accurate when his sister is killed and left in his backyard. Peaches is strongly protective of her father, and she finds that she actually can use some of her memory tricks to help solve the murder of her aunt. Along with her close friend Ted, a semiretired history teacher, Peaches learns how to use newspaper database searches to do research on similar crimes. These charming, light cozies have interesting settings in the mountains of North Carolina and they offer fun advice on how to improve a wayward memory. In *Remember the Alibi* (Berkley, 1994), Peaches gets involved in a search for a serial killer who may be stalking her father. The killer befriends elderly people, persuades them to invest their money in dubious schemes, then kills them in a way that makes it look like they're committing suicide. By the time of *Memory Can Be Murder* (Berkley, 1995), Peaches has gained a local reputation as the absent-minded sleuth. A cousin asks her to help with a difficult personal situation involving a man who is locally notorious for his study of magic and Satanism. Murders begin to occur and occult symbols abound, and eventually, Peaches and her cousin are embroiled in a situation that threatens their own lives. Squire spins an interesting plot, with thought-provoking commentaries on modern superstition and regional customs.

Readers may enjoy other mysteries set in North Carolina, like those of Margaret Maron and Toni Kelner, and Sharyn McCrumb's wonderful Appalachian ballad series. Mysteries with newspaper backdrops include those by Lilian Jackson Braun, Carolyn G. Hart (the Henrie O series), and Celestine Sibley.

Stabenow, Dana. Stabenow writes a highly atmospheric series of mysteries set in Alaska. The heroine is Kate Shugak, who is a former investigator for the District Attorney's office in Anchorage. Kate, an Aleut, has retreated to live in the bush after being seriously injured while trying to stop a father from sexually abusing his daughter. Her throat was cut, so she has trouble with her voice, but she is still curious and vital. The first two books in the series are set in a fictional national park that covers thousands of acres of mountains, glaciers, and forests. In the first book, *A Cold Day for Murder* (Berkley, 1992), Kate needs to find out what has happened to a missing park ranger and an investigator sent in after him. *A Fatal Thaw* (Berkley, 1993) begins on the first day of spring with multiple murders. The mass murderer confesses immediately, but forensic tests show that one victim was killed by a different gun. Kate is hired to find the hidden killer, and during her search she discovers many of the concealed activities that go on daily in the bush country, like growing marijuana and poaching protected animals. In *Dead in the Water* (Berkley, 1993), Kate goes undercover on a fishing boat to find the killers of two crewmen. Kate is assisted in her investigations by Mutt, her half-wolf, half-husky dog; her on-again, off-again lover Jack Morgan; and Bobby Clark, a raucous, intelligent, and wheelchair-bound black Vietnam vet. The novels are notable for their vivid descriptions of the Alaskan bush, Aleut towns, and the fiercely independent bush dwellers. The reader is held by the fascination of such an exotic setting for mysterious events.

A Cold Day for Murder won an Edgar Award for Best Paperback Original.

Readers who enjoy Stabenow's books should try the Alaskan crime novels of Sue Henry and the legal mysteries, set in Seattle, of Janet L. Smith. Chelsea Quinn Yarbro and Jean Hager write mysteries with Native American sleuths.

Stacey, Susannah/Eyre, Elizabeth. Jill Staynes and Margaret Storey are former teachers and lifelong friends who are the joint authors of two series of crime novels. In America, their books are published under the Stacey pseudonym; in Britain, the books appear under the names of Staynes and Storey. They write a series of police procedurals with a continuing protagonist in Superintendent Robert Bone. He appears to be a typically quiet, omniscient English policeman. Tragedy has affected Bone deeply, however; his wife has been killed in a car accident and he is bringing up his teenage daughter, Charlotte, alone. Charlotte has a speech impediment and other injuries from the accident, and she is a strong and charming character in the novels. Bone works out of Tunbridge Wells, and the mysteries he solves occur in the villages and countryside of Kent. The people he encounters in the course of his investigations are idiosyncratic individuals whose psychology Stacey explores as an integral part of her plotting. For example, an intelligent and charismatic rock star, Ken Cryer, appears in several stories. The first Superintendent Bone mystery is *Goodbye Nanny Gray* (Summit, 1987). A nanny is murdered, and there are many suspects in this well-done English village mystery. *Grave Responsibility* (Summit, 1990) is a bleak and rather gory tale of multiple murders that occur within the very peculiar Clare family.

Under the pseudonym of Elizabeth Eyre, the writers have begun a new series of historical mysteries set in Renaissance Italy. Sigismondo, the Duke of Rocca's agent, is an enigmatic sleuth in the atmospheric *Death of the Duchess* (Harcourt Brace Jovanovich, 1992) and *Curtains for the Cardinal* (Harcourt Brace Jovanovich, 1993). The authors' plots reflect the conspiracies and the Machiavellian scheming of the times, along with detailed historical settings.

Fans of Stacey's mysteries should try the works of P. D. James, M. C. Beaton, and Ruth Rendell. Jean Hager writes about a policeman, Mitch Bushyhead, who is a devoted single father to a teenage girl. Kate Sedley, Margaret Frazer, and Sharan Newman write medieval mysteries.

Stallwood, Veronica. A resident of Oxford and a former librarian at the Bodleian Library and Oxford's Lincoln College, Stallwood writes a series of mysteries featuring novelist Kate Ivory. In her first appearance, *Death and the Oxford Box* (Scribner, 1993), Kate becomes involved in an odd scheme to help a fellow member of the Fridesley Road running group retrieve a valuable antique, the eponymous Oxford box. The husband of a group member has recently left her, taking with him half of her valuable collection of antique boxes. The group hatches a scheme to steal them back, giving one another alibis. But the scheme goes awry when murder intrudes, and Kate turns detective to discover who in the group is a murderer. In her second outing, *Oxford Exit* (Scribner, 1994), Kate ventures back into the library world to help the Oxford University libraries discover who is stealing books and manipulating the library's on-line system to cover his or her tracks. A bit of a loner, Kate is a quiet, somewhat offbeat character, who offers wry and sometimes acerbic commentary on her world. Stallwood's first novel, *Deathspell* (Scribner, 1992), is more in the psychological vein than her series about Kate Ivory.

L. R. Wright also features a librarian in a prominent role in her series. Readers might also try Nora Kelly, Anna Clarke, and Celia Fremlin.

Staynes, Jill. See **Stacey, Susannah.**

Stewart, Mary. Stewart began her writing career in the 1950s and eventually she became the foremost practitioner of the romantic suspense novel. She is known especially for the use of exotic locations and for her masterly descriptions of landscapes. Several of her novels, such as *The Moon-Spinners* (Mill, 1963) and *This Rough Magic,* (Morrow, 1964) are set in Greece, but her stories also take place in Scotland, France, Lebanon, Austria, and England. *My Brother Michael* (Mill & Morrow, 1960), one of her best, brings together brooding, austere Greek backgrounds with a twentieth-century revenge tragedy in the shape of a wartime murder and a postwar search for justice and vengeance. In many of her novels, Stewart uses the archetypal Gothic plot device of a young woman caught in a dangerous situation from which she uses her own agile wits to escape. But she brings to this classic form her own touch of magic, exemplified in her elegant and educated use of language and history. A superior example is *Nine Coaches Waiting* (Mill & Morrow, 1959), set in the French Alps, which tells of a young boy protected by his teacher from the ill will of his evil relatives and a series of potentially fatal mishaps. Stewart's recent novel, *The Stormy Petrel* (Morrow, 1991), is an impressionistic story of mysterious events on a small island off the west coast of Scotland.

Stewart also has written an admirable set of historical novels that weave together the legends of Merlin, King Arthur, and Mordred, with her own splendid evocation of fifth-century Britain.

Stewart's first novel was *Madam, Will You Talk?* (Mill, 1956). Her first Arthurian novel was *The Crystal Cave* (Morrow, 1970).

Many later writers in the field have been influenced by Stewart's style and popularity, including Caroline Llewellyn, D. F. Mills, Phyllis Whitney, Victoria Holt, Elizabeth Peters, and Dorothy Cannell.

Storey, Alice. See **Shankman, Sarah.**

Storey, Margaret. See **Stacey, Susannah.**

T

Taylor, Elizabeth Atwood. Taylor writes a series of mysteries with heroine Maggie Elliott. The first novel, *The Cable Car Murder* (St. Martin's Press, 1981), has a San Francisco background of wealthy couples with spoiled children and snobbish friends. Maggie is a young widow who has spent her recent years drunk, depressed, and increasingly impecunious. However, her half-sister is killed under a cable car, and the grisly death brings Maggie out of her inertia. Maggie teams up with Pat O'Reagan, a retired cop, to investigate her sister's murder. They do so well at their sleuthing that they decide to open a private eye agency. In *Murder at Vassar* (St. Martin's Press, 1987), Maggie returns East for her Vassar College reunion, only to find more murder and her first solo assignment as a professional investigator. *The Northwest Murders* (St. Martin's Press, 1992) is about the murder and scalping of a hiker on the Pacific Crest Trail near the California-Oregon border. Maggie is staying in a backwoods cabin, borrowed from O'Reagan, while she recovers from chronic fatigue syndrome. She is hired to find the killer after a local man is falsely accused of the murder. As a backdrop to the detection, Taylor paints a vivid portrait of the Pacific Northwest woods and their Native American inhabitants. The historical prejudices against the local Karuk and Shasta Indians, and against immigrant Chinese workers in California, become an integral part of her mystery plot.

Other writers who set mysteries in San Francisco and northern California include Janet LaPierre, Chelsea Quinn Yarbro, Susan Dunlap, and Marcia Muller. Isabelle Holland and Joan Smith also write novels with heroines who, like Maggie, are intensely self-reflective.

Thomson, June. Thomson has the distinction of being perhaps the only current mystery writer whose series detective has a different name either side of the Atlantic. Known to British readers as Inspector Finch, the character had his name changed to Rudd in the United States because Thomson's longtime American publisher, Doubleday, already had a detective named Finch on its list (the Inspector Finch of the novels by the late Margaret Erskine). Finch/Rudd first appeared in *Not One of Us* (Harper, 1971). From the beginning, Thomson demonstrated a keen insight into the psychology of her characters, many of whom live in the smaller towns and villages of England. Her writing style is succinct, with no excess verbiage to trim, particularly when compared to that of P. D. James, but, at her best, Thomson is no less compelling nor less psychologically acute. Finch/Rudd is an intriguing and believable character, and Thomson gives him tantalizing puzzles to solve. Especially noteworthy are *The Long Revenge* (Doubleday, 1975) and *The Habit of Loving* (Doubleday, 1979).

Readers of Thomson generally also will enjoy the work of her peers Patricia Moyes and Dorothy Simpson. Other writers who make effective use of the small towns and villages of England for their crime-writing are Susan B. Kelly, Anthea Fraser, Marjorie Eccles, and Clare Curzon.

Trocheck, Kathy Hogan. Formerly a reporter for the *Atlanta Journal-Constitution*, Trocheck has turned a sharply observant eye on life in the modern South in a new series about former cop and not-quite-former private eye, Julia Callahan Garrity, "Callahan" to her friends. Burned out by the male-dominated worlds of the police and the private eye game, Callahan has gone into business with her mother, Edna Mae Garrity. As owners of House Mouse, Callahan and her mother, along with a deliciously funny staff of "mice," clean houses in some of the best sections of Atlanta. In the first book of the series, *Every Crooked Nanny* (HarperCollins, 1992), Callahan takes on a cleaning job for an old sorority sister, Lilah Rose

Beemish, who soon turns to Callahan for help with more than just overgrown dust bunnies. Her family's Mormon nanny has absconded with jewelry, furs, and files of a secret business deal that could land Lilah Rose's husband in deep trouble. Callahan dusts off her private eye license and tries her best to help the obnoxious Beemish family. Callahan Garrity is smart, funny, and tenacious, whether she's tracking down a murder suspect or trying to get that noisome stain out of the living room carpet. With helpers like Neva Jean, one of her cheerfully "white trash" House Mouse employees, the elderly black sisters, Sister and Baby Easterbrook, and the irrepressible Edna Mae Garrity, Callahan has her hands full solving crimes in Atlanta. Trocheck's trenchant humor takes no prisoners when it comes to the idiosyncracies of modern American society or of Southern culture. The second novel in the series, *To Live and Die in Dixie* (HarperCollins, 1993), was nominated for an Agatha Award for Best Novel.

Readers acquainted with Trocheck's books might try Kay Hooper, Sarah Shankman, Celestine Sibley, and Patricia Houck Sprinkle, all of whom use Atlanta as settings for their books. For other Southern series with satirical overtones, readers should look for the work of Sharyn McCrumb and Charlaine Harris.

Truman, Margaret. Truman writes mysteries in the classic puzzle whodunit mode, all set in and around Washington, D.C. The novels have murders committed in Washington landmarks: the White House, the Supreme Court, the Kennedy Center, the National Cathedral, and so on. A dash of romance between male and female investigators often accompanies the working out of the plot, and politics is always present in the story. Truman has an insider's knowledge of government and the political process, especially as practiced in the Washington corridors of power. She shows her acquaintance with the details and minutiae of White House life, for example, in *Murder in the White House* (Arbor, 1980). Oddly enough for a president's daughter, Truman doesn't even mind casting revered and august figures like the President or the Chief Justice of the Supreme Court (in fictional form, of course) as murder suspects.

Another offspring of a president has written Washington mysteries: Elliott Roosevelt's series of mysteries depicts his mother,

Eleanor Roosevelt, as the sleuth. R. B. Dominic (aka Emma Lathen) writes a series with a congressman-sleuth that readers may enjoy.

Tucker, Kerry.   Tucker's series heroine is Libby Kincaid, a photographer. In the first mystery, *Still Waters* (HarperCollins, 1991), she is taking photographs of celebrities for a glitzy New York magazine when her brother dies in southern Ohio. Libby goes out for his funeral and discovers that not everyone is convinced that he committed suicide and tried to shoot his beloved dog as well. As she cleans out his belongings and stays in his house, mysterious events begin to happen. Tucker's second book, *Cold Feet* (HarperCollins, 1992), is set in New York City during a brutally hot summer. Libby is on leave from her magazine job and she is taking a series of photographs of a group of jazz tap dancers. Her life is consumed by her project, at least until murder occurs and her wandering father reenters her life in a dramatic fashion. As well as creating lively mystery plots, Tucker provides a detailed view of how Libby thinks about her art and how she handles the technical aspects of her photography.

Susan Moody's heroine Penny Wanawake is also a photographer. Sandra Scoppettone's richly detailed New York City settings also might prove enjoyable for readers of Tucker's mysteries.

Uhnak, Dorothy.   New Yorker Uhnak spent fourteen years with the city's Transit Police, won several medals, then quit because of sex discrimination and wrote *Policewoman: A Young Woman's Initiation into the Realities of Justice* (Simon & Schuster, 1964). She has since written a number of realistic police procedurals set in New York and with prominent female characters.

Her first novel, *The Bait* (Simon & Schuster, 1968) won an Edgar Award for Best First Mystery and introduced a series character, Christie Opara. Opara is an NYPD detective who encounters sexism and violence routinely in her job. In *The Ledger* (Simon & Schuster, 1970), for example, Christie uncovers the story of a mobster's girlfriend who became a prostitute after starting out in a convent. *The Ledger* won the Grand Prix de Litterature Policiere.

False Witness (Simon & Schuster, 1981), one of Uhnak's most acclaimed works, involves Lynne Jacobi, a bureau chief in the New York District Attorney's office. Lynne, in the midst of an affair with a subordinate, is assigned to the case of a top-ranked black fashion model and part-time revolutionary talk-show host who, in the novel's opening scene, is assaulted with particular savagery. *False Witness* is memorably successful in fooling the reader about the identity of the culprit.

Victims (Simon & Schuster, 1985) is the story of a brutal killing of a young woman on a middle-class street in Queens, where no one helps her or even calls the police. Uhnak shows why each witness refused to help and how people become brutalized through the difficulties and crime of contemporary urban life. *The Ryer Avenue Story* (St. Martin's Press, 1993) is Uhnak's first book in almost a decade. It begins in the Bronx in 1935 with a brutal attack on a drunken man. Six neighborhood kids are involved, and one of their fathers is executed for the crime. Uhnak's story covers the children as they grow up and as social customs change. Uhnak's stories are often violent and portray the world of big-city politics and police work with a gritty frankness. She vividly depicts New York's ethnic groups and neighborhoods.

Readers also may want to try the realistic urban novels of Lillian O'Donnell, Soledad Santiago, Teri White, Dorothy Salisbury Davis, Wendy Hornsby, and Katherine V. Forrest.

Van Gieson, Judith. Hard-boiled, atmospheric mystery novels are the metier of Van Gieson. Her series with lawyer and investigator Neil Hamel is set in a vividly realized New Mexico landscape. Neil has a small, slow law practice with an ineffectual law partner, Brink, and an equally inept secretary. She chiefly handles divorces and real estate closings. This leaves her plenty of time to get caught up in causes, like reintroducing an endangered species of wolf to its former habitat in *The Wolf Path* (HarperCollins, 1992), or opposing urban redevelopment in *The Other Side of Death* (Harper-Collins, 1991). Aside from her casework, Neil has a young Mexican lover known only as The Kid; he's her auto mechanic but also the person who gets her through bad times and lonely nights. Essentially a loner, Neil tries not to rely on him or on the tequila she drinks so much of when she's feeling morose. Van Gieson's descriptive powers bring home to the reader the heat and the austere beauty of the desert Southwest, although most of *Raptor* (Harper & Row, 1990) is set in Montana. Throughout the series, Van Gieson's writing is spare, economical, and often cynical.

The first Neil Hamel novel is *North of the Border* (Walker, 1988). *The Lies That Bind* (HarperCollins, 1993) was nominated for a Shamus Award for Best Private Eye Novel.

Other novelists of interest include Lia Matera and Mercedes Lambert for their depictions of hard-boiled female lawyers, and

Jane Langton, Nevada Barr, M. K. Wren, and Janet LaPierre for environmentally oriented mysteries. Cecil Dawkins also sets her mysteries in New Mexico.

Vine, Barbara. See **Rendell, Ruth.**

Walker, Mary Willis.   Texas writer Walker has quickly become well-known, for her first two novels each won prestigious awards in the mystery world. Her first book, *Zero at the Bone* (St. Martin's Press, 1991), won the Agatha, tied for the Macavity, and was nominated for the Edgar for Best First Novel. Her second novel, *The Red Scream* (Doubleday, 1994), won the Edgar for Best Novel. *Zero at the Bone* features dog trainer Katherine Driscoll in a novel about mysterious doings at the mythical Austin, Texas, zoo. Austin is also the chief setting for Walker's series about true crime reporter, Molly Cates. In *The Red Scream*, Molly is excited about the publication of her first true crime book, on a notorious Texas murder, when the case grabs her attention again. The murderer, Louie Bronk, is slated for execution soon, and Molly wants to do follow-up interviews with the family of one of Bronk's victims. The family happens to be headed, however, by a wealthy and powerful Austin businessman who doesn't want Molly to stir up the case any further. When someone starts carrying out copycat-style murders, Molly can't help but become involved, no matter the threats to her personal safety. In *Under the Beetle's Cellar* (Doubleday, 1995), Molly tries to discover everything she can about the leader of a religious cult that is holding a group of eleven schoolchildren and their bus driver hostage. Molly is stubborn and dogged on the trail of a crime; she's haunted by the memories of her own father's unsolved murder years before.

Walker knows how to kick the suspense into high gear, and Molly Cates is a tough and memorable heroine.

Readers looking for other Texas series should try the work of D. R. Meredith, David Lindsey, and Lee Martin. D. F. Mills also writes suspenseful stories set in Texas, and Mills's *Deadline* also features a true-crime writer.

Wallace, Marilyn.   With her debut novel, *A Case of Loyalties* (St. Martin's Press, 1986), Wallace won the Macavity Award for Best First Novel. This book also introduced her series characters, Jay Goldstein and Carlos Cruz, who work out of the Oakland, California, Police Department's homicide division. Goldstein, who likes to spend his spare time reading philosophy, comes from a prominent Bay Area family; his father is an influential lawyer. Cruz is a family man with two sons and a working wife. Both men, despite their widely differing backgrounds, are dedicated to their work and their ideals of justice, and they balance each other's weaknesses with their strengths to make an effective team. Wallace tells her stories through multiple viewpoints, allowing the reader to have a wider view of the story than just through the eyes of the detectives. This is particularly effective in *Primary Target* (Bantam, 1988), in which a mysterious group named the Brotherhood of Men attacks the presidential campaign of Congresswoman Jean Talbot. Most recently, Wallace penned a suspense novel, *So Shall You Reap* (Doubleday Perfect Crime, 1992), somewhat in the vein of Barbara Michaels. Wallace writes crisply, with intelligence, and her stories are suspenseful and absorbing. Wallace has also edited the *Sisters in Crime* anthologies (Berkley) and coedited the *Deadly Allies* anthologies (Doubleday).

Those who have enjoyed Wallace and her Bay Area settings might try the work of Shelley Singer, Marcia Muller, Susan Dunlap (the Jill Smith books), and Linda Grant. Those who have read *So Shall You Reap* might try the work of Barbara Michaels, Phyllis A. Whitney, or Caroline Llewellyn.

Walters, Minette.   With *The Ice House* (St. Martin's Press, 1992), Walters won the John Creasey Award for Best First Novel, bestowed by the British Crime Writers' Association. Upon first look, *The Ice House* appears to be a fairly conventional English mystery. A body has been discovered in the abandoned ice house on an estate in

Hampshire. Could it be the body of the estate owner's husband, who disappeared ten years ago? Or does it belong to someone else? From this starting point, Walters takes the conventions of the traditional English mystery and turns them topsy-turvy, sideways, and any-which-way she pleases, and the result is a compelling and engrossing story that never takes the tack the reader expects.

With her second novel, *The Sculptress* (St. Martin's Press, 1993), Walters explores our modern fascination with brutal murderers. Roz Leigh, a journalist whose life is in a shambles, reluctantly agrees to write a book about Olive Martin, a monstrous young woman who murdered her mother and sister, then calmly dismembered their bodies before calling the police to confess the crime. Fascinated by Olive, Roz delves further and further into the background of the crime to understand why it happened, and she finds herself drawn deeper into Olive's disturbing world.

Walters's third novel, *The Scold's Bridle* (St. Martin's Press, 1994), won the Gold Dagger for Best Novel. An elderly woman is found naked in her bathtub, wearing a medieval device forced on women who nagged their husbands too much. Did she commit suicide or was she murdered? Walters conjures up a dark and brooding atmosphere in her novels in which nothing and no one are ever quite what they seem. Since each of her first three novels has been awarded a major prize from her peers in the mystery world, Walters has obviously established herself as a major force in the field.

Like Minette Walters, Ruth Rendell, in her non-Wexford books and as Barbara Vine, writes novels that playfully stretch the conventions of crime fiction. Readers who enjoy such novels as these might try in addition the work of B. M. Gill, S. T. Haymon, Frances Hegarty, Margaret Millar, and Rosamond Smith.

Webb, Martha G. See **Wingate, Anne.**

Weir, Charlene. Weir's *The Winter Widow* (St. Martin's Press, 1992), won the St. Martin's Press Malice Domestic Best First Traditional Mystery Award. Susan Wren has quit her job as a police officer in San Francisco to move with her new husband Daniel to his hometown of Hampstead, Kansas. Daniel, who is the chief of police in Hampstead, is killed right after they move back, and the town makes Susan the temporary acting chief of police. Susan is in shock, and Weir's evocation of her grief and bitterness is powerful and memorable. Susan must investigate her husband's murder as her first order of business, but more mundane problems, like dealing with pigs let loose in the town's main street, keep interfering with her quest. Weir has written a strong and effective first novel.

In *Consider the Crows* (St. Martin's Press, 1993), Susan has stayed on in Hampstead and is trying to reconcile her big-city background with small-town crimes and gossip. A woman who has recently arrived in town disappears, and Susan is searching for her, when she finds that another local woman, an administrator at the college, has disappeared as well. Weir's characters are interesting, and she provides a fascinating backdrop of small-town Kansas, with all of the vagaries of Kansas weather. *Consider the Crows* was nominated for an Anthony Award for Best Novel.

Weir's third mystery, *Family Practices* (St. Martin's Press, 1995), is an engrossing tale of twisted family relationships and murder. Several of the five Barrington siblings are doctors or are married to doctors, and the oldest sister, Dorothy, is in control of the family medical practice and their parents' substantial inheritance. Susan is baby-sitting Jen, a neighbor's child, and when she brings her in for treatment, someone breaks into the clinic, murders Dorothy, and seriously wounds Jen. Susan has begun, cautiously, to learn to care about another person again, and her attachment to Jen gives her a personal stake in finding the murderer. All of Weir's books are intense studies of character and setting, and the sequence of the novels follows and describes the sequence of Susan's mourning period for her dead husband.

Other books with Kansas settings include Nancy Pickard's *Bum Steer* (Pocket, 1990) and Earlene Fowler's *Kansas Troubles* (Berkley, 1996). Other writers who use small town settings effectively are Janet LaPierre and Katherine Hall Page.

Wesley, Valerie Wilson.   An editor-at-large at *Essence* magazine and the author of several books of fiction and nonfiction for younger readers, Wesley has begun a series of novels starring African-American private eye Tamara Hayle. Based in Newark, New Jersey, Tamara is a divorced mother trying to make a living for herself and her teenage son Jamal in *When Death Comes Stealing* (Putnam, 1994), the series opener. Jamal's father, DeWayne Curtis, comes calling upon Tamara for help. He is convinced someone is murdering all his sons from previous marriages and liaisons, and he wants Tamara to find out who's doing it before Jamal becomes the next target. In *Devil's Gonna Get Him* (Putnam, 1995), Tamara is hired by Newark's wealthiest black businessman, Lincoln Storey, to get the scoop on the relationship between his stepdaughter and a documentary film maker, who just happens to be an old flame of Tamara's. When Storey drops dead at a political fund-raiser, Tamara keeps digging to protect the young sister of a good friend accused of the murder. Wesley brings a trenchant voice to the private eye novel, with Tamara's observations on being black and female in today's world, and she also offers a stark portrait of contemporary Newark and its environs. *When Death Comes Stealing* was a Shamus Award nominee for Best First Private Eye Novel.

Readers who have enjoyed Wesley might also try Eleanor Taylor Bland, Janet Evanovich, Barbara Neely, and Sara Paretsky.

Wheat, Carolyn. A former defense attorney with the Legal Aid Society in Brooklyn, New York, Wheat uses her extensive knowledge of the law and of the court system to lend a sometimes harrowing authenticity to her novels about Cass Jameson. When the series begins, with *Dead Man's Thoughts* (St. Martin's Press, 1983), Cass, like her creator, is a lawyer with Legal Aid. One day Cass finds her lover and colleague, Nathan Wasserstein, murdered in his apartment in an apparent gay killing by a young Puerto Rican hustler. Cass refuses to believe what looks like a setup to her, and she turns detective to clear Nathan's name. By the second book, *Where Nobody Dies* (St. Martin's Press, 1986), Cass has left Legal Aid and set up her own practice, but she finds herself visiting all the familiar places of the system from her days as a Legal Aid attorney. Cass is tough, principled, compassionate, and committed to seeing that justice is done to the best of her ability. The plots of the novels are neatly and tightly constructed, an excellent blend of the traditional mystery plot with contemporary, well-rounded characters. *Dead Man's Thoughts* was nominated for an Edgar for Best First Novel.

Readers acquainted with Carolyn Wheat might try the series of Janet L. Smith, Julie Smith (the Rebecca Schwartz books), Frances Fyfield, and Dana Stabenow, all of whom have women lawyers as main characters.

White, Gloria. White's series protagonist, Veronica "Ronnie" Ventana, is a private eye in San Francisco. Her parents were well-known cat burglars who were killed in a car crash just before their trial. Ronnie has learned some tricks from them, like the ability to pick almost any lock, that she now uses to do security checks for her legitimate clients. Ronnie's sidekick is sexy sixty-five-year-old Blackie Coogan, an ex-boxer, heavy drinker, and fellow private eye. The first novel in the series is *Murder on the Run* (Dell, 1991), which was nominated for an Anthony Award. Ronnie is running one morning, when she inadvertently becomes a witness to a murder. She sees someone throw a man into San Francisco Bay, and she must find the murderer before he finds her. Ronnie then helps an old college friend who is afraid that the Mob is after him in *Money to Burn* (Dell, 1993). In a complex plot, a woman appears to be luring men who date her to their deaths, and crimes of passion may be intertwined with white-collar financial crime. In the Edgar-nominated *Charged with Guilt* (Dell, 1995), Ronnie is hired to test the security system at the house of a state senator, but it turns out to be an elaborate frame-up when she's caught breaking in and the senator is found electrocuted in his bath. To clear herself of suspicion, Ronnie must investigate. Ronnie is an intrepid, fearless investigator, who never carries a gun and prefers to use her quick mind and her ability to do break-ins in order to solve crimes.

San Francisco has always been rich territory for private eyes, covered by the likes of Marcia Muller's Sharon McCone, Linda Grant's Catherine Sayler, and Elizabeth Pincus's Nell Fury.

White, Teri. White writes hard-boiled, gritty suspense novels and police procedurals. Her books often concentrate on the psychological dynamic of male bonding, and they generally feature a team of men, either cops or criminals. White's first novel, *Triangle* (Ace Charter, 1982), won an Edgar Award for Best Paperback Original. The plot follows two Vietnam vets, Johnny and Mac, who hire out as a team of hit men. As part of a Mob rubout, they kill an undercover cop. The cop's partner, Simon, abandons everything else in his life to seek his partner's killer.

Bleeding Hearts (Mysterious, 1984) introduces Blue Maguire and Spaceman Kowalski, detective partners in the Los Angeles Police Department; *Tightrope* (Mysterious, 1986) continues their adventures. Maguire is rich, educated, and angst-ridden; Kowalski is a tough, macho, streetwise cop. The evolution of two such different individuals into an effective team is set against a bleak backdrop of bloody, hideous L.A. crimes. *Tightrope* is a particularly unusual book; it's one of the very few caper novels written by a woman.

Max Trueblood and the Jersey Desperado (Mysterious, 1987) is the story of two New York City police detectives (one veteran, one novice) and two Mob hit men (again, an old-timer and his protégé). In this novel, White has written effective underworld scenes in New York and New Jersey, with authentic-sounding dialogue.

Readers also may want to try hard-edged urban mysteries by Wendy Hornsby, Dorothy Uhnak, and Faye Kellerman.

Whitehead, Barbara. After publishing several Regency romances, Whitehead has written what is described as the York cycle of mysteries. The cycle is notable for her vivid descriptions of the city of York and its magnificent cathedral, the York Minster. *Playing God* (St. Martin's Press, 1988) is set at a summer theater festival of medieval mystery plays, performed in the ancient parts of the city. Poison Peters, a punk rock star, is brought in to play the part of Christ. A storm of protest, attempts on his life, and an eventual murder are played out against a religious and theatrical background. Whitehead turns to the secular world for the setting of a police procedural, *The Girl in Red Suspenders* (St. Martin's Press, 1990), and an atmospheric mystery set in a family-run chocolate factory, *Sweet Death, Come Softly* (St. Martin's Press, 1993). She returned to a religious setting for *The Dean It Was That Died* (St. Martin's Press, 1991), which revolves around the mysterious death of the dean of a cathedral during a church service. Canons Grindal and Oglethorpe and Lucy Grindal, who appeared in *Playing God*, become key characters here as they discover a group of criminals that is attempting to use the church for evil purposes.

Whitehead has also written a book about Charlotte Brontë.

Readers may enjoy the clerical mysteries of Isabelle Holland, Kate Charles, Veronica Black, and Mollie Hardwick.

Whitney, Phyllis A. Named Grand Master by the Mystery Writers of America in 1988 and given an Agatha Award for Lifetime Achievement by Malice Domestic in 1989, Whitney has been producing entertaining mystery fiction for adults and young adults for five decades. Her first novel was *Red Is for Murder* (Ziff Davis, 1943). Along with Mary Stewart and the late Victoria Holt, Whitney was a regular on the best-seller lists of the late 1960s and 1970s, the heyday of what is called romantic suspense. These mysteries with a romantic twist remain popular, as evidenced by the longevity of such practitioners as Whitney, Holt, Stewart, Barbara Michaels/Elizabeth Peters, Velda Johnston, and Mary Higgins Clark. One of the hallmarks of Whitney's fiction is its strong sense of place. Born to American missionaries in Japan, Whitney was a world traveler at an early age, and this taste for unusual and interesting places makes a distinctive contribution to her work. Her novels vary in setting from Turkey, South Africa, Greece, Japan, and various parts of the United States. Along with an expertly sketched setting, Whitney gives her readers entertaining stories with a masterful sense of pace and suspense. Whitney's heroines are generally young, sometimes a bit inexperienced, but always with a sense of self-responsibility and the courage to carry them through often life-threatening situations. Among Whitney's best mysteries are *Emerald* (Doubleday, 1983) and *The Glass Flame* (Doubleday, 1978).

Those who enjoy Whitney for her sense of place might also try the work of M. M. Kaye, whose novels of far-flung places are a nostalgic and evocative travelogue of a vanished world. The novels of Mary Stewart also are set in the most of exotic locales. A newer writer, Caroline Llewellyn, is a bright new voice in this same tradition. Another new writer, D. F. Mills, writes convincingly about young women caught up in mysterious events seemingly beyond their control.

Wilhelm, Kate. Winner of the two most prestigious prizes in science fiction, the Hugo and the Nebula Awards, Wilhelm is perhaps better-known as a science fiction writer. But her very first novel, *More Bitter Than Death* (Simon & Schuster, 1963), was a mystery. Conventional in plot and setting, this book exhibits the staple elements in Wilhelm's later mystery novels. There is a strong sense of place, underscored by the belief that environment plays a significant role in the shaping of character. Wilhelm pays much attention to the development of her characters, creating her people through disciplined, descriptive language.

First introduced in a short story, the husband-and-wife team of Charlie Meiklejohn and Constance Leidl has featured in several novels, beginning with *The Hamlet Trap* (St. Martin's Press, 1987). Charlie, a former New York City arson investigator, now works as a private investigator, and Constance is a professional psychologist, a

Ph.D. with impressive credentials. In combination, these two make a very effective team, and their relationship provides a strong emotional core to the novels.

Wilhelm is not afraid to experiment, as with *The Dark Door* (St. Martin's Press, 1988), a Charlie and Constance novel that blends science fiction and mystery, or *Death Qualified* (St. Martin's Press, 1991), a highly unusual legal mystery. Other books, such as the recent *Seven Kinds of Death* (St. Martin's Press, 1992), are more traditional, though Wilhelm remains strongly individual, whatever she writes.

Those who have enjoyed Wilhelm's mysteries might try the series of P. M. Carlson, M. K. Lorens, B. J. Oliphant/A. J. Orde, and Mary Monica Pulver.

Wilson, Barbara. Seattle writer Wilson is cofounder of Seal Press, which happens to be the publisher of Wilson's two series of lesbian, feminist mysteries.

Murder in the Collective (Seal Press, 1984) introduces Pam Nilsen, who with her twin sister Penny, has turned their family business, Best Printing, into a collective after the death of their parents. The collective receives an offer to merge with lesbian-owned B. Violet Typesetting, and the stage is set for murder. As she sorts warily through the tangles of politics and sexual relationships among the collective, Pam also seeks an answer to her own troubling questions about her sexuality. In subsequent books of the series, Pam adjusts to her new identity as a lesbian and finds her attention captured by murders that help her explore her beliefs as a feminist. Teenage prostitutes are the theme in *Sisters of the Road* (Seal Press, 1986) and pornography and lesbian sadomasochism in *The Dog Collar Murders* (Seal Press, 1989).

With *Gaudi Afternoon* (Seal Press, 1990), Wilson introduced Cassandra Reilly, globe-trotting Spanish translator, who dashes through her paces in a delicious comic thriller set in Barcelona. This novel won an award from the British Crime Writers' Association for Best Crime Novel with a European Setting.

Whether writing about Pam or Cassandra, Wilson has a crisp style. She mixes characters with differing political viewpoints with ease and makes them articulate and believable.

Readers who have enjoyed the work of Wilson might try writers such as Ellen Hart, Katherine V. Forrest, Claire McNab, and Sandra

Scoppettone, all of whose characters are lesbian amateur or professional detectives. Readers looking for Seattle settings might try the work of Mary Daheim and Janet L. Smith.

Wiltz, Chris. Native New Orleanian Wiltz has set her series of hard-boiled private eye novels in the Crescent City and endowed them with that special flavor that can belong only to New Orleans. Wiltz's detective is Neal Rafferty, who grew up in the tough, wrong-side-of-the-tracks area known as the Irish Channel. A cop like his father and his grandfather before him, Neal leaves the force after the murder of his lover, a prostitute Neal believes was killed by the powerful district attorney. Since striking out on his own as a private cop, Neal finds it difficult to get along with his father and his father's cronies on the police force. Neal Rafferty exhibits many of the characteristics common to the hard-boiled private eye. He drinks and smokes too much on occasion, he sometimes gets involved with the wrong woman, and he's stubborn about doing things his way. Wiltz makes New Orleans as much a character in the series as any person, and this gives the books a strong sense of place. First in the series is *The Killing Circle* (Macmillan, 1981). The most recent novel, *The Emerald Lizard* (Dutton, 1991), has as an underlying theme the seductiveness of violence, and this book displays Wiltz's skills with people and place at their best.

Readers looking for other series set in New Orleans and Louisiana might try the Skip Langdon novels of Julie Smith, the work of Tony Fennelly, and the series about lesbian private eye Micky Knight, written by J. M. Redmann.

Wingate, Anne. Wingate is actually the third literary incarnation for this prolific mystery writer who has a Ph.D. in English. She began her career as Martha G. Webb, penning three novels. About the same time as Webb appeared, Lee Martin published her first novel, then a few years later came Wingate, her real name. Several characteristics are common to all three, including Texas settings. The veteran of eight years of police work, mostly with the major crime scene unit, Wingate uses her experiences to lend an authentic feel of police procedure to her novels.

The Lee Martin books feature Fort Worth homicide detective Deb Ralston, who first appeared in *Too Sane a Murder* (St. Martin's Press, 1984). Deb is called to a horrifying crime scene in which a young man, previously diagnosed as a schizophrenic, has allegedly murdered five members of his family.

As Wingate, the author introduced Mark Shigata in *Death by Deception* (Walker, 1988) as an FBI agent based in Bayport (on the Gulf Coast near Galveston). Shigata in the second book, *The Eye of Anna* (Walker, 1989), copes with his duties as the new chief of police in Bayport as a hurricane rages.

Whether writing as Webb, Martin, or Wingate, this author packs her novels full of authentic police procedure and rapid-paced action. An underlying theme of antiracism lends a strong message to the books. For example, Shigata is Nisei, and Deb Ralston and her husband have three adopted children of different ethnic backgrounds.

In addition, Wingate has recently published *Scene of the Crime: a Writer's Guide to Crime-Scene Investigations* (Writer's Digest Books, 1992).

Those who have enjoyed any of the works of this author might try the various series of Elizabeth Linington, Dell Shannon, and Lesley Egan, the novels of J. A. Jance, the Skip Langdon series of Julie Smith, Dorothy Uhnak, Medora Sale, and Lillian O'Donnell.

Wings, Mary. Wings has written a series of mysteries with lesbian sleuth Emma Victor. The first Emma Victor novel is *She Came Too Late* (Crossing Press, 1987). Emma is a former publicist and activist, now suffering burnout and working at the women's hot line in Boston. A woman who calls for help is murdered, and her death leads Emma into a shadowy world of biological engineering and drugs. In *She Came in a Flash* (New American Library, 1988), Emma has moved to California and is doing publicity for an old friend. Her friend asks her to look into the death of a religious cult member as a favor, and Emma becomes involved with the activities of a self-absorbed rock star, Nebraska Storm. The claustrophobic atmosphere of the cult is conveyed forcefully, and Emma is a strong female investigator in the classic hard-boiled mode.

Divine Victim (Dutton, 1992) has the unnamed narrator traveling with her new lover, Marya, to clean out an old house in Montana that Marya has recently inherited from her aunt. The novel is full of religious intensity as the narrator slowly uncovers the story behind the aunt's obsession with images of the Virgin Mary and female saints, and reveals her own dangerous activities.

Other lesbian sleuths have been created by Ellen Hart, Sarah Dreher, J. M. Redmann, and Lauren Wright Douglas.

Wolzien, Valerie.   Susan Henshaw, the housewife who serves as Wolzien's series detective, inhabits a world in suburban Connecticut that many readers well may envy. The wife of a highly successful advertising executive, Susan has a beautiful home, two children, and a loving and generally attentive husband. This is a world where husbands might give wives expensive vintage automobiles for Christmas, or where families might spend as much on Christmas decorations as many people make in one year. Beginning with *Murder at the PTA Luncheon* (St. Martin's Press, 1988), Susan becomes involved with the fatal goings-on in her suburban corner of the world, and she proves that the ability to run a successful household evinces some skills at solving domestic murders. The woman who becomes Susan's best friend, Kathleen Gordon, luckily has experience as a police detective and private security consultant, and Kathleen's professional knowledge, linked with Susan's in-depth knowledge of the inner workings of suburbia, make an effective combination.

Other writers who set their series in suburbia include Jill Churchill, Caroline Crane, and Susan Isaacs. Readers might also try the series of Elizabeth Travis and Katherine Hall Page. Best-selling suspense novelist Mary Higgins Clark has also effectively mined the suburban setting for several of her successful novels.

Woods, Sara.   The late Sara Woods wrote some forty-eight novels featuring barrister Antony Maitland, his wife Jenny, and Antony's uncle, Sir Nicholas Harding. Using her own experience of having worked in a solicitor's office, Woods made the English legal mystery particularly her own, and Antony Maitland is perhaps the character in English mystery fiction closest to Erle Stanley Gardner's Perry Mason. Maitland has a definite nose for crime, for he has hunches that nearly infallibly tell him when something is odd about a seemingly straightforward case. Courtroom scenes are often a part of the action in these novels, and Wood handles them with considerable aplomb, building tension in a manner worthy of Gardner himself. Through the course of the series, readers find out tidbits of the lives of the Maitlands; one book, *They Love Not Poison* (Holt, Rinehart, & Winston, 1972), takes the reader back to a period before Antony has qualified as a barrister and is thus a prequel to the rest of the series. Wood's literate style, attention to detail, and generally complex puzzles will appeal to readers who like their mysteries English and traditional. *Bloody Instructions* (Harper & Row, 1962) is the first in the series. Woods also wrote as Anne Burton, Mary Challis, and Margaret Leek.

Readers interested in English legal mysteries might try the work of Frances Fyfield, Ann C. Fallon, E. X. Giroux, the late Anthony Gilbert, and M. R. D. Meek.

Woods, Sherryl. Woods writes romantic mysteries as well as romance novels. The heroine of her first mystery series, Amanda Roberts, is a former New York hotshot journalist, who followed her husband to a job in rural Georgia. The husband rapidly decamped, and Amanda now yearns for a more exciting career than working on a country weekly. The initial novel, *Reckless* (Warner, 1989), begins with the famous chef Maurice keeling over dead into the chocolate soufflé at a cooking demonstration. Amanda hopes that if she can solve the crime and write a prizewinning story she can get out of her dead-end job. However, Joe Donelli, a former Brooklyn cop, is unofficially helping his friend the sheriff with the investigation. Inevitably, he tries to thwart Amanda's sleuthing at every turn. Subsequent books chart a relationship that develops between Roberts and Donelli.

Woods's second romantic mystery series is set in South Florida. *Hot Property* (Dell, 1992) introduces Molly DeWitt, a single mother who finds a man dead one morning in her condominium card room. Homicide detective Michael O'Hara is the drop-dead handsome Cuban cop assigned to the case. In *Hot Secret* (Dell, 1993), Molly is working as a publicist in the Miami/Dade film office, and a famous film director is found dead on a location shoot that Molly has arranged. O'Hara turns up again to argue with Molly and to listen to her discoveries.

Readers who enjoy Woods might want to try Mignon F. Ballard, Caroline Llewellyn, and Kay Hooper.

Wren, M. K. Wren is the pseudonym of Martha Kay Renfroe, a West Coast writer and artist. Her mysteries star Conan Flagg, a bookstore owner in Holliday Beach, Oregon. Conan has a private investigator's license, the existence of which he usually tries to keep quiet, and he is a former intelligence agent. The independently wealthy heir to a ranching fortune, Conan is also one-half Nez Percé Indian, a collector of art, and the possessor of a classic Jaguar XKE and a luxurious beach house. As a sideline to his bookstore business, he helps out people who come to him in trouble. In *Nothing's Certain but Death* (Doubleday, 1978), for example, Conan helps a friend who is suspected of murdering an IRS agent. *Seasons of Death* (Doubleday, 1981) is set in a ghost town in Idaho, where Conan investigates a forty-year-old murder. Conan sets out to ensure justice when a friend is killed in *Wake Up, Darlin' Corey* (Doubleday, 1984). Wren uses the Oregon environmental movement as a backdrop to her story of greed and vengeance. In all of her mysteries, Wren is particularly adept at creating atmospheric settings, especially in the Oregon beach areas and the desert.

The first Conan Flagg novel is *Curiosity Didn't Kill the Cat* (Doubleday, 1973). Wren has also written a science fiction trilogy, *The Phoenix Legacy* (Berkley, 1981), and *A Gift upon the Shore* (Ballantine, 1990), a science fiction novel.

Carolyn G. Hart, Joan Hess, and Sheila Simonson write about booksellers turned sleuths. Jane Haddam (aka Orania Papazoglou) features Gregor Demarkian, a former government agent turned private detective, in her cozy mysteries. Janet LaPierre creates mysteries noted for their vivid North Coast settings and environmental concerns.

Wright, L. R.   The *L* stands for Laurali, who is a journalist and novelist. Canadian Wright struck gold the first time out with a crime novel, *The Suspect* (Viking, 1985), which won the Edgar for Best Novel. Two elderly men are having a conversation, and suddenly one of them strikes the other dead, then toddles off home. Called in to investigate is Staff Sergeant Karl Alberg of the Royal Canadian Mounted Police, stationed in the town of Sechelt on Canada's Sunshine Coast. In his late forties, divorced, but delving into the dating game again, Alberg is a shrewd, laconic detective. He works slowly through the evidence to identify the killer and the motive in this absorbing, inverted murder study. Subsequent novels in the series demonstrate Wright's interest in the reasons ordinary persons commit crimes. Each novel is in some ways a character study, either of a victim or a perpetrator, and of the people involved in the situation. As the series progresses, Alberg develops a romantic relationship with Cassandra Mitchell, the town's librarian. Thoughtfully and compassionately, Wright looks into the nastiness in the human heart and creates fascinating novels of suspense. The Sunshine Coast is a vital part of her tapestry of crime, and her evocative descriptions of the area lend a strong sense of place to her work. In addition to her crime novels, Wright has written several novels of straight fiction.

Those who have enjoyed Wright's crime novels might try the work of English writers Ruth Rendell, P. D. James, Frances Fyfield, and Margaret Yorke, or the Toronto-based series of Medora Sale.

Yarbro, Chelsea Quinn/Fawcett, Quinn.   Yarbro is a prolific author of science fiction and children's books, as well as mysteries. She has created a series that features Charles Spotted Moon, a San Francisco attorney and Ojibwa tribal shaman. In each novel, courtroom scenes and legal details alternate with Charlie's independent investigations. In order to establish a client's innocence, he sometimes goes on Ojibwa spirit walks to hear how a murder happened by listening to the voices of the dead. The difficult and sometimes gory realities of contemporary urban life often contrast with Charlie's clear awareness of his positive spiritual life.

The first book in the series is *Ogilvie, Tallant & Moon* (Putnam, 1976), also published as *Bad Medicine* (Jove, 1990). Yarbro also has written numerous volumes of a historical horror series featuring the Comte de Saint-Germaine, a vampire.

Yarbro's latest mystery series, published under the name of Quinn Fawcett, begins with *Napoleon Must Die* (Avon, 1993). The protagonist is Madame Victoire Vernet, an amateur sleuth in the court of Napoleon Bonaparte.

Readers who enjoy legal maneuvering also might try Sara Woods's series with British barrister Antony Maitland. Susan Wolfe and Lia Matera have written crime novels about San Francisco attorneys. Jean Hager writes about Cherokee traditions, and Dana Stabenow about Aleuts.

Yeager, Dorian. Yeager's protagonist is Victoria (Vic) Bowering, a New York City actress. Vic is tall, redheaded, and eternally anxious for acting jobs. She is a funny, acerbic, larger-than-life character, with many eccentric friends. *Cancellation by Death* (St. Martin's Press, 1992) is about the murder of a soap opera star. Vic is about to be amically divorced, and she already has two suitors, including a police officer involved in the murder investigation. In *Eviction by Death* (St. Martin's Press, 1993), Vic is threatened with eviction, along with others in her building. Vic is head of the tenants group, and she hates the unscrupulous landlord. Several people in his apartments die under suspicious circumstances, and Vic becomes the prime suspect. The Vic Bowering books are light, amusing tales of criminal events in the life of a starving actress.

Yeager has started a new series featuring Elizabeth Will, an artist who also works a fishing boat with her father, and her friend Ginny, the local police chief. In *Murder Will Out* (St. Martin's Press, 1994), Elizabeth and her father find a dead body one day in one of their lobster traps. Yeager provides good descriptions of the cold, hard work of fishing, and of working-class life in Maine. She creates a tangled plot, with plenty of gritty New England atmosphere.

Mystery writers who set their books in Maine include J. S. Borthwick, Susan Kenney, and B. J. Morison. Heroines who are actors can be found in the works of Jane Dentinger, Stefanie Matteson, and P. M. Carlson.

Yorke, Margaret. Yorke began her mystery-writing with a series of conventional detective novels featuring Oxford don Patrick Grant, whose first appearance was in *Dead in the Morning* (Geoffrey Bles, 1970). Handsome, learned, and incurably nosy, Grant is much in the mold of the gifted amateur detective, and in his five appearances he serves as an entertaining, if not compelling, sleuth.

After her fourth novel about Grant, Yorke wrote a novel that was to signal the direction of her career in crime. *No Medals for the Major* (Geoffrey Bles, 1974) is set in a much more contemporary edition of the traditional English village of the crime novel. In this setting, Yorke has full range for her considerable talent in observing the ordinary routines of life and how these routines and the people who effect them can be altered by crime. Yorke's world is no St. Mary Mead, and she mines this ground time after time with quiet effect. She focuses on ordinary people, not the psychopaths so beloved of her peer Ruth Rendell, and she demonstrates to the reader just how easily crime can upset the delicate balance of an ordinary person. Other excellent examples of Yorke's craft are *A Small Deceit* (Viking, 1991) and *Criminal Damage* (Mysterious, 1992).

Readers who have enjoyed the crime novels of Yorke might try the novels of Anna Clarke, Sheila Radley, Rosamond Smith, Celia Fremlin, Margaret Millar, June Thomson, and Ruth Rendell.

Z

Zaremba, Eve. Zaremba's series heroine is Helen Keremos, and she is one of the earliest contemporary hard-boiled women private eyes. In *A Reason to Kill* (Markham, Ontario: PaperJacks, 1978), Helen is living in Vancouver when a college professor in Winnipeg contacts her about a job. His son has disappeared in Toronto, where his mother lives. Helen drives across Canada to investigate, and discovers the son's potentially scandalous secret. She also meets Nate Ottoline, a rather shady but influential figure in Toronto's gay community. Zaremba's plot takes many turns, with a classic twist at the end. The atmosphere is distinctly '70s, and reflects many of the trends and the slang of the time. We learn little of Helen's personal life here, and the fact that she is a lesbian is distinctly downplayed. Toronto is the setting again when Helen returns in *Work for a Million* (Toronto: Amanita, 1986). Helen is investigating the harassment of a singer who has won a million dollars in a lottery. She has a circle of friends and hangers-on plus an ex-husband, and it could be any of them. We learn more about Helen; she is tough, she is attracted to her client Sonia, and she prefers action to pondering lists of suspects. Nate Ottoline reappears and Helen welcomes his help. In *Uneasy Lies* (Toronto: Second Story, 1990), Helen gets a temporary job filling in for a vacationing head of security for a condominium development in the Toronto suburbs. Inevitably, the body of a resident is found in an empty apartment. The dead man was an environmental lawyer who had been working on an environmental assessment of a nearby piece of land on which the condominium company had proposed to build the second phase of their development. Is there toxic waste on the site? Was he bribed to approve the project by the developers? Helen is tough and persistent in her quest for the truth of the matter, and the Toronto setting is strong and colorful.

Other Canadian mystery writers include Gail Bowen, Ellen Godfrey, Medora Sale, and Alison Gordon. Writers with lesbian protagonists include Sandra Scoppettone, Val McDermid, Lauren Wright Douglas, Mary Wings, and Elizabeth Pincus.

Zukowski, Sharon.   Zukowski writes a series of mysteries with New York City private eye Blaine Stewart. Blaine and her sister Eileen, a lawyer, own a large company that specializes in civil and criminal law and corporate investigations. Blaine's husband has been murdered, and as the series opens, she attempts to deal with her grief through overwork, alcoholism, and chain-smoking. In the first book, *The Hour of the Knife* (St. Martin's Press, 1991), Blaine has gone to a small town on the Carolina coast to deliver a security report. Her clients are an old college friend and her husband, who now own a computer business. Blaine's friend is killed and Blaine stays on to investigate. *Dancing in the Dark* (St. Martin's Press, 1992) concerns militant animal rights organizers who are protesting a Texas beef company that is just about to start trading on the stock exchange. Blaine also gets involved with a sulky teenager whose grandfather has died in a suspicious fire. *Leap of Faith* (Dutton, 1994) has perhaps the most absorbing plot device in its story of a pregnant surrogate mother who runs away rather than give the child up at birth to the genetic mother. In an interesting variation on the classic search for a missing person, Blaine's firm, Aldridge and Stewart, is hired by the genetic mother to find a baby who is not yet born. Zukowski also does a good job of portraying the moral quandary of surrogacy.

Readers may want to try other books with New York sleuths, including those by Dorian Yeager, Jane Dentinger, and Sandra Scoppettone.

Authors Included in the First Edition

M. J. Adamson
Gloria Dank
Jean Femling
L. B. Greenwood
Mary Bowen Hall
Kay Hooper
Vicki P. McConnell
Deborah Powell

Erica Quest
Annette Roome
Diane K. Shah
L. V. Sims
Dorothy Sucher
Elizabeth Travis
Deborah Valentine

Anthologies

This list includes important short story anthologies of women mystery writers.

Crimes of the Heart, edited by Carolyn G. Hart. New York: Berkley 1995.

Deadly Allies, edited by Marilyn Wallace and Robert Randisi. New York: Doubleday, 1992.

Deadly Allies II, edited by Robert J. Randisi and Susan Dunlap. New York: Doubleday, 1994.

The Fourth Womansleuth Anthology, edited by Irene Zahava. Freedom, CA: Crossing Press, 1991.

Lady on the Case, edited by Marcia Muller, Bill Pronzini, and Martin Greenberg. New York: Bonanza Books, 1988.

The Ladies' Killing Circle, edited by Victoria Cameron and Audrey Jessup. Burnstown, Canada: General Store Pub. House, 1995.

Lethal Ladies, edited by Barbara Collins and Robert J. Randisi. New York: Berkley, 1996.

Malice Domestic 1, presented by Elizabeth Peters. New York: Pocket, 1992.

Malice Domestic 2, presented by Mary Higgins Clark. New York: Pocket, 1993.

Malice Domestic 3, presented by Nancy Pickard. New York: Pocket, 1994.

Malice Domestic 4, presented by Carolyn G. Hart. New York: Pocket, 1995.

Malice Domestic 5, presented by Phyllis A. Whitney. New York: Pocket, 1996.

More Ms. Murder, edited by Marie Smith. Secaucus, NJ: Carol, 1991.

Ms. Murder, edited by Marie Smith. Secaucus, NJ: Citadel, 1989.

Ms. Mysteries, edited by Arthur Liebman. New York: Washington Square, 1976.

Out for Blood: Tales of Mystery and Suspense by Women, edited by Victoria Brownworth. Chicago: Third Side Press, 1995.

Reader, I Murdered Him, edited by Jen Green. New York: St. Martin's Press, 1989.

Reader, I Murdered Him, Too, edited by Helen Windrath. London: Women's Press, 1995.

The Second Womansleuth Anthology, edited by Irene Zahava. Freedom, CA: Crossing Press, 1989.

Sisters in Crime, edited by Marilyn Wallace. New York: Berkley, 1989.

Sisters in Crime 2, edited by Marilyn Wallace. New York: Berkley, 1990.

Sisters in Crime 3, edited by Marilyn Wallace. New York: Berkley, 1990.

Sisters in Crime 4, edited by Marilyn Wallace. New York: Berkley, 1991.

Sisters in Crime 5, edited by Marilyn Wallace. New York: Berkley, 1992.

A Suit of Diamonds: a Commemorative Volume of Specially Commissioned Short Stories Published to Celebrate The Crime Club's Diamond Jubilee. New York: Dell, 1991.

The Third Womansleuth Anthology, edited by Irene Zahava. Freedom, CA: Crossing Press, 1990.

The Web She Weaves, edited by Marcia Muller and Bill Pronzini. New York: Morrow, 1983.

A Woman's Eye, edited by Sara Paretsky. New York: Delacorte, 1991.

The Womansleuth Anthology, edited by Irene Zahava. Freedom, CA: Crossing Press, 1988.

Women of Mystery, edited by Cynthia Manson. New York: Carroll & Graf, 1992.

Women of Mystery II, edited by Cynthia Manson. New York: Berkley, 1995.

Index by Series Character

INDEX BY SERIES CHARACTER

261

INDEX BY SERIES CHARACTER

Geographic Index

Isaacs, Susan
Kelman, Judith
Lathen, Emma
Logan, Margaret
Lorens, M. K.
Maiman, Jaye
Maron, Margaret
Matteson, Stephanie
Meyers, Annette
Michaels, Barbara
Monfredo, Miriam Grace
Neely, Barbara
O'Brien, Meg
O'Connell, Carol
O'Donnell, Lillian
Papazoglou, Orania
Paul, Barbara
Piesman, Marissa
Roberts, Gillian
Scoppettone, Sandra
Scottoline, Lisa
Smith, Evelyn
Sucher, Dorothy
Travis, Elizabeth
Truman, Margaret
Tucker, Kerry
Uhnak, Dorothy
Wallace, Marilyn
Wesley, Valerie Wilson
Wheat, Carolyn
White, Teri
Yeager, Dorian
Zukowski, Sharon

South
Adams, Deborah
Ballard, Mignon
Brown, Rita Mae
Buchanan, Edna
Cornwell, Patricia D.
Drake, Alison

Fennelly, Tony
Friedman, Mickey
Harris, Charlaine
Hart, Carolyn G.
Hess, Joan
Hightower, Lynn S.
Hooper, Kay
Janeshutz, Trish
Kelner, Toni
MacGregor, T. J.
Maron, Margaret
McCafferty, Taylor
McClellan, Tierney
McCrumb, Sharyn
Michaels, Barbara
Peters, Elizabeth
Redmann, J. M.
Shankman, Sarah
Sibley, Celestine
Smith, Julie
Sprinkle, Patricia H.
Squire, Elizabeth Daniels
Trocheck, Kathy Hogan
Wiltz, Chris
Woods, Sherryl

Midwest
Baker, Nikki
Braun, Lilian Jackson
Borton, D. B.
Brod, D. C.
Carlson, P. M.
Churchill, Jill
D'Amato, Barbara
Elrod, P. N.
Gosling, Paula
Hager, Jean
Hart, Ellen
Jacobs, Nancy Baker
McGiffin, Janet
Morgan, Kate

Paretsky, Sara
Pickard, Nancy
Pulver, Mary Monica
Weir, Charlene

Southwest and Mountain
Albert, Susan Wittig
Cooper, Susan Rogers
Dain, Catherine
Davidson, Diane Mott
Douglas, Carole Nelson
Dreher, Sarah
Hager, Jean
Jance, J. A.
Lackey, Mercedes
Landreth, Marsha
Martin, Lee
McConnell, Vicki
Meredith, D. R.
Millhiser, Marlys
Moffat, Gwen
Oliphant, B. J.
Orde, A. J.
Prowell, Sandra West
Sandstrom, Eve K.
Van Gieson, Judith
Walker, Mary Willis
Webb, Martha G.
Wingate, Anne

California
Beck, K. K.
Burke, Jan
Dawson, Janet
Dunlap, Susan
Forrest, Katherine V.
Fowler, Earlene
Girdner, Jaqueline
Grafton, Sue
Grant, Linda
Green, Kate

Hall, Mary Bowen
Hornsby, Wendy
Jackson, Marian J. A.
Kellerman, Faye
Kijewski, Karen
King, Laurie R.
Kraft, Gabrielle
Krich, Rochelle Majer
LaPierre, Janet
Matera, Lia
Maxwell, A. E.
McKenna, Bridget
Millar, Margaret
Muller, Marcia
O'Callaghan, Maxine
O'Marie, Sr. Carol A.
Padgett, Abigail
Pence, Joanne
Pincus, Elizabeth
Pugh, Dianne G.
Roberts, Lora
Rosenberg, Nancy Taylor
Rothenberg, Rebecca
Sawyer, Corinne Holt
Shah, Diane K.
Singer, Shelley
Smith, Julie
Taylor, Elizabeth A.
Valentine, Deborah
Wallace, Marilyn
White, Gloria
White, Teri
Yarbro, Chelsea Quinn

Pacific Northwest
Beck, K. K.
Daheim, Mary
Henry, Sue
Jance, J. A.
Smith, Janet L.
Stabenow, Dana

McCrumb, Sharyn
McDermid, Val
McGown, Jill
Meek, M. R. D.
Melville, Jennie
Mitchell, Kay
Moffat, Gwen
Morice, Ann
Moyes, Patricia
Myers, Amy
Neel, Janet
Perry, Anne
Peters, Elizabeth
Peters, Ellis
Peterson, Audrey
Quest, Erica
Radley, Sheila
Rendell, Ruth
Robb, Candace M.
Ross, Kate
Rowlands, Betty
Shepherd, Stella
Simpson, Dorothy
Slovo, Gillian
Smith, Joan
Stacey, Susannah
Stallwood, Veronica
Stewart, Mary
Thomson, June
Valentine, Deborah
Walters, Minette
Whitehead, Barbara
Woods, Sara
Yorke, Margaret

AUSTRALIA

Day, Marele
Geason, Susan
Greenwood, Kerry

McNab, Claire
Rowe, Jennifer

REST OF WORLD

Arnold, Margot
Beck, K. K.
Coker, Carolyn
Dunnett, Dorothy
Fallon, Ann C.
Friedman, Mickey
Gilman, Dorothy
Gur, Batya
Hadley, Joan
Langton, Jane
Livingston, Nancy
Leon, Donna
Llewellyn, Caroline
McQuillan, Karin
Moyes, Patricia
Nabb, Magdalen
Newman, Sharan
Peters, Elizabeth
Robinson, Lynda S.
Stewart, Mary
Whitney, Phyllis
Wilson, Barbara

HISTORICAL SETTINGS

Beck, K. K.
Brightwell, Emily
Davis, Lindsey
Douglas, Carole Nelson
Elrod, P. N.
Eyre, Elizabeth
Frazer, Margaret
Greenwood, Kerry
Greenwood, L. B.
Jackson, Marian J. A.

Index by Type of Detective

ACTORS/THEATRICAL

Babson, Marian
Barnes, Linda
Brennan, Carol
Carlson, P. M.
Dentinger, Jane
Hart, Ellen
Matteson, Stefanie
Meyers, Annette
Morice, Anne
Paul, Barbara
Yeager, Dorian

AMATEUR DETECTIVES

Adams, Deborah
Atherton, Nancy
Babson, Marian
Ballard, Mignon
Beck, K. K.
Bowen, Gail
Boylan, Eleanor
Brightwell, Emily

Brown, Rita Mae
Cannell, Dorothy
Charles, Kate
Churchill, Jill
Clark, Mary Higgins
Craig, Alisa
Crane, Hamilton
Daheim, Mary
Dank, Gloria
Davis, Dorothy Salisbury
Dunlap, Susan
Ferrars, E. X.
Fowler, Earlene
Granger, Ann
Gray, Gallagher
Hadley, Joan
Hager, Jean
Harris, Charlaine
Harris, Lee
Hart, Ellen
Isaacs, Susan
Johnston, Velda
Kelman, Judith

ARCHAEOLOGISTS/ ANTHROPOLOGISTS

ARTISTS

BOOKSTORE OWNERS

BUSINESSPEOPLE/OTHER PROFESSIONS

Femling, Jean
Fennelly, Tony
Girdner, Jaqueline
Godfrey, Ellen
Gray, Gallagher
Hager, Jean
Hall, Mary Bowen
Hardwick, Mollie
Hart, Ellen
Lathen, Emma
Law, Janice
Maxwell, A. E.
McClellan, Tierney
McQuillan, Karin
Meyers, Annette
Pugh, Dianne G.
Travis, Elizabeth
Trocheck, Kathy Hogan
Wilson, Barbara

CLERGY

Black, Veronica
Davis, Dorothy Salisbury
Frazer, Margaret
Gallison, Kate
Greenwood, D. M.
Harris, Lee
Holland, Isabelle
O'Marie, Sister Carol Anne
Peters, Ellis
Whitehead, Barbara

COOKS

Davidson, Diane Mott
Laurence, Janet
Myers, Amy
Page, Katherine Hall
Pence, Joanne

Pickard, Nancy
Rich, Virginia

ETHNIC DETECTIVES

Adamson, M. J.
Baker, Nikki
Bland, Eleanor Taylor
Buchanan, Edna
Femling, Jean
Hager, Jean
Hornsby, Wendy
LaPierre, Janet
Moody, Susan
Muller, Marcia
Neely, Barbara
Shannon, Dell
Singer, Shelley
Stabenow, Dana
Wallace, Marilyn
Wingate, Anne
Woods, Sherryl
Wren, M. K.
Yarbro, Chelsea Quinn

FANTASY/SCIENCE FICTION DETECTIVES

Elrod, P. N.
Hightower, Lynn S.
Huff, Tanya
Lackey, Mercedes

GOVERNMENT AGENTS/ WORKERS

Barr, Nevada
Cooper, Natasha
Dominic, R. B.
Edwards, Ruth Dudley

Maiman, Jaye
McConnell, Vicki
McDermid, Val
McNab, Claire
Pincus, Elizabeth
Powell, Deborah
Redmann, J. M.
Scoppettone, Sandra
Wilson, Barbara
Wings, Mary
Zaremba, Eve

LIBRARIANS

Harris, Charlaine
MacLeod, Charlotte
Monfredo, Miriam Grace
Morgan, Kate
Peters, Elizabeth
Wright, L. R.

MUSICIANS

Douglas, Carole N.
Neel, Janet
Paul, Barbara
Peterson, Audrey

OLDER SLEUTHS

Arnold, Margot
Borton, D. B.
Boylan, Eleanor
Burden, Pat
Christmas, Joyce
Comfort, B.
Ferrars, E. X.
Gilman, Dorothy
Godfrey, Ellen
Gray, Gallagher

Hadley, Joan
Hall, Mary Bowen
Lorens, M. K.
Matteson, Stefanie
Morgan, Kate
Rich, Virginia
Rowlands, Betty
Sawyer, Corinne Holt
Squire, Elizabeth Daniels

POLICE

Adamson, M. J.
Aird, Catherine
Bannister, Jo
Beaton, M. C.
Belfort, Sophie
Bland, Eleanor Taylor
Burden, Pat
Butler, Gwendoline
Carlson, P. M.
Cleeves, Ann
Cooper, Susan Rogers
Craig, Alisa
Crombie, Deborah
Curzon, Clare
Dewhurst, Eileen
Drake, Alison
Dunlap, Susan
Eccles, Marjorie
Edwards, Ruth Dudley
Forrest, Katherine V.
Fraser, Anthea
George, Elizabeth
Gosling, Paula
Graham, Caroline
Granger, Ann
Green, Christine
Greenwood, Kerry
Grimes, Martha
Gur, Batya

PRIVATE EYES

Jacobs, Nancy Baker
James, P. D.
Kijewski, Karen
King, Laurie R.
Lackey, Mercedes
MacGregor, T. J.
MacLeod, Charlotte
Maiman, Jaye
Maxwell, A. E.
McCafferty, Taylor
McDermid, Val
McKenna, Bridget
Muller, Marcia
O'Callaghan, Maxine
O'Donnell, Lillian
Paretsky, Sara
Pincus, Elizabeth
Prowell, Sandra West
Scoppettone, Sandra
Slovo, Gillian
Sucher, Dorothy
Taylor, Elizabeth A.
Trocheck, Kathy Hogan
Wesley, Valerie Wilson
White, Gloria
Wilhelm, Kate
Wiltz, Chris
Wren, M. K.
Zaremba, Eve
Zukowski, Sharon

SCIENTISTS

Rothenberg, Rebecca

TEACHERS AND PROFESSORS

Arnold, Margot
Belfort, Sophie
Borthwick, J. S.

Bowen, Gail
Clarke, Anna
Cross, Amanda
Ferrars, E. X.
Hornsby, Wendy
Kelly, Nora
Kenney, Susan
Langton, Jane
LaPierre, Janet
Lorens, M. K.
MacLeod, Charlotte
Peterson, Audrey
Roberts, Gillian
Singer, Shelley
Smith, Joan
Wilhelm, Kate
Yorke, Margaret

WRITERS

Bannister, Jo
Conant, Susan
Cooper, Natasha
Cooper, Susan Rogers
Daheim, Mary
Holt, Hazel
Kelly, Susan
Kittredge, Mary
Lorens, M. K.
Maiman, Jaye
McConnell, Vicki
McCrumb, Sharyn
McDermid, Val
Moffat, Gwen
Paige, Robin
Roberts, Lora
Rowlands, Betty
Sandstrom, Eve K.
Smith, Julie
Stallwood, Veronica